RANDOM HOUSE

LARGE PRINT

THE
ROOM
OF
WHITE FIRE

THE
ROOM
OF
WHITE FIRE

T. JEFFERSON PARKER

RANDOM HOUSE
LARGE PRINT

Copyright © 2017 by T. Jefferson Parker

Published in the United States of America by Random House Large Print in association with G. P. Putnam's Sons, an imprint of Penguin Random House LLC, New York.

Cover design by Eric Fuentecilla
Cover photograph © Leszek Glasner/Shutterstock

The Library of Congress has established a Cataloging-in-Publication record for this title.

ISBN: 978-1-5247-7840-8

www.randomhouse.com/largeprint

FIRST LARGE PRINT EDITION

Printed in the United States of America

10 9 8 7 6 5 4 3 2 1

This Large Print edition published in accord with the standards of the N.A.V.H.

In memory of Roberta and Jack Sharer

1

Once upon a time they would have named it Pines Asylum or Mountain View Sanitorium or even Lifespring Hospital, but now it was just Arcadia. It was hidden in the mountains of San Diego County, near Palomar Observatory. A patient had left the grounds and I'd been offered the job of finding him.

The last five miles of road wound through trees that broke the late-morning light. Slats of sun and green. A guard at the gatehouse took my driver's license, checked my name against his appointment list, entered something on a tablet and seemed to ponder it. He handed the license back, eyes steady behind yellow glasses. "Dr. Hulet will meet you in the lobby. Surrender all weapons and cell phones to security."

I nodded.

"Welcome to Arcadia, Mr. Ford."

Another steep half mile up the road stood the main building, a beveled structure of concrete and smoked glass cut into the mountainside. An expanse of lawn, parking places, groomed walkways. Flower beds waving with Iceland poppies. And seating areas, some made of carved and varnished tree stumps, where men and women of various ages talked and drank from colorful plastic tumblers. Most wore casual or business clothes, with others—both male and female—in white work pants and tucked-in white shirts. A few of them watched me as I got out and turned off my phone and set it inside the large tool chest bolted to my truck. Placed the phone next to my sidearm, then closed and locked the heavy lid. A white-haired man in a sport coat and bow tie gave me a thumbs-up. The April day smelled of pines.

My cursory Internet search of Arcadia hospital—buried deep down in the search engine listings—had revealed a state accreditation link, a few breezy mentions in blogs and social media, and a one-page website that declared it to be **an exclusive wellness community for treatment of mental and emotional disorders.** The only website graphic was a watercolor of a Grecian temple on a hillside surrounded by trees. No physical address, no photographs, no additional information. A phone number and an email address and that was all.

The lobby was cool and filled with natural light steeping through the glass. Modern Scandinavian style, beige leather and chrome. Wall-mounted screens showed **Curious George** on

KPBS San Diego. A professional-looking woman caught my eye from beyond the security gate. I emptied my pockets and removed my belt and boots and watch before stepping through the scanner. Got my things back on as she came toward me, her hand out. "I'm Dr. Paige Hulet," she said. "Sorry for the airport welcome."

"The in-flight snacks must be something."

"I can offer you coffee or water, Mr. Ford."

She looked about my age, thirty-eight. Medium height and weight, brown hair and eyes. Black pantsuit with a white collared blouse buttoned to the top. Hair up and firmly secured, a cool hand. We walked a short hallway to a door, where she swiped the ID card on her lanyard through the lock.

We stepped into a towering atrium. Six floors up was a glass ceiling, beyond which hovered blue sky. Zigzagging ramps linked the floors all around us. People were out and about, going up and going down. "We have elevators, or the ramps."

"Ramps, please. I see you let the patients dress as they like."

"We call them partners, but yes. We encourage them to express themselves through dress and grooming. Most do. This way."

As we climbed I saw that the room doors and windows faced the open atrium, as in a hotel. The doors were painted in repeating red, yellow, and blue. No curtains or blinds. Two patients and two staffers passed us on the left, heading down the ramp, all talking loudly about a new San Diego Chargers running back. One of the patients wore a Chargers jersey and helmet. The other wore a San Diego Padres baseball cap and jersey—#51, no less—that of the great pitcher Trevor Hoffman. I tried to think of them as partners rather than as patients. In this American hour words meant everything and nothing.

"Sixty beds," said Dr. Hulet. "Men on floors two and three. Females, four and five."

"Is it unusual to mix male and female partners?"

"In a private community like this, no," said the doctor. "And we have almost a one-to-two staff-to-partner ratio, so it's never a problem. One of our pillars of treatment is to create an environment that signifies normal. Dr. Briggs Spencer is our founder. He's a bit of a renegade, as you probably know."

"I didn't realize this hospital is one of his."

Dr. Hulet gave me a **Now you know** look. "He keeps a very low profile. For the families. Our end mission here is discharge and reintegration, when possible. We try to prepare our patients for life on the outside."

"You used the wrong P-word."

"I do it all the time."

Through a fourth-floor wall of smoked glass

I looked down at the flank of the mountain and the winding road that I'd driven in on, and the heavy blanket of oaks and manzanita and conifers. Boulders the size of cars, tan and rounded, some stacked, some strewn. Directly below us I saw a kidney-shaped swimming pool, blue and shimmering, with a few swimmers and waders overseen by white-clad attendants.

The patient in question had "left the premises" two days ago, as Dr. Hulet had told me the previous evening by phone. When someone escapes from a place like Arcadia, the hospital will rarely call law enforcement. Too many potential embarrassments and liabilities. Mental illness still brings fear and shame, especially to the rich and powerful. Police draw media, which draw the public. So a missing patient is the responsibility of either hospital security—which had failed to find the man—or a private locator, such as myself. Looking down on the dense forest surrounding Arcadia I saw that our AWOL patient could easily be hunkered within a mile of the building and it might take a bloodhound to find him.

Dr. Hulet's office was a corner with floor-to-ceiling windows. Waiting for us was Alec DeMaris, a wedge of muscle in an expensive suit, who introduced himself as Arcadia's director of security. Hair short and curly, face set. His handshake was intended to punish so I punished back. Men. We sat across from Dr. Hulet, who rested her elbows on the green-marble desktop, working a never-sharpened yellow pencil with both hands. She pointed the eraser end at Alec.

"His name is Clay Hickman and he's twenty-eight years old," said Alec. He was a notch older than me and his voice was sharp, martial. "Missing at the lunchtime head count two days ago, Monday. We searched the compound and grounds and found where he'd dug out under the security fence. Rough country out there. I hired a bloodhound handler from Ramona. We got some clothes from Hickman's hamper and the dog took off down a dirt road on the other side of the fence. Then the dog turned around and brought us back to the escape hole and went yapping up the road the other way. So we figured our boy had gotten into a vehicle. The road is public but unmaintained and not used much. Tried the dog at the three nearest gas stations down-mountain, the Amtrak stations from San Diego to Oceanside, the Greyhound station in San Diego. No scent. Nada. That went into Tuesday afternoon. The handler wanted to try a different dog but I fired him and we called you. Why you, Mr. Ford? You've only got five years of experience as a PI and a rocky history with the San Diego Sheriff's. But I can tell you why you—because of your good reputation as a locator, and your service in Iraq as a United States

Marine. Fallujah, I gather. I was a lieutenant during Operation Iron Harvest in Iraq, a little after your time. The taking-out-the-trash phase. So here we sit, brother."

They say once a Marine, always a Marine, brothers for life, always faithful. I say fine, but don't let it cloud your judgment.

I looked at Dr. Hulet, then out the southern window for miles and miles, to where the pale desert waited. "Why is Clay Hickman in this place?"

Dr. Hulet's gaze was calm and direct. "Schizoaffective disorder, the bipolar subset. He has been delusional, paranoid, and at times violent. He was admitted to Arcadia three years ago as a danger to himself and others. Clay Hickman is the son of Rex and Patricia Hickman—yes, of Hickman Homes. Like you two, Clay served our country in the second Iraq war—Air Force. He returned home in late 2009, rented an apartment in San Diego. He found some security work but was soon exhibiting symptoms of what was assumed to be PTSD—hypervigilance, sleeplessness, anxiety, and depression. It escalated. He experienced his first psychotic break six months after coming home. He was stable for a year and a half, then broke again. The next two episodes came just six months apart. Erratic behavior. Fighting. One charge of assault with a deadly weapon—he struck someone with a gun. Shoplifting, drunk in public, resisting arrest. Alcohol and drugs. Unaccounted for, weeks at a time. His sixth fifty-one fifty landed him in Patton State for observation. That's what it takes for a disturbed person to get help these days in our system. Even a veteran of war. That would have been 2014. Luckily for Clay, his family brought him to us. Mr. Ford, I want you to know that Clay Hickman—when he's taking his medications and keeping himself active here in a structured setting—is a peaceful, deep-feeling, generous young man."

Dr. Hulet took a deep breath and let it out slowly. "Two years ago, when I took over his therapy here, I began to suspect that he was suffering what is now called 'moral injury.' From the war. Some therapists call such psychological trauma a soul wound. It is caused by something you **do**. Not by something done **to** you. I've published on the subject. It is very different from PTSD. They are not the same."

DeMaris deadpanned her.

I watched a vulture fly by the window, up close to the smoked glass. He seemed to eye his reflection, then continued his reconnaissance. As nature made him. Clay Hickman sounded a lot like some veterans I knew from my Marine days. As a veteran I wondered for the millionth time why some of us had such profoundly bad reactions to war but others did not. Why some had lost their bearings while others had managed to move on to the next thing. As nature made us? As war changes us? Either way, stress was a constant torment to all of us, and maybe an excuse to some.

"Is he suicidal?"

"He's shown the ideation but has made no attempt," said Dr. Hulet. "Suicide is one of my biggest concerns now, with Clay in a totally foreign environment and his medications and therapy abruptly suspended. We cannot allow Clay to end his life. Veteran suicide rates run roughly double those of the general population, as you might know."

A moment went by. I knew a Marine who killed himself after coming home. Lenny. From Biloxi, Mississippi. Both legs amputated above the knee. Didn't want to live like that. I knew others—some disabled—who wanted very badly to live. I think I understood both sets of mind—opposite sides of the same hard coin.

I watched the trees outside swaying in the breeze. The low temperature up in these mountains last night was thirty-nine. Not that I thought Clay Hickman was out there in the forest. I had the feeling he had covered some miles in the last two days. But it was just a feeling. "Are you his lead doctor?"

Dr. Hulet nodded. "As well as Arcadia's medical director. His leaving surprised me. In all the hours I've spent with him, he rarely talked of a life outside or of running away. I think he felt safe here."

Hard to believe, I thought, that an airman locked in a hospital, swank or not, wouldn't want to fly away. Having been married to a recreational pilot, and still being a pilot myself, I know something about flight. Flying toward or flying away. Either way, it gets into your blood and stays there. Flight is more than freedom. You are subject to nature, your own limitations, the whims of the gods. You are free to fall. "You told me yesterday that Clay is not voluntarily here. That his father is his conservator and makes decisions on his son's behalf."

"That is true," said the doctor.

"Had his behavior changed lately?"

"He was restless. Not at peace. I felt that he was coming to a crossroads that he couldn't articulate."

DeMaris loudly cleared his throat. "Mr. Ford? Or can I just call you Roland? Roland, we've come to the part of the program where you tell us if you're going to take the job we've offered you. Daylight's a-wastin' and our man is in the wind. His family is extremely worried, and so are we. It was good of you to fax us your contract yesterday. Dr. Spencer has approved it and Dr. Hulet and I will sign it. But I do need to ask you, why do you only take cash?"

"Why wouldn't I?"

"We report every penny."

"So do I."

"And you're awfully damned expensive, too. I know. I'm familiar with your world and your type."

"Then maybe you can explain me to me sometime."

DeMaris opened his mouth to speak, came up empty.

"That would be my job," said the doctor.

"I'll find Clay Hickman."

2

r. Hulet again pointed her pencil at Alec De-Maris, who pulled a fat envelope from his suit coat pocket and plopped it down. She slid my contract across the marble and handed me a pen.

I signed. Finding missing persons can be difficult when they don't want to be found. Locating is my specialty. To begin this kind of work for a corporate client, I charge three eight-hour days at one hundred dollars an hour. I refund the balance if we get results fast. For families, the hourly goes down, sometimes way down. For political and most religious organizations, the hourly goes up, sometimes way up.

"Thank you," she said. "I have the pictures you said you would need."

She handed me a legal envelope, unsealed. I pulled out the photographs, head shots, one in color and one black-and-white. PROPERTY OF ARCADIA—NOT FOR RELEASE OR CIRCULATION stamped on the backs. Clay Hickman had an open face, a high forehead, and straight white hair. In the color picture I could see that he had a hazel left eye and a blue right one. His expression was alert but calm.

"What was he wearing?"

"Tan cords, a black T-shirt, a brown cardigan sweater, and dress shoes," said Dr. Hulet. "They were caramel-colored, or maybe camel. I'm not sure exactly what they call it. We have video of him taken at eleven fifteen that morning, before he left the grounds."

"Chestnut on the shoes," said DeMaris. "And expensive. The Hickmans do not allow their son to dress down, even here on the funny farm. Hickman, by the way, is five-ten, one seventy. He's fit from the gym, and running and biking around the grounds. Supervised, of course. We encourage exertion. Gain through pain for our insane. That's my joke and don't repeat it. I'll take you out to the wire when you're ready."

I looked at Dr. Hulet. "I'll need the names and numbers for friends he's made here. And all recent visitors—dates are important. I'd like access to any staff he trusted, or talked to. His family, of course."

"The family might be a problem," she said. "Very private people. I'll talk to them again. Anything else?"

"Clay Hickman's medical history."

"We can't let you have that," said DeMaris.

"Of course we can," said Dr. Hulet.

"Paige, don't be foolish."

"I've already cleared it with Dr. Spencer."

DeMaris sighed and stood and went to the window.

I pocketed the money. Felt good. "Did you find a shovel?"

"Negative," said DeMaris.

"I'd like to see his room."

Hickman's room was 25, second floor, a yellow door that DeMaris unlocked with a key card. Inside it was decent-sized and set up like a hotel suite. A window looked west over the mountains and some of the trees were close enough you could ID the birds in them. The walls were bare. No kitchen. There was a desk by the window and a laptop computer on it. I thought he would have taken it with him. I nudged one corner of the laptop but it did not move. "We bolt them to the desks," said De-Maris. "Had an incident."

"You can log on to it, see what he's been doing online?"

"Remotely or right here," said DeMaris. "Care to take a peek?"

"Later, from my office, if possible."

"Can't let you do that," said DeMaris. "Our network isn't secure if we give out usernames and passwords." He gave the doctor a preemptive look.

In the small bedroom the bed was tightly

made, as a former airman might do. There was a dresser against one wall with pictures on it—matted but no glass—long-ago shots of Clay Hickman as a boy with his family, mom and dad, two sisters, varying dogs through the years. A dock with a boat, a swimming pool, a tennis court. Clay was the baby. As a child he looked unhealthy and unhappy. Not like the sisters. The older he became the better he looked. "How often do they visit him?" I asked.

"Once a year," said Dr. Hulet.

"That's all?"

"It's difficult for all of them. Their visits bring great anxiety to Clay. Very destabilizing."

"Once a year when?"

"Spring. Usually April. Their visit was scheduled for next week."

"Who all comes to see him?"

"Mr. and Mrs. Hickman and the older sister, Kayla. Never the younger sister. I believe she is estranged from the family. Her name is Daphne."

"I want their numbers."

"Daphne's, too?"

"Hers especially."

A beat. Then, "Of course."

"Show me where he dug out."

"I'll leave that to you two," said the doctor.

———

DeMaris bucked the quad along a path through the trees to the property line, driving stupidly fast, as guys like DeMaris do. The chain-link fence was ten feet high and topped with strands of razor wire thoughtfully tilted inward toward a would-be escapee. A standard correctional setup, nonelectric. DeMaris's security people had already filled in the escape hole, though its shape was plainly visible. I contemplated it. Big enough for a man to climb in, wriggle under the fence, then climb up and out again on the other side. Digging it had been a big job, done quickly enough to foil security. Which meant that another person was likely digging from the other side. Both of them feeling the pressure, with Arcadia staff soon to catch on to Clay's absence.

I toed through the top few inches of soil with my boot, found it typical for this part of the county—decomposed granite and scattered quartz. I saw bloodhound tracks and shoe prints around the hole, and bike or motorcycle tracks on the firebreak that paralleled the fence. The Arcadia property was sixty acres, according to DeMaris, and this section of fence stood some five hundred well-wooded yards from the main building.

"How did he evade you guys?" I asked.

"Used the after-breakfast transition," said DeMaris. "Lots of patients on the move, too many for staff to monitor individually. At some point you really have to give these nutcases a little trust. So we didn't catch on until the post-lunch head count."

"Did he sneak off often, try to lose you?"

"Not until recently. He got away from us twice in the last month. Found him still on the grounds. He knew this property, and he was getting to know the security patterns. Some of our cameras are hidden pretty damned well. For exercise he liked to run the fence line around the property. We always sent someone with him. He ran fast, good endurance. Some of my day-shift guards brought running shoes to work, liked the workout."

I looked at the rough dirt road on the other side of the fence. Public but unmaintained looked about right. Ruts and rocks, coyote scat, more paw and footprints. There were vehicle tracks, too, difficult to make out on the hard, rough road. "Sounds like he was practicing up for a getaway."

"I think so," said DeMaris.

"You're sure he doesn't have a phone?"

"Our body and room checks are thorough. But someone could have smuggled one in. It happens."

I pictured someone bringing Clay a shovel, and maybe one for himself, and them digging under the fence just enough for Clay to squeeze out. I saw them toss the shovels in the car and hit the road. I imagined them driving fast, laughing low and quietly. Clay smiling. You bet he'd be smiling—the airman flying his coop.

"Just to clarify the obvious, Mr. Ford. When you locate Clay, you contact me. No one else. Here's my card. Use the cell number."

We rode back. Through the trees rushing past I saw a pod of five patients on bikes on the concrete path, led and followed by white-clad Arcadia staffers. The bikes were big-tired beach cruisers with high, swept-back handlebars like I used to ride as a kid growing up on the California coast.

Back in the hospital, Dr. Paige Hulet gave me a folder containing Clay Hickman's medical charts, USAF service record, arrest reports, and a list of friends and family and their numbers.

She escorted me through the lobby and outside, into the bright early-afternoon sun. Mountain sunlight always seems stronger than sea-level sunlight, especially in spring. On a sunny patch of lawn, four partners had squared off for a game of horseshoes, plastic. Concentration, then laughter. Dr. Hulet waved to them as we walked toward the parking area, and two of them waved back, smiling.

"I thank you again for helping us, Mr. Ford."

"Thank you for the work, Dr. Hulet."

We walked at a thoughtful pace. A warm and somehow promising day. Spring had arrived without resistance after another parching winter. Sixth year of the Great Drought. We came to my truck and stopped.

"This would be more than mere work to you," she said. "If you knew him. All my patients are important, but Clay is dear to me. I feel responsible for him."

"In the sense that he served your country and appears to have lost his mind for his trouble?"

"Yes. Yes. I feel as if I personally sent him into all that."

"All what?"

Dr. Hulet squinted up at me. "Iraq. Clay is very closed about what he did there. But I know that he was damaged."

"Where was he stationed?"

"Ali Air Base. He was a mechanic. It's in the file I gave you. Where were you, Mr. Ford, in that war?"

"First Fallujah."

"The door-to-door campaign?"

"Yes."

"A dark chapter."

"Dark book."

She peered at me. "How does it make you feel to see Fallujah in the news again?"

Took me a minute to find the words. "Fooled. Pissed. A lot of good people suffered for nothing."

"Are you at peace with what you saw and did there?"

"At peace because I surrendered," I said.

"To the facts of what you saw and did."

I let a moment pass, for some reason unsure of how to say yes.

"I've never been to war," she said. "Yet, I've become a student of what it does to the mind."

"There is nothing comparable."

"No. Mr. Ford, I want to ask a favor of you. When you locate Clay, call me first. Before you call anyone else. Do not call Alec DeMaris until you and I have talked."

"He told me just about the opposite."

"I expected that."

"Why?"

Still squinting up at me, she raised a hand to shade her eyes. A small tear had formed in the corner of one.

"I beg your pardon, Dr. Hulet," I said, taking her shoulders gently. I turned us away from the frontal sun and released her. She stood still, then took my shoulders and reversed us back into the piercing light, raising a hand to shade her eyes again.

"Because it would be in Clay's best interest,"

she said. "To call me first, when you locate him, and not Alec and not Dr. Spencer."

"Just take your word for it?"

"I'm asking you to, yes."

"I'll think about it," I said. I'd dealt with multiple masters before and no good had ever come of it.

"What we just did made me realize something," she said. "Moving in and out of the sun like that? I haven't danced in five years."

"I'm a good dancer. Let me take you sometime." The words came out as I thought them. I regretted them instantly. Professionally perilous, just for starters. The whiff of need. Not very Roland Ford.

She studied me for a long beat. "I'll think about that, too." Then she turned and strode back toward the lobby, heels brisk on the asphalt and a glint of spring sunlight off her neatly packaged hair.

I watched her. Pretended to wonder what had gotten into me. I looked for clues in the truck window reflection. Same old face. Some dings and a faint forehead scar from the ring. There's a story behind that scar, a story about Roland "Rolling Thunder" Ford. For what little it's worth, I **am** a good dancer. I took it up after boxing. For a big man, it turns out, I have good balance, and when I dance I feel light and graceful. Temporarily. But then, everything is temporary. The trick is letting temporary be enough.

I knew damn well what had gotten into me. Just surprised by the intensity of it. I hadn't asked a woman to dance in two years. Gave myself fifty-fifty odds on the invite.

3

stashed the papers with the gun, put the phone in my pocket, and locked up the heavy toolbox again.

Under the gaze of two orderlies, I strolled past the Iceland poppies and followed the path across the big lawn. Then into the trees. The spring afternoon had gone cool in the shadows and soon I felt free of the men and women in white.

Ten minutes later I came to the perimeter fence and the freshly filled escape hole. From under a big oak tree I looked at the fence and the hole and the rough dirt road on which Clay Hickman and at least one confederate had driven away. I lit a cigarette and gave it a good deep draw.

A beaten black economy car popped along the road, picking through the ruts. Bad muffler. The girl driving waved out the window and kept on going. I took a knee under the oak, considered calling in my own bloodhound man, whose dogs I had seen work near-miracles. I wished Clay had a cell phone so I could get an old sheriff's deputy friend to ping it for me, but no such luck. I watched a pair of mountain quail hustle along the road, topknots upright and feet just little blurs. Soon they'd have chicks, then late in summer they'd covey up with other families. Safety in numbers. Sometimes that worked. I stood and ground out the butt nice and deep, swept some dirt over it like a cat.

The noisy black car came back in the opposite direction, which made me think of the bloodhound going up and down that road, faithful to his best sense, as far as it could take him. The car stopped not thirty feet from me and the girl left the engine running, got out and came to the fence. I walked over.

She was skinny and orange-haired and didn't look twenty. Denim shorts with frays and holes, a red plaid flannel shirt with the tails knotted at her navel and the sleeves rolled up, hiking boots. "Are you one of the crazies?" she asked.

"I just look that way."

"You can't tell by **looking.** Security?"

"No."

"But you're camped out by that hole wondering where so-called Jason got to."

"So-called Jason. Exactly."

"Why?"

"I want to help him. But I have to find him first."

"You don't look like a doctor."

I shrugged. A shrug to a human is a shiny object to a crow.

"Jason is a sweet guy. He said he'd be my friend if I brought him a shovel so he could dig out. I wasn't looking for a friend. But I sensed something good in him. So I brought two shovels and helped. That was Monday." She held up her small white hands, each palm with a big blister, one of the bandages hanging half off. "When we got back to my place I went to use the bathroom and he took sixty bucks out of my purse and went off in my truck and I haven't seen him since. This here's my sister's car, which I'm borrowing."

"So you'd talked to him before Monday."

"Twice. First time we met was right here at this fence. I'd stopped to look at a snake on the road and he was running. For exercise, I mean. I asked him where he was going and he said, 'Crazy, wanna come?' I said maybe, and came back the next day, same time and place."

"After you dug him out, did he say where he was headed?"

She squinted at me, then tried to push the bandage flap back onto her skin. "No. He did call a couple of hours later, though—from a pay phone. Didn't think they had 'em anymore."

"You're just the young lady I've been looking for."

"That's what he said, too."

"I'm a private investigator."

"I sell plush toys at the Wild Animal Park. In the Primate Palace."

"Can we talk?"

Her name was Sequoia Blain and her home was a leaf-littered Airstream trailer in a park about a mile down the mountain. The trailer park was called Lazy Daze.

"Small but cheap, and they pay the propane," she said, climbing the steps of a wooden deck. "I'm from eastern Oregon. I hate cities and can barely tolerate a town. Let's sit outside."

She tried to brush off the seat of a resin patio chair for me to sit in but flinched and waved her hand in the air as if to cool it. "Nothing worse than a blister you keep hittin'. Except for maybe a drunk boyfriend that keeps hitting **you**. Which I've had the last of."

I swiped off the seat with the photo envelope and Sequoia went inside, screen door slamming. There were eight other trailers scattered in the oaks, all facing west, downslope, which gave way to chaparral and eventually the ocean, and probably some killer sunsets.

The screen door slammed again and Sequoia handed me a can of root beer. She set her phone on a small pine-needle-littered table and popped open her can. "I first saw him about a month ago. This lousy road is actually a shortcut to the highway from where I live. He was running along the nuthouse fence with one of the white nurse guys behind him. But he was a good-looking guy and he ran really fast and muscular. The nurse was huffing away. I didn't know he was Jason then, of course. 'Jason Bourne is my full name,' he told me later, 'exact same as the movie hero,' and I just said, 'Oh, crap—how dumb do you think I am?' But he was all 'No, no, no—that's my real name, swear to Christ in heaven it is.'"

"Well, it's not," I said.

"Duh."

"Try Clay Hickman."

She nodded and took a sip of root beer. "Well, that's a cool name, too. He didn't seem that crazy."

I handed her the envelope and she looked at the pictures. "These make him look kind of stoned. In real life he's happier, but pretty random, too."

"Random how?"

"His mind won't stop for long. The spider monkeys at my work have more focus than him. Really. But he's upbeat. Maybe he's always that way. I mean, I only spent a few hours with him."

I told her what I could about him, which wasn't much. Prosperous family, military service, a diagnosis of schizoaffective disorder, sometimes delusional and violent.

"Jeez, for reals?"

"Really. When did you next talk to him after the 'Crazy, wanna come' line?"

"The very next day. I was curious, you know. So I drove back at the same time and waited a while, and there he came, running again. I got out of the car and yelled out, 'Nice day, isn't it?' He came over, breathing hard, pretty sweaty. He asked if I had any water in my truck and I did. So I got a bottle and tossed it over the fence and he drank it half down. He said his name was Jason. He asked me if I lived around here. Then he finished off the bottle and tossed it back. One of the guys in white came running out of the trees about then, way behind. Jason asked if I could meet him the next day, same place and time. So we did. And that's when he told me how he needed to get out of the hospital but they were keeping him prisoner and he'd pay me a lot of money for a shovel. I said I'd bring him the shovel but not for money. I had a good feeling about him from the very start. I've always been an excellent judge of character. Except once, actually, when I was a really bad judge."

"Do you have any idea where he went?"

She looked out to the oaks and the distant chaparral. "He said his parents were rich. Own the Family Suites hotel chain, and I know they got one of those down on Hotel Circle."

From what had been suggested about his family, I figured the Family Suites might be the last place Clay Hickman would land.

Sequoia set her can on the table with a tinny knock. "What he talked about was his mission. Which was to bring white fire to Deimos. 'My mission is to bring white fire to Deimos.' He said Deimos was the Greek god of terror, which I barely remembered from Miss Benson in high school. Clay—I still want to call him Jason—but **Clay** said he was almost clear on how to accomplish his mission. And when the meds finally washed out of him he'd see everything perfectly, like he used to. He said that he'd built up resistance to electroshock but the doctors didn't know it. I didn't think they did electroshock anymore. Shocking another human being's **brain**? No animal in nature would do such a cruel thing to another."

I thought of what young male lions do to the cubs when they take over a pride. And weasels in a henhouse. Feuding chimpanzees. But also of a torture basement I'd seen in Fallujah where the loyalists worked over the local Shia. Bloodstains on the walls and floor, several coats. Smell of burned flesh. They had a car battery rigged with cables but it wasn't for jump-starting vehicles.

That got to me, that battery. Humans. Animals. The human animal. Where's the big difference? Maybe Sequoia had a point.

"He could have made that up," I said. "About electroshock."

"Why would he do that?"

"Good question."

She considered me. "He didn't seem, like, delusionary at all to me. Just . . . excitable. But my mom? She took some heavy meds for depression and she could fool people. I remember how convincing she could be, even when I knew she was making stuff up. To her it was true. That's a terrible deal, when a mind turns down reality and makes things up instead. Like there's a little devil up in your skull, directing his own movie for you to see."

I got Sequoia's phone, driver's license, and plate numbers, and a description of the missing truck—a "trashed" silver Nissan with a lowland gorilla key chain dangling from the rearview mirror. She had not reported it stolen because she didn't want to get Clay in trouble, but I encouraged her to file the report because if Clay Hickman did anything illegal, then she could be considered an accomplice. And in case he abandoned it, she could get it back. And because the truck was, well, stolen. She agreed.

She put both of my phone numbers into her phone. An office landline and a cell. I gave her my email address, too. She promised to call me immediately if she had any contact with Clay whatsoever.

"Hey, can I have one of those pictures of him? The color one? I love his different-colored eyes."

I slid the picture back out of the envelope and set it on the table by the empty root beer cans. "I really need that call from you, Sequoia. So does Clay, whether he knows it or not."

She studied me. "Maybe he just wants to be free."

"Some people can't handle freedom."

"Well. Okay."

"Be very careful with this guy if he contacts you again. Your job is to contact me. He has a history of violence. Don't be alone with him."

"I'm nineteen and I can take care of myself."

I gave her a hyper-dubious look. "Drunk boyfriend."

"You don't have to bring him up. I learned."

I was forty miles from the Family Suites on Hotel Circle. I picked my way down the mountain to the state routes and finally to the interstate and hit the city at rush hour. Hotel Circle is pretty much what it sounds like, a loop of chain hotels set up for San Diego's tourists. Beaches, zoo, Chargers, Padres, trained killer whales, more beaches. We've got it all. A large white charter bus was pulling out of the Family Suites lot as I squeezed in. A group of maybe sixty tourists was checking in but I managed to catch the eye of a tall young man who waved me to the end of the desk and welcomed me to his hotel. His badge said PETER. I showed him the picture of Clay Hickman. He turned it over and read the PROPERTY OF ARCADIA claim, then looked at the face again.

"He was here Monday evening, say six o'clock. He came in and looked at me, then at Lannie— she's one of the other night clerks—and I remember it was slow right then and we both said 'Welcome to Family Suites' at the same time. Me and Lannie laughed but the guy didn't. He turned around and hurried out. We joked about him all that shift, how we scared him off with too **much** hospitality. I remember him because the moment was funny and weird. What did he do?"

"He's on the run."

"A criminal?"

I pictured Sequoia Blain's trusting face, and remembered that Clay had pistol-whipped someone before being committed to Arcadia. "Not yet."

I left Peter my card with both numbers and a twenty, and he said he'd call if he saw Clay Hickman again.

Hotel Circle is too big to walk so I drove from

hotel to hotel, all the way down, across the interstate, then all the way back up on the other side. Those bloodhounds and me, down and up, then up and down. I saw no trashed silver Nissan pickup with a gorilla key chain hanging from the rearview in any of the lots.

4

I live sixty miles northeast of San Diego, fifteen miles from the coast. The property is oak woodland and has been in my wife's family for almost a century. Twenty-five acres, nearly perfectly square on the plat map. The main structure is a 1922 adobe-brick house that holds the high ground, and downslope are six casitas built around a spring-fed pond. There's a barn and a paddock. It has a name, possibly pretentious: Rancho de los Robles—Ranch of the Oaks. The nearest town is Fallbrook.

The entire rancho became a wedding gift to Justine and me—just a little something to get the newlyweds started—and when she died a year later I tried to give it back to the Timmerman family because it seemed like the right thing to do. But they said no—I was family and it was mine now. It was one of several Timmerman properties in the American West. Two years now since Justine's death. I feel both surrounded by her and abandoned by her, a form of torture familiar to anyone who loses someone they love. To all of us, sooner or later.

Oaks and sycamores, sage and grasses, and dramatic outcroppings of granite boulders. No neighbors for miles. It's potentially good farmland—avocados and citrus do famously well in Fallbrook. But no one in the Timmerman clan, certainly not us newlyweds, could ever muster the time or energy to tame this place. Justine and I were much too busy being young and ambitious. She was five years younger than me, a public defender. She had a good moral compass, an impressive memory, and was born to argue. I was three years into private investigations after resigning from the San Diego County Sheriff's Department. I had a gift for finding people and was doing well at it. She owned a Cessna 182 when we first met, which she had painted pink and named **Hall Pass**. She taught me to fly **Hall Pass**, too, and we soared all over the Southwest for that one perfect year we were married.

Our plan was to live forever or die trying, and we thought we could pull it off. We were bullish. Timmerman brains and Ford brawn. All four grandparents alive on both sides. Sky the limit and no end in sight.

We all make assumptions and that's where we go wrong. Sometimes they crash. As did **Hall**

Pass, with Justine alone at the controls. Into the Pacific, off Point Loma. Mechanical failure. She was celebrating a little plan we'd hatched, and I had stayed on the ground because I had work to do. **Work.** I could never say no to work back then. Still can't. That day, I had been thinking of her up in the great blue, at just about the time **Hall Pass** went down. My thoughts had been pleasant ones—not a premonition among them. Picturing myself as a dad someday. I was a trusting soul back then. That day is the river that divides my life. A river, or a wall topped with broken glass. If it's anywhere close, I can recognize the throaty rumble of a 182 in the sky.

A year after her death I bought another Cessna, same year and model as Justine's plane, and christened it **Hall Pass 2**. I fly it now and then for business but mostly for what is supposed to be pleasure. To remind me of her and those few fine days. Sometimes memory is a blessing and other times it's a curse. On a given morning you won't know which it will be.

The truth is that Rancho de los Robles was in need of serious work when we first moved in. Still is. Foundation splitting faultlike. Adobe bricks of the main house cracking and crumbling. The twice-updated electrical prone to overload. Plumbing startlingly loud and undependable. Roofs leaking. Outbuildings dilapidated. The drought had killed off most of our fruit trees and pretty much every species of plant that hadn't been established here five hundred years ago. At certain times of the day, in certain light under certain skies, the property looks like it blew in from the Dust Bowl.

The main house is too big to keep clean. I barely even knock down the cobwebs. Lizards get in under the doors, but at least they eat some of the spiders. This home still contains much of its original, very old furniture—all vaguely Franciscan and not quite comfortable. There are rough-hewn oak tables, chairs, and trunks; crude wooden chandeliers; dark velvet drapes; heavy cushions. Dusty now, and hushed. You half expect Father Serra to come down the hallway with a tallow candle. Justine and I had happily romped and partied amid all this history, two randy cherubs making hasty plans to modernize our home when the excitement cooled a little, if it ever did. But how could it?

Sometimes I wander from room to room, each with its own history and climate. Outside I can see the rolling oak savanna and distant groves of oranges and avocados. By night I can see stars and the scattered lights of Fallbrook. But generally I leave the drapes drawn. Though it may have been a gift, this house feels assigned. Everywhere I look I see a wisp of Justine—a flash of red hair, the hem of a favorite dress vanishing around a corner. Never the whole her. And I hear her voice, its rhythm and timbre, hidden under the groan of the plumbing or the drone of the air conditioner or the rumble of the Camp Pendleton artillery in the distance. Never a whole sentence.

I try hard to remember, and to forget.

I locate people for a living, but the person I want to locate most is the one I will not find.

I work when I'm needed, but there's not always enough work that pays. The six casitas: I rent them out to add to my unpredictable income. I haven't touched Justine's life insurance money. Like I haven't touched the clothes in her closet. And the things on her dresser. Can't touch, can't let go.

Near the center of the property, in the large shaded barbecue area between the pond and the casitas, I've posted rules for my tenants:

GOOD MANNERS AND PERSONAL HYGIENE
NO VIOLENCE REAL OR IMPLIED
NO DRUGS
NO STEALING
QUIET MIDNIGHT TO NOON

RENT DUE FIRST OF MONTH
NO EXCEPTIONS

Interesting crew. I call them the Irregulars.

In casita number one, Grandpa Dick Ford. On the opposite end of the pond, in casita number six, Grandma Elizabeth. Liz. They don't get along often, but they raised three children and spoiled six grandkids to the best of their abilities. Their son—my father—is traveling the world with my mother now, in well-deserved retirement.

In casita number two is Lindsey Rakes, a former Air Force lieutenant and drone pilot. A Reaper sensor ball operator, to be exact, flying missions in the Middle East from a trailer at Creech AFB outside Las Vegas. CIA stuff, of course, secret missions, twelve-hour days, six days a week, both good and bad kills. Drove her bats. She's unemployed just now, with a gambling problem and too many local Indian casinos for her health. The night I met her she was too drunk to drive so I offered her a ride to her home and on the way she broke the news that she didn't really **have** a home. She's trying to get shared custody of her young son from her ex-husband. The boy is five and I question the wisdom of her being more involved.

In casita number four is eighteen-year-old

Wesley Gunn, scheduled for an eye surgery that might leave him blind. Tumors in both eyes—retinoblastoma. Six weeks from now his left eye will have to be removed. The doctor will try to spare the right eye as he removes the tumor that, if left untreated, will spread and kill Wesley. There's a ten percent chance that the surgeon will need to take that right eye, too, but he won't know until he gets inside. Wesley is a local kid, a high school senior and all-conference quarterback. Then the blurring vision and diagnosis. I offered casita four to him for free because that's what you do for a young man who, it turns out, has a rotten home life and is facing blindness. He's an outdoorsy guy, wants to spend his last few sighted weeks where he can watch nature. Plenty of birds, bobcats, coyotes, cottontails, ferrets, squirrels, reptiles in these hills. Right now—spring—is the time to see them. Wesley spends lots of his waking hours back in the arroyos with little more than water, binoculars, and a camera. I used to barely keep up with him when I tagged along. But he's slowing down.

Casita five is Burt Short, a fifty-something man I know almost nothing about. He read my ad in the Fallbrook paper and filled out an application listing his occupation as "outside sales" and offered to pay rent in cash. Told me he grew up locally but told Lindsey Rakes he was raised in Alaska. Where he worked most of his life as a fishing guide. But I overheard him tell someone on his phone—sounds carry easily through the barbecue area because of the pond—that his arbitrage days are over. And Burt Short **is** short, and built like a bull. Top-heavy and powerful, a big head. Smile that shows bottom teeth on one side. Mischief or derangement. His hair is dark and cut close. He's the only one who pays on time and in full, first of the month.

Casita three is vacant but listed.

I'm a landlord because I need the money. Can't remember a single time when all of my tenants—not counting Wesley Gunn—paid their rent on the first of any month.

At any rate, this was home and I was happy to be there. I poured a large bourbon on ice, wiped a lemon wedge around the rim of the glass, gave it a squeeze and dropped it in. I like alcohol as much as I like tobacco, which means I have to say no to myself a lot. I'm fair at that. I nuked some good barbecue leftovers that probably Lindsey Rakes had put in the fridge for me.

I fully reclined in the living room reading chair with Clay Hickman's file on my chest. Judging by weight, Paige Hulet had done a good job on the file. Maybe used all the time she saved not dancing. She'd assembled not only a detailed treatment history at Arcadia, complete with Hickman's long formulary and notes from her sessions with him, but also his DoD service record and medical charts subsequent to his discharge from the Air Force. Plus, a good accounting of Clay's run-ins with the law, via police reports and court records.

I tore through the bio all the way to where Clay Browne Hickman was born to Rex Gayle Hickman and Patricia Browne Hickman on October 7, 1988.

When my phone rang deep in some uneasy dream, I read the time as I answered it: 3:55 a.m.

"Mr. Ford, it's Sequoia. My truck just drove up so I think he's here. I better go."

5

I made good time, turning from the state route onto Sequoia's dirt road in the dark of five in the morning. I cut the headlights and clipped right along, the rocks rapping the underside of the truck like small-arms fire. The first two years after my tour of duty I heard those pops everywhere I went, even in my dreams. Less now.

Coming around a bend I saw the Lazy Daze sign lit from below by one weak floodlight. Beyond the sign stood the squad of Airstream trailers, faintly luminescent in the trees. A light was on inside Sequoia's trailer but there was no small silver pickup truck in sight. What looked like Sequoia's sister's car waited in the faint porch light downslope, beside another Airstream.

I turned slowly into Lazy Daze and picked my way past the unlit manager's residence. I parked and zipped my jacket against the mountain cold. Things felt nervy and wrong. Scar on my forehead was tingling, never a good sign. Clay Hickman had apparently come and gone and . . . done what? I was responsible for Sequoia Blain, and it was on me if Clay hurt her. Or worse. She was a free-spirited girl and he was a physically fit psychotic male with a history of violence. She'd quickly allied herself with him against odds and logic, as only a free-spirited nineteen-year-old would do.

In the rearview mirror I saw a pale SUV cruising slowly down the dirt road from the direction I'd come, raising a little cloud of dust behind it. Ten seconds later a bulky, dark muscle car—looked like a Chrysler—followed through that diminishing cloud, leaving one of its own.

I crunched across the pine needles and down a short pathway to Sequoia's deck. Took the steps quietly and stood close enough to the trailer to feel the cold coming off its body. Heard nothing inside. The door handle turned freely and the door opened: small dining area, light shining softly down. Empty table, bench seats. Down the short hallway to my left, the bedroom door was open. I looked behind me to the parking area and the dirt road beyond it, then stepped inside the Airstream.

Smell of coffee and dish soap. "Sports fans? Just your friendly neighborhood PI here. Sequoia? Clay?"

Stone silence, so I walked two short steps down the hallway, felt the whole trailer rocking with my weight. Turned on the bathroom light, saw little, then took another step and squeezed through the bedroom doorway. Found the light, picked up the faint scent of laundry soap and bleach. Closet open: two pairs of green cargo pants and two tan short-sleeved blouses with Wild Animal Park emblems on the sleeves. Parting the window curtain slightly, I looked out to the manager's cabin, where a light was now on. No movement inside. Dirt road, pines against the gray sunrise.

Back to the bathroom, oddly empty. No toothbrush or toothpaste, no shampoo, no deodorant, no perfume.

No problem. I'm hearing you, Sequoia.

Kitchen again. Fridge lightly stocked. By the sink a plastic grocery bag stuffed with more plastic grocery bags. Coffeemaker grounds still warm and damp.

Off on an adventure, I thought. Home and job now distant blips in the rearview of a trashed silver pickup. Plastic bags for luggage, a cute hunk calling himself Jason Bourne for company. What more could a girl ask for?

I crunched across the needle-covered grounds to Sequoia's sister's trailer. No light on, no car out front, and no one answered the door. A squirrel undulated across the grounds and climbed a tree, pausing to consider me, tail waving.

When the manager answered her trailer door, she looked and smelled as if she'd slept through a fifth and a beer or two. She hadn't seen Sequoia since the day before, had neither seen nor heard anything unusual earlier this morning. She studied my card as if it were a complex legal document. "I sleep like the dead," she said.

I nodded.

"Don't worry, Mr. Rolando. Sequoia's a good girl. Early riser. You don't worry about her. I'll have her call you."

I started up my truck and checked my phone. Watched the rearview for a minute for a pale SUV or a black muscle car, saw only the dirt road and a pair of crows squabbling in the trees beyond. I wondered what exactly they had to argue about, but every creature has its grievance. I had mine right at that moment: It annoyed me that my target, Clay, and my semiresponsibility, Sequoia, were now in the wind together, not far from here, in a vehicle that would be easy to find. Easy if you're a cop, that is. As a deputy I'd have hot-listed the truck plates and stood a good chance of it being pulled over within an hour. I miss that power sometimes. But I had not been a good team player. I would have loved to have had some of that power again just long enough to find Clay Hickman and get him back to Arcadia.

I thought of calling Sequoia, but that could surprise or anger Hickman. I didn't want an angered psychopath driving around with a trusting teen.

I called Dr. Paige Hulet and told her I'd be at

Arcadia by nine that morning to talk to some of Clay Hickman's friends.

"Yes, yes, Mr. Ford, I'll make sure. That he's available. There's one best friend, really. I can do that." She sounded flustered and short of breath, or both.

"You're okay, Doctor?"

"Yes. Of course. I'm on the treadmill."

"Aren't we all?"

She rang off.

6

Clay's best friend at Arcadia was Evan Southern. Dr. Hulet introduced us out at the pool. Mid-morning, and the April day was sunny and cool, showers in the forecast. Southern wore seersucker shorts and leather deck shoes and a white pullover sweater with navy trim on the cowl and cuffs. His tortoiseshell glasses magnified his eyes, which were blue. He was deeply tanned and parted his hair, dark brown, in the middle. He looked to be in his late twenties. Evan removed his earbuds and rose slowly from the thick blue pad of the chaise longue. "A friend of Clay? Why, this is a pleasant surprise. Where has that boy gotten to?" I heard the South in Southern's speech.

Dr. Hulet excused herself, then walked away along the pool edge. Evan watched her, exhaled audibly, and offered his hand. "I'm not surprised by Clay," he said, not much above a whisper. "We need to talk. But we need to move. There are microphones and cameras hidden in the trees, and some of the birds you see are actually surveillance drones. So speak quietly and face the ground if possible. Come."

We left the pool area. Evan took one of the gravel pathways around the main building, then another across a big sloping lawn on the eastern side. He walked slowly, bent at the waist, with his hands held loosely behind his back. A white-clad attendant trailed us a hundred feet back, gave me a brief salute when I turned.

"Explain your presence here," he said, more to the path than to me.

I told him my profession and that I'd been hired to find Clay Hickman.

"I sensed that he would do this," said Evan. "Clay is utterly tormented by the ghosts of the war. I sensed an awakening in him over the last few months. He told me he had a mission. He wants to bring 'white fire to Deimos.' Deimos, you may not know, is the Greek god of terror, but it's also a nickname for someone Clay knew in the war. Do not look up now but there is a camera in the jack pine coming up on our left, twenty feet up, right side, near the trunk. Where the branches are trimmed. You can't even see all the mics. Be silent as we go by."

When we came to the tree I looked anyway, and saw a small video camera strapped to a truncated branch. When the path forked just past the camera tree, Evan went left, west into the forest.

"I wasn't able to unravel his metaphor," he said, glancing at me. "I see no relevance between Deimos and Clay and white fire, whatever that might be. Clay insisted that he has friends to help him. I heard that he slipped past his guards before lunch, threw a blanket over the razor wire, and climbed over. Is that true?"

Do you tell the truth to a crazy man in a crazy place? Will it make him free, or are you inviting harm to him and others? I thought about that and said nothing.

"If you don't tell me the truth I can't help you find him."

"He dug out," I said quietly, facing down. I realized how suddenly and easily I'd entered his world.

"Did his friends help him?"

"I don't think so."

We walked deeper into the forest, which I noted, upon this second tour, was cleared of brush and saplings. There was no thick bed of pine needles as an authentic forest would have, no fallen trunks or drying branches, no tangles of old growth or dead limbs. I saw that most of the trees had been laced so they were balanced and attractive and nonwild looking. **Arcadia,** I thought. **A region of ancient Greece known as a place of simple pleasure and pastoral quiet**. I looked back at our keeper, still a hundred feet behind us, now with a phone to his head. Deeper in, the forest was less groomed, darker. We came to the firebreak and the chain-link fence topped with coils of razor wire, maybe two hundred yards from the escape hole that curious Sequoia Blain from Oregon had helped Clay dig. I hadn't seen a camera along the last hundred yards of trail, and saw none on the fence. Maybe DeMaris's security team figured they were too expensive to install this far out. Large and heavily wooded, the Arcadia grounds would be very difficult to fully secure without towers and guards.

"See that hummingbird hovering over the razor wire?" asked Evan. "It's not a hummingbird. It's a surveillance drone. They send information from sensors in their eyes back to the main computer in the security room."

I looked up. The tiny bird was whirring in place as hummingbirds do, maybe twenty feet away from where we stood, near the top of the razor wire. A male, by the bright, metallic-red blazes on his head. Evan Southern's magnified blue eyes were excited and calculating. He seemed to be waiting on a decision from me.

"Who told you that?" I asked him.

"Everyone knows. Just climb up there and scare it off and you'll see it's a drone by the way it flies."

"Why don't you climb up and see what it does?"

"Because I already know what it will do."

It sounded logical and doable enough. The worst that could happen was I'd climb up part of the fence, scare off a hummingbird, and have a lunatic down on the ground laughing at me. I turned and looked at our escort again. He'd stopped his usual hundred feet away, crossed his arms, and now stood watching us. I found a rock and lobbed it up near the hummingbird.

The bird didn't dodge it. So I got a big pine-cone and arched it closer, just a couple of yards from the bird, more than close enough to scare most hummingbirds I'd seen. The bird moved slightly. I looked back at our guard.

"He won't mind," said Evan. "Mickey is an Alabama gentleman, like myself."

The fence was the good-quality chain-link, with rubberized black coating, which would be easy on the skin. I spread my hands and legs, got my fingers and toes set, then began pulling and toeing my way up to the bird. Halfway there it flew off. I clung there mid-fence, craning my neck to watch it disappear into the trees behind me. It didn't make the usual low thrum of a hummingbird, but rather a high-pitched whirr. And it didn't fly in swift, bottom-heavy swoops like hummingbirds do, but in a straight line. Its wings looked weird. It was one of the strangest things I'd ever seen. I lowered myself a foot or two, pushed off, and landed with a puff of dust.

I waved at the guard. He shook his head slowly.

"See?" asked Evan.

"I saw."

"I can let you examine one later if they haven't found it yet."

"You caught one?"

"Two. They found the first one in my room but I put the second one in a much tougher place to find. I do love hiding things from these people. It's one of the little pleasures of captivity."

"Why did you bring me all the way out here?"

"The farther you get from the hospital the less surveillance. That is why. And because I wanted to tell you that before Clay came to Arcadia, his very favorite place in San Diego was the Waterfront Bar and Grill. I'm sure you know of it. He went there often when he returned from Romania."

"He was in Iraq."

"No. Romania. Somewhere in that dark and humble country, home to vampirism and werewolfery, lie the seeds of Clay's madness. I think you might actually locate him at the Waterfront."

"Thank you. I appreciate your help."

"If you have anything to ask me, especially if it's secret or very serious, you should do it now, away from the cameras and mics and surveillance drones."

"Did he tell you where he was going?"

"No, only that he had the mission."

"Was Clay given electroshock therapy here?"

Evan fixed me with a stare from behind his thick lenses. There was nothing playful in him now as there had been when he challenged me to climb the fence. Instead, there was something frightened. "I'm certain of it. Without his informed consent. They will deny it." He seemed ready to add something, but did not. "The Waterfront, Mr. Ford. The Waterfront is the best lead I can give you."

We stood in awkward silence, both looking back at Mickey, our overseer, as the hummingbird motored back into view, stopped and hovered above us, then whirred off into the forest again.

"Let's head back, Mr. Ford. I want to show you the art studio."

We were still in the trees when we came upon three all-white-clad orderlies looking up into a large sycamore with low-hanging branches. Halfway up a young man was crouched in the crook of two branches. He had something in his hands, a phone maybe, or a remote control. One of the orderlies, a thin black man, called up to the man in the tree, asking him to come down safely and right now.

"That's Remsen," said Evan. "They blame the

drones on him and his friends. Handy, don't you think?"

The art studio was a big room on the first floor. The entire north-facing wall was solid glass. There was only one artist at work when we walked in, a woman standing at a high table, forming a pot with her hands. She looked from the pot to us, a gray slurry dripping off her wrists, then dropped her attention back to her vessel. Easels stood throughout the room, some holding works in progress, others empty.

"Clay and I dabble in the fine art of painting," said Evan. "I prefer portraiture, whereas Clay is more of an abstract expressionist, with maybe some Bay Area figurative thrown in. But should we categorize art or just make and enjoy it? Here's one of mine."

The painting was maybe two by two feet. An oil. From the canvas Evan's face looked back at me. The eyes, nose, and mouth were clear, detailed, and realistic, right down to the glimmering trapezoids of light caught on the lenses of Evan's glasses.

"Nice," I said. "Very you."

"Thank you. It's hard to be objective about oneself. But it helps the art to detach and examine, just as Dr. Hulet says detachment and examination help a person understand himself. Isn't she one of the most attractive women you've ever seen?"

"She's easy on the eyes."

Evan fixed me with a look. "More like a direct assault on mine. But a most welcome one."

The potter looked over, hands still working the vessel. "You're nothing to her but a case number. A nutcase number."

"Julie, you charmer you! This is the famous private investigator, Mr. Roland Ford. Star of film and TV."

She ran her eyes up and down me just once, then turned back to her work. "I only watch PBS."

"Let's see Clay's work," I said.

"Over here."

Our watcher from the forest looked in from the doorway, caught my eye briefly, then backed off. Evan put a hand on my shoulder as if we were old friends, guided me to the far side of the huge glass wall. We picked our way through the easels and paint-splattered worktables and stools. Through the floor-to-ceiling window loomed the mountainside, sharp with pines.

Clay's painting was on an easel near the window. It was small. It looked complete but unclear. Against a black-orange background—a burning black curtain, a cave wall lit by a bonfire?—a figure stood above another figure lying on the ground. They had elongated, almost pointed heads. Human or simian, I couldn't tell. No faces. Both were dark, twisted, and anguished, as if writhing in a fire. But somehow resigned, too. A performance or a ritual? I stared at it for a long time.

"What's going on in the painting?" I asked.

"Clay's mind."

"Are those people?"

"Clay will have to tell you. I can't. I just know that when we paint, Clay is very involved. He never paints from a model. Or uses a picture. It all comes from memory."

Evan led me to the back of the room, where dozens of canvases leaned against the wall. Clay's were not hard to find, two rows of four, all small in size. I knelt and flipped through them. The dark, longheaded figures repeated painting to painting. The backgrounds differed, though: some had similar red-black interiors, others brightly illuminated by what looked like cold white sunlight, and still others were dense, constricting fields of green that might have been forest or woods. But all of them featured the same two skinny, possibly charred but living figures.

"A fucked-up mind imagined that," said Evan. "Pardon my language. Where I grew up they'd bullwhip you for using a word like that."

"Alabama, right?" I asked absently.

"Shelby County. Hill country."

I finished studying the last painting in the second row, tilted the canvases back against the wall. Then I went to the first row and looked at every painting one more time. I didn't know why I couldn't take my eyes off them, only that I couldn't. Painful stuff. Pain itself. They had the simple brute allure of a highway wreck. Another way into the mind of this strange creature I'd been hired to bring back to the world. I stood and looked around. Back to this, I thought. His world.

"Do you think he's capable of violence, Evan?"

He studied me, blue eyes narrowed, wheels turning inside. "His violence is not upon others. He smashed one of his paintings not long ago. Kicked a hole in a door."

"Do women set him off?"

"No, Mr. Ford. He's a gentleman or he wouldn't be my friend. Anyway, that's our art studio. Like to see that hummingbird drone in my room?"

Evan's room was similar to Clay's but looked considerably more lived-in. There were curtains over the big window with the nice forest view, several posters of Civil War–themed movies—**Cold Mountain**, **Glory**, **Gettysburg**, **Sherman's March**—taped somewhat randomly to the walls. I guessed that poster glass or even plastic was prohibited. I let my eyes wander the living area while I listened to Evan rooting around in the bedroom. He had a desk, a laptop computer, and a printer, as had Clay. Also on the desktop was a loose stack of white printer paper and dozens of crayons of various colors and use. I nudged the laptop but it was fixed to the desk as firmly as Clay's had been. And like Clay's room door, and undoubtedly all the others, this door was lockless.

Evan came from the bedroom with a grin on his face and a small hummingbird-like thing riding on his palm.

7

We do have a drone-flying club here at Arcadia," said Dr. Hulet. "One of Dr. Spencer's interests. That's what you saw." I was back in her sixth-floor office. I'd told her about the strange little drone and Remsen in the tree.

"The pilots are supervised, of course. The drones have to be small and harmless. No cameras. The partners fly them around and end up crashing most of them. Evan of course knows all this but prefers a grand surveillance conspiracy."

A drone-flying club at Arcadia. It didn't sound as reasonable as an art studio. Or a nice swimming pool, or a play-money casino and a walk-in aviary where patients—**partners**—tended to small, frightened birds. And certainly our security escort wasn't concerned when I climbed the fence to better see the bogus hummingbird.

Paige Hulet was wearing what I figured to be her standard work uniform: black pantsuit and shoes again, white blouse. This blouse had small black accents on the collar and buttonholes. Her hair was up in a tight bundle identical to the one she'd worn before. Her makeup was light or she wasn't wearing any, and I thought of her tread-mill voice early that morning.

"Where's your power pencil?" I asked.

"I don't think it would work on you. I use it on Alec because it helps keep him on task. Something to do with his Marine training?"

"Carrying out orders is what we do."

"You don't seem like a Marine."

"I'm pretty ex, to tell the truth."

She sat back in her black padded chair and looked at me for what felt like the first time since giving me Clay's medical diagnosis the day before. I watched her gaze drift to the scar on my forehead, then lower. "As far as Evan's claim about Clay being in Romania, that goes against all of the DoD information I was given. Of course, Evan Southern is delusional. He's from Pasadena, California, not from the Alabama hill country. His name was Edward Frizell until he changed it. His accent and manners, the whole Civil War fixation—it's imaginary. He probably didn't have time to tell you about his great-great-great-grandfather who died at Antietam Creek."

"No."

"Evan has other identities, too."

"This is a confusing and maddening place."

"I love your choice of words. One of the lon-gest discussions in mental health treatment is whether our help does more harm than good.

Whether we're just making them worse in places like this. I wrestle with that. I really do."

"Clay Hickman told a lady friend of his that he received electroshock therapy here."

She gave me a long, frowning look. "A lady friend? Someone outside Arcadia, then? So you've actually seen him?"

"Not yet. Back to the electroshock, Dr. Hulet. It isn't mentioned in Clay's file. The one you gave me."

"It's called electroconvulsive therapy, or ECT. It is a modality we use. Sparingly and judiciously. And generally with success. Dr. Spencer demands unilateral placement of the electrodes, never bilateral. Far fewer side effects."

"Did you personally conduct the ECT on Clay?"

She stared at me. "Yes, of course. It's not in the treatment history for reasons of confidentiality."

"Clay also told his friend he'd built up resistance to the shocks."

Paige Hulet looked hard at me again, then closed her eyes and slowly shook her head. She opened her eyes and I saw the moisture on them. "Very unlikely. Maybe Clay was just trying to . . . impress his lady friend."

"What is it between you and Clay?"

"What do you mean by that?"

"You seem inordinately focused on him."

She fixed me with her dark, no longer moist

eyes. "I am his doctor and I am **ordinately** focused on him, Mr. Ford. He's a wonderful, troubled man. And though it is absolutely none of
your business, I'm going to share something personal with you. I live for my partners. They are
what I have and what I want. I have never married and have no children. When I hired you, I'd
hoped you'd see my passion for my work. And
respect it. I'd hoped you'd prove to be more than
a base-model hominid just up from the mud."

I thought about that a moment. "No. That's
me. But I meant no offense, Doctor. I like it that
your voice rises slightly in volume and you blush
and your blood pressure probably goes up when
you talk about Clay Hickman. I like it that you
like him and he moves you and you seem to
want what's best for him. Maybe I'm even envi-
ous. Maybe I want a doctor like you."

Slowly, very slowly, Dr. Hulet's look went from
staunch defense to acceptance. I wasn't sure just
what she was accepting. Whatever it was it took
a while. She sighed. "You come at me from so
many directions. And are much closer to being
fired than you seem to know."

"Well, why not just get it over with?"

"**I want you to succeed.** Yes, okay. I **am**
wound rather tight, Mr. Ford. I understand that.
And I meant no offense, either, about your ape
likeness."

"I couldn't handle working here for long."

"There are, well, rewards and punishments."

I hesitated. In for a penny. "Have you given any thought to my invitation to dance?"

"None. I'm so sorry, but when I said I would think about it, I was trying hard to be polite but not leading. It's a difficult balance with men."

Ouch. But never with women. "No apology needed, Dr. Hulet, but you were the one who brought up five years of dancelessness."

It was the first time I'd seen her smile. A ray of sunlight in a cloud. "That's not even a word."

I shrugged. "We both know what it means. What do you think Clay Hickman's paintings mean?"

"Your mind jumps from thought to thought."

"Who cares what my mind does?"

A shadow of gravity on her face. "I find the paintings disturbing. Those same two figures, trapped over and over in varying postures. Their pointed heads. They made me think of hell. You?"

I stood. "The same. Can I ask you a question about this place?"

"Of course."

"How much do people pay for their loved ones to get treatment here?"

"I'm not authorized to discuss costs. That's a very personal thing for the families, Mr. Ford. You understand."

"You told me that Arcadia's goal was discharge and reintegration."

"When possible."

"What percentage of partners go back into normal life?"

"It's in line with other institutions like ours."

"Can you ballpark it for me?"

"Again, not my information to give."

"So, Arcadia is more of a residence than a treatment center."

"Words can be slippery."

"So let's use the right ones."

A hard, brown-eyed stare, analytical but not unkind. "Like 'dancelessness'? Now I have a question for you, Mr. Ford. Have you given any thought to calling me first when you find Clay? Not Alec. Not Dr. Spencer. **Me?**"

"I'm still considering. Your signature is on the contract but Briggs Spencer is your superior."

"It would be in Clay's best interest."

"So you've said."

"You must do the right thing for Clay. I'm banking on you."

"You're smart to. Because I'm Roland Ford, the go-to hominid."

8

A knot began forming in my throat as I walked toward the Waterfront Bar and Grill in downtown San Diego. The knot tightened as I climbed onto a familiar stool. I knew the odds were small that Clay Hickman and Sequoia Blain would just come strolling in, arm in arm, but Evan Southern had vouched for Clay's enthusiasm about this place before he was committed to Arcadia. So maybe Clay would show up and make my job easy. Maybe, now free after three years of confinement, he wouldn't be able to resist his favorite drink at his former favorite watering hole.

Sergio, one of the Waterfront's senior bartenders, was on duty that evening. He's an easygoing, quick-to-smile man, well fitted to a place that is often crowded and rowdy. He made me a light bourbon and soda and we talked Padres until he got busy. The TV news was speculating on who would be the new secretary of Homeland Security. Springtime, I thought, and like everything else in spring, our new president is moving and shaking. New policy. New people. New words. Then a brief story on the latest bloodshed in Fallujah. Nothing new there, I thought. All that flesh and blood. That belief. Wasted. Forget.

But remember: I had spent more than a little time here at the Waterfront the first year after Justine died. Some of it on this very stool. It had seemed important to be out of my depressing house, somewhere out in the open, where I couldn't overdrink and hide from a world I wanted no part of. Another life. I felt that knot in my throat again. I realized that Clay Hickman's time here in the Waterfront wasn't that much earlier than my own. He had checked into Arcadia a year before Justine had died and I had checked into my own private, inner asylum. According to delusional Evan Southern, on good authority from possibly delusional Clay Hickman, this had been Clay's downtown haunt. And mine. We'd barely missed each other.

Sergio was twisting a white towel inside a beer glass as I held up the picture that Paige Hulet had given me. The towel stopped. "Rick Sims," he said.

"Seen him lately?"

Sergio's brow furrowed as the towel started up again. "Six hours ago."

I tried to sound casual. "With a girl?"

"Yeah. I carded her and she made an excuse and ordered an Arnold Palmer. What's up with

him? Haven't seen him in three years. The day
Tony Gwynn died. Big Tony fan. Nice guy. Serious." Sergio looked down at me, nodding, his
brow furrowing again. "Is he all right?"

"Not fully."

Sergio shook his head quickly and unhappily,
as if shaking off a bad thought. "Today I didn't
think so. Too happy. Too loud. Not like he was.
The girl kind of pulled him out of here."

"Any clue where they were going?"

"None. I just served them drinks while they
waited for a table and he talked at her. Is he in
trouble?"

"Headed for that neighborhood."

"Where's he been the last three years?"

"Back east. I'd appreciate a call if you see him
again. An immediate call, Sergio."

"Sure, okay."

"How about a table and a menu?"

The table was just big enough to hold another
bourbon and Paige Hulet's file on Clay Hickman.

The Hickman family had its roots in
nineteenth-century Boston banking, then mi-
grated west and branched into railroads, lumber,
and construction. Damon Hickman, a Navy
lieutenant, had settled in San Diego after World
War II, going into residential and, later, hotel

development. By 1953, Hickman Homebuilders was Southern California's fifth largest contracting company, and later, when Damon's son Rex became chairman of the board at age thirty-five, it had risen to third place in the hottest home-building market in the country. Clay was Rex and Patricia Hickman's third child, born prematurely and with a faulty left ventricle, not expected to survive. No pictures of baby and mother after birth. No announcement.

But Clay Hickman survived not only his early birth but an early heart surgery, too. He grew healthy. In junior high school he was a scholar athlete in spite of his short stature and light weight (five feet three inches tall; one hundred and five pounds). He graduated from high school with honors and lettered varsity in four sports. He had added six inches of height and fifty-five pounds by graduation. A middleweight.

Three weeks later he joined the United States Air Force.

According to my DoD file, Clay Hickman had undergone basic training, then trained for a year in tactical aircraft maintenance. He was then deployed to Ali Air Base in Iraq to work on AC-130U "Spooky" gunships. I knew from my own tour of duty in Iraq that the Spooky is very spooky and more, a menacing nightmare belching out six thousand machine-gun rounds per minute through electric Gatling guns. From the air it is both deafening and surreal, but from the ground it is very real, and the last thing many people hear or see. It also carries a 105mm Howitzer cannon and a 40mm armor-piercing machine gun. It was known in Vietnam as "Puff the Magic Dragon" because its dense exhale of lead could rain down death on so many humans at once. Clay had serviced and maintained the Spookies, apparently with neither distinction nor demerit, during 2007. But as I noted in the poorly lit Waterfront bar, Clay's final two years of service had been blotted out by half a page of heavy black ink, from which Clay did not emerge until late 2009, honorably discharged from the U.S. Air Force, as Dr. Hulet had told me. So, almost two missing years.

I sipped the bourbon and called my flight instructor at Oceanside Airport. He taught both Justine and me to fly—Justine first, years before I met her. Chuck Graff was Air Force back in Vietnam, piloting F-16s. He had spent his last three active decades with the Air Force Office of Special Investigations in Washington. Then he'd retired and come west to teach people how to fly for pleasure. He was crushed when Justine's plane failed. They had spent a lot of hours together in the blue. We're not friends, but I'd done him a favor during the divorce of a friend of his.

We caught up just a little, then I told him who

I was looking for and the reason why, and what the DoD file on 2A3X3 Clay Browne Hickman had said. "What it didn't say is what I'm most interested in. Two years gone. Blacked out. I'm just after the basics, Chuck."

"I can't help you with that," he said. "They redact those records for good reasons."

I waited a beat. "I understand. But would you look over his file anyway?"

"With an eye for what?"

"For helping me find him."

"I'd do you more good flying search over those mountains."

"He's out of the mountains by now." I told him about Sequoia Blain, letting my worry about her come through.

A long wait. "Well. Don't expect much, if anything, Roland."

"I appreciate it."

"Call me in an hour."

I called him a dinner and a bourbon later. I had to put the file on the seat across from me while I ate. Chuck told me that no Clay Hickman had been deployed in Iraq as an aircraft mechanic by the USAF during the years in question.

"Was Clay Hickman deployed to Iraq as something else?" I asked.

"Not deployed to Iraq at all."

"Then I have a falsified file?"

"Correct." Chuck went silent. I could almost

hear his brain whirring. "Clay Browne Hickman was part of the aircrew protection program—survival, evasion, resistance, and escape. SERE. It may ring a bell. It's based at Fairchild AFB outside of Spokane. He graduated from the program and immediately went to work as a Fairchild trainer. I'll deny telling you that until the end of time."

I knew that SERE prepared at-risk airmen for survival, capture, and interrogation. "Was he still at Fairchild in 2008 and 2009?"

A long pause. "I hit the same block you did."

"Redacted into the great black yonder?"

"Sorry, I tried."

"Thanks, Chuck."

"Roland, little bit of advice? Clay's file tells me that he probably stepped into something that's hard to step back out of. Trespass at your own risk. Better yet, don't trespass at all."

I said nothing for a long beat.

"Roland? Who gave you that document?"

"It came from Arcadia. A private sanitorium out by Palomar Mountain."

"I've never heard of it."

"It tries hard not to be heard of."

"Forging military records is a felony."

"I'll point that out to them."

"Good luck. Come out to Oceanside and we'll have lunch."

I hung up, paid up, waved to Sergio, and got

out. I walked half a block down Kettner, stopped and lit a smoke. The promised rain had not come but the fog was thick enough to wrap the street-lights in gauze. A white Range Rover and a black Charger came down Hawthorn, passed Kettner, headed toward the harbor. There are hundreds of such vehicles in San Diego County, but few of them travel in pairs, and this was the second time in two days I'd seen two of them doing just that. The windows were all blacked out and the windshields darkened so I could see nothing of who was inside. I walked half the block toward Grape, changed sides of the street, and finished my cigarette. Sure enough, a moment later the happy white Range Rover and black Charger came rolling east on Grape, making me the approximate center of their rectangle.

Back at my truck I knelt both front and rear, scanned my phone flashlight across the under-carriage, found no radio transmitters that might account for my company. Tomorrow I'd get under it and really look. I cussed myself for let-ting myself be tailed. Once from Fallbrook to Lazy Daze, once from Fallbrook to downtown. The last time I'd been tailed was during my In-ternal Affairs interviews regarding the shooting of Titus Miller, an erratic but nonthreatening, armed black nineteen-year-old citizen. My part-ner had killed him with five shots and I had chosen not to fire. Back then, the tails were fellow Sheriff's Department deputies trying to harass me. It worked. Followed me everywhere, it seemed. Made me angrier and more spooked than usual. Trouble sleeping. Bourbon and regret. During that harassment I relearned my most important lesson from Fallujah: To stand by me. To watch my own back. Be my own ally and friend.

After the transmitter check I sat in the cab of my truck, blasting the heater and defroster. Based on what Sergio had said, I decided it was safe to text Sequoia. A gamble, because if my text set something bad in motion, it was all on me.

I thought for a minute and came up with:

> **7:21 PM**
> **Just saying hi ☺. Primate Palace misses U. Call me when U feel like it. Bye 4 now**

9

Back in my heavily draped, ponderously furnished, Justine-haunted home office I poured
another drink and began hunting down the
basics of the survival, evasion, resistance, and escape program of which Clay Hickman had apparently been a part.

SERE had been created by the United States
Air Force during the Korean War to help airmen who might get shot down over enemy terri-
tory. The Air Force suspected that Koreans, like
Japanese, would use hideous tortures to get what
they could out of the captured U.S. airmen, and
reasoned that the airmen's best chance was to be
prepared. Later, the program was adopted by the
Navy, Army, DoD civilians, and private military
contractors with a "high risk of capture."

SERE was mostly what you might figure: wilderness survival in various climates, emergency
first aid, land navigation, camouflage methods,
communication, and how to improvise tools.
Former prisoners of war taught the resistance
and escape classes, based on their own hard-

earned wisdom. Just as Chuck Graff had said, it was headquartered at Fairchild AFB.

Early rumors held that resistance to "Chinese brainwashing" was the main focus of SERE's "psychology of captivity" training, though Air Force spokesmen denied this. Details of the training were, of course, classified. SERE's broadly stated purpose was to "provide students with the skills needed to live up to the U.S. Military Code of Conduct when in uncertain or hostile environments."

I hadn't thought about the Military Code of Conduct since I studied it as a boot camp wannabe grunt in 2001. Some parts of that document never leave my mind. **I am an American, fighting in the forces which guard my country and our way of life. I am prepared to give my life in their defense. I will never surrender of my own free will . . . If I am captured . . . I will make every effort to escape . . . I am required to give name, rank, service number, and date of birth. I will evade answering further questions to the utmost of my ability . . . I will never forget that I am an American, fighting for freedom, responsible for my actions . . . I will trust in my God . . .**

I was twenty-two years old when I studied that code. We memorized and were tested on it. I had nothing but eighteen years of innocence and four years of college to bring to the altar. A history major! But still I committed myself to the code with all of my heart, truly and without reservation. The reservations started coming soon thereafter, when I saw that a code required action. Kind of like stepping up to the edge of the Grand Canyon and looking down. It was that way for a lot of us. We didn't talk about it until later, when we were on our way out of the war. Maybe twenty-two is the oldest you can be and still believe absolutely what a government tells you to believe. I have regrets in my life, and some of them are substantial, but none of them came from my allegiance to that code of conduct.

Clay Hickman was even younger—eighteen—when he joined the Air Force and memorized the Code of Conduct. In Dr. Paige Hulet's file, Clay's military ID picture had him looking more like sixteen, with different colored eyes, an oily complexion, and a buzz cut that had a small white tuft up front. He stood five foot nine and weighed one hundred and sixty pounds. In spite of his prosperous and influential family, Clay had enlisted.

I wondered what Chuck Graff had found so ominous about the more modern-day SERE. It seemed to me a good idea to prepare airmen for survival and captivity, especially American airmen flying over murderers, torturers, beheaders. Reading further into the articles, I found two interesting entries under "Controversies." The first was a 1993 incident at the Air Force Academy, where USAF cadets in the program claimed that they were sexually assaulted during their SERE "Resistance to Sexual Assault" classes. According to the cadets, the "playacting" instructors had gotten out of hand. Air Force spokesmen denied the allegations but modified the program. A three-million-dollar settlement to one cadet was reported but not corroborated.

The second controversy was murkier and darker. In 2006 the ACLU obtained a sworn statement in which the former chief of Interrogation Control Element at Guantánamo Bay said that SERE instructors taught "interrogation techniques" to Guantánamo military personnel, and that these physical and mental techniques were "mirror images of SERE resistance training."

The upshot, in the words of more than one journalist, was that SERE instructors had "reverse engineered" their resistance methods into interrogation methods—training military interrogators to use the same dark arts of persuasion that they had been teaching Americans to resist if captured. They had turned from defenders to attackers. Their methods were said to include waterboarding, beatings, mock executions, and sleep deprivation, among other "enhanced techniques" recommended on a SERE-approved twenty-item "menu."

SERE came up again in the big ugly blast that hit the news late in 2014. In December the Senate Intelligence Committee published its report after nearly five years of investigating the CIA-run detention and interrogation programs in Iraq and Afghanistan. Reading those "torture report" headlines again was its own kind of torture:

SENATE FAULTS CIA FOR LIES AND TORTURE—"A scathing Senate report says the brutal methods yielded no useful intelligence and were badly managed."

FACE-OFFS WITH CIA INTERROGATORS—"Key Sept. 11 figure seemed to take pride in his ability to endure waterboarding, Senate panel's report says."

INTELLIGENCE GAINED FROM TORTURE FOCUS OF DEBATE . . .

AIR FORCE SERE PROGRAM DIRECTORS QUESTIONED . . .

PANEL FAULTS CIA OVER BRUTALITY AND DECEIT . . .

THE HORRORS IN AMERICA'S "DUNGEON" . . .

AL-QAEDA MASTERMIND WATERBOARDED 183 TIMES . . .

DETAINEE LEFT TO FREEZE TO DEATH . . .

DETAINEE KEPT AWAKE FOR SEVEN STRAIGHT DAYS . . .

STRESS POSITIONS . . .

MEDICALLY UNNECESSARY RECTAL FEEDING . . .

RECTAL HYDRATION . . .

TOTAL CONTROL OVER DETAINEE . . .

THE SALT PIT . . .

It took a few more days for the SERE connection to the CIA interrogation program to bubble back up into the headlines. But there it was again, right in front of me, glowing from my computer monitor in the evening gloom of my crumbling home.

THE ARCHITECTS OF TORTURE . . .

**EX–AIR FORCE DOCTORS RAN
PROGRAM FOR CIA . . .**

**EXPERIMENTS IN TORTURE HAVE
ROOTS IN U.S. MILITARY . . .**

**DOCTOR'S ROLE IN TORTURE
DETAILED . . .**

I scanned through these articles, too, feeling those dark pages of history flapping around inside of me. As a combat Marine, I'd had a pretty good idea what was going on in the so-called black sites. Wasn't proud of it, just aware. War is hell—no excuse, but a fact. Later, I had actually tried to forget it. Yes, Roland Ford, private investigator—with a history degree and a concealed-carry permit—was more interested in forgetting than remembering his own country's recent past.

And then I found exactly what I thought I'd find, something half forgotten, which is also something half remembered.

**FORMER AIR FORCE PSYCHOLOGISTS
WROTE TORTURE BOOK FOR CIA . . .
AND TOOK HOME A FORTUNE . . .**

**Fourteen years ago psychologists Briggs
Spencer and Timothy Tritt were buddies**

at Fairchild AFB in Washington State, "master trainers" in a program to help captured U.S. servicemen survive captivity and torture. Now the just-released Senate report on CIA Detention and Interrogation programs for the wars in Iraq and Afghanistan is naming them as co-authors of one of the darkest chapters in American history—the torture of hundreds of detainees in "secret" CIA "black sites" scattered throughout the mid-East, Europe and Asia . . .

I remembered Paige Hulet's description of Arcadia's founder: **a bit of a renegade.** Which made Paige Hulet as understated as she was neat and pretty. My search engines fired on all eight cylinders with "Briggs Spencer" and "SERE" as fuel. He was a doctor of psychology but not a medical doctor, born and raised in ritzy Newport Beach, California. He was fifty-eight years old, twenty years my senior, had attended Cal State Fullerton on a baseball scholarship, helping the team to its first College World Series championship in 1979. He played first, threw and hit left, had a .314 lifetime Titan batting average. He was dark-haired and big-jawed, with merry eyes and a cheerful, harmless smile. He looked like he would be popular.

Spencer was described as "athletically gifted and outgoing," "a fair student," "a team player." He was Air Force ROTC. After college baseball he married high school sweetheart and cheerleader Dawn Foxx, got a masters in psychology, then a PhD. A **Military Times** article noted that psychology was not an approved ROTC major, but for Briggs Spencer—and others— exceptions had been made. At age twenty-six he graduated from Officer Training School and was quickly assigned to the SERE program at Fairchild AFB.

I scanned through Spencer's time at Fairchild. He left the USAF in 1995 but was rehired as a civilian consultant to continue teaching SERE. His salary was classified, but an anonymous source put it at triple his Air Force pay. In 2002, not long after 9/11, he and another SERE senior trainer, Timothy Tritt, incorporated under the name Spencer-Tritt Consulting and, in 2003, shortly after the invasion of Iraq, moved their offices to Washington, D.C. A badly focused picture showed an older version of the hard-hitting first baseman.

Besides his fleeting notoriety from the Senate Intelligence Committee Report on Torture, there was little hard biography on Spencer to be found. But I found plenty of up-to-the-minute buzz: Spencer's "tell-all" war memoir, **Hard**

Truth, was due out later this month. **Can life lessons learned in a secret prison change your life for the better?** Schedules of his media appearances and book tour were posted. He had dates on CNN, MSNBC, and Fox News, and had a **60 Minutes** feature in the can. His book tour was twelve cities, coast-to-coast, starting in his hometown of La Jolla. Much was made of Briggs and Mrs. Spencer flying from city to city in one of his "several" helicopters. There were lots of pictures of him—Spencer in a ruggedly handsome headshot, Spencer loping from one helo or another, Spencer on the tarmac in front of Air Force One with Bush and Rumsfeld, all three of them red-eared in overcoats against some biting winter wind. A major studio had purchased movie rights to **Hard Truth**, Russell Crowe attached.

Next I searched to see if the paths of Clay Hickman, SERE program graduate, and Briggs Spencer, "master instructor," had crossed early on. If so, I couldn't find that crossing. Not at Fairchild, from which Briggs Spencer departed long before the arrival of Clay Hickman, at the ripe old age of nineteen. Not in Iraq, where, according to Chuck Graff's DoD source, Clay had not set foot. While Doctor of Psychology Briggs Spencer was commuting from black site to Langley and back again, Clay Hickman was officially nowhere from late 2007 until his discharge at the end of 2009. Then came Clay's troubled years, as documented in Paige Hulet's file. Until 2014, that is, when he was committed to Arcadia, a for-profit hospital recently founded by Briggs Spencer. In a low-percentage play, I replaced "Clay Hickman" with "Rick Sims," then "Richard Sims," but nothing popped.

I stood up from the rustic old table that was my work desk, went to one of the tall windows and looked out at the dark hills to the west. Rain was falling. I remembered flying through a rainstorm with Justine one night, coming home from Palm Springs. We'd ignored the forecast in our usual manner, and sure enough, by the time we began our descent into Fallbrook Airpark the rain was heavy and the thunder booming and the lightning splintered yellow in the west. She landed **Hall Pass** beautifully and the rain poured off the plane's wings as we taxied toward the hangars. We got the Cessna into her place and secure, then ran through the rain to the car. It was late and dark and we were alone in the parking lot so we made love in the back while the storm bore down. We had music on. I can remember the songs but not the order in which they played. I used to know. Every small loss takes you further away from what you loved. But how else do you go forward without forgetting some? You can't carry all of it.

Now in my darkened study I watched the rain.

A scientist on the radio said there's always the same amount of water on and in the earth, it just changes places. I wonder what good this knowledge does. Tell that to someone in a flood. Or in a drought. Soon water was tapping on the old oak floor. I got a red plastic bucket from under the bathroom sink and toed it into place. The drops kept a beat, slower and louder than the raindrops hitting the roof. Quietly, from under those wonderful syncopated rhythms of water, came Justine's voice, just its sound, no words.

My phone buzzed in my pocket. The text said:

12:38 AM
All good. Sleeping. Must leave
soon. He will talk to u. Use this
number, Walmart cheapie no GPS.
He's afraid of ping

12:39 AM
Where are u now?

12:40 AM
No. Trust us.

12:41 AM
Where are u going?

12:41 AM
TRUST US!

12:42 AM
Must see him. Any time or place.

12:43 AM
You sleep tight 2 ☺

Fat chance. I kept picturing Clay Hickman's paintings. And Sequoia's neat little Airstream. And wondering about all the things that might happen when you put Clay and Sequoia together in a tight space and shook them up a little.

I sat up late with my grandparents Dick and Liz, under the big palapa out by the pond, watching the rain. The raindrops sparkled on the surface of the pond and raised a faint mist. Even light rain like this seemed like a major weather event after so many years of California drought.

Grandpa Dick sat to my left, drinking scotch and grousing about the democrats ruining his country, berating Grandma Liz for her drinking, and complaining about the slippery shower floor in his casita.

Elizabeth sat to my right, drinking wine and griping about the republicans ruining her country, belittling Dick for his drinking, and me for not fixing the electricity in her casita.

"This whole place is a disgrace," she concluded. "You should sell."

"I can't leave it, Grandma."

"But you won't fix it."

"You can't leave it and you can't fix it, but you can't **stand** it, either, can you?" asked Grandpa.

"Sell, Rollie," said Liz.

"It is California real estate!" said Grandpa. "Hang on to it."

"And run it into the ground?" countered Grandma.

Grandpa said nothing, just shook his head, as if his wife of fifty years were daft. "So what in hell have you been up to, Rollie? Haven't seen much of you around here the last couple of days. Staying busy?"

"The usual."

"Exactly what usual?" he asked.

"I'm looking for someone who doesn't want to be found."

"That's everyone, if they're truthful," said Grandma.

"Speak for yourself."

"I knew he was going to say that. I knew it."

I watched the rain fall on the water and saw for one brief second the little rowboat we had, Justine at the oars, swimsuit, looking back at me from beneath one of her floppy sun hats. Bright water. That was in September, our perfect year. I heard her voice on the water, then no voice, only the raindrops boiling the pond.

Trying to shake that, I trotted out into the rain and pulled my truck into the barn, which had been fitted with a hydraulic vehicle lift years ago by a car-tinkering great-great-uncle of Justine's. Once I got it up I took a powerful shop light and examined the underside of the truck.

I found the transmitter tucked up on the foreside of the gas tank, screw-clamped to a metal strap. I wondered when they had put it on. More important, who they were. Lots of **they**s out there, if you let your imagination run, which I am not in the habit of doing. Good for an artist, maybe, but not a PI.

My first thought was Alec DeMaris's security team at Arcadia. Why would they follow their own expensive, cash-only private investigator? Good question. Arcadia security had had access to my truck twice—most recently for several hours today. A guy who knew what he was doing could have clamped that little tracker on in less than two minutes. Lunchtime would have been good, because the partners were all bellied up in the mess hall instead of roaming the grounds. Maybe less than one minute.

I unlocked and opened the tool chest in the bed of the truck. It's one of those big metal wall-to-wall chests that contractors bolt to their trucks and features not one but two lockable latches. I set the transmitter down inside of it with the jumper cables and road flares and watched its steady blue light. For now I'd let them enjoy following me, whoever they were. Drawing them along might come in handy, or it might not. If not, I could be rid of the thing in the time it would take to pull over and open a lid.

10

It descended through the sunrise, shiny as a new penny, engines humming and the quad rotors whapping the sound that makes people love helicopters. A svelte little Sikorsky 434 turbine with a bright copper paint job, darkened canopy windows, and the words HARD TRUTH painted on the pilot-side door. The letters were black and forward-rushing, and had tails to make them look like speeding bullets. Landing near the pond, the helo kicked up little dust, courtesy of last night's rain. It settled on its skid tubes.

I set my coffee cup on the long communal picnic bench. The chopper's rotor blades were still slowing when a man pushed open the door, looked at me through yellow-lensed aviators, then dropped to the ground and ducked beneath the blades, headed my way.

He looked to be near sixty, solidly built, and when he cleared the rotors I saw that he was tall. He came to the picnic bench where I sat, spread his hands on the tabletop, and leaned toward me. "Dr. Briggs Spencer," he said. His smile said, **You're going to like me**.

He still had the heroic jaw. Since the war he'd grown his gray hair long enough for the helo blades to throw it around. I could see blue eyes behind the yellow lenses, nearly blanched of color, roaming my face as if looking for a way in.

A long beat.

"Come on, I'll take you up. You can explain to me how Clay has managed to secure a girl-friend and a truck in less than the forty-eight hours since I hired you to find him. Don't mind heights, do you?"

"I like heights. But I'm not a fan of torture."

The good doctor lay a hand on my shoulder and took another while to study me. The hand was heavy. He tilted his head down to look over his glasses at me. "Mr. Ford, people change. Come on. Get in."

I didn't move. I had told Paige Hulet about Clay's "girlfriend" but nothing about her role in his escape or her subsequently stolen truck. Which meant the doctor had sources other than Paige Hulet and me. Sometimes people hire PIs to watch their PIs. I wondered if Briggs Spencer's other sources of information drove a white Range Rover and a black Dodge Charger.

I finished my coffee, and followed the man to his helicopter.

We rose swiftly into the early-morning sky. I had that funny gut-drop you get in a helicopter, like some part of yourself is still on the ground and you want to go back down and pick it up. My property got smaller as the world got bigger. I saw Lindsey Rakes standing in front of her casita, looking up, shading her eyes. I thought of buzzing the rancho with Justine in **Hall Pass**, how she'd bring it in just over the pond, touch and go on the little strip we'd dozed, then go screaming into a climb. Being in the air makes me feel close to her, makes my problems on earth seem smaller. Less bound by the laws below.

The S-434 was configured for four, but we were alone. It had dual flight controls. The cabin noise wasn't bad for a light turbine chopper and Dr. Briggs Spencer's voice was clear and forceful, but we used headsets anyway.

"I didn't learn to fly until I was in my forties," he said, banking hard to the west. "I was stationed at Fairchild outside of Spokane and I knew some Apache pilots. Off-the-radar kind of arrangement, literally. Now, that is one enormous head-and-body rush that you'll never forget—flying a gunship. I'd buy one, but it wouldn't be practical for business. Terrible fuel economy. Check this out, though."

He nodded to a holster bolted to the helo frame on his left, in which rested a large semiautomatic handgun. Spencer smiled, leaned back a little, and reached to the fuselage just above the weapon. He slid open a small window, not much larger than a gas-tank lid, made a gun of his forefinger, and pointed it out the hole. That cheerleader-winning smile again. "Coyotes," he said. "There's hillsides near my home crawling with them. At night I get down low, hit the spotlights, and give them hell. Nice to be a southpaw sometimes."

"Odd hobby for a psychologist."

"I told you, people change. There's a gun port on your side, too. Maybe we'll go out some night, shoot some varmints."

"No, thanks. Did you buy this helo with your money from running the torture programs?"

"Don't be squeamish. It wasn't torture. It was detention and interrogation."

Words, meaning everything and nothing again. "Bullshit is bullshit, whatever you call it."

"Yeah, well, I made an ungodly sum from it. CIA just threw money at us—at everyone over there. Our base contract was worth eighty million, and we were paid bonuses for what they called 'useful intelligence.' Bear in mind that I'm nothing but a garden-variety psychologist graduated from a state school. A decent first baseman with a GPA of two point four. My only gifts are a stubborn streak and that people like me. Now, some of that government money I used for black-site maintenance, bribes, subcontractors—everything you'd expect. But Tim and I cleared about twenty mil each. We closed Spencer-Tritt Consulting in 2009, one step ahead of Obama. When DoD came after me for breach of contract, the CIA paid the legal fees. Five million. I won. Invested in some lucky IPOs that went huge, opened the door to start-ups. At that level it's who you know. Allowed me to get into things I love. Which is tech and medical—drones and drugs. Medevac hardware conversion—helos again. Pharmaceuticals, mostly psychotropic therapies for schizophrenia and depression. I founded residential mental illness facilities where we actually make you better, not worse. Got three of them up and running and the fourth underway. Exclusive and expensive because exclusive people **demand** expense. I made a fortune off the United States government and turned that into a hundred fortunes more. Funny part is, the CIA always thought of me as a bargain. And let me be extremely clear on one thing—we did **not** torture. We applied enhanced interrogation techniques, developed by Dr. Tritt and myself. They were rational and legal and they worked. They saved American lives. Don't believe the gutless media or the politicians. Nothing they say about us is true."

Only a guilty conscience talks that long without being asked a question. "Except the eighty million."

"Yes, good, the money was very true. But believe it or not, I didn't bring you all the way up here to talk about myself. Have you seen Clay?"

"Not yet."

"Paige told me you've discovered a lady friend of his. Is this a friend from his past or a new acquaintance?"

"New, unless she's a good liar."

"How long have they known each other?"

"One month of talking through the fence at your hospital."

"But no past connection?"

"Not that I've found."

"Give me her name. I'll run it through DeMaris."

"She spoke to me confidentially."

"Is she a hostage?"

"She doesn't think so."

"How did you know to look for them at the Waterfront?"

I shrugged and looked down at tawny foothills buttoned by dark green oaks. I had to conclude that the tail cars at the Waterfront were his, but I said nothing. I'd had employers like Briggs Spencer before—controllers who want to know not only everything you've learned but how you learned it. It's their way of confirming that they could have learned it themselves if they'd only had the time, thus you are an overpaid fool. "So, Doctor, does Arcadia offer a military discount?"

The psychologist peered at me again over his glasses. "You mean for Clay? I can't do that. Rule number one: Business is business."

He drew the stick back and shoved it right. My body swayed left, inner gyros working, then I felt the gut-drop again as the light craft banked into heavy air. It was like one of those carnival rides that go around fast and pin you to the wall. "But I can tell you, the profit I make on Arcadia and my other hospitals is pocket change compared to other things I do. It's more a passion than a business."

"What's the monthly charge for a partner to live in Arcadia?"

Spencer looked at me. "That's not something my conservators want disclosed. And more important, implied when you admit a loved one to Arcadia is the idea that **this kind of shit doesn't happen.** Partners don't just walk off, Mr. Ford. I **promise** their families they can't. Now Rex Hickman is putting enormous pressure on me to find Clay and return him to Arcadia."

I waited for his disapproval of my not having delivered Clay to him already, his subtle employer's threat. And I didn't care if the psychologist fired me on the spot, as long as I got a ride back home. I looked down on Vail Lake, a sapphire-blue gash in the hills. Compared to the torturer beside me, Clay Hickman was more forgivable. Clay was an earnest overachiever most likely driven crazy—truly, actually, crazy—by war. Violent? Yes. Dangerous? Maybe. But this wasn't the first time I'd been hired to find someone more admirable than the people looking for him. I didn't care if I worked another day for Briggs Spencer or not.

Then he pushed the stick down and left, which dropped the little Sikorsky into a steep descent. It looked like he was aiming for the lake. He pegged the engine, earth on tilt, chopper shuddering.

"The first goal of interrogation is to establish control over the partner," he said. "When the control is total, his will dissolves. He must come to see you as controlling every element, from what he hears and sees to what he feels and thinks. What he eats and drinks. When his diapers are changed. When he is slammed into a wall or left overnight chained naked to a concrete floor. Finally, the detainee must see that you control whether he lives or dies. When he knows that you are in control of his life, he will begin to feel helpless. We taught our partners helplessness, Mr. Ford. **Learned helplessness**. Our goal was not simple information and confession, but **exploitation**. The full exploitation of the partner—for propaganda, recruiting, penetration. It all derives from helplessness, which can be taught. No one understood us, though our success was visible everywhere you looked. I say it all the time and I'll say it again: We saved American lives. But enough. It's all in my book. **Hard Truth**. Out this month, huge media, big tour. The times have caught up with Briggs Spencer. I got a nice advance, and film rights went big. I'm getting sequel offers, speaking offers. The new president has reached out to me for cabinet recommendations. Heady stuff. And I intend to profit from every bit of it."

I watched the earth rising up at us. The little Sikorsky wasn't built for this kind of thing: the dizzying, disorienting yaw, and the g-force pressure. But he wouldn't see me sweat. I focused my attention on the rough hills beneath us, grass and chaparral. This season's rain was poor again, and by summer a spark would be all it would take to set it off. **Whoosh**. Adios north San Diego County.

Then, time to jab: "Was Clay a part of your program?"

"No. He was a flight mechanic in Iraq. I didn't meet him until three years ago, when his father asked me to examine him at the state hospital. Rex and Patricia Hickman wanted something better for their son. Something that would help him. I had opened Arcadia two years earlier."

I wondered if Spencer had fallen for the same

falsified service record that I'd been handed by Paige Hulet. Then I wondered if Spencer had created that record himself. If so, he was a solid liar, both on the page and now. I wondered how such a skill might have influenced **Hard Truth.**

Spencer smiled at me, eased out of the dive, then pointed the helo back toward Fallbrook. He turned and gave me another long look. "You don't scare easily. I know you've played in the sky before."

"I've got good insurance up here. You."

"Soundly reasoned."

"Why are we here?"

"I need two things, Mr. Ford. One is to find Clay. I want one hundred percent of your time devoted to him. Your pay is now doubled, to guarantee your full attention. Two, I need you to call me immediately when you've located him. Do not call Paige. Do not call DeMaris."

If I'd had any doubt how badly Briggs Spencer wanted to find Clay, my unasked-for raise erased it. And his demand that I call him first, not his director of medical services, not his head of security. Their three-way competition was more than just intriguing. It seemed desperate. Even in a quick glance I saw the intensity on his face. And the coldness in his eyes through the chilly yellow light of his aviators.

"Why **not** call Dr. Hulet or DeMaris?" I asked.

"Because you work for me, not them. It's best for Clay. DeMaris is a dullard. And Paige is scary smart but she tends to take her partners too seriously. Too personally, for her own good. Clay needs a steadying hand."

"And then what? I locate Clay, you come take him back to Arcadia?"

"That's what the Hickmans want. It's where he belongs. Best treatment in the world and a damned nice place to get it."

From what little I'd seen of Arcadia and its staff so far, I could have agreed. Though the idea of a private asylum run by a bona fide ex-torturer seemed more than a little off to me.

"I want to put an idea in your head," he said.

"I don't want your ideas in my head."

"Listen. There are rewards to be gotten on earth—genuine treasures—far beyond your paltry hourly wage. Beyond what you imagine is possible to attain. Beyond that vast ache you feel in your heart for Justine."

Rage, Wrath & Fury rose to attention inside me. They are the rude, ugly creatures who clambered into me the moment I heard that Justine was dead. I named them. They haven't left since. Right then, in that helo with Briggs Spencer, they were very angry. Even for them. A lot of things set them off, Justine's name among them. "Don't say her name again."

"I say what I want in my own helicopter."

"Not her name." I set my right ankle over the other knee, let the cuff of my pant leg reveal the gun.

Spencer took a long look at it, then at me. "You surprise me. I could make a call and have your license for this. And up here in the sky, I'm your lifeline. So all you're really doing is bluffing."

"It's up to you."

He looked ahead, not at me. He glanced at the gun on his left. "You keep her alive inside you. Don't you understand that? You control who she is and who she becomes."

"Don't say her name again."

"No, **hell** no. You win. But thank you. I understand you better now."

The sun was a fat orange ball in the eastern sky. Below us, Interstate 15 traffic was humming along smoothly. Fallbrook came into view. A minute later I could see my hills and the thickets of oak and sycamore and the random network of narrow two-track roads that linked Rancho de los Robles together, then the house and the barn and the pond.

"Roland, you've impressed me today. I see that, after you've gotten Clay back, I might need you on my team again. Where you would have a chance to flourish, and become familiar with those treasures I mentioned."

I ignored him. We came in low over the water.

The rotor chop dashed the reflections of the willows and cattails on the banks. I saw my tenants sitting around the picnic table under the palapa, their five curious faces all tracking the approach of the shiny Sikorsky.

Spencer set the craft down softly. He worked a card from his wallet and wrote something on the back and gave it to me. He looked at me once again. "My Air Force friends? They called the action 'smoke.' Put me in the smoke, Mr. Ford. I love it there. Find Clay Hickman and lead me to him. It would be the best thing for everyone involved."

11

"What kind of crackpot paints his helo copper?" asked Grandpa Dick. "And what's so hard about the truth?"

Breakfast time under the big palapa by the pond on Rancho de los Robles, all Irregulars present. Dick and Burt Short were the breakfast team most days, which meant scrambled eggs, sausage, bacon, ham, tortillas, and salsa.

"It's a new book by a psychologist," said Burt Short, giving me a flat look. "And that Sikorsky 434 turbine will set you back nine hundred and thirty thousand new."

"A book about Operation Iraqi Freedom," Lindsey Rakes said absently. The cuffs of her fine cowgirl shirt from the night before were rolled up, her hair lopsided from sleep, her sunglasses dark. Apparently she'd run the gauntlet of casinos between her lawyer and here without success. "Pass the tortillas."

"Here you go, honey," said Grandma Liz. "I can make you a Bloody Mary that might help."

Lindsey stared at Liz but said nothing.

"Anyone wants to hike after breakfast let me know," said Wesley Gunn. "I'm down to a hundred and fifty-seven days with both eyes."

"I still think that Tijuana doctor I know could do you some good," said Burt. "How about you skip the hike and I'll drive you down for a consult?"

"All Mexican doctors are quacks," said Dick.

"Of course they're not," said Liz. "Some are educated in America."

"Illegally and for free," said Dick.

"Don't you two ever stop?" asked Lindsey. "You're worse than a hangover. You **are** a hangover."

Wesley Gunn regarded Burt from behind the very dark lenses of his prescription glasses. "Okay. Let's go see the Mexican doctor."

Burt set his coffee cup down and smiled. He's a round-faced little man with a raspy voice and laugh. "Let's finish breakfast and mosey south. I'll call him."

"Can I go?" asked Lindsey. "I don't have anything else to do."

I loaded up my plate and poured another cup of coffee. During good weather we spent more time here at the picnic table than in the cavernous dining room inside. I sent a text message to an acquaintance at the **San Diego Union-Tribune** to whom I had spoken frankly and on record about the shooting of Titus Miller. I asked him if he could get me an early copy of **Hard Truth**. He said he'd send the paper's review copy along, but I told him I'd pick it up instead.

When my phone buzzed I stepped away from the picnic table to answer. The voice I wanted to hear most was Sequoia Blain's. Wish granted. But I braced myself for the worst.

She sounded worried but said she was okay. Was with Clay in a motel in Ojai—a three-and-a-half-hour drive north from Fallbrook. Not sure why they were there. Not afraid, exactly, but she was worried because Clay was agitated and emotional and he was definitely coming off his meds. He'd been using her phone, but was secretive about who he was contacting.

She gave me the name of the motel and room number, and said Clay thought he was ready to meet me, but I had to call when I got there. In case he changed his mind. "He wants you to bring a voice recorder. Mr. Ford, you're not just going to show up with the cops and arrest him, are you?"

My temper was rising and Clay was the target. His demands and evasions. Sequoia's protective complicity was wearing thin, too. "If he hurts you I will."

"Because he's . . . breakable. You know what they did to him in that so-called hospital? **Arcadia?** They shocked him and drugged him for three years. He's afraid no one will believe him."

I rallied my patience because I thought it would get me closer to Clay faster. "I'll be there as soon as I can, Sequoia. Tell him I'm depending on him to protect you. Tell him very clearly."

"You can't take him back to the hospital. What **are** you going to do?"

I didn't know the answer to that. But Sequoia was wrong: I **could** take him back to Arcadia. I'd contracted to do just that, so profession and compensation came to mind. The Hickman family apparently wanted him to stay in that swanky prison of a hospital—and as conservator, Rex Hickman was in control of almost every aspect of his son's life. Legally, Clay was powerless. There was the very real possibility that Arcadia was still the best place for him. No power was granted to me except fulfilling the terms of my agreement with Arcadia, and a moral obligation to keep Clay Hickman from hurting himself or Sequoia or anyone else.

"I'll hear him out," I said.

"I want you to. But his mind changes fast."

I grabbed my work travel duffel—packed and waiting under my bed—then drove fast to the **Union-Tribune** office in San Diego and picked up the swank readers' copy of **Hard Truth.** On the cover was a moody black-and-white photograph of Briggs Spencer trotting handsomely beneath the blades of a helicopter. Resolution on his face. Gray hair tousled, and tie streaming, a blurred gallery of darkly overcoated men in the background, watching Spencer while he looks into the camera.

I hit Fallbrook Airpark an hour later, taxied **Hall Pass 2** down the runway. As I climbed into the blue western sky I saw a white Range Rover and a black Dodge Charger sitting side by side on the far edge of the parking area, facing opposite directions. Two men leaned on the driver's-side doors, looking up at me. They looked like cabbies waiting for fares. When I was out of their sight I cleared myself in all directions, dropped the Cessna into a steep descent, and buzzed the cars low and fast. One of the men clambered back into the SUV. The other, Alec DeMaris, leaned casually on his car and looked up at me, shaking his head. The airpark manager could have my hide for the stunt, but I didn't care. I banked and buzzed them once again, then climbed steeply and set my bearings north.

An hour and nineteen minutes later I was touching down on a private landing strip two miles from Ojai. It was owned by a friend of Pete Bagnoli, who is one of my hundreds of confederates in the very loosely organized Private Investigators Group—which we affectionately call PIG. No dues, no officers; nothing but a not-easy-to-acquire directory of PIs who might be inclined to help one another. Quite a variety of characters. We meet once a year, in Denver, whoever can make it. Young and old, male and female. Most are working professionals, a few are amateurs, others no more than crackpots with stories to tell. But I've met hundreds of PIs at the Denver confabs, everyone from marathon runners to skydivers to master marksmen to salvage divers. Some are vets like me, and plenty are former cops and deputies. Some are geeky tech wizards. Two collect stamps competitively.

Some even have access to landing strips. I'd met Ojai-based Pete once in Denver, and an hour and a half ago he'd been happy to offer me his friend's landing strip. He said he'd leave a car there for me, too—keys on the right rear tire.

PIGs roll together. And I had the feeling I'd need all the luck that brotherhood could buy me.

12

I locked up **Hall Pass 2** and called Sequoia. Got voicemail; texted and got nothing back. It took me ten minutes to get to town. Ojai sits on the tip of the Santa Ynez Mountains, north of Ventura, twelve miles from the Pacific. It's a Spanish Revival–style town with a nice arcade and campanile, photogenic, and popular with tourists, motorcycle clubs, and golfers.

The Regal Motel was just off Matilija. I drove Pete's aging Taurus through the crowded little parking lot until I saw Sequoia's silver truck. A gorilla key chain from the Primate Palace hung from the rearview mirror. I found a space across the lot with a good view of the truck and backed in. The Regal Motel was two stories, and their room was ground level. In the middle of the parking area, a big valley oak grew behind a low concrete wall. A gray cat sat on the wall in the shade, licking its paw on this warm April day. I felt clear in the head and ready to meet my opponent, still not sure what I was going to do with him.

I texted Sequoia again and waited. The curtains in room 104 were drawn, the air conditioner dripped. No reply.

Ten minutes later they came out. Sequoia pulled the door closed snugly, then they walked all of the ten feet to the truck, Clay's arm draped lightly over her shoulders. I watched for signs of fear or coercion but they looked like lovers and nothing more. In the moment. Appreciative of this time together. Sequoia was dressed much as I'd seen her before—denim shorts with fashion tears in them, a baggy plaid shirt with the sleeves rolled up, hiking boots. Clay Hickman wore what looked like the same clothes he'd ditched Arcadia in—tan cords and a black T-shirt, dressy shoes. He opened the passenger-side door and she got in.

When they turned onto Matilija I followed them to the exit, then let two cars get between us for cover. Clay drove carefully, working his way north and east through town. He picked up Highway 33, leading me past Matilija Canyon, then Dry Lakes Ridge, headed toward steep and rugged Los Padres National Forest.

The highway was heavily forested and climbed steadily in elevation. I kept a car between us. Nothing in Clay Hickman's driving suggested evasion or even much precaution. Then, abruptly and without signaling, he turned right onto an unmarked dirt road. I had no choice but to slow down with the cars in front of me, then continue on past the turn. As I went by I could see the silver truck trundling away, puffs of dust coming off the tires. A half mile farther, I U-turned and backtracked. The unmarked dirt road was oiled, well kept, and winding.

Two hundred yards from the highway I came to what looked like a very large gravestone lying on its side. I stopped and studied it. It was set levelly into the earth, and a modest bed of daisies had been maintained around its base. The stone itself was a red granite rectangle approximately six feet long, four feet high, and at least six inches thick. It was polished and clean. One word was cut into the stone in graceful cursive letters:

HICKMAN

I took a picture with my phone and continued on. The trees were dense and the curves were narrow. Half a mile farther I climbed a gentle rise and came to a stop. From there the road ran straight through the forest toward green, rounded mountains. Low on the flank of the foremost mountain, partially hidden by trees, stood a large white farmhouse. Black trim. Outbuildings painted similarly. Reminded me of homes

I'd seen once in Pennsylvania Amish country. I could see what looked like a barnyard or a large lawn. In front of this was a rolling, white-fenced pasture where horses grazed in the sunshine. On the road, midway between the house and the pasture fence, stood a guardhouse, the white crossbeam lowered over the road.

Sequoia's aging silver pickup idled at the guardhouse, then the arm rose and the truck went ahead. I backed Pete's car into a highway-patrol turn, then picked my way back down the road until I found room in the trees. Got my binoculars from the trunk, hiked back up the rise, and glassed the scene.

The silver truck was parked near the house with three other vehicles—a Tesla, a Porsche Cayenne, and a BMW X5. Beside them the little truck looked like a family secret. The guardhouse crossbeam was down again and a uniformed man stood with his back to the front window of his booth, looking up at the house, a cell phone to one ear. He was older, heavy. Seemed to be listening intently. Then he was shaking his head firmly in the negative. Then another long listen before shaking his head in the affirmative and clicking off. I noted the time: 2:24. He dialed and waited, phone to his ear.

The afternoon sun had started its downward roll, splashing light on the white house and the white fencing and the green pasture and the cars. The Hickman home was a beautiful estate in a beautiful setting and it tried to tell me that nothing could ever go truly wrong there: it was a simple factory for producing privileged human beings. I lit a smoke and wondered how it was going in there between Clay and his parents, assuming that Rex and Patricia were home. I could wait and wonder. Or drive right up to the guardhouse and announce myself. Or finish the cigarette.

With the binoculars up again, I glassed the forested mountains and the wispy cirrus clouds above and suddenly I thought of Wesley Gunn, eighteen years old and less than half a year away from losing half—perhaps all—of his eyesight. Rage, Wrath & Fury started up. Very protective of Wesley. I pictured him down in Mexico right now with Burt and Lindsey, searching for a miracle. And I thought of what the poet had written about the dying of the light and I wondered what kind of god would shoulder a bright and untested young man with such a dark and permanent burden. Leaving him rage instead of vision? What good would rage do Wesley? It wouldn't stop the dying of his light. Wesley wasn't even angry yet. He was mostly bewildered, and only lately starting to feel the yoke of fear fitted to his young shoulders. Even Justine had gotten her thirty-one years. And to be truthful, Justine had tempted her Lord. Tempted Him by flying close to His sun, showing Him her skill and courage, by being unafraid of what He might do. By **enjoying** it all—the risk, the thrill, the victory of staying alive. Wesley hadn't done anything brasher in his life than throw footballs for touchdowns.

I sat there for a good long while, watching the house and the surrounding mountains, willing Rage, Wrath & Fury to pipe down. I'm better now at shutting them up. They grew still. In the welcomed quiet, a Cessna 182 passed by overhead, Lycoming engine growling right along. I watched it disappear in a cloud.

The guardhouse crossbeam lifted. I looked behind me, back down the drive leading in, and saw two black, dark-windowed SUVs moving toward the house. I glassed them and saw that each vehicle carried two men, and that these men wore sunglasses and were neither talking nor moving except with the bounce of the road, and looking nowhere but straight ahead. Presumably armed. I swung the glasses to the guardhouse again and saw him step out, pushing red twelve-gauge loads into the breech of a pistol-grip shotgun with a stub barrel. Nothing like a shotgun to make the heart jump. I got my phone.

3:03 PM
Four men coming. Guns probable.
Surrender immediately. Do not resist
in any way. This is a direct order.

The two SUVs cruised along, not quite fast,
as if this thing would unfold exactly on their
schedule. They stopped at the booth. The guard
stepped to the lead vehicle and the driver's-side
window went down. A heated exchange, the
guard jabbing the gun toward the house.

The driver pushed him away and the SUV
lurched forward, followed closely by the second.
On they went. The guard lumbered after them
for a few yards, then gave up, an old dog out-
run by rabbits. The two vehicles picked up their
pace. It looked like half a minute to the house,
another ten seconds to get in, and after that
they'd probably clear the place like we did in
Fallujah, one room at a time, all screaming and
arm language, room to room, then to another
and another. There are few things more intense
and adrenaline-spiking in this world. Carrying
life and death in your hands. Yours and those of
others. Making all that follows back home feel
dull and inconsequential.

3:06 PM
Men coming! Do not resist. DO NOT!

I figured if Clay was packing by now, or even Sequoia—through some understandable lapse in a nineteen-year-old's judgment—there would soon be a brief firefight and two young lovers, or whatever they were, would be left lying side by side and forever dead.

Then: movement up by the house. I swung the binoculars onto the silver truck, which came accelerating down the drive, fast. The SUV drivers swung across the narrow road and parked. The four men dropped out and ran to cover in the trees, two on each side of the road. One with a handgun drawn. Clay charged toward the roadblock. I could see him behind the wheel, hands at two and ten, sunglasses on and his white hair bouncing. Beside him, Sequoia sat low, her head jammed back against the rest, hands braced on the dash.

On approach Clay downshifted, snaking right then left as he looked for a way through the blockade. From my higher view I saw the way. Clay did, too. He accelerated with a scream of engine, skidded around the first vehicle, shot the gap between, fishtailed around the second SUV, then gunned his truck down the tree line. The men held their fire.

The truck slid back onto the road and sped toward the guardhouse while the men scrambled into their vehicles. The guard had lowered the gate arm again and taken a position in the tree line. He knelt, heavy and off balance, trying to steady the buttless weapon with both hands. When the truck was a hundred feet in front of him, he fired into the air high above it. Clay didn't slow down. The guard was clumsily jacking in another round when Clay splintered the gate and roared past the guardhouse. By the time the old man got himself up and turned and ready to fire again, Clay and Sequoia were out of range. The guard slammed the gun to the ground.

Moments later the silver pickup truck sped past me. My gut reaction was to give chase, but even if I managed to pull them over, then what? I could neither detain nor arrest. Could I talk enough sense to calm down a psychotic young man, off his meds, who has just been shot at? I didn't think so. My first moral responsibility was still Sequoia's safety.

The two SUVs skidded to stops at the guard gate and the men got out. The guard started yelling, then everybody was yelling at everybody. Their voices came to me as distant yelps. The BMW from the big house came barreling down, and it skidded to a stop, too, and a late-fifties-looking couple jumped out.

I watched the truck bouncing back toward the highway, Clay essing along in gentle left and right swerves, enjoying the getaway. **Enjoy it,**

I thought. **You are very lucky to be turning that wheel rather than bleeding on it.** I had to shake my head as Clay and Sequoia disappeared around a curve.

The man I assumed to be Rex Hickman punched a finger into the old guard's chest. The presumed Patricia Hickman grabbed her husband's arm. The two SUVs hauled down the drive after the silver truck, and a moment later the BMW tore back uphill toward the house. No one saw me or paid Pete Bagnoli's semi-hidden Taurus off in the trees any mind.

I waited a few minutes, then called Rex Hickman, told him who I was, that I was in the neighborhood, and would like to talk to him.

Hell no, he said, bad timing.

I told him I'd seen the shooting that had just transpired outside his home.

"Those men are mine," he said. "And so is this property. Stay off it."

"I'm on my way," I told him. "Tell fatso not to shoot me when I come up the drive."

13

I stood on the Hickman porch and listened to the voices, upstairs and distant. Rex hollering in torrents, Patricia silent, then shouting back. Couldn't hear the words, but things were escalating by the sound of it. I rang the doorbell once more, waited, then called Rex again.

A few minutes later he swung open the front door. He had a **Kick your ass** expression on his face and a derringer dangling from one hand. Medium height, short brown hair, and pointed ears.

I overrode my instinct to go after him. "Cute gun, but I come in peace."

"What in hell do you want?"

"To help your son. You don't mind, do you?"

A few steps behind him materialized Patricia— tall, blond, workout clothes. She stared at me from behind his shoulder. "We don't, do we, Rex?"

Without another word they led me through the foyer. He wore a purple polo shirt, shorts, and deck shoes. He looked as harmless as a man with a gun can look. The nylon soles of his shoes tapped on the hardwood floor as we walked past a great room with a towering ceiling, nineteenth-century portraiture, and a central flower arrangement the size of a Christmas tree.

Then into a study. Walls of bookshelves and a cavernous fireplace, picture windows facing west and south. At a bar beneath one of the windows Rex set the gun down and poured a glass of red wine for his wife. And what looked like a scotch and soda for himself. He took the wine to Patricia, who had encamped near one of the windows. I declined the drink they didn't offer.

From here the Hickman grounds looked pastoral, as if nothing had happened. No gunfire. No car chase. No crazy son on a crazy mission. But here in the study, in close proximity to Rex and Patricia, I felt as if some flammable gas had pooled and a spark could set it off.

"Look, Hickmans," I said. "You can stay on mute as long as you want, but I'm trying to find your son and bring him to some kind of safety."

"My men will do that," said Rex. "They'll return him to Arcadia, where he's safe and well taken care of."

"I wonder why he ran away, then."

"Not for you to know," he said.

"Do you?"

He pondered this. "This is what I know. I know the quality of care he gets. His quality of

life. And I know how much money I spend to
provide it for him."

"Honey."

"Try twenty-five thousand dollars a **month.**"

I did try it, and it came to three hundred thousand dollars a year. At that rate, Arcadia's sixty
patients brought a breezy eighteen million dollars annually to "Dr." Briggs Spencer, who also
owned two other facilities. I remembered that
he'd called his hospital profits "pocket change."
I smiled at the stubbornly cheap natures of so
many very rich men.

"What is it that you find funny?"

"Let's be frank, Mr. Hickman. Twenty-five
grand a month doesn't even budge your bottom
line."

"It certainly doesn't help it. But really, how
far out of your way will you go to miss a point?
The point is, Clay is a very troubled young man,
and he has been that way for a long time, and
Pat and I have done **everything in our power**
to get what is best for him. And now Clay has
had yet another break. His medications have become toxic or obsolete. Again. His mind is fir-
ing wrong. Again. Whatever was keeping him
stable—relatively stable—has somehow gone
wrong."

Half a mile down the road I saw the heavy old
guard come from the booth, look down at the

broken barrier lying in the grass, then go back inside. "Has Clay ever complained to you about his treatment there?"

Mr. and Mrs. Hickman exchanged looks. "All we know is he was stable," said Rex. "Then this."

"Why did he come here today?" I asked.

"Because we're his parents and we love him?" Rex asked.

My turn to ask the obvious. "If you love him, then why don't you see him more than once a year?"

Rex colored, then drank. Patricia turned her back to us and looked out a big window. I hadn't wanted to bring that up yet, but their armor was hard and I needed something strong to get through it.

"He loves us," Patricia said to the glass. "But few and brief visits are all he can stand of us. He experiences terrible anxiety when we visit. Once, he chewed himself like a dog, the day before we were to see him."

"So we stay away," said Rex. "Even the once-a-year is . . . difficult."

"Why?"

Rex set his drink on an end table, put an arm around his wife. They were the same height. When they whispered it sounded like the same whisper. Questions and answers. I had the feeling that they were saying things they had said many times. Had the feeling that Patricia was winning this negotiation. They turned to me together.

"Clay was born with a bad heart," she said. "And they said he might not live. There were complications over the years, but he wanted to be strong, like his sisters. So he compensated. He compensated so hard you wouldn't believe it. There was never a boy who worked harder to be strong and smart. He read and read, and studied and studied, got tutors, always took the hardest classes. He ran for miles and lifted weights and played sports and went to summer school, and there was never one day of his life that Clay wasn't striving and straining and sweating to be stronger and smarter and better. He—"

"Overcompensated, is what Pat's trying to say." Rex cleared his throat. "I did some of that myself. When I was young. Winning became everything to him—beating Kayla and Daphne. But the war changed him. He felt he had lost. He thought he'd let us down somehow. Then came all this crazy behavior. Seeing us now reminds him of his failure, of how far he has fallen. So he doesn't want to see us."

"He was set for Stanford but he joined the Air Force instead," said Patricia.

"Nine-eleven," said Rex. "He was only thirteen, but the attacks fit right into his mental picture of becoming Superman. For his country."

"He was one of the best aircraft mechanics in Iraq, wasn't he, Rex?"

Rex held my stare. "Ali Air Base. He worked on the Spookies."

"So," said Patricia. "That's why we can't see him as much as we'd like. It's a sacrifice we make for him. If he was more comfortable around us, I'd move him into this house, get the security better and plenty of nurses, and maybe—"

"Enough, Pat. This is ground we have agreed not to walk upon."

She nodded, resigned.

"Believe me," said Rex. "We'd be at Arcadia once a week."

At the bar Rex freshened his drink, then refilled his wife's wineglass and brought it to her. "I'd offer you a drink, but it's late."

I checked my watch to confirm it was only four in the afternoon, but let that slide. "Less than an hour ago there was gunfire here, directed at your son and an innocent girl. Now I show up, trying to get Clay back to his hospital, and you want to kick me down the road. Why?"

Hickman gave me a cold stare but no information. I rolled with his silence and turned to his wife. "Mrs. Hickman, were you looking forward to your annual visit with Clay next week?"

"Get out," said Rex.

Patricia Hickman smiled. "Very much, Mr.

Ford. I've purchased a new Max Azria for the occasion."

He gave her a tough glance. "Dear? Please shut up. Beat it, Ford. The Ventura sheriffs can get here in a hurry." Rex jammed a hand into his shorts pocket and drew his phone.

"Just a couple of things, Mr. Hickman, then I'll leave you to your busy evening. Did you have any contact with Clay in 2008 or 2009?"

"Why, of course," said Patricia. "We talked three or four times a week when he was overseas."

"Did he ever send you anything physical, a letter or a postcard or a package? A gift, maybe? Not electronic, but something with an origin?"

Patricia seemed guileless and Rex overheated and I didn't think they were lying to me about Clay being at Ali Air Base. They'd fallen for the same invented war story that Paige Hulet had given me. "Clay only got us one gift from the war," said Patricia. "But he didn't mail it. He brought it home in his duffel."

"What was it?" I asked.

"Pat? Stop."

"It's okay, Rexie. Dolls, Mr. Ford. Two dolls, fighting with swords. Villagers of some kind. Soft, with ceramic faces. Less than half a foot tall. Clay thought we would like them. We kept them upstairs in his room."

"Christ, Pat."

She looked at him, then down at the floor. "The dolls were genuine folk art, and they showed us he cared. Honey, Mr. Ford really should know that the longer Clay was at war, the less we heard from him. And how, by the last year of his deployment, we were down to maybe an email or text every other week. Or once a month."

"It's none of his business how much our son did or did not write us," said Rex.

A heavy silence settled over the room. I felt very grateful that I was not either one of these human beings. "When Clay first saw Arcadia, what did he think of the place?"

"Clay liked it," Rex said. "He wanted to live there. But we didn't discover it—it discovered us. People like Briggs Spencer look out for people like me. Now, excuse me while I call 911 to report your invasion of my home."

"What did Clay want today? Why did he come here?"

Hickman looked up from his phone with all the menace he could find. It might have been terrifying from across a boardroom table. I did not laugh in his face. It always surprises me how successful in life angry, small-minded people can be. I must underestimate these virtues.

"He wanted the fighting dolls I just told you about, Mr. Ford," said Patricia. "And he took them."

I paused and considered. "After three years in a private hospital, he dug out and came all the way up here to retrieve two folk dolls that he'd brought home from the war. Can you make some sense of that for me?"

"He also needed money," said Patricia. "So he took five thousand from our what-if jar."

"Damn it, Pat!"

"We're as puzzled as you must be," she said. "But Clay gave us something back. He gave each of us a big strong hug. For the first time in years. My heart felt so full and light. But then he took the gun from Rexie's nightstand. It's loaded. He seemed so eager to have the gun. Which frightened both of us half to death."

I felt a jagged surge of adrenaline. Now the violent schizoaffective Clay Hickman was armed, financed, and shielding himself with a nineteen-year-old girl who thought she'd found a friend in him. He had risked her life just an hour ago. He was off his meds and in the wind again and his stolen firearm was loaded.

"Clay needs to be stopped," I said. I set a business card on an end table. "He's crazy, off his meds, and dangerous. Neither of you see how wrong that could have gone."

Rex tried to stare me down again but his fighting spirit had flown. He slipped the phone back into his pocket. "I want to get one thing straight before you get off my property."

"Straighten away."

"I love my son."

Once in a while, I get an inspired idea. "Would you like Clay back here? Under this roof again?"

"Yes!" cried out Patricia.

I don't know what I was expecting from Rex. Spontaneous combustion, or a backhand to his wife's cheek, or at least another ugly stare-down. Instead, he looked at her with thirty-plus years of hard-won understanding. "We would consider that. Yes."

"Please give us that chance, Mr. Ford," said Patricia.

had just climbed into **Hall Pass 2** when the message came through from Sequoia.

6:25 PM
R ok. Dents in truck from gun.
Driving north to find old war friend.
Won't say name or why. U saved us.
Clay thanks and me 2.

6:26 PM
Game over. Clay, we
need to meet. You are
going to hurt someone.
Don't want it to be S.
You owe her! Help me
help you.

I leaned my head back against the rest and closed my eyes and waited.

No reply.

No surprise.

Justine was all I could think about on the flight home. I cruised just offshore, with the lights of the coast and the great black Pacific beneath me. I let the growling power of the Cessna engine vibrate through my body, the same power that had hummed through me the first time Justine had taken me up. I'll never forget the charge of it back then, and the charge of what I was already feeling for this beautiful, bright, unpredictable woman. Back then, those two charges had combined to form an irresistible current. Now, flying over the Palos Verdes Peninsula, I remembered it very clearly. But I couldn't feel it. Justine was gone and even **Hall Pass 2** couldn't make up what was missing.

14

Paige Hulet stepped inside Clay's room at Arcadia and held open the door. "Clay texted me one hour ago," she said with a small smile. "He's fine. I'm so relieved. So very happy."

I stepped in. It was Saturday but Arcadia seemed no different than during the week. Through the window I saw the morning sunlight on the green flanks of the mountains. The room was warm and I caught the doctor's light scent in the still air. She wore the usual black pantsuit and a white blouse and her hair was up and snug. Predictable, like the morning paper—black and white and neatly bundled—day after day after day. She had a small black satchel over one shoulder. She turned on the lights and set the air conditioner, then leaned over the front of Clay's computer. I stood and watched as she started it up, entered a password, waited for it to boot.

"Clay said he was fine and would be in touch," said the doctor. "You don't seem nearly as pleased as I thought you would."

I nodded to the reading chair by the window. "Would you sit down for a minute?"

Dr. Hulet sat, swung the satchel across her lap, and regarded me. "I have to be in therapy in twenty minutes. What's on your mind, Mr. Ford?"

"Are we on mic or camera?"

"No. We turn off the room feeds when a partner is absent."

"Clay and his lady friend surprised his mother and father yesterday. Have you talked to them?"

She had not, so I told her about Clay's visit to Ojai, the security blitz, the gunfire near the guardhouse, Clay's acquisition of a gun, cash, and souvenir fighting dolls.

"But Clay is okay?" asked the doctor. "He said he was okay."

"He's fine. So is the girl, in case you're concerned. Her name is Sequoia. I'm not clear on why Clay really went there. But it made me realize how little contact the Hickmans had with him here."

"I told you it was only once a year."

"I assumed it was their preference—trying to forget about him, too painful. Something like that."

She shook her head. "No. The infrequent visits were at Clay's insistence. He thought his parents wanted to turn him over to the state. I don't know where he got that idea."

I thought back to the Hickman couple standing in the study—Rex livid with helplessness, and Patricia trying to find her courage. I thought of Rex's parting words. **I love my son.** One thing I didn't get from them was any hint that they wanted to wash their well-moneyed hands of Clay. "They said Clay's fear of them began when he was deployed. Over his last two years, especially."

"Clay and I have talked about it in therapy. He feels that in the war he let his country down, and his airmen buddies, and his family. During his last two years of deployment, his feelings of failure grew and grew. Once he was back home he was better—as you know from the medical charts. Then the first psychotic break. Along with the drinking. And it all seemed to focus on what he'd done—and failed to do—during his time overseas in Iraq."

"Clay was never at Ali Air Base in Iraq, Dr. Hulet, as you and your alleged service record claim. He wasn't a flight mechanic, either."

Silence hung between us like a heavy black curtain. Then it vaporized with her voice. "Really. It says so, right—"

"The record is invented." I told her about Clay's attendance and later his teaching at the SERE program at Fairchild AFB from 2006 through 2007. Then his abrupt "disappearance" from 2008 until his discharge in late 2009.

Paige Hulet colored, like she had before when talking to me about Clay. "Well, Alec gathered up all of the military information. I can ask him where he got it."

"You two can point fingers at each other all day. What good would that do anybody?"

"I resent your implication, Mr. Ford. I certainly did not falsify Clay's service record in any way, and I doubt that Alec did, either. It was probably the DoD itself. Isn't that what they do when it's convenient? Redact documents? Rewrite history?"

"Clay never mentioned SERE or Fairchild?"

"No, never. He talked about fixing those big gunships, the Spookies, at Ali Air Base. However . . ." She stood, looked uncertain what to do with herself, then sat back down and set her satchel on her lap again. "**However,** Clay didn't offer many details of Ali. His memories seemed neither vivid nor emotionally grounded. There was something rote about them. Which made me suspect that his experience there was too painful for him to recount. Or perhaps untrue. It would not have been his first elaborate fabrication."

I felt something snap inside me. Like what snaps when you get a runaround at the DMV, but worse. DMV cubed. Enough is enough, and one more word lights your fuse. "What about Clay's last two years overseas? Did he ever talk about 2008 and '09? I need something true from you, Dr. Hulet. Not more of your live-streaming nonsense about him being a flight mechanic in Iraq."

She gave me a power scowl. "I've told you what I know."

"No, you haven't. And Spencer hasn't, either. Doctor-patient confidentiality? Maybe. But why did he dig out of this place? Because he couldn't stand visits from his parents? I doubt it. You've been in therapy with him for two years and you couldn't tell he was ready to run? And what about those paintings of Clay's? What goes through your mind when you look at those things? You care about Clay Hickman. You blush when you talk about him. You probably know him better than anyone in the world. Speak true words."

She pulled her phone from her jacket pocket, checked something, gave me another stony look.

"Let me guess," I said. "Our time is up."

"Yes, it is. You're a blunt man, Mr. Ford, but not a stupid one. Two years ago when I came here as the new medical director I assumed oversight of sixty mentally disturbed patients. Clay was by far the most heartbreaking because he had struggled so hard to make something of himself. Struggled for life and health, accomplishment and recognition. For his country. He had soared, then fallen. To me, he's the definition of a hero. I saw the damage done to him, but I didn't understand it all. I still don't. I know I'm blushing now and I just don't care."

She wiped the corner of her eye with a finger, then took a deep breath and let it out in one loud huff. "Speak true words? Okay. I have to be careful what I say here. I will do no harm. In therapy with me, Clay has claimed that, during 2008 and 2009, he was assigned to a secret prison in Romania named White Fire. He has also denied ever setting foot in Romania. I don't know what is true and what is only in his mind. Yet."

I took a hop of faith. "Romania. Where he met Briggs Spencer."

"Clay says he did, then denies it." Paige Hulet sat looking at me with an oddly hopeful expression.

I remembered what Evan Southern had said of Deimos. **A nickname for someone Clay knew in the war.** Made another hop: "Deimos is Spencer."

"Deimos and Phobos," she said, "are nicknames Clay uses for Briggs Spencer and his partner, Timothy Tritt. They ran this alleged prison. They were identified in the Senate report on torture, as you know. But again, at other times Clay says he has never been in a secret prison in Romania or anywhere else."

Suffocating, this tangle of contradictions. "Is Clay in therapy with Spencer here?" I asked.

"Irregularly," she said. "Neither man has acknowledged those sessions to me."

I tried to collect this disorderly information into an orderly whole. It was like trying to herd lizards. "What is the white fire Clay wants to bring to Spencer?"

"He has not spoken to me of bringing anything to Spencer," she said.

"He told Evan. And Sequoia."

"Maybe he trusts them more than me."

"Is that what his paintings are about? White fire?"

"I don't know yet," she said. "He gives up so little at a time."

"Did he ever mention dolls to you? Folk dolls—swordfighters he'd brought home and given to his parents?"

Her brow bent with confusion. "Never."

I went to the window and looked down at the glittering swimming pool and the partners wading around in it, and the white-clad staff maintaining order. I looked at her and she must have seen the cynical amusement on my face. "Anything else in his file that might be just a little bit made up?"

Dark eyes, dark flash. She stood, flipping open the satchel. "I've told you what I know. And I hope you find what you need on his computer."

She told me how to get printouts from Clay's

laptop through the security office, if needed. Floor six. Then pulled a visitors' clip badge from her satchel and dropped it to the computer desk.

"You asked about medications," she said. "The next meds break is in half an hour, in the Lyceum. You'll need this to be anywhere on the grounds unescorted. Clay was always good about taking his medications. But you should ask the dispensary nurses about that, since I'm so difficult to believe."

"I will."

She reached into the satchel again and set a thick envelope next to the badge. "Yours, complete with Dr. Spencer's raise. Cash. Maybe you should put it in a bank. Or are bankers as difficult to trust as doctors?"

"Far easier, Doctor."

"You're being an ass just to anger me."

"I've been downgraded from hominid to ass."

She shook her head and held my gaze, and I could feel her hostility waning. Instead of hostile she looked undecided, as if she'd caught herself in the act of something and wasn't sure how she would be judged. She struck me as a person long on trial with herself. She latched the satchel, smoothed her pants somehow primly, though they were without a wrinkle. "I'm afraid for Clay," she said.

"I'm afraid for the people around him."

"I hope you find him in time."

"In time for what, Dr. Hulet?"

"I don't know. The worst fears come from what we do not know."

I doubted that, shrugged.

"And Mr. Ford? I have a few more true words for you. My name is Paige Ann Hulet. I don't think you are an ass or an ape. And it's been five years, but I used to be a good dancer."

The sound of her words seemed to hover for a moment before being consumed by the sound of the air conditioner in Clay Hickman's room. "I don't get you," I said.

"Truths are always complicated."

"Some are simple."

"Tell me if you find one."

15

Clay's laptop computer, bolted to the desktop for security, was an older machine. He had scratched elaborate doodles on it with a sharp object. So much for pen and pencil forfeiture. But the laptop had medium-speed Internet capability, good graphics, and email set up with an Arcadia.org address. His desktop wallpaper was an Air Force SERE emblem featuring an eagle trapped within barbed wire. The slogan at the bottom read: RETURN WITH HONOR.

I saw that his last email had been sent on the previous Monday at 8:05 a.m., the day he escaped. I recognized the recipient—San Diego KPBS TV host Nell Flanagan. I was a fan of her show.

```
Dear Ms. Flanagan,

I enjoyed yesterday's piece
about the Navy dolphin train-
ing program. I would like to
```

remind you again of the much
better story that I have to
tell you. (See my earlier
email.) I may be out of touch
for a few days and wanted to
give you plenty of time to
consider.

Best,
Clay Hickman

The next-to-most-recent email was sent just
ten minutes earlier, to one John Vazquez.

Yo Vazz,

Just checking in. Head is
clearing as the walls close
in. Gods on the lawn and
black hoods in the shadows.
Dr. Paige my guiding light.
White fire to Deimos!

Soon,
Clay

The word **soon** jumped out at me. How soon?
And was John Vazquez an old war friend? **The**
old war friend?
Vazquez had replied two hours later, about

the time Clay and Sequoia Blain were digging Clay out of Arcadia.

```
Hey Claymore,

They're working me to death
here but I got nothing bet-
ter to do. Laura mostly happy
and Michael is great. Have
yourself a kid some day. Glad
the head is clearing. Mine
okay. Miss the smoke but any-
thing beats White Fire. I can
come down to San Diego and
see you sometime. Don't say
"soon" if you don't mean it!

Later,
Vazz
```

In Clay's address book I found John Vazquez in Redwood Valley, California. North of Ojai, in the direction Clay and Sequoia were headed. I emailed Vazquez on my phone, told him Clay Hickman was in trouble and I was trying to help him. I told him there was a possibility that Clay was on his way there. I asked Vazquez to contact me immediately.

More silence from Sequoia. I texted her again:

```
Where are you and where are
you going?
```

Back on the computer I scrolled through Clay's sent and received emails over the last months, noting that John Vazquez was his most frequent correspondent. Clay's second-favorite correspondent was Daphne, the estranged sister who had never visited Clay in Arcadia.

Hi Clay,

I like the pictures of your paintings but I wish you were happier and could paint happier subjects. Maybe if you got yourself some yellows and whites you'd find yourself with more optimism. I'm glad you have a good doctor. I miss you but I understand why you don't want to see me. I am happy now that I've separated myself from Rex and Patricia and Kayla. So relieved to be free of them. Mel and I are very happy and my own paintings are selling very well at the gallery. I can't believe I'm 30 this Wednesday!

Hugs,
Daphne

I noted that there were no solicitations and no junk mail, and that Clay's trash box was empty. It figured that DeMaris, and probably Paige Hulet, screened his correspondence, trying to keep Clay insulated from the world.

Randomly, I read some of Clay's sent mail, going back in time from his Monday email to John Vazquez. Names I recognized: Paige Hulet, Evan Southern, and Timothy Tritt—Briggs Spencer's former partner.

Also, another email to the TV host Nell Flanagan, in which Clay said he had a story that would "melt your face":

> It involves a secret part of the Iraq War that took place in Romania. It is 100% true. There is a graphic component. My story also involves a San Diego—area celebrity who is not a baseball or football player. I have written to you before about this and would appreciate that you write back. I am ready to speak on the record. I am ready to bring the fire.

White fire to Spencer?

Nell Flanagan had not responded. I wondered why not.

Sampling the emails randomly, I saw that many were vague, somewhat premonitory, and occasionally ominous.

To Vazquez:

```
I feel the changes coming
on inside me. I don't know
whether to dance or gouge out
my eyes.
```

Or to sister Daphne:

```
I heard this song about how
it takes a lifetime to get
some things right. I believe
this. I believe I still have
time to get things right.
```

To Vazquez again:

```
Monstering wasn't for me.
That was one of the differ-
ences between us Air Force
guys and the rest of them.
The contractors scared the
shit out of me. No rules but
the ones they made.
```

I forwarded twenty emails to the sixth-floor security office to be printed. Then copied Clay's inbox and outbox logs and sent them, too. I imagined Alec DeMaris or one of his security people examining each page as it came off the printer. I figured a fifty-fifty chance that someone would shred them and make me start over.

Next I snooped through Clay's documents. He had been keeping notes for all of his three years at Arcadia. I scrolled through scores of them, some brief, some long.

Written during his first week here:

I like Arcadia, after all the cells I've been in the last two years. You expect rough treatment from police and mental ward workers because they're all afraid of you. Which makes you want to put a real scare into them. Here it's different. Who do I run into my first day? Morpheus! He hadn't changed a bit since White Fire! Arcadia must screen the employees for happy attitudes. Happiest-place-on-earth kind of thing. I like my doctor. Calvin Whipple, old guy. He's got these tiny little eyes like a chameleon and I want to laugh. And guess what? I still can't get rid of Sox the cat! From White Fire, remember him? Later, when I came home and got the apartment in San Diego, Sox was there, waiting for

me. When I got thrown in jail, he'd be there, too. I went to the ding wing out in Chino and there he is, Sox the cat again. Waiting for me! Now he's here in Arcadia. Skinny and sitting there staring at me just like always. Black, white feet and tail tip, green eyes. Same Sox. Remember? Bizarre. Just when I think my brain boil is simmering down, Sox shows up and reminds me what a nutcase I am!

I picked out another file, dated nearly two years later:

And just when I look up at the mountains here around Arcadia, just when I feel the sun on me, and I've talked to Dr. Hulet and I'm just chillin' with Evan, all of the damn sudden there's Aaban, chained up by his wrists, screaming at us to let him use his bucket. What incredible willpower he had. What strength.

Or this:

Dr. Hulet has me on a new combination of drugs but they don't seem to be helping. I feel like I'm dreaming all the time. I don't fully understand how all of them work and I have been prescribed so many. Back when Dr. Whipple was in charge he told me not to worry about my meds—we could always adjust and find the right mix. Morpheus still slips me some of the good stuff. But sometimes it makes me feel earthquakes in my skull. Once, a voice told me to eat myself, so I tried. But Dr. Hulet explains the drugs to me, and she shows me on the computer how the molecules are put together, and how they interact in the body. It's a lot to keep track of. She sometimes seems puzzled by how I react to the drugs. There are lots of side effects. I believe in her. She is trustworthy and beautiful and the best thing that has happened to me since I joined the Air Force. I'd ask her to marry me if I weren't insane!

I browsed some of Clay's downloaded picture files, too. There were scores of drawings of Greek mythological characters, photographs of ancient Greek statuary, current-day travel and tourist information for Greece. Clay also had modern illustrations of Greek characters, many of them monstrous in ancient, prehuman ways. Some were suggestively sexual, some more overt. There were also photos of rock and hip-hop artists he liked, baseball and basketball stars. Tropical sunsets, bright reef fish, coral, and eels.

Still no word from Sequoia, so I tried again:

11:05 AM
Where are u?

I went back to Clay's computer. Another collection of Greek imagery. A photograph of a statue of Pan having intercourse with a goat gave me the creeps. The look on Pan's face. I found images of Deimos and Phobos.

Deimos.

Briggs Spencer answered on the first ring. "Have you located him?"

"Why did you lie about Clay and Romania?" I asked.

"Clay is no longer in Romania, Mr. Ford, if you haven't heard. He's in California and you're supposed to find him."

"You were Deimos, god of terror. Living it up at White Fire, the not-so-secret prison."

Spencer chuckled. "Mr. Ford, you only know one small portion of the truth. Your minor role in this story is to find Clay and return him to Arcadia, where he can get the finest care in the world."

"In a hospital run by a torturer."

He was wordless for a while. "We all have our pasts. In the wars I spent some time with the human soul. I know exactly how to break it or to heal it. I have chosen to become a healer."

"Your partner ran off on you, healer."

"And you ran off on **your** partner, Mr. Ford. I'll be honest with you—my biggest question in approving your hire was what you did that night in San Diego. Was your partner right in shooting Titus Miller? Did he save your life? Were you right to not fire? Did you risk the life of your partner? Were you right in saying that the shooting was undue force? Or should you have bowed to the blue religion and covered your partner? I still don't know. That is your past. I hired you to locate, not to judge. So, can you bring me Clay Hickman or can you not? The decision is yours and I won't ask again."

"I'll honor the contract."

A pause. "Good. You may still see those treasures I spoke of earlier."

"I don't want your treasures."

"No matter how much he has, a man will always want more."

"You're the proof."

"I am that."

"What's white fire?" I asked.

He was quiet again. "Capitalized, it was CIA code for the prison. We also came to use those words to mean something irresistible, or unbearable."

"Like one of your 'enhanced interrogation techniques'?"

"We were so much more than that."

"Because Clay wants to bring it to you. The white fire."

Another silence. I'd never been more curious about what thoughts were streaking through someone's silence. I had the feeling that Briggs Spencer was on the ropes. "I know. I've offered to meet with Clay. But he's refused. He says he's not ready. But I have no idea, Mr. Ford, what he is getting ready **for**."

"You must have some idea."

"Here are two: Do your job. And stop wasting my time and money."

16

The pre-lunch medications break in the Lyceum was one of four such sessions offered every day at Arcadia. The Lyceum was large and sunny, with views of the mountains through two glass walls. TV monitors were suspended from the ceiling as in airport waiting areas, all tuned to children's programming.

Four round tables stood in the middle of the room, each with a tall sign: A–G, H–N, etc. At each table waited an all-white staffer, a small bouquet in a plastic vase, a snack basket, and a plastic tub filled with drinks.

Also a stainless steel case about the size and shape of a shoe box, where, I assumed, the drugs were kept. Psychotropics, sedatives, stimulants, anticonvulsants, antianxiety drugs, mood stabilizers, pain-numbing opioids, and who knew what else. I had been surprised at the number of drugs in Clay Hickman's formulary. Next to the pill lockers stood inverted stacks of small white cups.

I took a seat under a sunny window, arranged

my visitor's badge to be visible, and watched. Music played softly—rock melodies on synthesizers, lyrics redacted like the last two years on Clay Hickman's service record. The patients and the staffers carried on polite, familiar conversations, which gave the room a subdued, professional hum. Could have been a convention of pediatric oncologists or funerary wholesalers.

I couldn't get Paige Hulet's simulations of truth out of my mind. I wondered what she was hiding. The only solid fact I'd really gotten from her was that she cared deeply for Clay. Fine. But why had she given me a falsified service history? Did she really not know? Why no file notes on Clay's "rote" details of Ali Air Base? Why no mention of electroconvulsive therapy? I also couldn't help wondering what, exactly, she meant by saying she'd once been a good dancer. Ready to try again? Well, **that** was a changeup.

It was strange that all three of the deities here—DeMaris, Hulet, and Spencer—had insisted that I notify **him, her,** or **him** first when I'd located the man they all wanted to find. **Me. No, me. No, me.**

And it was beyond strange that Clay's soon-to-be-a-celebrity, multimillionaire healer had once been his superior at a black-site prison in Romania.

My brain swimming with bullshit and prevarication, I looked out at the weird opulence of Arcadia's "med hour," where fifty-nine ailing pilgrims would soon be downing the powerful drugs that shaped their lives.

Two beefy white-clads stood at ease along each wall, hands folded in front of them and eyes sharp.

Alec DeMaris strode in, packed into a trim brown suit and flanked by two more white-clad orderlies. He seemed to be making an important point. When he saw me, he stopped, dismissed the men, and came over. Sat one chair away.

"Darn, Roland—you've got two strikes. One at the Waterfront and another up in Ojai. Don't tell me we have to double your pay again."

"That's okay, Alec. I'm making a fair wage."

"But what are you doing here in the one place you know Clay Hickman isn't?"

I looked over at him. "They call this Investigation 101, Alec. You ask questions and sometimes you get surprising answers."

"Surprise me, then."

I ignored him instead.

Mostly the partners were entering the room alone. Some talked and pointed and nudged each other. Some raised their chins and strode to their destinies. Most were dressed casually, though there was one Native American woman in beaded buckskin, a tiny old ballerina, and the two young Charger and Padre fans I'd seen before.

"The Jock Brothers," said DeMaris. "I caught them snorting Ritalin in the toolshed not long ago. I heard them inside—arguing National League versus American League pitching."

They came in our direction and stopped in front of us.

Charger leaned over and looked at me. From the recess of his helmet stared two curious blue eyes. I saw that the helmet had been signed by Philip Rivers. "Chargers?" he demanded. "Or Padres?"

"You know it," I said. "Go Bolts. Go Friars."

"What else is he going to say?" asked De-Maris.

"He's just checking," said the one with the Hoffman jersey. His cap looked like a real MLB issue, right down to the red clay ground into the fabric.

"Why don't you gutterballs go harass someone else?" asked DeMaris.

Hoffman chortled. Rivers stood up straight, chest out, turned to DeMaris. "You may be head of security, but you have no right to treat nobody like anything," he said.

"Not so sure I'm clear on that, Phil," said De-maris. "Move along, you two."

"Nice to meet you," said Hoffman, offering me his hand. I shook Rivers's hand, too. Hoffman put out his hand again, so I shook it once more.

"Enjoy the games, gentlemen," said De-Maris, standing. "You, too, Ford. Get in line. Score yourself some fentanyl if you want to feel like you're having sex on a cloud while eating a cheeseburger. At least, that's how I've heard it described."

Edward Frizell from Pasadena—otherwise known as Evan Southern from Alabama—spotted me and took the chair beside me. He wore a light blue seersucker suit, a button-down white shirt, and a regimental tie. In one hand he carried a neatly folded **San Diego Union-Tribune**. Between the first two fingers of his other hand was a handsome tortoiseshell cigarette holder that matched the frames of his glasses. The cigarette itself, I noted, was candy, with a dab of red dye for an ember. He crossed his legs, rested the paper atop one knee, and drew on the mouthpiece. "Should I conclude that you haven't found him?"

"I missed him by six hours." I told him about the Waterfront, Clay's new friend, his Ojai run.

He pursed his lips. "I suspected he'd seek out female companionship."

"Why is he so afraid of his parents?"

Evan looked up toward the ceiling, seemed to be scanning it for something specific. Cameras, mics, and drones, I thought. "He dreaded their visits. He would have seizures beginning a week or two before they were to take place."

"But **why**?"

Evan tapped his cigarette, made as if to grind its ashes with his toe. His shoes were pale blue suede wing tips, and his socks were a blue-and-cream argyle pattern, and all of them matched the color of his suit. His eyes were almost exactly the same shade of blue, behind the magnifying lenses of his glasses. "He thinks he failed them in the war. Clay had banked everything on winning that war. Not only our country winning, but he himself. Winning personally. He wanted citations and medals. He wanted to find those WMDs and chemicals, smash Saddam and the terrorists. Clay Hickman, from one of America's wealthiest families, enlisted in the Air Force and deployed to war with high resolve." Evan made a fist of his free hand and coughed into it, a soft smoker's cough. "That's the truth. And what brings you here?"

"I wanted to see where he got his meds."

Evan's gaze roamed the room. "Every once in a while someone panics in here and won't take their pills. Things can escalate rather quickly. That's why they have the gorillas watching. You don't mess with them."

The music played and the patients and nurses

chatted and joked quietly, and the meds went down the hatch with no trouble at all. "Who is Morpheus?" I asked.

"Greek god of dreams, of course." Again he gestured to the room.

"You mean all these drug-induced dreamers?"

"Well, no," he whispered, leaning close. "The man at the table, right there. **That's** Morpheus."

I followed Evan's line of sight to a middle-of-the-room medication station, H–N, presided over by a white-clad man about Clay's age. He was temporarily alone at the table, tapping something into his computer tablet. When his next partner, an older woman, came to the table, Morpheus set the device aside, rose, and pulled out the chair for her. She wore a black dress, a black funeral hat, and a veil that covered the top half of her face. She smiled and sat.

"That's Veronique. She mourns for her husband, who died young and tragically." Evan drew thoughtfully on his cigarette holder, squinted his eyes as the smoke rose.

"How did he die?"

"She poisoned him. **That** old story. Small doses over months, until he became tolerant. When the dose got high enough, Veronique cut it down to nothing and he died within days. Extreme agony. No trace of poison in his system, of course. Acute renal failure. Possibly hereditary. A natural cause. Much later, tormented by her conscience, she told his family. Guilt is a stern confessor."

Veronique and Morpheus looked like old friends as they talked. While she chatted away, Morpheus checked his computer tablet, then thumbed the combination lock on the pill case and opened the lid. He fingered through it, front to back, deftly removing and opening a bottle, shaking pills into one of the small paper containers. Capped and replaced each bottle before taking out another. By the time he was finished, Veronique was about to take five different kinds of pills. He set them in front of her. Veronique continued her narrative as Morpheus opened a small green apple juice can from the plastic tub and set it beside the pills.

"His name tag says 'Donald T.,'" said Evan. "Staff last names are confidential so we maniacs won't know much about them. His last name is Tice, if you're interested."

Tice looked over as if he'd heard us, even though Evan's voice was a whisper. Veronique spilled all the pills into her mouth before raising the can and chasing them down in two long gulps. Tice turned back to his partner.

"Why do you and Clay call him Morpheus?"

"It's his nickname from the war."

"From White Fire."

Evan looked at me, raised one eyebrow, and tapped his cigarette. "Clay never said those words to me. He implied a house of detention of some kind. Or perhaps worse. In Romania. The men running it gave nicknames to themselves. For . . . anonymity, said Clay. Morpheus was the medic in charge of drugs. For both prisoners and keepers. He prescribed everything from antibiotics for infections to amphetamine-adrenaline injections that kept detainees conscious during long and painful 'procedures.' For the Americans, he had black-and-red capsules they called bliss bullets. It was a titrated opioid combined with the antipsychotic medication ziprasidone. The bullets would let you sleep and have pleasant dreams. They were extremely popular. The sleep it brought on was relatively light sleep, too. So Clay could be rousted at any hour to work or fight or evacuate."

I watched Veronique nod at Donald T., then adjust her prim black hat and veil. She ate something off the snack platter. "What was Clay's nickname in Romania?"

"Asclepius. The Greek god of healing and medicine. Asclepius healed a divine snake, which gave him secret knowledge. He brought people back to life. Zeus killed him for meddling in the underworld. A shame."

"Why 'Asclepius'?"

"Obviously Clay saw himself as a healer."

"In a place like that?"

Evan shot me a skeptical look, then pulled the

candy cigarette from his holder, ate one half of it, then the other, crunching quietly. From his pocket he brought out fresh candy, carefully working it into the holder. "I was struck by that irony, too."

Morpheus opened his pill locker again and reached far back. He removed a bottle and dropped the pills into a fresh paper cup and handed it to the old woman. She took an overly casual look over one shoulder before lifting her green can.

"Evan, it looks to me like Morpheus is up to his old tricks again—handing out goodies." I wondered what bonus meds he supplied to Clay. **Morpheus still slips me some of the good stuff.**

"As an 'H,' Clay went to Morpheus's table every day," said Evan. "Personally, I try to keep my own meds to an absolute minimum. I am down to two antipsychotics, an antianxiety medication, one anticonvulsant, a daytime sedative, and a light sleeping aid."

Veronique set down the can and paper cup and stood. A dapper older man pulled out her chair. He was dressed for golf. He pulled a flower from the bouquet and handed it to her. She worked the flower between her hat and hair and strode away. The dapper man took her place.

"I should go get mine," said Evan, standing.

I looked up at Evan's blue eyes, which struck

me as remote and resigned. "Did Clay ever mention the dolls he brought home?"

"Dolls? Never."

"Thanks again for the Waterfront tip," I said.

"Glad to be of help."

I had a thought. "Are you going to read that newspaper?"

"Be my guest," said Evan, holding it out to me. "Please do contact me when you've located Clay. I worry about him. The world is too hard a place for his gentle spirit."

"I'm more worried about the people around him."

17

I wandered the Lyceum for the next few minutes, security goons surveilling impassively, Alec DeMaris keeping an eye on me. I mingled among various patients, most of whom looked briefly at my visitor badge, then at my face, then away. The old ballerina sobbed to one of the all-whiters. Evan sat at the O–S table, legs crossed, puffing thoughtfully, nodding to his staffer. Rivers and Hoffman stood near the middle of the room, face-to-face, in intense discussion, Rivers with his helmet under one arm and his hair plastered to his head.

As I worked my way over to them, they fell silent and watched me approach.

"Any luck finding Clay?" asked Rivers.

"Not yet."

"He'll be in the last place you look," said Hoffman. The two men laughed, and Rivers backhanded his friend in the ribs, not hard.

"Hope you don't feel harassed by us," said Hoffman. "Like Alec said."

"He can't stand us," said Rivers.

"Or your teams," I said. "He told me the Chargers are nothing but a billionaire's toy, and the Padres are strictly triple-A."

"Oh, Jesus."

"That's just . . ."

"Exactly what I thought," I said. "Forget where you heard it."

We tapped fists and they wandered slowly away, leaning close together as in a huddle or a pitcher-catcher conference. Tapping the folded newspaper against my leg, I wondered what kind of strategy they might be cooking up, hoping it would fit in with mine.

I came to Donald Tice's table, from which another satisfied customer had just departed. Morpheus eyed me with a pugnacious expression. He looked younger up close than from a distance. His hair was blond and thinning and he wore a stainless steel Rolex.

"Any progress on Clay?" he asked.

"Some progress, no Clay."

"Get him back here. Or he'll freak out and do something bad."

"Any idea what?"

Tice closed the pill box lid, spun the combination lock absently with his thumb. "The trouble with psychotropic drugs is, you can tolerate them and they can help stabilize you for a certain period of time. Then that period is over. But no one knows when. It can happen fast."

I put on a thoughtful expression. "How long have you known Clay?"

He drummed his fingers on the pill box, looking up at me. I could almost hear him weighing his answer. "I was hired to open this hospital and Clay was one of our first partners. So, three years now."

"Did you sense that he might make a run for it?"

"You're always ready for it in a place like this. But, no. I saw nothing that pointed to an escape." Tice glanced at his watch.

"What drugs was Clay taking?"

He looked at me with contempt. Huffed and nodded, as if he'd been waiting for me to ask such an impossible question. "Come on, man. His formulary is confidential information. You of all people should know that."

Past Donald T.'s shoulder I saw Rivers and Hoffman moving toward DeMaris, who was at the T–Z table, talking to the dispensing nurse. The quarterback and pitcher had a sense of purpose about them. Rivers had his helmet back on.

"I also know you want to get him back here," I said. "It would really help if I knew what drugs he was taking, and how often, and what happens when he stops."

"Talk to Hulet. She prescribes them."

Rivers and Hoffman had come to a stop twenty feet or so behind DeMaris. Rivers cleared the patients around him. They cooperated, standing aside, waiting and watching. DeMaris continued his conversation with the nurse. Hoffman lowered his cap and looked in for the sign. He shook it off, then another. Into the stretch. A glance to first. Then, with a high leg kick and a practiced turn of body, he fired a green juice can.

Donald saw my expression and sensed something amiss, turning just before DeMaris wheeled around and the can flew past his head. DeMaris charged the mound. The security men crashed in from the peripheries. Shouts and shrieks blotted out the music.

Donald jumped and his chair clattered to the floor. Elbows up, he barged through the throng of patients who were closing in on the action. Rivers stepped into the pocket and bounced a green bullet off DeMaris's chest.

When the first security guard got to Hoffman, the reliever screwed himself into a martial arts fighting stance, yelped, kicked, and missed. The goon pulled up short and raised his hands for order, but Dressed for Golf issued a weirdly savage war whoop and tried to tackle him. The security man threw him to the floor and Hoffman piled on. Then Donald. The tiny old ballerina clenched her fists to her chin and screamed.

DeMaris slammed into Rivers, carried him along for five yards, then crashed him onto table

A–G. The drink bucket jumped and the cans and ice sloshed out and the snacks and flowers popped into the air.

I set my **Union-Tribune** over Morpheus's tablet, picked up paper and computer together, and walked toward the nearest exit. I turned to see three big security men bury DeMaris and Rivers in a mountain of white. Cries and cheers and laughter from the crowd. An alarm wailing and fire sprinklers raining down.

Back in Clay's room I searched the tablet and found his formulary for the last three years. Not wise to send any of it to the Arcadia security printer, so I used my phone to photograph the tablet screens and email the pictures to my office. Took me a while, with my big man's fingers and my heart loping right along. Kept waiting for Donald or DeMaris to walk in on me. When I was finally done I wiped down Morpheus's tablet and wrapped it in the newspaper. Then sent another message to Sequoia.

2:28 PM
   Talk to me.

By the time I got back to the Lyceum the med-break tables had been righted and rearranged, the chairs pushed back to one wall. Two all-whiters with shop vacuums slurped up the fire-sprinkler water from the carpet. I chose my moment, set the tablet and newspaper on Donald T.'s table, then headed back to security to pick up my printouts.

E njoy the show, Ford?" asked DeMaris. His coat and tie were gone and his white shirt was stained with what looked like fruit punch.

"Clutch tackle."

"Linebacker, Florida State," he said. "Around here, you think everything's fine, then the nuts go nuts. They're strong. Fuckin' lunatics are always strong."

DeMaris led me through a small lobby, then into a roomful of monitors. An all-whiter sat at a booth well back from the screens, a control console before him, eyes up. With twenty-four cameras going, he had plenty of Arcadia to keep track of. Most of the locations were interior, but the pool area and some of the outside grounds were video-covered, too.

In the next room a woman sat at what looked like a studio mixing board, with speaker buds in her ears and a very large digital recorder on the desk in front of her.

"How many mics?" I asked DeMaris as we passed through.

"Classified. And quiet, please."

"It's my job to ask questions."

"I can't believe Spencer doubled your pay."

"And I don't even get pelted with juice cans."

"I looked at the stuff you printed from Clay's computer," he said. "If it was up to me, I wouldn't let you take any of it. I wouldn't even let you in here."

"Just follow orders and keep the cash coming."

He stopped and turned and looked at me. "Things will get settled between us. Don't worry."

He opened the door to a smaller back room, where Paige Hulet stood near a printer stand, flipping through a sheaf of paper.

"Pardon the riot," she said. "It's unusual here." A strand of her hair had come loose from the usual tight knot to dangle out of her vision. I'd never seen her so recklessly presented. She must have felt the coil bobbing because she pushed it back into place, but it fell out again.

"Your partners sure take a lot of drugs," I said.

"You know why we prescribe them, don't you? Because they work. Laypeople don't realize that lithium beats cold-water dunks and straitjackets every time."

"I'm lay as they get. So I may have some questions about those drugs."

"I can answer them. We've come a long way in treating mental illness, Mr. Ford. But we're not perfect."

I considered her, felt that basic instinct a person can only resist with effort. It had been building for some time, since that first day I'd tried to move her out of the sun and lost my cool. Now I made no effort at all to resist. "You're pretty close."

She stared back, her eyes forceful against mine. "I haven't been accused of that for a while."

Her eyes pried, then loosened into skepticism. I stepped closer, into that space where everything changes. Her eyes drew in the light and threw it back. There was a very small flaw in her iris.

"I know what happened to your wife, Mr. Ford. From the news. I'm very sorry." She held out the papers and I took them. She made another long appraisal of me. "And I accept your invitation. The dance thing."

I set the papers on a table, moved closer still, put my right hand just above her hip.

"No, definitely not **now,**" she said. "This is highly insecure. For us being in security, I mean. I could lose my job."

"No you couldn't. We're model citizens."

I waltzed her around the small room—one **two** three, one **two** three—my favorite dance, barely missing the desks and tables, really just an extended version of my moving her out of the sunlight that first day we'd met, and her moving us back into it, which had prompted her confession of the five-year dance drought, which had quietly thrilled me, and led directly to my invitation, which had led to this. We were clunky at first, opposing forces, but we evolved. The small of her waist fit full in my hand, and her weight, once I gained her trust, shifted easily with mine, and her scent, so much a woman's, went straight into my thick male skull. She held her cheek almost to my chest. One **two** three. It was odd and good to dance in silence. Justine in our bedroom. Memories bouncing off the present. Sometimes dancing feels like flying. Then she pushed me away, gently but firmly. "Take me dancing sometime. Properly."

My phone rang and I recognized the number. "Hello, Mr. Vazquez."

"Clay is on his way here."

18

John Vazquez lived in Redwood Valley, 60 miles inland from the Mendocino coast and 124 miles north of San Francisco. He told me he had served with Clay during the war in Iraq but didn't say where. He was now managing a large vineyard owned by Briggs Spencer. The property had an airstrip and a helipad. Vazquez gave me the GPS coordinates, said he'd meet me on the strip.

Easing **Hall Pass 2** down, I could see tawny hills and dark green valleys, vineyards large and small. Highway 101 to the west, Clear Lake bright as a mirror in the late afternoon sun.

The breeze was stiff and tricky on the approach. **Hall Pass 2** skittered and shied like a spooked horse. I set her down with a rasp of tires, braked, and coasted under the shadeport as John had instructed. No Vazquez. I climbed down and called him. Left a message. I stood in the shade and smoked while **Hall Pass 2**'s Lycoming crackled and cooled. Afternoon leaned into evening.

Up a wide dirt road, atop a gentle hill, surrounded by row after row of grapevines, stood a boxy, standard-issue 1950s stucco house. A pickup truck and a minivan parked in front. A child's bike resting against a porch beam. Two big oaks towered over the house for shade, a tire swing hanging from one of them.

The wind whipped a dust devil across the road and the bright green grape leaves fluttered and swayed. Zinfandel, Vasquez had told me—certified organic. Pride in his voice. Not far from the house stood a large yellow barn. Its breezeway door was open and the top half of the paddock door had come unlatched. Opening and slamming shut in the wind.

In Fallujah in 2004—in April, in fact, this same month—just after the Blackwater contractors were killed, dragged through the streets and hung off a bridge over the Euphrates, we Marines spent days trying to find those responsible. Tall order, considering we were the enemy and even the Shiites, who had suffered so long under Saddam, were beginning to hate us. At one point it was our job to go door-to-door, handing out leaflets, asking for Fallujahns to help us root out the guilty. It was a very strange time in the war, a turning point—they say now—during which "insurgents" from all around the Middle East began moving in to fight us. It was no longer the U.S. "liberating" Iraq from Saddam. It was the

U.S. "occupying" a sovereign Muslim nation—
which had become a deafening call for jihad.

This was when we realized we were targets,
not liberators. Going door-to-door with those
pamphlets had suddenly struck me as both op-
timistic and groundless, an example of the very
American idea that anything can be fixed by
throwing enough hope and force at it. Late on
that first day of pamphleteering in Fallujah we
pounded on an already beaten wooden door in
a poor section of the city, and something in the
silence that came from behind that door told us
that we were about to be greeted by something
terrible.

The family—mother, father, three young
children—had been hacked to death. Recently.
The bloodshed was indescribable and the pain in
that house was like a living thing. Some strong
men lost their stomachs there. I lost something
else. Some portion of belief. Because I knew that
this family had been murdered for helping us.
Whether they actually had helped us, or not.
The slaughter was their price for the Iraqi freedom we were dying to deliver.

One month later, in May, we turned over operations to the newly formed Fallujah Brigade.
We armed them to the teeth, then withdrew.
America had lost twenty-seven servicemen in
that first battle of Fallujah, and the four Blackwater men. The news said we had killed two

hundred insurgents and five hundred civilians. By September, the Fallujah Brigade had surrendered all the weapons we'd given them to the insurgency. Now Fallujah was back in the news. Under siege again. As if the Blackwater civilians and the Marines and the slaughtered family and everyone else who lost their lives in that ancient, cultured city in the war of 2004 had died for— what? Nothing?

Standing in the shadeport now, I had the same feeling I'd had outside that house in Fallujah. Maybe it was the slamming of the Dutch door. Or the wind in the grapes, or the way the tire swing turned on its rope. I've had that same eerie feeling several times since Fallujah and found nothing wrong at all. Other times, well . . . I waited a few minutes, ground out my smoke, and kicked some good rich Mendocino County grape-growing soil over it.

Then I opened up **Hall Pass 2**, slipped my sidearm behind the waistband of my jeans at the small of my back. I own four handguns. This one was a Model 1911 .45 ACP with a standard single-stack magazine that holds eight rounds.

Up the dirt road to the barn. Wind strong, crows wheeling over the grapes. The Dutch door banged and the weather vane on the roof kept shifting directions. I caught the top door mid-slam and latched it open. The sun was behind me, lighting the interior: two full-sized tractors, one with a backhoe and the other with an auger for setting line stakes. A mud-spattered Bobcat sat beside them like a dirty infant. Tools, implements, more tools.

Inside smelled of gasoline and sulfur. I walked lightly, noting the pallets of supplies—bird netting, shade cloth, training stakes, end posts, crossarms, a drip irrigation line, connectors, and emitters. A workbench lined one wall, with a mounted table saw, a drill press, a grinder/polisher, and overhead fluorescent shop lights for the craftsman.

Nothing seemed unusual or out of place to me until I came to the shiny puddle on the cement floor. The puddle sat in a well-used parking place, judging by the old oil and power-steering and transmission-fluid stains around it. Decades of faint black tire tracks lined up perfectly with the sliding breezeway doors—easy in and easy out. I squatted and touched my fingers to the liquid, which was neither oily nor coolant-green. Condensation from the air-conditioner compressor, I thought. Like any vehicle would leave. Left recently, however. Recently enough that it hadn't evaporated. I watched through the open Dutch door while I called John Vazquez again. No answer, didn't leave a message.

Then to the house, past the oak trees and the truck tire turning slowly in the breeze. The pickup truck out front was older and had a ZIN

LIVES! bumper sticker. The minivan was late-model and there was a child seat in the second row, behind the driver. The family must be home.

The house blinds were drawn. No one answered my knock so I used the doorbell and waited. The knob turned freely and I pushed open the door. "John! John Vazquez!"

Silence.

No sound from the back of the house, no lights. Sunset was half an hour away but the western hills blocked most of the sunlight. The entry and living room stood half in darkness.

I stepped in and called his name again. I saw the baby grand piano covered with framed pictures, and the wood-burning stove and sofas and the big TV. A ceiling fan whirred and the control chains swayed and twitched. I saw a door, ajar, and what looked like a half bath. On the far side of the living room was a small breakfast counter and three bar stools, and beyond that the kitchen and a dining room. On the dining room floor was a dark colored carpet and on the carpet, lying still, was a man. I dropped to one knee, gun raised in both hands, viewing the world beyond a sight notch and a vertical post. A gun in your hand changes who you are. Heart thumping fast, I was thoughtless but sensory. Movement beyond the man: a white cat outside, looking at me through a sliding glass door. Movement above the cat: the breeze in a pine tree. Oddities of the door glass: two round shatters around two small holes.

I scrambled across the floor. The man was faceup—arms out and legs spread as if he'd landed mid-stride. A revolver lay a few inches away from his open right hand. His eyes were open to the ceiling. I pressed two fingers to his neck—no reaction, no pulse. Through the glass the cat looked at me, tail twitching. I reached over with my .45 and nudged the revolver away. He was trim-faced, dark haired, thirty-something. Dead eyes. I saw the family in Fallujah. And blood on the hardwood kitchen floor. I sat there on my haunches for a minute, low and partially covered by the wall of the breakfast bar, listening and thinking. Outside, the wind hissed in the oaks. The cat paced, head low, looking in. The glass surrounding the bullet holes looked like frost.

Then a sound came, carried in by the wind it seemed—a faint vocal tone that at first sounded very much like the way I hear Justine's voice now. A tone and syllables but no words. Next was a dull thump—something dropped, maybe—but barely audible over the breeze and my steady heartbeat. The wind whooshed through the trees, and when it stopped the house was quiet again.

19

I set my gun on the floor and worked the wallet from the man's back pocket. His driver's license was in a flap with a clear window: John A. Vazquez, brown and brown, 5'11", 185 pounds. His DOB made him thirty-one. In the photo he was smiling.

I heard the sound again. Slightly clearer now while the wind caught its breath. It sounded as if it were coming from somewhere closer—not from the outside at all, but from inside.

I stood and looked down at John A. Vazquez. His T-shirt was light blue and he'd been shot several times. I saw entry and exit wounds on his front torso, which could mean the gunman shot Vazquez coming and going. Or two gunmen. The thing I learned about death by gunshot—both with the San Diego Sheriff's and in combat in Iraq—is the absolute chaos that gunfire causes, especially in tight quarters. The facts of ballistics are complicated by astonishing bullet speeds; physical variables, from bones to belt buckles; as well as human reactions that often border on the impossible. I ran my gaze along the kitchen cabinets and walls, looking for more holes. Saw none.

I heard the thump again, something being dropped or struck. It seemed to come from under me. Gun up and finger on the trigger, I moved slowly and quietly down the hallway. Room to room. Cleared a home office, what looked like a spare bedroom, and a young boy's room. I looked at the Transformers toys and plastic weapons and the bats and balls and plastic dinosaurs littering the floor. I wanted very badly not to see that boy, lying like his father was. I didn't.

The master bedroom was spacious. The bed was made and there were no bodies. I'd worked myself up about that: no more bodies.

The voice came clear but faint. "John? John!"

Again the thump, which now sounded like a hard object being pounded on a wall or door. It came from below me, and no more than twenty or thirty feet away. Into the master bath: toilet room, twin basins, and a Roman tub. Off the bath was a big spa room with a whirlpool, skylights, and cedar walls sprouting bromeliads and orchids. There was a door. Bromeliads and orchids on it, too. If not for the slender pull handle, I might not have seen it. The sauna, of course. I pulled open the door and found not a sauna but a landing, and a steep spiral staircase, leading down. Being in wine country, I understood.

The voice was clearer now, and much closer. "John? Is that you? Please be you."

"I'm a friend of Clay Hickman." Silence. "I'm coming down, Mrs. Vazquez. Don't shoot me. I'm a friend of Clay Hickman."

"Is John there? Is John okay? There were men . . ."

"With guns!" A boy's voice. **"And masks!"**

"Hush, Michael! Are you one of them?"

"No. I'm here to help you."

"Why should I believe you?"

"Because they might come back."

A beat. "They locked us in. But I have a twelve-gauge shotgun. John keeps it down here."

"I'm trying to help you, not get killed."

"Where's John?" she asked.

I didn't know what to say.

"Where's Dad?"

"There's a spare key," said Mrs. Vazquez. "In the medicine cabinet over the right sink. Bottom row, far left."

"I'll be back with it."

"Where's John? Why won't you tell us? Are you one of those goddamned sons of bitches?"

"With guns?"

I got the key, then hustled down the steep, circular stairs to a cozy tasting room that smelled of cigar smoke. Wall cubbies stacked with bottles, a tasting bar with wine goblets racked overhead, wine barrels for tables, stools. It was cool and I could hear a built-in air purifier humming in the ceiling.

Mrs. Vazquez and her son had been locked in what I assumed was the wine vault. Concrete-block wall, rustic oak door, a wrought-iron lock and pull handle.

I stood to the side and explained to Mrs. Vazquez that I was about to crack open the door but wouldn't let them out until I had the gun. "Got that? You have to stay cool."

"Okay."

Key in quietly. "I'm cracking the door. All I want to see is the barrel of that thing."

"Okay."

I unlocked the door, leaving the key in, then stood aside. Planted my foot as a brake. Pulled the door open six inches and waited. "The gun please."

With only moderately good guesswork, Mrs. Vazquez could have blasted me through the door. Instead, a shotgun barrel came through the crack. As soon as there was enough, I grabbed it and yanked hard. It came loose and the door swung open and a terrified woman backpedaled away from me, nearly knocking over a boy no more than ten years old. The boy got his balance and held up his fists, ready to fight.

She tried to run past me. I caught her wrist, let her get past the door, then slammed it on the boy. She threw a wild punch with her free hand, so I set the shotgun against the cement wall and grabbed that wrist, too. I shook her firmly and got up in her face. **"Listen to me. Listen!"**

She struggled, grunting, but I half-turned her and marched her across the tasting room to one of the barrel tables. I let go of her, stepped back, and raised my index finger to my lips. She watched me for a long moment, then slowly put aside her fight. "John's dead," I whispered, glancing at the vault in which her son waited silently. "He's . . . in the kitchen. You probably don't want the boy to see that."

"My god . . ."

"Go up there if you need to, Mrs. Vazquez. No one says you have to. But remember, they could come back if they left something unfinished or have a change of mind. I'll try to talk to your boy."

She flew up the spiral stairway and out of sight. I heard the spa door open and slam shut, then footsteps dimming fast. I didn't know how to break the news to Michael that his father had been murdered. Opened the vault door and looked in. Cases to the ceiling, poor light. He sat on a step stool, chewing a thumbnail. Looked at me and stopped.

"I'm Roland and I'm a good guy."

He blinked. "Mike."

"Do you box?"

He took his time answering. "Dad's teaching me. We watch on TV."

"I boxed in the Marines."

"Were you good?"

"Not bad."

"Heavy or light heavy?"

"Heavy. My best weight was two-oh-six."

"Muhammad beat Liston at two-oh-six. In the rematch. He was Cassius Clay then. Um, how's my dad?"

Through the loudest of storms only the heart can be heard. Its roar almost deafened me. "They killed him, Mike."

He looked down at his hands, nodding slowly. Tears jumped from his eyes. "That's not true, is it?"

"It's true. I'd give anything to say it isn't."

"Mom's up there with him?"

"Yes."

"I hear her."

So did I, a high, seemingly distant keening.

"I don't want to go up there."

"Don't. Nothing will change, and you'll see things you don't need to see."

His face caved and shifted as emotions surged through him. "Did they shoot him?"

"Yes."

Eyebrows raising, tears falling. "What did he do?"

"Your father did nothing to them. This is about someone else."

"Then . . . why?"

"I don't know. But I will find out."

The tears poured down his cheeks and Michael brought his hands to his face and screamed. Loud. He ran for the door. I blocked him and held him back while he flailed at me with his fists, blubbering, his bloodshot gray eyes dilated with wild grief. He punched himself out in a brief fury and dropped to his knees, sobbing into his small fists.

Helplessness is worse than fear. Fight and flight are easier than facing a suffering human being you can do almost nothing to help. Ask any combat medic or corpsman. So I stood there in all my tall heavyweight **semper fi** adult uselessness, looking down on this child, feeling the tears in my own eyes while Rage, Wrath & Fury writhed and bellowed away inside me.

"I won't keep you from going up there," I said.

He looked up at me. I knew I'd offered him a heart-splitting choice. It was too much to lay on a ten-year-old, and his decision would last a lifetime.

"Blood?"

"There's a lot, Michael."

"What do I do?"

"Stay here and wait for your mother."

"I can't."

"I understand."

"I'm afraid."

"You will never forget what you see."

"Go with me?"

I offered my hand and he shook his head no, then stood and led the way.

We covered John Vazquez with his favorite Pendleton blanket. I figured the crime scene elves would have to live with it. Mrs. Vazquez—Laura—and Michael brought over dining room chairs and sat with him, sobbing, while I called the sheriffs.

Next I sent a text to Sequoia, having jumped to a conclusion that I dreaded she would confirm:

> 7:28 PM
> Did you see Vazz?

> 7:29 PM
> No. Shots inside! We sped off!

> 7:29 PM
> Where and when?

> 7:30 PM
> Vazquez house. Less than an hour ago.

7:31 PM
Where are you now?

7:32 PM
We are ok.

7:32 PM
Need to see Clay
tonight. No excuses,
S!!!

7:36 PM
Clay says no. We are in this
together now. I love him.

My heart slumped.

While we waited for the sheriffs to arrive, I was able to get Laura Vazquez and Michael to tell me what had happened. They'd come home from running errands in Ukiah and walked in on two men with guns. No car parked outside to warn them. The men wore black balaclavas. One big and in charge. The other short and stocky. John was on the couch, hands bound behind him with plastic ties, afraid and alive. The two men—dressed in casual clothes—took Laura and Michael at gunpoint to the wine cellar and locked them in. The men were calm and courteous.

Half an hour later, both Laura and Michael heard car tires screeching near the house, then shouting from the direction of the kitchen or dining room, and thumping sounds, like a fight. Urgent voices. Tires screeching away. Then silence. When John didn't come for them, they thought something terrible had happened to him and they were going to be killed. Approximately an hour later they heard my voice—faint but audible—calling out John's name from above, probably through the front door.

So: two men, armed, equipped, polite. They had seen John Vazquez's pickup truck parked by the house and figured the rest of the family was gone. They'd parked in the open barn to be out of sight—where I'd seen their leaked coolant—and knocked on Vazquez's front door. Guns drawn or friendly? Either way, they'd gone inside and bound him. Why? For transport? Interrogation? To scare something out of him? To wait for . . . what?

All good, until Laura and Michael came home and walked through their front door.

Then a sudden memory from grade school— "The Highwayman," a poem in which the bound heroine warns her approaching lover of the ambush waiting for him. Warns him with her death.

So who were these men and what did they want that was worth killing for? No obvious signs of drugs or other illegal business going on here. My quick background check of Vazquez—just before leaving for the Fallbrook Airpark—had come up clean. A family man.

From Laura's description, the two men weren't local bangers or junkies looking to fund their next fix. They were professionals of some kind—trained, prepared, and purposeful. Whose arrival here, at the same time as Clay Hickman's arrival, was no coincidence. One link was Briggs Spencer, owner of Arcadia, owner of Vazquez's home and livelihood, former operator of White Fire, a secret prison in which Clay and Vazquez had worked. The man to whom Clay was going to bring something unbearable. A man connected to some of the more ruthless organizations in the republic.

Which led me to the white Range Rover and the black Charger, whose drivers had tailed me to the Waterfront and, later, to the Fallbrook Airpark. And planted a GPS locator in my car. Specifically, Alec DeMaris and an associate. I also considered Rex Hickman's private security team. Trying to intercept Clay? Leading to a dispute with Vazquez, who was apparently armed? I circled back to "The Highwayman": Had Vazquez been shot while trying to warn off Clay Hickman and Sequoia Blain?

Three Mendocino County prowl cars barreled

onto the property, funneling in from the entry road, lights flashing but running silent.

I knew I'd be there for a long time.

I quickly texted Sequoia.

7:48 PM
You know they
killed Vazz.

7:50 PM
They wanted Clay.

7:50 PM
Why did Clay go
there?

7:51 PM
For part 2 he says

7:51 PM
Of WHAT?

7:52 PM
He won't tell. He trusts me,
then doesn't.

Through a window I watched one of the Mendocino Sheriff cars stop down by the barn, and two deputies jump out. The other two vehicles slowed and crept toward us.

7:52 PM
People are dying!
Bring me to Clay. Do
the right thing.

7:53 PM
What is the right thing?

> **7:54 PM**
> Turn himself over
> to police or me.
> He'll be safe.

7:56 PM
I DON'T WANT SAFETY,
MR. FORD. I WANT THE
WORLD TO KNOW THE
TRUTH.

A strong but surreal sensation, to be communicating with Clay Hickman for the first time. Before that moment he had seemed only partial. Now I felt his full perilous presence. I responded quickly:

> **7:56 PM**
> Tell me your
> truth and I can
> help you tell the
> world.

7:57 PM
That is a crude trap. Sequoia
said you were a good man.

Outside, the two patrol cars stopped on the driveway, well apart from each other, and well short of the Vazquez home. No lights now, no sirens. Four deputies fanned out and came toward us, one of them carrying an assault shotgun. Behind them I could see two deputies trotting from the barn back toward their vehicle.

> **7:57 PM**
> **Tell me your**
> **truth, Clay.**

7:58 PM
Don't you understand?
It isn't my truth to tell.
The world must hear it
from the God of Terror.

> **7:59 PM**
> **Bad things**
> **happened in**
> **Romania. I get that.**
> **But you need help.**

Through a window I watched the deputies converging on the front porch. Laura and Michael sat in silence, holding hands and watching them, too.

7:59 PM
You have no idea, amigo.

> **8:00 PM**
> **You are responsible for S.**

8:00 PM
I will protect her with my life,
as Vazz did for me.

8:01 PM
Meet me tonight.

Silence.

An idea came to mind. A way to get Clay to **want** to meet me. It wasn't quite legal and it could backfire spectacularly. But now was not the time. Right now, he'd smell it out. Missing persons are good at smelling things out, no matter how desperate and confused they are. Though I wasn't sure that Clay was either of those things.

I exchanged a look with Laura Vazquez, then walked toward the sharp rapping on the front door.

20

ours later, one of the sheriff's detectives dropped me off at a motel in Ukiah on his way back to headquarters. His name was Polson. He had conducted my crime scene interview, certain that I was withholding information, which in fact I was, due to my contract with Arcadia and my ethical obligations to Clay Hickman and Sequoia Blain.

None of which meant anything to Polson or the law. I did tell him the basics of what I'd been hired to do. I referred him to Alec DeMaris. I told him I'd call him if I thought of anything else that might help them identify John Vazquez's killers and I meant it. Polson said he'd charge me with obstruction of justice if I didn't. He said incompetents didn't belong in law enforcement and the San Diego Sheriffs deserved better than me.

Now I sat at a small table in my room at the Days Inn in Ukiah, having forwarded my images of Clay Hickman's formulary to Paige Hulet before calling her. I didn't tell where I'd gotten them. And I said nothing about John Vazquez.

The silence at her end was a long one. I heard the ice clinking in her glass. Finally, she spoke. "This is not Clay's formulary. These are not the drugs I've prescribed for Clay. Some go back before my time at Arcadia, but . . . What **is** this? Where did you get it?"

It took me a second to get my brain around that idea. If the drugs on the dispensary computer tablet were not prescribed by Clay's physician, who **were** they prescribed by? "What are you giving him now?"

Another silence. I poured a second light bourbon. Through the crack I'd left between the heavy curtains, I saw a Mendocino Sheriff's prowler moving down State Street.

"Two years ago," she said, "when I joined Arcadia and took over Clay's treatment, I thought his diagnosis of schizophrenia was questionable. There were manic episodes that didn't fit, and his responses to the meds were erratic, so I reclassified Clay as schizoaffective disorder, bipolar type. He was exhibiting sustained bursts of goal-oriented hyperactivity. To answer your question, I went to lithium and paliperidone, antipsychotics. His anxiety was very high. The benzodiazepines are often a good answer for anxiety. They seemed to work for a while. Clay stabilized. His anxiety subsided, the manic phases shortened. The risk was mood cycle acceleration or medication-induced psychosis. Clay showed neither for, well, a while."

"How long a while?"

"One year. Then his paranoia and anxiety came back again, especially pronounced just prior to a visit from his family. Those visits were a huge stressor. So I moved him to aripip-razole. The danger there was extrapyramidal symptoms—tremors, restlessness, akathisia."

"Akathisia?"

"Literally, akathisia is the inability to sit. In the medical sense, it's a compelling need to be in motion. It's a common side effect of many antipsychotics."

"What did you make of his behavior, given those meds?"

"Overall? It was somewhat bewildering. So I tried another approach. I discontinued paliperi-done and aripiprazole in favor of olanzapine. It's a good medication but you've got to watch for weight gain and increase in blood sugar. I took Clay's blood twice a week. When his psychosis became treatment-refractory I went textbook—clozapine, which has less side effects and is also indicated for suicidality. As I told you before, Clay ideated suicide—but never acted. Your turn, Roland. Where did you get this bizarre formulary I'm looking at?"

I told her it came from the computer tablet assigned to one of the staff dispensers, Donald Tice, who was almost always assigned patients with last names beginning with **H.**

"But these are not Clay's prescriptions," said Dr. Hulet. "I **write** his prescriptions."

"What do they do, these drugs?"

A pause. "I'm only familiar with some of them. Others, I've never known to be compounded and are not commercially available."

"Lysergic acid diethylamide is LSD."

"Yes—still manufactured for research. Experimental microdosing to aid in creative thinking."

"Jesus, Paige—he's been taking acid, just for starters."

"No! They are **not** his prescribed meds. He cannot have been taking them."

"Don't you get it? It's why his responses were so wrong. You thought you were treating Clay but you weren't. Someone else had complete control over his meds. And some of them were drugs **you've never even heard of**."

"Impossible. Arcadia has checks and bal—"

"I saw it with my own eyes. Tice got every pill and dose straight off his computer tablet. That's where I got the formulary. What are you people trying to do to Clay Hickman?"

I hung up, went outside, and lit a cigarette. Felt my heart knocking against my ribs. The night was cool and damp and I thought of John Vazquez lying on his kitchen floor while his wife and son covered him in a blanket. I was angry at Paige Hulet and whoever was drugging Clay behind her back. I was also tired and hungry and mean. Felt like hitting somebody who deserved it, eating a decent dinner, and getting a good night's sleep.

Ten minutes later I was back inside and Paige called. "I've read through Donald's formulary," she said. "Unacceptable. I was prescribing Clay's medications while Donald was dispensing others, and I failed to understand what was happening. But it tracks. For instance, in April of last year, when Clay began to trust me in therapy, Donald commenced twice-weekly doses of LSD. And if you look back at the last two Aprils—which coincides with visits from Clay's family—Donald had been giving him four hundred micrograms of LSD every day! Thirty doses in April of last year. Not only that, but Donald suspended Clay's antianxiety meds for the whole month. It's as if Donald is trying to make Clay anxious and hallucinatory just before his parents arrive. As if Donald doesn't **want** Clay to see his own mother and father."

I wondered if Donald Tice had also told Clay that his parents wanted to put him in a state institution. Parents who still believe that their son was an aircraft mechanic in Iraq, I thought. Who might not even suspect that Clay was in a black-site torture chamber for two years, working under Briggs Spencer and Timothy Tritt— Deimos and Phobos, gods of terror and fear.

When Paige spoke again, her voice had risen and I heard the bitterness in it. "Roland, I ran scores of scans on Clay. I did EEGs and blood work, sometimes twice a week, just trying to figure out why my medications weren't **helping** him. I tested him for drug allergies, food allergies, pollen allergies—you name it. I made sure he had good vitamins and herbal teas, for god's sake. I've been deceived. I feel sick. Truly sick."

I thought back to my conversation with Evan Southern as we watched Morpheus dispensing his potions at Arcadia. "Did you know that Donald Tice was with Clay and Briggs Spencer in Romania?"

"Donald in Romania?"

"Spencer-Tritt recruited him. Along with other loyal young men who would do what they were told and keep their mouths shut. Like Clay Hickman and John Vazquez."

All she offered then was silence. So I improvised a little. "Briggs Spencer knew what Donald was doing with the meds behind your back, Paige. He knows everything that happens at Arcadia, through Alec and his security people, and the cameras and microphones. Briggs Spencer probably created Clay's formulary himself. Donald is just his employee. Still."

I listened to her breathing. And the hum of the mini-refrigerator in my room. "Roland, could I count on you to testify to having seen Donald Tice dispensing from his computer tablet?"

"It wouldn't matter. I didn't see him give Clay anything."

"But it might give the state medical board enough to open an investigation. Or even the San Diego district attorney. Who knows what Tice would tell them? They damaged my patient while he was under my care. I can testify that Clay's behavior was not what it should have been, had my prescriptions been used. Would you do it? Would you testify to what you've seen?"

I had to think on that. For the first time since I'd set foot in Arcadia, I saw that Clay Hickman—the missing lunatic with violence in his past—was a victim as well as a menace. "I'd consider."

"I'm taking that as a yes. Now do you see how important it is, Roland? That you call me first when you find Clay? Not Alec or Briggs?"

"How well do you know Spencer?"

It took her a while to answer, and she commenced at the end of a long sigh. "After hiring me he professed a . . . romantic interest. I professed none back. He was separating from his wife. We talked, often and sometimes long. I noted that he did not seem to have genuine emotions for things and people outside himself. He presented as a sociopath—what we call anti-social personality disorder. Subtly at first, then not. As many of them do. He patched his marriage back together. He totally shut me out. I was thankful for that. The only reason I stayed at my job was my partners."

Another long silence. When she spoke again it was no more than a whisper. "I'm very, very tired."

"Then sleep."

"Do you think of your wife before you fall asleep?"

Again I listened to the slow in and out of her breath. I wanted this woman to know my wife's name, but had been ready to shoot Briggs Spencer for even saying it. "Her name was Justine."

"How beautiful. Do you work hard and constantly to avoid thinking about her?"

"I think of her anyway."

I heard the ice hit her glass again. "That is a healthy thing. Roland? There's something I'd like you to know about me. I was married once. His name was Daniel, though he preferred Dan. A beautiful man. I loved him. Cancer, age thirty-four. Five years ago."

That rocked me. "I'm sorry. Why did you lie to me about him?"

She had to think about her answer, which seemed odd. "He is hard for me to talk about. I know. A shrink who doesn't want to talk can't be a real shrink. But his death was a long and sometimes brutal thing. It colored the way I consider the world, and love. I wanted not to be colored for you. For reasons I don't yet fully understand."

I heard the glass and ice again, but no words. We let the time pass in our connected distance. "I enjoyed our dance," she said.

"Let's add music next time. A waltz or two."

Briggs Spencer answered on the first ring. "What were you doing on my property?"

"Trying to get there ahead of Clay," I said. "Vazquez was shot dead in your kitchen. What do you know about it?"

"Why would I know anything about it?"

"Because I'm not the only one you've recruited to find Clay Hickman, am I? You also sent idiots who played it heavy. DeMaris and his sidekick? Whoever it was, it blew up when Laura Vazquez and her son came home."

"That's not the narrative."

In the ring, I was never much of a believer in feeling out an opponent. Just wanted to get right into it. "How's this narrative? You were Clay's superior in Romania. You know from his emails that Clay was talking to Vazquez about bringing you a dose of something you don't want—white fire. What you **do** want is Clay back in his psychotropic haze at Arcadia, where he can't bring anything to anyone. I know about Donald and the formulary. Clay wasn't taking Paige Hulet's prescriptions, he was taking yours."

"Stirring!" he yelped. "Except Paige Hulet is the medical director at Arcadia and prescribes for Clay. I'm a mere psychologist. I can't prescribe drugs in the state of California. It's against the law."

"You've been letting Hulet prescribe medications for Clay for two years," I said. "But behind her back, Tice has been giving him other drugs the whole time."

"Utter fabrication. Do your job and find him."

I considered resigning my commission. Letting Clay bring white fire to Deimos. Whatever white fire was, Briggs Spencer deserved it. But I couldn't let Clay go back to Arcadia. I needed to know if he was a menace or a victim. And, menace or victim, I wasn't going to abandon Sequoia to him—in love with Clay or not. Briggs Spencer heard my thoughts.

"Thinking of quitting? Maybe doing a tell-all with that reporter who gave you a copy of **Hard Truth**?"

"If you didn't send those men to Redwood Valley, who did?"

"Find out."

He clicked off.

I thought a moment, declined another drink from the bartender who follows me everywhere, then pulled Clay's printed address book from my briefcase. I wrote Timothy Tritt a brief text explaining my position and requesting an interview as soon as possible.

21

Timothy Tritt lived in a yellow barn in Bishop, California, on the eastern slope of the Sierra Nevada Mountains. The barn sat in a meadow with a creek winding through it and thirsty black cottonwoods following the curves of the water. The main ranch house was a hundred yards upstream. The Sierras stood jagged and black against the western sky, with the White Mountains to the east, the two ranges facing off like enormous chess pieces. I'd landed at Bishop Airport and taken a taxi to this, the north end of town.

We sat on tree-branch chairs in the shade of the barn, a blue cooler with a white top between us, and six dogs alternatingly panting or sleeping close by. The morning was warm. Tritt was skinny and bearded, hair long and yellow as the faded barn. Cargo shorts, a cheap plastic watch, and a black bandana rolled into a headband. Skin dark and wrinkled by the sun. He wouldn't look at me. He popped the caps off two more beers and swung one over.

"Terrible about John Vazquez," he said. "We weren't close but I loved the man just the same."

"They shot him up like a paper target. Who would do that?"

Tritt shook his head, drank. "He could have been mixed up with bad people. Drugs. Weapons. I don't know."

I had considered those things, too, but Clay having been at Spencer's ranch at the same time was too big a coincidence. And nothing I had seen of John, Laura, and Michael Vazquez looked like a drugs or weapons kind of life.

Tritt sighed and continued. "Spence was always an easy guy to like. We were SERE instructors at Fairchild, both married. He was always picking up the tab for the beers and burgers. He played ball in college and tried out for the pros but didn't make it. So he coached Spokane Little League. He adored his wife, Dawn. Respected her. They couldn't have children. Then one morning the world changed."

I nodded.

"Spencer and I were past fighting age when they bombed the Trade Center, but we wanted to fight terror and protect American lives. Wanted to get into the smoke. Terrorists can't **do** that to Americans. We saw a chance to make our own war on terror. We left SERE and started Spencer-Tritt Consulting. We would train military and diplomats for danger zones. Private contractors, too. We'd give everyone the best tools we knew for avoiding capture and surviving interrogation. We'd been teaching those things for years at SERE. And Americans were being dished up for torturers and executioners, right?"

I said nothing, not wanting to derail him. He scratched a dog's belly with his toe. "Then one night Briggs and I came up with a great idea— why not play some offense, too? Why not reverse engineer our resistance techniques into methods for extracting good intel **from** detainees? Spencer-Tritt would be the cutting edge in getting high-value, actionable intelligence. Naturally, we would have to charge very good money for this expertise. Well, when the CIA heard our pitch, they lit up like a million-dollar slot machine. They had even less of an idea than we did on how you actually interrogate a human being. They didn't **want** to know. So out came the checkbooks and we were on our way."

A long silence. A hawk wheeled and keened, one of the dogs snored. I tried to put myself into the mind-set of a psychologist going into the interrogation business while his country declared its war on terror. I'd enlisted in December of 2001, three months after the attacks, recently graduated with a bachelor of arts in history. I was twenty-two and had no real prospects. Like

Tritt, I was angry and wanted to do something. Military service was a tradition in my family. So I understood Tritt, so far.

"They sent us to Guantánamo for a trial run at the al-Qaeda guys," he said. "We had no experience at all in the Middle East. No knowledge of the history or language or customs. We had no experience as interrogators, either, except in role-playing scenarios at SERE. Hell, we taught survival in the wilds. Evasion from capture. Resistance in captivity. And escape."

Tritt drained most of his beer in one long gulp. "But Briggs and I made up for it with attitude and showmanship. We had both written 'scholarly' papers for the SERE instructors under us. One of mine was called 'The Psychological Aspects of Captivity.' Twenty pages of psychobabble. But I updated the title to 'The Psychological Foundations of Enhanced Interrogation Techniques,' and made it required reading for the Guantánamo staff. We were arrogant and aloof. We acted like experts. We **wanted** that job."

"How'd you do?"

"At Gitmo? Fair. Nobody there was impressed by us at first. Everybody thought **they** were experts on interrogations. You tell a seasoned military interrogator that you're a psychologist, they don't exactly salute you. But we were energized by the idea of how far we might be able to take things. And how much money we could turn it into.

"We were selling our souls, but we didn't know it yet. I can't speak for Briggs, but as of our last day at Guantánamo I could still stand the sight of my own face in the mirror. After? Now? Well."

Tritt finished the beer, dropped the bottle into the cooler, and brought out another. A wrinkled, short-haired mongrel heard the clink and lifted his sleep-flattened face to the sound.

"Luckily, some of the rogue Bagram interrogators were at Gitmo, so Briggs and I learned fast. They showed us how the everyday tools worked."

"Everyday tools?"

"Oh, the basics, I mean. The restraint chairs and iso boxes, which aren't much bigger than a coffin. The hoods. And the basic physical techniques, too, like walling and peroneal compliance blows. Those are when you knee a detainee on the outside of his thigh. You know, right here, where it's all gristle and tendon against the femur." He tapped the outside of his thigh. "You knee the guy really hard, and as often as you need to. It hurts like hell, especially if they're suspended by chains. This one detainee at Bagram, a taxi driver named Dilawar, he died in the chains. When we took him down, we found out his legs had turned to mush from the compliance blows. Surprised us."

Tritt took a deep breath and let it out slowly, looking down at the label on his beer bottle. "And we learned all the other basic techniques that seemed to be working—the chains and stress positions, hooding, light saturation, sleep deprivation. Loud music for hours on end. We renamed some of the basics, took credit for them with the new guys. Over the years, Briggs and I got credit and blame for all sorts of things we didn't do. But there were two **big** things we did that made enhanced interrogation techniques better. One was we learned to combine. Throw the book at 'em. You keep a guy awake for thirty-six hours, chained to the ceiling in a cold cell, throw on some ice water every few hours, make him listen to death metal the whole time, and he'll pretty much tell you anything you want him to. Of course, he's got to have that thing to tell."

22

The pitch of Tritt's voice rose and his words came faster. "The other revolutionary thing we did had actually begun at Navy SERE training, where we'd taught resistance to waterboarding. Briggs and I remembered how much our men hated waterboarding, hated it more than anything else. They said the only thing that kept them from cracking was being able to thrash around, you know, just fighting for breath. **The fight kept them sane.** So Briggs and I invented this two-man procedure, 'Constrictor.' One of us would get the subject in a headlock, and the other would put the wet towel over his face, then get the stream going. Hold the bucket up high for maximum pressure, of course. And we'd just fill the guy up with cold water. Cold water worked best, retarded the gag reflex. And not being able to thrash around to try to get breath because of the headlock, well, that just drove the detainees crazy. They'd break their wrists in the restraints. It's been called simulated drowning, but there was nothing simulated about the way we did it. It was a good way to get a subject to what we called 'the point of distortion.' That was an amalgam of physical and psychological force that, when applied at the right time, distorted the detainee's reasoning to the point where he could see no options. No options. End of hope, end of resistance. All he could do is tell us what we wanted to know. If he knew it. But . . . waterboarding was just the beginning. It was nothing compared to other things we did."

"Spencer mentioned the menu."

"Oh yeah. The **menu.** We had nineteen EITs approved by Rumsfeld and the lawyers. We even used insects. 'Plague of Insects,' we called it, where you put a detainee's head in a pillowcase filled with the ugliest, meanest bugs you can find. Which are plentiful in tropical and desert countries. The key to Plague of Insects was forcing the detainee to look into the bag first. Later, in places like Romania and Poland, we had trouble finding good biting and stinging insects, especially in cold weather, so Plague of Insects wasn't used as much. Mice worked on some detainees. You'd be surprised how often the biggest, strongest guys are scared of mice. The lawyers didn't approve the mice, but if they worked, well . . . One detainee broke down completely when we moused him. God, we laughed. Sometimes, laughing was all you could do to keep your sanity. Don't forget, we were working and living in a torture chamber."

"No, I won't forget that."

"Another thing that kept Briggs and me sane was reminding ourselves that we were running a business. This was our **career.** So we not only strategized on how to get actionable results with enhanced techniques, we also figured out how to report the results in order to get bonuses. We killed a Yemeni man in Poland on the waterboard. It happened on the one hundred and forty-fifth time we did him. He had denied knowing anything about al-Qaeda. He prayed to Allah but never gave us one shred of actionable intelligence. So we kept filling him up with cold water and one day his heart just stopped. So, the question was: How could we turn that dead guy into a useful intelligence bonus? Well, I'll tell you how—just call his death **proof that the detainee had no meaningful information to surrender.** Which justified the torture, of course. So we reported that case as 'resulting in useful intelligence,' which earned Spencer-Tritt the bonus pay. We did that a lot. After all, we were our own overseers, our own watchdogs and analysts. I remember the man we drowned. Jamal. Proud guy. Hated us."

Tritt finished his beer in one long gulp and had another open before I was half done with mine. The alpha dog, a nice-looking yellow

Labrador named Chief, came over, sat with ears cocked, and looked at his master. Tritt's tone of voice had changed once again and Chief had heard it, and I'd heard it, too.

"Even Chief hates these stories by now," said Tritt. "I tell them to the dogs all the time. That keeps all the old wounds open and fresh, which keeps me sorry and miserable. The main reason I haven't killed myself is because I believe I deserve the pain of remembering all the pain I caused. But you didn't come here to hear about my gloomy little psyche."

I noted that Tritt still hadn't looked at me since I'd arrived, not directly, not even when handing me a beer. I wasn't sure why his voice had changed—excitement? Passion? Revulsion? Shame? The thrill of confession? I watched him in profile. His eyes were trained slightly up, and apparently far away, maybe on the sharp tips of the Sierras, or the sky beyond.

"I volunteer at the vet center once a week," he said. "And at the parish food hall once a week. And the dog pound two days a week, which is where I got these brutes. And the hospital. Every Monday through Friday. I put in a good hard volunteer day. Hard as I can. My personal take from Spencer-Tritt was twenty million. Well, I gave most of it away. To the Catholics, which is what I am. Used to be."

I let that observation hang. Chief lay down

in front of Tritt, who seemed to wrestle his attention off the distant peaks to look down at his dog. He worked a weather-beaten bare foot against the dog's ear.

"Tell me about Clay Hickman," I said.

"Clay? Good kid. One of Spencer's. He was assigned to a Romanian site in Bucharest—code name White Fire. Centuries ago it had been some nobleman's estate, then a hotel that Ceauşescu turned into a communist interrogation center. Closed for years after his people executed him. Outbuildings, basements, smokehouse, a big wine cellar. It was still almost stately. But crumbling and haunted, too. It fit in with the rest of the hood, so we were hidden in plain sight. Big property, fenced, heavily wooded. And of course those stone walls kept the noise down. The Dambovita River wasn't far. The Romanian Foreign Intelligence Service gave it to us because Romania had applied for NATO and wanted U.S. support. I say they 'gave it to us,' but of course we paid handsomely for it. I helped lug the suitcases of CIA cash. A few of us got to open one and gawk at it. Three million in five different duffels. Big, heavy duffels. Like most of us, Hickman thought he could save America from terror if he got the right intel out of the prisoners."

"What do you mean that Clay was one of Spencer's?"

"We had three teams. Briggs and I each had one, and a CIA guy named Bodart led the third team. Bodart's guys called themselves the Wranglers, and they dressed up like cowboys sometimes. Sheesh, that was funny. There was overlap and some filling-in between the teams, too—it's not like we couldn't switch personnel around if we needed to. But it gave us three eight-hour shifts per day, seven days a week. We were competitive, and each team had a different set of, well, skills. Spencer's and my team used nicknames. It made the whole experience more livable. The nicknames gave a sense of playacting. Distanced us from what we were doing. My idea. Our teams used the names of Greek gods and heroes. For narrative authority. I was Phobos, god of fear. Briggs was Deimos, god of terror. I think Clay was Asclepius, the god of healing."

It was making more sense. "Clay says his reason for escaping is to 'bring white fire to Deimos.'"

Tritt raised his beer, drank most of it down, then lowered his head and the bottle. "Well, we'll see."

"Explain."

"Like I said, White Fire was Langley's code for our particular site in Bucharest. Then 'white fire' got to be our slang for something that couldn't be resisted, or withstood. Then Briggs claimed the words 'white fire' for an original enhanced interrogation technique he was developing. He wouldn't tell me much about it, but Bodart was in on it. Anyway, Spencer's white fire was based on a father's love for his son. The son was the fire that you held your detainee up to. The fire was what you, as an interrogator, learned to exploit."

Tritt dropped the empty in the cooler and looked up at the mountains again.

"Exploit the son?" I asked.

"Exploit the son. Yes. That was Spencer's white fire."

23

Finally, Tritt looked at me. Handed me another beer. His eyes were armor-gray in the sunlight, spoked and small-pupiled, like those of a snapping turtle.

"To understand white fire," he said, "you start with Aaban. Aaban was Spencer's. Middle thirties, a Dari Afghan. His name meant Angel of Iron. He was strong, good-looking, hateful. We believed that Aaban knew bin Laden. Aaban's grandfather had fought with bin Laden in the wilderness days. Aaban openly associated with Wahhabi jihadis. We had some intel that Aaban might have been in contact with bin Laden.

"So Briggs applied our standard menu. Got nothing useful. He stayed patient. He got creative with the menu combinations and still got nothing of value. Aaban gave us nothing but lies and minor truths we already knew, and half-truths that took hours and hours to verify or finally disprove. He cursed Briggs. Spit on him. Plague of Insects? Nothing. Wallings, sleep deprivation, death metal 24-7? Nothing. Aaban became the man Spence couldn't break. Aaban survived one hundred and ninety-six waterboardings, personally done by Briggs Spencer. Up to ten sessions a day. We jacked him with amphetamine and kept him awake in a restraint chair for one hundred and eighty hours—that's seven and a half days. Twice. His legs were pulped by compliance blows. He was chained naked to the ceiling just short of strangulation for days at a time. During the chain sessions, he got little water and no food. Not even diapers. We kept his bucket just out of his reach. We hydrated him rectally, mainly for the humiliation it brought him. It was cold in there, the cellar of an old smokehouse. But Aaban gave us exactly no useful intelligence. Do you find it unpleasant to hear this story?"

"I'd rather listen to a World Series game."

"Try being there with us. Try hearing and smelling it. Try **doing** it."

"I wouldn't want to."

He turned those armor-gray eyes on me again. "Not many people would. Although we didn't hear much in the way of thanks after America found out what we were up to."

I took a long swig of the beer, Tritt-style.

"Briggs was worried he'd kill Aaban, making Aaban the victor. So he decided to try something outside the menu. A new technique. It took him six months to locate, detain, and transport

Aaban's eleven-year-old son from Afghanistan to White Fire. Three thousand one hundred and seventy miles."

Chief rose from sleep, shook off the dead grass, and lumbered off toward the creek. Two of the other dogs followed; the last three lifted groggy heads and stayed put. I felt like going to the creek myself, washing off in cold, clean water. I envied the dogs, fearless and lazy, with no comprehension of death.

Rage, Wrath & Fury mustered, ready to unleash themselves on God for how He treats the innocents. For allowing whatever it was that He let happen to Aaban's son, though I hadn't even learned the boy's name yet.

"Roshaan," said Tritt. "Skinny, shy, terrified. They took him to the smokehouse and put him in with his father.

"A week went by. Life at White Fire proceeded as usual—quiet for short periods, then alive with wailing and music. And the trains and their horns. And the muffled screams from the smokehouse. The pain was . . . tangible. Even in the dead of night you could feel the ebb and flow of it, like a tide. **Oh,** I'd think, **that's Bodart's people rectally hydrating old Mohammed.** Or, **That must be my guys, walling Qahtani again.** I saw less of Briggs, but I knew he was out there in the smokehouse cellar with Aaban and Roshaan."

I heard those faint cries from the Romanian smokehouse. They came not from the Angel of Iron, but from his son, Roshaan, as he watched. From the boy—innocent, unprotected, and damned. My friends couldn't control themselves. They screamed: What kind of God are you? How did You allow that to happen? **Why?**

"Another week went by," Tritt continued. "When I'd ask him how it was going out there, Briggs would shrug and stare at me. He started losing weight. He developed a bad case of acne on his nose. He began eating his meals alone. He made me post the twice-daily TPUs—the team progress updates—which used to be his job. He became almost silent. He cut his own hair, with an electric clipper, very, very short, but he'd miss places. It looked like he was shaving his face every few hours, because it was always razor-burned and nicked. The only people out there in the smokehouse with him were Clay Hickman and John Vazquez and a couple of others. None of them were talking details. They kept to themselves. Another week went by, and another.

"Then, five weeks after the arrival of Roshaan, our routine started returning to normal. Briggs began attending the TPUs, then presiding again. He and Clay and the others rejoined us at meals. He let his hair grow, quit shaving. Once in a while, he'd talk baseball, or even make a joke, like the old Spence. What happened in the smokehouse? I don't know. I never saw Roshaan again."

"With all respect, Dr. Tritt, I find it hard to believe. That you don't know what happened to the boy."

Again the hard gray eyes, roving over me. "Spencer would say nothing about him. None of them would. Absolute lockdown, total silence. When I saw Aaban again, he acted as he always did—ferocious and proud. Angel of Iron was right. We moved him and the others out of White Fire just before Obama closed it. He's at Gitmo, as we speak. I still don't know what Spencer did with Roshaan. He refused to tell. It was as if the boy was never there."

I watched the three dogs in the creek, heads hung to the water, backs lit by the sun. The dark Sierra Nevada and the pale White Mountains were still facing off across Owens Valley, while between them a vulture circled precisely in the blue.

"Bullshit," I said. "You know what happened to Roshaan."

Tritt said nothing, and I understood that he had come to the end of his speakable truth on this subject.

He shook his head slowly, as if answering no to a question only he could hear. "Spence knew he was being carried off. By the time the government closed the black sites and put us out of work, Briggs Spencer was a changed man. Maybe not even so much because of what he did, but because of what he **believed** about what he did."

"Which was what?"

"That we were American doctors who had saved American lives and protected the safety of Americans at home using enhanced interrogation techniques."

"What do you believe?"

Tritt helped himself to another beer but didn't offer me one. He opened it and poured half of it down. "That some men lose their souls but keep their minds. While others keep their souls but lose their minds. We were basically just citizens who tortured people to little effect but made a lot of money. We rigged the results, and the CIA pretty much sang along. I can certainly make excuses. We had to deal with the languages and the dialects and the interpreters and detainees. They were endlessly evasive and inventive. What do you expect them to say under excruciating pain? Most of them screamed out **something** when they couldn't take anymore. Something they thought we'd like to hear. Most of them didn't know what we wanted them to know."

There was a long silence then while Tritt stared out at the Sierras and dangled his half-empty bottle by its neck. His tone of voice was softer now, more intimate. "I was very concerned about the costs to my people. Most of our CIA officers were poorly trained and inexperienced. But they meant well. They were innocents, in their own self-serving ways. And some of the enlisted men we drafted into Spencer-Tritt, guys like Clay, they were just so damned young. I wondered right off what White Fire would do to them. I have a pretty good idea by now. See, Mr. Ford—most people can't endure a place like White Fire for long. It's the equivalent of a psychotic break, but you don't come out of it. We lived in a world of constant pain and light and sound. A world of anguish and hopelessness. Our nightmares were not just in our heads while we slept, they surrounded us every waking minute of every day. They were real. The torturer is tortured. You do not drown a man strapped to a board without drowning yourself.

"Today, Briggs will claim that none of what we did bothers him. That everything we did was necessary. That we saved American lives with torture. He can't name one American saved by torture, and not because the name is classified. You will search **Hard Truth** in vain for one such name. I spent time at every site. I know. Spencer will bring up bin Laden's courier. But they'd been watching that courier for **months.** They had him cold. Ghul? The al-Qaeda agent? He'd identified that courier **weeks** before we got our chance at him. No EITs needed—Ghul just

sang. Our little parakeet. We tortured him anyway, just in case there was more. There wasn't.
But everyone thought, at the time, that it was
the right thing to do."

Tritt opened the cooler, pushed his empty
bottle into the ice, and came up with another.
"You have to understand our circumstances.
The pressure on us was enormous. We kept
wondering when the next terrorist attack would
come. Not only that, but innocent Americans
were dying every day in the wars. I remember May 31, 2007. I was in Alexandria, Vir-
ginia, dining rather splendidly with some of
my government bosses, having just gotten a
five-hundred-and-forty-seven-thousand-dollar
paycheck for one month of work. And a story
came on the bar TV—one hundred and twenty-
six U.S. servicemen had been killed that month,
the deadliest month in Iraq thus far. Eleven
more in Afghanistan. Even half drunk I couldn't
escape those young deaths. Then I was back at
White Fire. American death hung over us like
a curse. How many more? What's bin Laden
going to do next? We needed to torture harder,
torture longer, extract more intel—pull it out of
them like teeth."

Tritt paused and turned his hard, small eyes to
me again. I would hate looking into those things,
hour by hour, while he prolonged my agony.
"So, you see, this difference between Briggs and

me—in the way we see what happened in the war—is everything. It is why he can fly through the skies and make millions more dollars with the money we made selling torture. And why I sit in this meadow, drinking with the dogs. We are different alloys forged in the same fire."

He swept his hand around the inside of the cooler but came up empty. Something in his mechanics told me he knew the beers were gone. He wiped his hands together, then drew them down his sun-wrinkled face.

"Clay told me something once," he said. "It stayed in my mind because I could never figure it out. I had gone to see him in Arcadia, and near the end of our visit he told me he had 'gotten half of Spencer's white fire.'"

I waited for the explanation and got none. "What did he mean?"

"I said, 'Clay, by "gotten" do you mean you **understand** half of Spencer's white fire, and what exactly had happened to Roshaan? Or do you mean that you somehow **have** half of it?' 'Yes,' he answered—he had half of Deimos's white fire in his possession—and Vazz had the other half."

"Clay had half of white fire, and John Vazquez had the other half? Help me out here, Doctor."

"I figured video," said Tritt. "Spence did, too. We shot quite a bit of it. The agency confiscated all they could find. Very dangerous material, to say the least. We had to close White Fire in a hurry. We figured someone could smuggle out evidence of what we did. We were just never sure who or what."

I let my memories of the last twenty-four hours blow around in my brain like leaves. Something in there that I needed. It took a while, but I saw it and grabbed it: what Sequoia had texted me the night before, when I'd asked her why Clay had driven all the way to Mendocino County to see John Vazquez.

7:50 PM
Why did Clay go there?

7:51 PM
For part 2 he says

For part two, I wondered.
Vazz's half of white fire?

From the shade of a cottonwood outside Bishop Airport I called Laura Vazquez and left a message.

The beer had left me dull but jittery. I kept seeing Tritt's dark, sun-brined skin, his gunmetal-gray eyes. I imagined hooded men in chains, writhing in pain—certainly the inspiration for Clay Hickman's obsessive paintings. I heard the sound of a human body flung against a wall, the gurgled thrashings of suffocation. I pictured young Roshaan and wondered why Tritt—who had offered me so much of his own tortured soul—still couldn't bring himself to tell me the boy's fate.

The ringtone of my phone startled me.

24

It was Laura Vazquez and I apologized for bothering her at such a difficult time. In a faint, stoic voice she thanked me for what I had done the day before and asked me what I needed.

I told her what Clay had once said to his old boss, Timothy Tritt, and asked Laura if she had any idea what her husband's "other half" of white fire might have been. I told her that I thought Clay might have come there yesterday in order to discuss that "other half" with her husband. I was crashing around for something, anything that would lead me toward Clay, and she must have sensed it.

She was quiet for a beat. "Mr. Ford—Clay left here just an hour ago. He was with a young woman named Sequoia. He asked me to see John's war trunk and I let him see it."

"What was in it?"

I pictured the contents as she listed them for me: his Air Force uniforms, rank insignias, training certificates, discharge papers. Commemorative plaques and medals. Some hats and T-shirts.

There were photo sticks and some photographs he'd printed.

"He never really got into that stuff," she said. "He seemed happy enough to forget it. The war. The trunk was down in the wine cellar, pushed into a far corner with fishing and viticulture magazines piled on top."

I'd seen it and not known what I was seeing. "Did Clay take anything from the trunk?"

"Dolls. From Romania, I believe. Two of them—colorful, folksy dolls. Mounted on the same wooden base, fighting with swords."

The jittery fog of White Fire vanished as a wave of adrenaline passed through me. "He left an hour ago?"

"Yes, no more than an hour ago."

"Did he say where they were going?"

"If he did I don't remember. I'm sorry, Mr. Ford. Today is the second-worst day of my life."

"Thank you, Mrs. Vazquez. Please give my best to Michael."

"I will do that."

My next call, to Sequoia, went straight to voicemail, so I sent a text.

4:46 PM
Where are you?

4:47 PM
Drawing closer to Deimos.
Sequoia drives and I plan.

4:48 PM
Hi Clay. How are
the dolls getting
along?

4:48 PM
You talked to my parents and Laura.

4:49 PM
Are the dolls valuable?

4:49 PM
Beyond value.

4:50 PM
Explain, please.

4:51 PM
Truth contained to be revealed.

4:52 PM
By Spencer? Because
the world must hear it
from the god of terror?

4:52 PM
☺

4:53 PM
Where did Roshaan go?

4:56 PM
☹ ☹ ☹

4:57 PM
We need to talk about
Aaban and Roshaan.

4:58 PM
I will tell you when and where.

4:59 PM
Remember you
are Asclepius, the
healer.

4:59 PM
I am he.

4:59 PM
Part of your mission is
to protect S.

5:01 PM
With my life. I love her. ☺

Then, the unforgettable sound. I turned to watch a late-model Cessna 182 taking off, the Lycoming turbocharger roaring to life.

I got home after dark. A fire raged in the pit, orange flames roiling upward, my five loyal Irregulars roasting s'mores on wire hangers, five inquisitive, up-lit faces watching me come up the walkway with my duffel. Led by tenor Burt

Short, they broke into the chorus of Warren Zevon's "Roland the Headless Thompson Gunner," their standard landlord welcome.

"We saved you one marshmallow and some chocolate dust," said Grandpa Dick. "But you'll have to make your own hanger."

"Pour him a drink," said Grandma Liz.

"You look like you've engaged the enemy," observed Lindsey Rakes.

Wesley Gunn handed me a wire hanger and I saw his two black eyes. I took his chin in one hand and turned his face to catch the firelight.

"Things went a little south, south of the border," said Burt.

"Drink, Rollie?" asked Grandpa, holding up an empty tumbler.

I declined, Dick eyeing me with concern. I set my duffel on one of the concrete picnic tables and looked out at the pond. Justine sat in the rowboat in her big straw hat. Looking my way, then gone. **Adios,** my living ghost. The pond lay flat and black and empty, and beyond it spread the hills and the distant scattered lights of Fallbrook. The night sky was gray and starless.

I lay back on a chaise longue and watched the smoke rise above the flame-lit silhouettes of my confederates. Burt took the adjacent chaise and filled me in on the Mexico run. As planned, he had driven Wesley and Lindsey down to Tijuana to a clinic once used "to great success" by an old friend of his. But, thirsty, they had stopped off at his favorite bar for "a" margarita, which had become "five," leaving them too jovial for the clinic but just fine for shopping, and, later, dinner at La Gaviota, Burt's favorite Tijuana club.

Later in the club cantina, after several more drinks—and the steady traffic of "distinguished professional women"—Wesley confessed that he was still a virgin. So Burt introduced him to one of the women. She was taken by strapping Wesley's boyish smile. Burt brokered a deal with the woman's "manager," which put Wesley and the woman together in an upstairs room for one hour. Burt had bargained the manager down from two hundred fifty to one hundred dollars, and sent eighteen-year-old Wesley on his mission with the money, as a "gift." At the end of the hour, the woman demanded two hundred fifty, then "feigned outrage" when Wesley offered all he had, which was Burt's one hundred, and thirty-six dollars of his own. Her manager appeared with two policemen, took the money from Wesley but knocked him to the floor, twice, before the cops dragged him downstairs and out. "So, it resolved as we'd hoped," said Burt. "Wesley gained black eyes but shed his innocence."

Behind the haze of woodsmoke, Wesley lifted a bottle of beer our way, offered a pained smile. "And how was your weekend, Mr. Ford?"

"Uneventful."

Wesley gave me a skeptical once-over. "Sometimes that's best."

I closed my eyes for a minute, listened to the conversations going on around me, then got up and collected my duffel from the table. Dick held up the empty tumbler again, an inquisitive look on his face. It drives him bats when I refuse alcohol. "Excuse me," I announced. "I have a date to get ready for."

"About time you had a date," said Dick.

"Excellent, Rollie," said Liz.

"She's not good enough for you," said Lindsey.

"Hope it goes better than mine," said Wesley.

25

Paige Hulet had accepted my dinner invitation and wanted to meet on "neutral ground." She'd arranged for a table at Tiburon on Fifth Avenue in downtown San Diego. I arrived on time and was seated. I wore a trim navy wool suit, a pressed white shirt, and a weirdly patterned necktie given to me by Justine. Tiburon was a handsome place, smoked glass and darkly burnished woods, with a wine list that weighed pounds.

She strode across the room in a black calf-length dress pleated from the waist down, a black-and-red woven shawl, strapped black heels, and a shiny red clutch. Hair up, a trace of lipstick, and a smile.

I stood. "Dr. Hulet."

"Mr. Ford."

She set her bag on an adjacent seat, then the shawl. Her shoulders and arms were graceful. I felt that hyperfocused energy of being with a beautiful woman who is there because of you. I sat across from her. "This is not like seeing you at your work," I said.

"Nor you at yours. Where did you get that wonderful tie?"

"Chinatown, L.A."

I saw a twinkle in her eye. "Do you like the restaurant?"

"Perfect, so far."

We ordered cocktails, made small talk, watched the sidewalk pedestrians through the darkened windows. The martini hit me like a punch. I felt the last two days trying to drag me under—the bloody murder of John Vazquez, the ragged wound his death would leave in the lives of his wife and son, Briggs Spencer's and Timothy Tritt's gothic horrors committed in the name of security.

Paige reached across the table and set a cool hand on mine. "I felt very bad for you Saturday night. I could feel your sadness for John Vazquez and his family, and your anger. And everything we're both feeling for Clay. And Sequoia. All from five hundred miles away. We don't have to talk about it."

I touched my glass to hers. Instead of murder, war, and moral injury, we talked about current events, books, sports. Careful with the politics. Then childhoods, friends, even futures. The future as What if? The future as Wouldn't it be great to? Future happy. Future lite. I realized she was not Justine and did not resent her for it. I gave in to the energy that she brought me, let my thoughts wander and my words play. We had another cocktail, ordered dinner, and made it last. Even the silences had comfortable shapes. I couldn't remember the last time I'd made so little effort and felt okay. We talked late, finished the wine, had a dessert liquor, and paid up.

"Let's walk," she said.

The April night was damp this close to the Pacific, and the electric "gas lamps" glowed in the mist. The Padres were on the road and Petco Park was dark. Spring Sundays draw out the locals, so the sidewalks were bustling. We got Jägermeisters at Bar Vie. Then a pedicab to take us past the aircraft carrier **Midway,** and the monstrous **Unconditional Surrender** statue pulsing in camera flashes.

We walked arm in arm downtown, past the library and stadium, no stated destination, no conversation. Paige stumbled slightly on a sidewalk crack and righted herself with my arm.

Then took my hand. Led me through an alley I wasn't familiar with, then back onto the avenue, where we came to a stop in front of the swank Glorietta Lofts. I looked up at the stainless deco building rising into the mist-pricked light of the streetlamps, then at Paige, close beside me.

"Oh," she said. "I must live here."

" 'Neutral ground'?"

"Are you up for a nightcap?"

A ripple of thrill. "I am."

She entered something on the keypad outside the lobby, held her thumb over a sensor, then swung the glass door open for me. I stepped past her. The lobby had a black marble floor, oak panels, gold light fixtures, and a large bronze pedestal-mounted catamaran tacking into the wind. A touch of class with a pinch of pretense.

"I could apologize for tricking you," she said. "But my heart wouldn't be in it."

We stepped into the elevator. She touched her thumb to another sensor on the control panel, then pushed the brass button for floor twenty-seven. The door shut and the car lifted off and Paige turned in close to me, hands on the shawl covering her shoulders. She looked at my face but not into my eyes. I could smell her light perfume, and a trace of liquor on her breath. When the elevator braked she tilted into me.

We entered her home and lights came on. In the foyer she draped her shawl and clutch on a coat rack, added my jacket. She led me into the living room. The shutters were open and I looked out over the Embarcadero, Coronado, and across the infinite black Pacific beyond. We were above it all.

The room was large and rectangular. An industrial feel. Pendulum lights hung from the ceiling and gas flames wavered silently in a glass-faced fireplace to my right. The floor looked to be maple. The furnishings were right-angled, sober, minimally padded. One entire wall was a bookshelf with a sliding stepladder to get up high. The large floor rug on which I stood had a crazed abstract pattern not unlike my necktie. The open kitchen looked sleek and neat. Paige went in and started on drinks. I could see the back of her reflected in the big window, her shoulders bare and calves flexed as she reached into a cabinet.

"Cold vodka with a twist okay?"

"More than."

A freezer rolled open and shut. I heard knife taps on a cutting board as she carved the twists, then the soft gurgle of liquid hitting glass. She came out with two frosted cocktail glasses topped with artful coils of lemon rind, spilling not a drop. We touched rims and drank. She turned and looked out the window so I did, too, and for a moment we stood separate but together, watching the city and the ships and the water. She took a sip, then set her glass on a coffee table and produced a remote control from between two neat stacks of magazines. Music poured into the room. She put down the remote and turned to me.

"You saved me a waltz," I said, setting down my drink.

Bracing herself on my shoulder with one hand, she unstrapped a shoe and let it drop. Then the other. Toed them under the table.

The waltz was from **The Princess Bride**. Just as in our nonmusical security-office dance, the first movements were clumsy, but soon we had that waltz all to ourselves. She followed well. The night's alcohol made me feel light. My dress shoes had good leather soles and they slid easily on the lunatic rug. I thought Paige said something and looked at her, but apparently she had not. Her gaze was level. Justine came to me in parts. Eyes but not face, voice but not words. Then drifted. To coalesce again. "Dancing with you makes me remember," I said.

"I remember, also."

She nodded against me.

One **two** three.

We glided around the funny-looking rug, took a side trip into the kitchen, around it and out, then along the face of the big window overlooking the world. A waltz is a heady dance, the play of weight and momentum. Formal and graceful. I learned by standing on Mom's feet when I was five.

"Dan's here right now," she said. "And just a second ago, before we started dancing, I sensed Justine, waiting just inside you. After years have gone by, here they are. Do they talk on the other side? Don't worry. I'm a scientist. I will not go supernatural on you. But I **know** they are somewhere. And that is good and okay with me." She touched her nose to my neck and inhaled.

Beat of heart, tingle of skin. "I thought I heard you say something," I said.

"Listen to what you don't quite hear, Roland. It's almost always something you don't hear **yet**."

"You pry right in."

"I'll shut up."

The room spun around us: window and city and lights on the water, bookshelf and ladder, foyer and fire, the kitchen, then window and city again.

"Can I take the comb out of my hair?"

I felt her arms release and her upper body lean away, but we kept our three-quarter time. Her arms reached to their task, and her fingers worked. A dark wave fell to her shoulders. She lobbed the comb into the kitchen, where it clattered on the floor, and took my hand again.

All the songs were waltzes. Some were uptempo and made me feel Austrian. Some were as slow as summer in Ventura, where I'd lived as a boy. Some had words and some not a one. My heart was beating strong after the first two, and my breathing was deep and good. So was hers. Five waltzes? Six?

She led me off the dance floor to the black sofa and collected our empty glasses. In the kitchen she rattled and banged, then came back with fresh glasses and twists, and the vodka bottle peeking out of a frosty stainless steel container— all balanced on a small tray. "I slung cocktails in college," she said.

She set it all on the table in front of us. Then sat down close to me and drew up her knees, letting her dress rise up her legs. I put my arm around her. She moved closer and rested her hand on the knot of my tie. She told me she saw something she liked in me that first day at Arcadia. Didn't say what it was. Less than a week ago. She laughed. I looked at her hair falling forward and her face and the shine of the light in her eyes. Small beads of perspiration had formed above her mouth and one drop made it down her neck and into the hollow of her collarbone.

"I'm nervous," she said.

"Me too."

"Did you dance with Justine often?"

"Often."

"Have you always been so angry?"

I shrugged. How to say, **It's for everything that happened to her and shouldn't have happened,** without ruining the evening?

"Do you blame yourself?"

A twinge of defensiveness. "I could have kept her on the ground."

"Do you blame her?"

I spoke before considering, and fumbled an unhappy truth. "I'm angry at her for trying to take a few hours of pleasure without me and not coming back. Logical? No. Anger does what it will."

"Fight it, Roland."

"With what?"

"Forgiveness."

She stood and picked up the remote, dropped it clatteringly to the hardwood floor, swayed unsteadily, then picked it up. Her hair fell forward around her face as she found the right buttons. The house lights dimmed while papery blinds hummed down the windows. She drained her glass and set it down and shivered. "Sorry. I need just a little more courage."

"Am I that scary?"

"Take me to my bed. It's thataway."

I walked Paige to the bedroom with one of her arms over my neck like a wounded warrior. She felt heavy and drunk. I helped her off with the dress and she hit the bed, dug under the covers and curled up, knees to chest. I lay on top of the covers, close beside her, and ran my fingers through her hair. "I'm so sorry," she whispered. "I can't drink that. Much."

"It's okay, Paige."

"Say no to anger."

"I will."

"But you still have to . . ."

"Have to what?"

"Call. Me first. When you find Clay. And testify. And make all the bad stuff. Go away."

Before I could tell her I hadn't agreed to either, her breathing had gone deep and fast. I
touched her face, pale in the moonlight. Ran a
finger along her jawline. I wanted her so bad it
hurt. I listened to her breathing. Took my hand
off her and sat up against the headboard. I heard
the San Diego traffic far below, watched a tug
pulling a Navy tender across the silver water of
the bay, felt weirdly crowded by the past, even
here, just two people, twenty-seven stories up in
a box of brick and glass with the lights off and
the nightshades down.

26

I found some bottled water in the refrigerator, took it back into the bedroom, and stood in the doorway for a moment. Her back was to me and she was breathing steadily. The bed-stand clock said 1:47. The bathroom night-light was on but I didn't want to wake her. Didn't seem like a thunderstorm could do that at this point, but . . .

So I crossed the living room to the other side of the penthouse and found the second bath at the end of the hall. It was good-sized, apparently set up to service two bedrooms, one on either side, with doors to each at either end of a long bathroom counter. There were twin sinks and dark blue tile. I hit the lights, splashed hot water on my face, then cold. The mirror displayed all my thirty-eight years in detailed relief—laughs and fights, highs and lows, truly a map deserved.

High on the left side of my forehead is the scar with the story behind it. Nickel-sized and Y-shaped. Faint, but in the right light it's clear. Got it in my first professional fight—just out of the corps and invincible. Roland "Rolling Thunder" Ford versus Darien "Demolition" Dixon. Part of the undercard at Trump 29 Casino, Coachella, California, 2005. Darien was twice the fighter I was and I knew it after the first thirty seconds of the fight. He had some fun with me. Finally put me down in the ninth with a jab, a cross, and a hook. I was a sack of gravel on the canvas, but still conscious. Watching the ref looming over me, counting. Lights bright, crowd loud. I knew I could get up, beat the count, and continue. Or I could stay right where I was and call it all quits. More important, I was astonished that this could happen to invincible me. Tough guy in school. Never knocked down in a Marine Corps bout. Door-to-doors in Fallujah and never caught a bullet or stepped on an IED. People around me shot dead from hundreds of yards away, others blown to shreds with one step. Twenty-six years of victory. But laying there as the referee counted, it all came crashing down on me at once and for the first time—the fact that I was utterly, spectacularly mortal. So **this** is how it feels. I was suddenly thankful just to be alive.

Of course, in accord with Ford spirit and Marine training, I got up at "nine," bounced on my toes, and glared at the ref, nodding. He took my wrists, stared into my eyes, and stepped away. "Demolition" hit me with a big right I just didn't have the legs to get away from. Saw it coming. The next thing I remember, a ceiling of faces was staring down at me in bright, bright light. Some I knew. I remembered where I was and what had happened. They helped me to my feet, then to my stool in the corner. I sat there, watching the world around me, feeling pleasantly outside myself, childlike. State of wonder.

Hospital, seven stitches and an MRI, out in a couple of hours.

Rolling Thunder's first defeat.

Mortality check.

Stopped fighting.

Began dancing.

I look at the scar sometimes to remind myself of that mortality. To know that sometimes it's good not to get up before the bell. Not to let your pride carry you into the big punch that puts you down. When I'm worried or afraid, the scar heats up. When there's something wrong that I'm not aware of, some trouble that has yet to register, the scar itches. And every once in a while—used to be once a year or so, but lately more often—I feel that same state of post-KO wonder come over me, and I'll want to sit on a stool in my corner and just watch the world go by. I asked a neurologist about it years ago and he told me not to worry—I probably hadn't taken enough punishment to cause chronic dementia pugilistica. That made the scar itch.

Which worried me. Had another scan, but he saw nothing unusual.

Still standing in Paige Hulet's guest bath, I checked my phone and found nothing, looked into the mirror again and shook my head.

I opened one of the bathroom's two interior doors because that's what I do. There was a light switch just inside. Paige's home office greeted me: a neat desk, a computer and peripherals, stacks of magazines. I stepped in. One wall hung with framed pictures, diplomas, certificates. On the desk a row of coffee cups bristling with pens and pencils and a large desk blotter dense with scribbles and drawings. There was a smaller version of the wall-sized bookcase, no ladder needed. A brown leather task chair sat before a desktop monitor. In the far opposite corner was a red leather recliner with a reading lamp behind it. A complex-looking treadmill faced the southern window. Through that window, the Grand Hyatt reminded me of the night I'd met Justine. I looked at it for a long while.

Then went to the bookcase to read titles and authors. Most of the volumes were hardbound books on biology, medical science, psychiatry, and philosophy. French literature, poetry, and drama. No PI novels.

I sat in the task chair in front of the desk, butt

low and knees high, found the chair's vertical control, and raised the seat bottom. For some reason I thought of me moving Paige Hulet out of the strong sunlight outside Arcadia, then her moving us back into it. I wondered if the sunlight was truth, or an irresistible illusion, or simply sunlight. Wondered if she was awake in her bed and maybe missing me. Smelled her body and perfume on me and silently apologized to Justine. It wasn't the horny foreplay that made me feel guilty, it was the reckless affection that Paige Hulet brought to me.

On the desk lay a short stack of the **Journal of Psychiatry,** all the same issue from three months ago, with "Soul Wounds" by Paige Hulet called out on the cover. I took one and flipped to the article and read a paragraph at random. I looked at her picture at the end. She looked better in real life. Especially with her dress off.

I rolled back from the desk for a wider view of Paige's work space. Stopped just short of the treadmill. Studied her diplomas on the wall, arranged at eye level above her computer monitor. Tustin High School valedictorian. UCLA, with a major in biology and a minor in French, summa cum laude. The Keck School of Medicine of USC. Columbia University Medical Center psychiatry resident. Proud of her achievements, I thought.

Around this core of lauds and laurels hung

framed photographs of Paige with various patients at Arcadia. Recognized some of them. It looked like the pictures had been shot spontaneously—some taken outside in the woods or around the pool, others in the art studio and the recreation rooms and the Lyceum. Most of the patients looked relaxed. Some looked wide-eyed with excitement, or maybe they were just aping the clichés about the mentally disturbed that they all surely knew too well. I saw trust on the faces of those men and women, and the satisfaction this trust was bringing their lovely doctor. Paige looked happy. Several were of Clay Hickman, who looked very much as he did in the pictures Paige had supplied to me: a young slender-faced man with a mop of blond hair and different-colored eyes. In one shot, she faced the camera while he looked at her, and the contentment in him was obvious. **The healer,** he's thinking. **My lovely healer.** She seemed as happy as he did. Something in her expression. Achievement. **See what I've done.** I looked at that picture for a long beat, wondering how a mind fails. Not like a heart, or a plan, or the fuel pump of an airplane. No. More complicated, maybe, or at least less understood. Sitting there, I felt humbled that, even through the sludge of psychotropic drugs and hallucinogens they were shoveling down him, Clay Hickman could still find moments of genuine joy.

Then, farther out from the doctor/partner shots, was Paige's personal history: as a girl with her mom and dad, beach trips, camping. Paige in a barnyard holding an orange cat, and tennis, tennis, tennis. Crestview League singles champion of 1992 and 1993. I was surprised that she was three years my senior. Didn't look it. She looked then like she did now: serious and smart. Paige looking up from a book. Paige with girlfriends. Later, Paige being graduated from UCLA, summa cum laude. Deans' lists. Not quite smiling. No boyfriends on that wall. And no Daniel that I could see. Only a few pictures of Paige as an adult, other than those with her partners at Arcadia. A few with Mom and Dad again, aging well apparently.

Back in the guest bath, I opened the door on the opposite wall of the two-sink counter, stepped in, and found a light. It was smaller than the home office and furnished very simply: a twin bed along one wall, a chest of drawers, a small desk with a wooden chair and a lamp. I turned on more lights. A French Open poster hung above the desk. I was pleased to see that its setting, Roland-Garros, was in big type. Beside it was a poster of Rafa Nadal sliding on clay. A window faced west and I could see the lights of the naval installations out on Coronado.

The room smelled fresh and clean, but felt un-used. I opened the closet: a few blouses and light jackets hanging at one end, jeans and trousers at the other. Shoes on the floor, sweaters on the shelf. I heard a siren wailing far down and away.

Back in the darkened living room, I found the remote and raised the blinds. Watched the lights of San Diego twinkle on the black surface of the bay. Considered the bottle of vodka, from which Paige Hulet had had to guzzle to attempt sex— after the restaurant cocktails, wine, and digestifs on the town. **Plenty of courage, Doctor.** She may have been the summa cum laude doctor of medicine and I just an average man, but it was pretty clear to me that she needed more than courage.

I went in and sat near her on the bed. She un-curled onto her back and I saw the faint sparks of light reflected in her eyes, and then they dis-appeared.

I kissed her lightly, lingering just a moment to gather in her breath, an undertow of alco-hol, and the smell of her body. I ran my fingers through her hair. Faintly and very far away, from under the hum of the sleeping city, I heard Jus-tine's voice. No words or syllables, even, just its rhythm and timbre. I felt noted by Justine, not blamed. Then she was silent. Don't go. Don't stay.

I walked around Paige Hulet's hushed lair

one more time, went into each of the rooms, just trying to register it all. Had the feeling that I wouldn't see it again.

Downtown San Diego was quiet at four in the morning. The moon was gone and the mist was April cool and the formerly busy sidewalks were all but empty. I backtracked my way through the alleys to Fifth, followed it to the parking lot. My truck was where I'd left it, one of only a few vehicles still waiting for their drivers. As I stepped onto the darkened lot I saw a figure on the far side of it, hands in his hoodie pockets, trotting away from me. Solid-looking guy, spring in his step. Then footsteps behind me. I turned to see a man in a ball cap hustling across the street ahead of a coming car. He glanced back at me and picked up his pace.

The newsstand across the street had opened. In the fog the gas lamps flickered and a man wrestled a bundle of newspapers from a truck. Coffee steam rose from a service window on the sidewalk. Another man stood near that window, sipping from a white cup, looking at me. Big fellow. A leather duster. Wide face, thick mustache, a shaven head that caught the flickering light. Calm, like he was daring me to connect him to the other two men who had slunk off into the darkness. A linen-supply truck parked along the curb in front of me. When I walked around it and looked over at the newsstand, Bald Mountain was still there, his back to me, choosing a paper off a rack.

THE ROOM OF WHITE FIRE

27

Shade goes well with a warm day, a cold beer, and a stack of almost-overdue bills. Reclining on a patio lounger under the palapa, I wrote out checks to SDG&E and for propane. Water and phone. I paused to look out at the pond and the rolling hills beyond. My mind drifted easily back to last night's strange twists and turns. Pretty, uptight Dr. Paige Hulet, dressed to kill, then undressed and drunk but still trying to heal me. Her past highlighted on the wall of her office.

Dick and Liz sat to my right, closer to the barbecue, and closely side by side, to better dispute and berate each other. Wesley Gunn lay on the chaise longue on the other side of me, fending off the bright sunshine with dark glasses. His black eyes were at their worst on this, the second day since his run-in with the Tijuana pimp. He had earbuds in and the player resting on his stomach and one foot keeping rhythm. Lindsey and Burt had gone into town.

I looked down at my stomach, shorts, legs, and feet. Pale from winter. Wondered what Paige Hulet had thought, then realized I'd never taken off my clothes. I thought about Bald Mountain and his two confederates waiting near my truck. Were they part of the Arcadia/DeMaris crew? If so, had they followed the transmitter on my car, or were they staking out Paige's penthouse? Possible. I had to figure that if Briggs Spencer was worried enough to follow his own PI, he was worried enough to surveil his own employee, too. Or, maybe some grudge from his unrequited passion.

"So, how'd the date go anyway, Roland?" asked Liz. "You didn't get home until sunrise. And you looked very **GQ** when you left here in that suit."

"Well, to be frank, Liz," said Dick, "Roland's three-button coat is pretty yesterday."

"She liked the suit," I said, opening the next bill—satellite for the TV I almost never watched.

"That's all you're going to say?" asked Liz.

"It was a good date."

"Just exactly how good?" demanded Dick.

"Let me run some figures on my calculator, and I'll get back to you."

I felt the afternoon warmth on my skin and finished paying bills. Picked up the **New York Times Book Review,** which always takes me a few days to get to. Full back-page ad for **Hard Truth,** Briggs Spencer's rugged face staring at me.

Felt drowsy. Drifted back to Paige Hulet. Dick and Liz argued men's fashions, then sex-or-not on the first date. Changed their own opinions and facts to create an argument. I wondered if Justine and I would have ended up like that. Didn't think so. Had so little time for it. Though I'll admit that, by now, at thirty-eight years of age, I've glimpsed myself in my parents and grandparents more than once. And every time I see me in them I vow to delay by any means possible their infirmities and combative dopiness and their frightening descents into habit. I also know by age thirty-eight that only time lasts forever.

One night after we'd made love, and not long after we'd met, Justine asked me to tell her seven things I believed in. Not believed, but believed **in.** They could be someone else's ideas, but I had to use my own words. No one else's. I tried and couldn't. She ran her fingers through my hair and laid her head on my chest. Rattled off seven things that she believed in. True and clear and simple. Her voice a whisper. Red hair on pale shoulder in the half-dark. "They'll keep you from going adrift. File your brief when you're ready. Take your time."

"Why seven?"

"Don't be extra thick. Work on them."

Never did.

When I woke up it was getting dark but someone had put a blanket on me and replaced my unfinished beer with a fresh bourbon over ice. I turned my head to see Dick wave at me as he sidled back to his casita.

I called Paige. She said she was driving down the mountain from Arcadia, on her way home. "When did you leave my place, Roland?"

"Just after four. How are you?"

"Profoundly hungover. God, I'm an ass."

I took a small first sip of the bourbon and closed my eyes. In a flash I was back in that twenty-seventh-floor condo, half carrying this beautiful woman to her bed.

"Where are you?" she asked.

"Home, by the pond."

"Not the pool, the pond. Do you live in the country?"

"Kinda. Rolling hills."

"Is the pond clean and pretty?"

"So far as ponds go."

"I'd like to see it someday. What did you do last night after I went MIA?"

"Took the self-guided tour."

A beat. "Find anything that interested you?"

"All of it. You were always smart and pretty. Didn't realize you were an athlete, too."

"I had no gift for tennis. Just worked hard."

"I wondered which pictures were of Daniel. Wondered why you didn't keep some of his things."

Paige spoke softly and deliberately. "I took the pictures down. Too painful. I threw out his clothing in a fit, a year after he died. Every last sock. A few days later I regretted it. That was four years ago, before I sold our Kensington place and moved downtown. As you probably know, the sudden throwing away of a loved one's things is a way of coping with loss. It is statistically common for widows and widowers."

I hated the word **widower**. Maybe I was statistically uncommon. Because Justine's closet was full. Not an item discarded.

I told her about the men loitering near my truck at four that morning, the big guy at the newsstand. "My first thought was they had tailed me there the night before. Then I wondered if they might have been set up around your place and I'd come up in the net."

Paige went silent. I could hear the ambient noise of her car on a road, the very distant swoosh of other vehicles around her. "I saw two men Friday morning outside my building. Not residents. Not merchants, not tourists. They looked and felt wrong."

I described Bald Mountain.

"Yes," she said. "My first thought was Briggs."

"Explain."

I listened to the road noise as she gathered her thoughts. "I told you most of it. Once I got to know him, Briggs struck me as morbidly detached and antisocial. He was very possessive, unreasonably jealous of me. And we were nothing. So would he send men to find out what I was doing, or who I was seeing? I think he's capable of that. I know he has contacts in the intelligence world. From the war. From the black sites he ran for the CIA. Don't people like that help each other to do ugly things and get around the law?"

"Sometimes."

"I'm worried for you," she said.

"They didn't touch me."

"It was intimidation. Now you'll be looking over your shoulder every waking minute."

"I do that anyway."

"Then you've chosen the right profession."

More road noise, a patch of static. Burt's car came up the drive, the sound of its engine overtaking Paige's. "Did Clay ever mention having evidence of crimes committed in Romania?"

"Not directly. But sometimes, in therapy, he would talk about revealing the truth of White Fire to the world. Implying that he might have some other kind of documentation of what went on there. Why?"

"I have an idea I want you to hear. Something I've been chewing on since Clay butted into my text messaging with Sequoia."

"Tell."

"Clay's a Nell Flanagan fan, right? He emailed her about telling his story on TV, on her show. He tried to persuade her with a 'graphic component.' But she didn't respond to him."

"I remember those emails. It upset him she didn't answer."

"Well, what if Nell changed her mind? And 'her story editor' is about to contact Clay about the story he wants to tell?"

Paige was quiet for a moment. "Sneaky."

"But Clay trusts you. So this story editor would need you on his side. For an introduction, I mean."

"Doesn't Nell Flanagan have real story editors?"

"Not credited. There's a producer, an assistant producer, and a director for each segment."

"What if he contacts KPBS and there is no you?"

"I'd tell him I'm not affiliated with KPBS. I'm one of three story editors working for Nell

Flanagan's management agency in New York. And **I** happen to be the one who read his pitch to Nell and smelled a knockout story. I'd advise Clay to keep his communication with Nell to a minimum until she green-lights this piece. I'd remind him that Nell is a genius, has roughly one million other stories to consider, and she abhors complication. And that it would make me look good at the agency to make this story happen."

"And if he calls KPBS anyway, and they put him through to her, and there's no you at her agency?"

"Then, well—just kidding, Clay. This is PI Roland Ford and I think you should come back to Arcadia with me."

"I won't allow it."

"It's up to the Hickmans. Not you."

Paige was quiet again at the other end. Her tone of voice went cool. "What's this alleged story editor's name and number?"

"First I'll need to set up one of my burners."

"Burners?"

"Throwaway phones."

"You keep them just lying around?"

"I have two in a desk drawer. Still in their boxes."

"And how many guns?"

"In the drawer? Just one."

"Funny. Will you have to get fake ID?"

"Already have some."

"You are a contradictory man. Risking wrong for right."

"Guilty as charged."

I heard the faint hollow sound of her car on the road. "I'm very sorry I drank so much and made a fool of myself last night."

"You weren't a fool."

"Of course I was. I'm not accustomed to what we did last night," she said. "Or didn't do. Does that make sense? Could we start over?"

I thought about that. "Might be easier to just continue."

A beat. "You're a good man," she said. "I hope I'm a good doctor. It's all I ever wanted to be. Is that enough to justify a life?"

"Being a good donut maker is enough to justify a life."

"I was trying to fix us last night. **Cure** us. So doctoral of me. So presumptuous." A pause. "Text me as soon as you've set up your phone and come up with a name. I want to hear from Nell Flanagan's 'story editor' as soon as possible. Let's get this show in the can, Roland. I want my partner safe and on the road to some kind of healing again."

"It won't be long."

28

8:02 AM
Dear Dr. Paige Hulet,
Thank you for responding to my
earlier email and for offering your
contact information. As I explained,
I am David Wills, story editor for
Nell Flanagan, multiple-Emmy-
winning KPBS show host. I would
like to communicate with Arcadia
resident Clay Hickman regarding
the story idea in his 4/3 email to
Nell. You now have my cell.

9:42 AM
Dear Mr. Wills,
Arcadia has procedures in place for
such requests. But I will happily tell Mr.
Hickman of your interest.

9:42 AM
Dear Dr. Hulet,
Appreciated and hopeful.

Clay's text message came through nine minutes later:

9:51 AM
Dear Mr. Wills,
Thank you for contacting my doctor.
I worked in a secret CIA prison in
Romania in 2008 and early 2009. I was a
United States Air Force airman assigned
to private contractors. My story is about
what happened to a high-value detainee
with important intel, or so we believed.
We subjected him to EITs (enhanced
interrogation techniques). Then other
events transpired. My story is true. I
have graphic evidence of key moments
in our procedures and of the tragedy
that unfolded. The graphic evidence is
video with sound. A San Diego–area
celebrity is involved. The detainee's
name was Aaban. This is a very
disturbing story and not for the faint
of heart. Nell Flanagan is my choice to
tell this story because she is smart and
kind to all people on her show.
Sincerely,
Clay Hickman

11:46 AM
Dear Mr. Hickman,
Stories involving national security
are tricky, at best. Federal
government/military are generally

unwilling to cooperate and can
make things difficult. Still, I will
communicate this information to
Nell Flanagan. She is extremely
busy and under constant
deadlines. I sense a good story
here. She will certainly have
questions, in particular, about
statements such as "then other
events transpired." And of course,
who is the San Diego "celebrity"
you mention? Can you write a brief
synopsis and make your graphic
evidence available to us now, as
a timely way of giving us a better
idea of the story possibilities?

11:47 AM
No. I can only do that when
I have a commitment from Nell.

      11:55 AM
      I understand, but hope that's
      not a deal breaker!

11:56 AM
Someone will want to air this story.

      12:20 PM
      I will present this in a positive
      light. We'll see what Nell says. Out
      of office today but will text late
      afternoon with Nell's response.

I sat at the picnic table, finishing lunch and reading the morning paper. The war on home-grown terror. Middle class sucks more wind. New Secretary of Defense. Padres picked to strike out in the NL West. Bad news makes bad thoughts. Such as John, Laura, and Michael Vazquez. What kind of god would let that happen to them? I thought: **Don't get me started.**

Because I felt my personal luck turning. The April day was clear and warm. Lindsey had not only made me lunch but paid her rent, only ten days late. On his morning hike, Wesley Gunn had shot video of a peregrine falcon taking a dove out of the sky. Clay Hickman had responded quickly to David Wills's interest in his story. Paige Hulet had couriered me another cash payment of forty-eight hundred U.S. dollars, reflecting Briggs Spencer's urgent doubling of my hourly wage. I regretted having taken his money to begin with, but until taking it I had never known the depth of his involvement in torture for profit. Let him get his damned white fire, whatever it might be. Morally, his cash would spend just fine.

So, I was ready for good things to happen. For Clay and Sequoia to return uninjured to civilization. For me to see Paige Hulet again. For science to find a cure for Wesley's eyes, for Lindsey to sober up enough to get joint custody of her son, for the Padres to win the wild card, for global warming to stop. My mother used to tell me I was too much of a softie to be a good Marine. Which I'm sure applied equally to being a good boxer, cop, or investigator. Maybe she was right. I sure didn't get much soft from her, however. She'd chew a lightbulb to get what she wanted.

And as often happens, while I was readying myself for luck, it struck on its own: a return call from Clay's sister, Daphne, in Laguna Beach. She told me that Clay had "showed up yesterday, out of nowhere," and she agreed to meet with me "very briefly" this afternoon. She didn't know where Clay was headed after Laguna, only "back south." She informed me she had dropped the name Hickman years ago and was just Daphne. Judging by her voice on the phone she wasn't looking forward to meeting me, but you take what you can get. I was never popular in high school and learned from the experience.

I showered and shaved and found good clothes. On my way out the front door I stopped at the hat rack in the foyer and put on my Carlos Santana shantung fedora, a gift from Justine, which she told me was lucky. **For you, Just.** I checked my look in the mirror, set the angle of the brim. White straw, cool band, pure luck.

Laguna was an hour's drive north for me. Daphne Hickman's Pacific Coast Highway home sat on a bluff overlooking the beach at St. Ann's Drive. I parked in the cobblestone drive under a canopy of king palms and stepped from my truck into the sweet Laguna air.

Daphne was tall and blond, a lithe, younger version of her mother. She welcomed me inside her home wearing blue jeans, a white halter, and no smile. The tops of her bare feet were tan and she wore a silver ankle bracelet on the left leg. I knew from her emails to Clay that she was thirty, two years older than he. The living room was white and sunny and hung with cheerful land- and seascapes of local scenes. All signed **Daphne.** I stood there, hat in hand, taking it all in. Sliding glass doors and a patio. An easel outside with a painting of Laguna Canyon taking shape. Beyond the painting, drooping telephone lines and palms and eucalyptus and blue ocean for as far as my eyes could see.

"I have water or iced tea," she said.

"Water, if it's not too much trouble. And I'd love to see some Hickman family pictures, if you have any."

She filled a coffee cup from the sink tap and even brought it over to me. She disappeared down a hallway and came back a moment later with a bulging plastic supermarket bag hanging from her index finger. We sat facing each other, Daphne giving me the ocean view. I thought of

Paige Hulet's twenty-seventh-story view of the same body of water. Body of Paige, too.

"How was your brother yesterday when you saw him?"

"Okay. Enthused but not agitated. Maybe stopping all the meds was a good idea. He looks fit and sane and tan. And he's got a darling young companion."

I nodded. "Did she seem okay?"

"Fine. Very stuck on Clay, by the way she looked at him."

"And all he said about his next destination was 'back south'?"

"Just like I said on the phone. The girl— Sequoia?—seemed pleased with that, since her trailer is there. Isn't that delightful, the great Hickman male hooked up with a girl who lives in a trailer?"

I said nothing, instead picturing a map of California in my head and drawing a bold black line from Arcadia, south to San Diego's Waterfront Bar and Grill, then north two hundred miles to Ojai in Ventura County, then north another three hundred miles to Redwood Valley in Mendocino. Since then, his known destinations had been farther and farther south—San Francisco and Laguna Beach. So, could "back south" from Laguna mean La Jolla and Briggs Spencer? Was Clay ready to bring him the white fire?

"Had you communicated with him since he escaped from the hospital? Before yesterday?"

"Of course. Text messages and email."

"What did he say?"

"He said he'd taken a leave of absence," said Daphne. "It was tongue in cheek. We both know that Arcadia is as much a prison as it is a hospital. He said he wasn't ever going back. He said he was on a mission, and when it was over he would come see me."

I asked if I could read the message chain with Clay but she said she'd deleted it, out of habit. She was not a message-chain saver. Her phone notified her of something. She checked it and set it back down on the table. "Gotta run soon."

When I asked her why she communicated with Clay but never visited him at Arcadia, she gave me a sharply disappointed look.

"I saw it once," she snapped. "Haven't you? It's a medication-fueled playground for dysfunctional members of the one percent. It angers me that Rex and Pat have put him there. What they really want is for Clay to go away. This big hero who Rex lived his fantasies through? Now he's just a shame to them. I'm fond of Clay. We used to laugh. We are both painters. In our different ways, we are both free. I don't consider myself a Hickman. Don't **want** to be. Maybe that's why Clay and I get along."

Daphne's disdain for her parents was fierce.

Unlikable people, I agreed, but I had read them differently. I saw decency and love behind their frustration with their son. Saw them trying to protect and even heal Clay in the best way they knew, not simply locking him away from the world. There had to be more beneath her anger than Clay being sent to Arcadia. I decided to come back to that. "Do you know anything about Clay's time in Romania during the war? From 2008 to '09?"

"I'm pretty sure he was in Iraq. A jet mechanic. I really do need to go."

"Have you met Briggs Spencer?"

"I don't even know who he is. I don't get out of Laguna very often, Mr. Ford. It's my cocoon. And that's just the way I like it."

"May I borrow these pictures?"

She stood. "You can have them. I've been wondering what to do with them for years."

"Please, think back to yesterday. Did he say anything about where he was going next?"

"Only south."

"Did he ever talk to you about Vazz and the fighting dolls?"

Daphne sighed impatiently and looked down at me with a surprised expression. "I have no idea what you're talking about."

"One more question?"

"All right."

"Why do you detest your parents?"

"I don't. I just will not be around them. The way he treats her. The way she lets him treat her. It's an alcohol-soaked knot they'll never untie. They don't want to untie it. Scenes and 'accidents' and dramatic apologies. Enough. I don't have to be around it. They can't stand my lifestyle anyway. And I'm not about to give up my right to love who I want to love."

I bagged the pictures and stood just as the front door flew open and a husky young woman barreled in. She wore a snap-brim panama and a smile until she saw me. Then she took off the hat, dropped the smile, and gave me an assessing stare. Her hair was razor-cut, and she wore baggy trousers, a white dress shirt with the sleeves rolled up, and a wide floral necktie.

"Just the PI," said Daphne, going to her.

The woman strode past her to me with her hand out. "Melinda Campbell. I own Daphne's gallery on PCH. How do you do?" Her shake was warm and firm.

"Very well, thank you."

"Have you found Clay?"

"I've practically got him surrounded."

She smiled. "He looked good yesterday. Of course, I don't know him as well as Daph. But he had peace in his eyes. Maybe that's attributable to not being in a mental institution any longer."

"Please call me if you see him again," I said, putting on my hat.

"Nice shantung."

"Thank you. It was a gift."

"I've got one kind of like it."

She gestured to the entryway rack, scarcely visible beneath all the hats.

"Any of them lucky?"

"All of them. But only on certain days. I've learned their powers over time."

29

headed south on PCH, pulled into a pay space, and sent a text message to Sequoia.

> **3:48 PM**
> **Where are u? I need to see Clay**

3:49 PM
I have changed mind. U must trick Deimos and bring HIM to ME

> **3:51 PM**
> **This is new, Clay!**

3:52 PM
Great ideas change. U work for him so he must trust u so easy to fool

> **3:53 PM**
> **If I can do that, where and when?**

3:55 PM
Must make arrangements, won't take long ☺

3:56 PM
What arrangements?

3:56 PM
Can Dr. Hulet come too?

3:57 PM
That is up to her but I
guess yes. Do u want me
to give her this number?

3:58 PM
No. Arcadia full of evil spies. No. No.

3:59 PM
Okay. Are you still in
California?

4:01 PM
In my own state of mind ☺

4:02 PM
S, are you okay?

4:03 PM
Not just okay. In love for first time

4:03 PM
BRING ME DEIMOS!!!

4:04 PM
Okay. When and where?

4:05 PM
I will say when time and place are right.

> **4:06 PM**
> What do you want from
> all this, Clay?

4:08 PM
To be a hero.

> **4:09 PM**
> Dr. Hulet says you
> are a hero.

4:11 PM
She has always believed in me. She
is the healer I always wanted to be.

> **4:13 PM**
> Heal yourself, Clay.

I waited twenty minutes. Listened to the news. A Laguna Beach meter maid came by and said she'd have to ticket me if I didn't move. I punched the truck down PCH toward Dana Point, phone on the seat beside me, ringtone and volume pegged on high.

But Clay had gone silent again.

I picked up Interstate 5 south, hit the eternal San Clemente jam-up, then a wreck at San

Onofre nuclear plant. Traffic inched. I pulled into the rest stop near Pendleton, walked out for a look at the Pacific, smoked a cigarette. I wondered how long Roland Ford would have to wait on Clay Hickman. Then weighed that against Clay's desire to tell his story to Nell Flanagan. **Okay,** I thought. **Time to pull this trigger.**

I got David Wills's burner from the glove box and sent Clay a message from Nell Flanagan's cagey story editor.

> **5:23 PM**
> Nell loves idea in spite of government hurdles and has asked me to audition you! This is first step in process. You and I will meet, you will tell me your story (off camera), and show me any relevant material you have (the video). Please be prepared and organized. If your story is as good as I think it will be, Nell will green-light the segment! FYI: In my two-plus years with Nell, she has NEVER ONCE declined to do a segment that I have personally endorsed. I can sell Nell! Thoughts?

> **5:24 PM**
> I am absolutely prepared and organized and ready to tell you my story.

5:26 pm
I am San Diego–based and can
meet at any reasonable time
and place. We need privacy and
quiet. Setting is not important as
we will not be final taping. I will
shoot some video on phone for
Nell. DO NOT bring any person,
as distractions ruin auditions.
DO bring your A-game.

Five minutes went by, then ten more. Big rigs
rolling in and out, people walking their dogs
to and from the "pet stop." I browsed through
the pictures Daphne had given me. The family
struck me as oddly ordinary, given the immense fortune that Rex Hickman had inherited
and multiplied. Clay looked just as I'd been told
and seen in other photos: sickly when young,
then growing healthier and stronger through the
years.

I checked my watch and I figured I'd lost him
again. I thought my impersonation of a story
editor was pretty good, but Clay was smart, borderline paranoid, and still coming off his meds.
But no. My notifications bell chimed and the
skies parted, a great light shone from above, and
I read:

5:48 PM
A-game ready, David. Room 14, Harbor
Palms Motel, Oceanside, 7 PM

I was right about my luck. After a week of near misses, of violence on the Hickman estate, and the murder of John Vazquez, I was now one hour and twelve minutes away from locating my missing person.

The only catch was, I didn't know what I was going to do after I'd let him tell his story.

I could shake his hand and walk out, call Briggs Spencer, find a safe place to watch the action, and never show my face. What might that action be? In my mind's eye I saw DeMaris knocking on the door of room 14, Donald Tice standing by with a tranquilizer gun, and the guys from the Range Rover and Charger ready for shock and awe. And of course Spencer himself, well back in the shadows, enjoying the capture.

I thought of DeMaris, ordering me to call him first when I located Clay. Why?

And Paige Hulet, Clay's lead psychiatrist, asking me to do likewise. Over and over. Again, why?

I thought of Rex and Patricia Hickman. If I'd heard them right that day, they were perhaps willing to take their son back into their home. Maybe.

Plots in motion. Human engines. Gears within gears.

I'm old-fashioned. I believe in doing the right thing, even if it's difficult and unprofitable.

But what was the right thing? What I came up with, sitting there in my truck in the I-5 rest area, lucky white straw fedora on the seat beside me, was Clay. What was best for Clay would be the right thing.

Returning him to his family seemed both practical and ageless. Brittle as they seemed, who could know better than blood what was best for him? Arcadia was out of the question. Paige Hulet seemed genuinely devoted to making Clay better, but what could she do? Hide him in her spare room? Should I just let Sequoia stash him in her Airstream?

Personally, I had little say in the matter. I'd never known Clay, or laid eyes on him, or even heard of him until seven days ago. And yet Clay Hickman had circled us all around himself—as if he were some beautiful and endangered creature and we were collectors, each wanting to put him into a different zoo.

In the end, this was Clay's show.

Switching phones, I called Rex Hickman.

"Ford. What do you have for me?"

"Do you want your son back?"

"Of course we do," said Hickman.

"I'll tell you what he decides."

"I expect good news."

"You've had twenty-eight years to earn his trust. I can't change his mind about you now."

I heard an amplified scuffle, then Patricia's voice: "Please bring him home."

"You'll hear from me either way."

I punched off, checked the time. One hour, three minutes. I clicked off Alec DeMaris's transmitter and set it back in the console.

The Harbor Palms Motel was on the beach side of the Coast Highway, south of the pier. It was 6:55 p.m. and the sun hung low over the horizon, spreading an orange blanket on the town. I drove past cafés, bars, convenience stores, surf shops, two exotic pet shops, a gun store, a bait-and-tackle store. There were plenty of military-specific retailers set up for the Camp Pendleton Marines—barbers, dry cleaners, used car lots, car rentals, new and used furniture—MILITARY WELCOME! Both U-Haul and Penske because the Marines are always on the move.

I passed the motel and found a parking place three blocks down. Pocketed the burner and locked my other phone in the truck-bed toolbox with my gun. Story editors rarely go to meetings armed.

I swung on my coat and headed down the sidewalk at a leisurely pace. Strolled past the motel, just another citizen doing who knew what. No sign of Sequoia Blain's beat-up silver pickup truck. I stopped outside a tae kwon do studio, admired my hat in the window. Watched the children practice their forms. Through the glass I heard the muffled snapping of the gis. I took a hard look up and down PCH. No silver pickup. A deep breath, the kind of breath you take getting off the stool for round one. If Clay had decided to include Sequoia in his audition, and she recognized me and failed to hide it, I would have to talk fast and hope for the best. I reminded myself that Clay Hickman had mental health issues, a mission, and a gun.

30

I stood straight and knocked firmly. The door opened a few inches, and the dead-bolt chain clunked straight. A vertically cropped face—one blue eye, one hazel—with weak orange lamplight in the background.

"David Wills," I said.

"Clay Hickman. I'll open the door."

The chain rattled away and I stepped in as Clay moved back. Curtains were drawn and the room was dim except the lamplight. I registered his face and the autoloader in the waistband of his jeans. A gun is an ugly thing unless it's yours. "You don't need the gun."

"I'll decide."

I held my coat wide open. "Nell hates guns."

"You're not Nell."

He stepped forward and tapped up and down my body with his free hand. Odd light in his eyes. Weird, the sudden closeness to a stranger who has consumed your life for an entire week. Someone you know much better than he knows you. In this small space I felt a jagged energy coming off Clay Hickman.

All in a glance: The motel room was cheap and simple and poorly lit. No Sequoia unless she was under the bed or in the bathroom. Two open suitcases on stands. Bathroom door open. A laptop computer open on a small desk. Desk lamp on. In the down-cone of lamplight, like on a stage, two cloth dolls posed in combat, swords raised. And next to them, two more swordfighter dolls locked in their own separate contest. Behind the desk was a mirror in which I could see the swordfighters and Clay looming above them. He looked no older than in the Arcadia head shots. Twenty-eight years, I thought. Still a young man, and his white forelock made him look boyish. He wore a tight gray T-shirt, the low-slung jeans, and a pair of desert camo combat boots.

"All I have is coffee and soda."

"All I want is a good story."

"I watched some Nell shows to see your name. You're not in the credits."

"I work for Nell, not the show."

This seemed to satisfy him. "How long?"

"Two years plus."

Clay stood lightly—arms relaxed, feet comfortably spread—a light heavyweight ready to hit and move. "Let me see your ID."

From my wallet I produced my David Wills

driver's license, a very good forgery made by a pro down in Otay Mesa. Wills was a well-rounded individual: criminal defense lawyer, reporter, financial adviser, MLB scout, owner of a chain of Tex-Mex restaurants, trucker, public relations flack, and now story editor.

Clay looked briefly at the CDL and handed it back to me. His hand was clean and his thumbnail trimmed back short. He ran his free hand over me again, said he was sorry. "Take off the hat."

I did, showed him the empty crown, brushed my hand through my hair.

"Okay. What do you know about me?"

"That you were in Romania during the war. That you are in the care of Dr. Paige Hulet of Arcadia hospital. That you are not supposed to leave that hospital and they are looking for you. That you have suffered psychotic breaks in the past but have been responding well to treatment."

He eyed me skeptically. "All true but the last. The drugs at Arcadia pushed me further and further underwater. Deep, dark, black fucking water. Full of voices and faces. Terrible visions, day after day. Real? Not real? It got worse and worse. Every med they tried. Even Dr. Hulet couldn't get them right. Then a force came into me. It told me to stop poisoning myself. Four weeks ago I started puking up the pills, back in my room. But there's a half-hour curfew after meds break to keep us from doing that. So most of it soaks in. Then, starting last week, no more meds at all." Clay spread his hands to show me they were empty.

"How are you doing, Clay?"

"How do I look?"

"Good."

"Sometimes I feel almost clear. Like I'm right on the edge of absolute clarity. But then it goes away without any warning. And I'm under the black water again with the voices and faces I've always seen and heard."

" 'Always'?"

"Since the war."

Clay turned and looked at himself in the mirror, then back at me. "You sit here at the desk. I'm going to sit on the bed against the pillows. I have a friend but she won't be back until much later. Do not touch the computer unless I say you can. I want to tell you a few things before I show you what I have."

I sat, took a small notepad and pen from my coat pocket. "Interesting dolls."

"Romanian. Dolls are a folk art there."

"Did you bring them home?"

"We hid flash drives in them," he said. "Sewed them into the undersides. The videos I'm about to show you."

" 'We'?"

"Me and Vazz. He's dead. They killed him."

"Who killed him?"

"Don't lead me ahead," said Clay. "Let me go at my own speed."

"Take all the time you want."

He looked down at me, then lay on the bed, his back against pillows and a headboard that creaked.

I asked him if I could record. "Nell wants authenticity," I added.

"I've got all the authentic she can handle."

"There. You're on, Clay Hickman." I tapped my recorder app and set the phone on the table by the swordfighters.

"I was born too early and wasn't healthy," said Clay. "Bad heart. So, operations. I spent my whole life working hard to get strong like other people. Like my sisters, then teammates, and then strong like Dad. In baseball I was all-league, all-conference, all-CIF as a senior. Third base. Then in the Air Force I was near the top in everything. I enlisted in 2006. Had to get Dad and Mom's permission because I was only seventeen. I didn't want special Hickman favors because of my family. I did really well in basic, was thinking pilot. But I really shined at the SERE training. That's survival, evasion, resistance, and escape. So they put me to work as an assistant trainer. Youngest one ever. I'm good at using the mind to overcome adversity. Because I'd spent

my whole lifetime doing it. There are similari-
ties between resisting pain and building a sound
body."

"I've heard the SERE is intense."

"Somewhat. I did mostly the simulations.
We'd make our students as frightened and miserable as we could. Within reason. You do have
to understand that none of it is like real detainee
interrogation or abuse. Did you serve?"

"Marine Expeditionary Force, Fallujah one."

"That was 2004," said Clay. "The Blackwater
contractors."

It told him I did a month of door-to-doors
looking for the guys who did it.

"I was still two years from enlisting," he said.
"Couldn't wait to join the Air Force. Nine-eleven
changed the way I saw myself, and the world. I
realized my country needed me."

"I thought that, too," I said. "I was just out of
college when they hit the Trade Center."

Clay seemed to consider this. He adjusted
himself against the pillows, and the headboard
squeaked. He worked the semiautomatic out of
his waistband and set it on the mattress beside
him. He looked into the bathroom for a moment,
then trained his attention on the curtained front
window. I noted that the curtain was open just
enough to let him see outside from where he sat.

It looked like two people had slept in the bed.
I glanced at the open suitcase on the far side of

it, up against the wall, saw the blow-dryer lying on top. A faint feminine smell hung in the small room. Like Clay, I could see the bathroom from where I sat. He had duct-taped a pink handheld mirror to the wall near the bathroom window. And wedged an empty toilet paper roll behind the mirror so he could see the window from the bed. An early-warning system. The window screen had been removed and set against the wall, behind the toilet.

"How is Nell?" he asked.

"Nell equals busy."

"But on TV she always seems so calm."

"She is, by the time she's on camera. A lot of actors and performers are that way," I said.

"Do you think she'll go for this?"

I opened my hands: **Hopefully.**

He looked to the window again, then brought his knees up and wrapped his arms around them. "Okay. One day at Fairchild—that's the Air Force base where the SERE school is—a big shot came to visit. Dr. Briggs Spencer. He was kind of a legend there. They talked about him and his partner—Dr. Timothy Tritt. They had been instructors there for years. Really got into it. Then after 9/11 they went private and helped start up the interrogation program at Guantánamo. Then Abu Ghraib. Then the black sites the CIA was allegedly in charge of. They were making a shitload of money. The rumor was,

Spencer and Tritt came through Fairchild every four months, looking for top recruits. Talented guys to put to work in the prisons."

"I remember reading about them."

"So, right in the middle of my 'Psychological Defense Against Mechanical Pain' class, the actual Dr. Briggs Spencer walks in and sits down in the back." Clay stared at me, nodding and smiling.

"Were you nervous?"

Suddenly he looked to the bathroom, his gaze raised high—window- and mirror-level. Then back to me. "No. I went on with my demonstration. One of the SERE methods was to use basic autogenics to create a useful dialogue between your conscious mind and your body to reduce the effects of stress. This was pure Spencer-Tritt. We had their training manuals. There was also a component of self-hypnosis. So, under stress, they taught, you focus your mind on a specific belief or idea or person that you are willing to undergo the torture **for.** For me personally, it had almost always been for my mom and dad and sisters. But you could pick a girlfriend or a buddy, or even a pet, and focus on that. Under interrogation, then, you would imagine that thing and you would create a conversation. You could even speak the words out loud if you wanted, which would generally confuse an interrogator, which we considered useful resistance. But I had added something of my own to that technique. Something I knew worked. If you, during pain, could combine that image and aural construct with three-part breathing—two short inhales through the nose followed by a fast loud exhale through the mouth—you were creating emotional resistance **and** a physical response. This satisfies the powerful fight-or-flight instinct. It gives you something to **do.** It's not unlike Lamaze for childbirth."

I was impressed by young Clay Hickman at SERE. "Nell is going to eat this up."

He smiled. "So did Dr. Spencer."

31

He pretty much hired me on the spot," said Clay. "I was still Air Force, but he got me reassigned to the Spencer-Tritt team. He got the brass to do whatever he wanted. They just shuffled some papers, sent me to Ali AFB for one week to learn my cover as a Spooky mechanic, then cut me loose to go to Romania. It's called sheep dipping. On that flight from Iraq to Romania, I thought I was joining the most elite team of specialists in the world. The absolute cutting edge—saving lives by asking questions."

"That must have been something, for a rich kid heading for Stanford a year before." I caught my misstep, hoped Clay did not.

"I never told you about Stanford."

"It was in Dr. Paige Hulet's background on you."

Clay looked at me for a long beat. I wondered how it must feel to have a receding tide of psychotropic drugs still eddying inside you. How it must feel to not quite trust the only mind you have.

"When we landed outside Bucharest it was early morning. First light. We traveled into the city in unmarked Romanian government vehicles. The black site was in the city limits, an old estate, set back from a road not far from the river. Going through Bucharest I saw the sun's rays on the buildings, and none of the trees had leaves. It was cold and bleak. And I felt this strange mixture of adventure and dread. I was excited and afraid."

"Describe the site."

"Seven acres, an old mansion and outbuildings. It had belonged to a nobleman, then became a hotel, then a communist torture chamber. Then it was abandoned. By the time the CIA got it for us, it was run-down. There were busy railroad tracks nearby, which covered some of the sounds. Thick walls, too. We drove through an electric gate and parked in the old livery. I watched the gate roll closed and learned my first lesson about working in a prison: You're a prisoner, too, man."

"What month was it?"

"March. It was always March at White Fire."

Clay picked up the pistol, casually moved the slide to check the chamber. The steel and springs, so well-machined, sounded loud and precise in the cramped room. He placed his index finger alongside the barrel as if to calm it, then set the weapon back on the bed beside him. He looked

out the front window, then back to the bathroom.

"Are you afraid right now?" I asked.

"Prepared."

"For what?"

"Mr. Wills—they are after me."

"Who?"

He shook his head slowly. "Please don't turn
out to be a fool."

I looked at the swordfighting dolls on the
desk not far from me, performing in the down-
glow of the lamp. Then across the room to Clay.
His shadowed face was unclear in the poor light,
but his eyes were bright flecks. In that moment
he looked no more than nineteen or twenty
years old. Sequoia's age. He seemed so partial,
so incomplete. I wondered how three years of
war and torture, followed by years of psychosis and commitment to Arcadia—an **exclusive
wellness community for treatment of mental
and emotional disorders**—where young Clay
Hickman was prescribed powerful drugs not to
help but to subdue him, could have left him so
strangely . . . What was the word . . . Blame-
less? Untouched?

For the next few minutes he described what
Timothy Tritt had talked about: the pressure
to prevent the next 9/11, to get bin Laden, the
American lives being risked and lost on bloody
foreign soil. He talked about the cold and filth

of White Fire, the incessant music and light, the compliance blows, sleep deprivation, waterboarding, walling, chainings. All of the monstering. And how the words **white fire** came to mean an irresistible torture, a kind of holy grail for the interrogators, a technique that, supposedly, no detainee could defeat.

"This is important background," Clay said. "Things Nell will need to know if she is to tell the story of Aaban properly."

Clay painted Aaban much as Tritt had—a large, proud, physically intimidating terrorist with personal ties to bin Laden and his organization. As in Tritt's telling, Aaban refused to break while they subjected him to the entire CIA–Spencer–Tritt "menu."

I tried my best to react as if hearing these things for the first time. I checked my phone to make sure it was recording, then looked again at the swordfighters. I noted that an opening on one fighter's baggy pants had been sloppily sutured with a rubber band, where one of the video sticks had been hidden all these years.

"Aaban is a truly fascinating character," I said.

Clay cleared his throat softly. "He might not even be in Dr. Spencer's book. Dr. Spencer will tell a story that makes a hero out of himself. But I know the true Aaban story."

I was tempted to confirm Aaban's absence from **Hard Truth**, based on the book's index.

"I want the world to see what . . . **we** did to Aaban," Clay continued. "This story is about me, too. Dr. Spencer was my supervisor at White Fire. This is about **us**."

He turned his head and stared dreamily at the mirror. I sensed him drifting away.

"Clay," I said. "It's important that we get to the video you mentioned. It will have to be clear and compelling for Nell and KPBS to even consider it."

"Don't rush me. I have the video. We recorded almost everything we did, to document our methods and successes and failures. We wanted a scientific record that could be built on in future wars. But some of it I recorded without Dr. Spencer knowing. Some of it Vazz recorded. Early in 2009, we were ordered to turn over any recorded material to the agency. Just before White Fire was closed. Vazz and I thought our secret videos would be destroyed, so we made copies, added some of the other recorded stuff, brought them home inside the fighting dolls. Something told me, even way back then in Romania, when I was nineteen years old and trying to gather actionable intelligence and save American lives, that everything we did was going to be denied. I already felt like I was beginning to lose it, Mr. Wills. Felt my mind slipping away, right into the cracks of those cold walls. I wanted a record of who I was and what we did. I didn't want to remember myself as a weak man living in a nightmare. There is roughly one hour of video I can show you."

"Roll it, Clay."

He hopped off the bed, pushed the gun back into the waistband of his jeans, went into the bathroom and realigned the mirror on the wall. "Can you see the alley from where you are?"

"Who are you expecting?"

"Dr. Spencer and his old agency employers. You can't conceive of my importance to them."

"Do they know what you have?"

"They suspect. That is their training and nature. I told Dr. Spencer I have 'white fire' for him. I didn't tell him exactly what it was. I want him to see it for the first time on Nell's show. With me. You don't see a problem with getting Dr. Spencer on the show, do you?"

I had to think fast on that one. "No problem at all. We just tell him it's to promote **Hard Truth**."

"Mr. Wills, it is nonnegotiable that Dr. Spencer be on the show with me. He must be."

"I'll make your wishes clear to Nell."

"He'll be surprised when he sees what I'm about to show you," said Clay. "But he will have the chance to explain himself."

Clay went to the front door, checked the flimsy

chain lock, and opened the curtain maybe one more inch. Then he sat down and tapped some keys on the laptop.

"Aaban came to White Fire in June of 2008. Now, the first thing you'll see is three guys shackled together in orange jumpsuits, being marched from a Romanian Foreign Intelligence Service SUV toward the detainee entrance to White Fire. ISIS now dresses their kills in orange as a reminder of how we dressed **them**. The detainee entrance was within a side courtyard, just in case neighbors or delivery people got curious about who we were and what we were doing. Aaban is the middle guy. The strong-looking one. Scared me when I first got up close to him."

32

See, right there," said Clay. He touched his finger to the screen but he didn't have to. Aaban was half a head taller than the two other prisoners, and he was just as tall and thick as the beefy young Americans escorting them from the vehicle. The prisoners were triple-shackled to each other—ankles, waists, wrists. Aaban glared at the video shooter as he walked past. He was hawk-faced, with a full beard and thick gray-black hair.

"Aaban means 'Angel of Iron' in Dari," said Clay. "When he walks by the camera he says, 'I will eat your eyes,' but you can't hear his voice very well. We always filmed the new detainees arriving so we'd have a chronological record of their progress. Before and after. Some of them you wouldn't even recognize after six months. Their whole posture changes. That's from stress positions and compliance blows. We put Aaban alone in the smokehouse cellar. It was the closest thing we had to a dungeon. Next, you'll see him getting walled the very next day, then chained to the ceiling so he has to stand up on the balls of his feet. That makes your arches cramp. Painful."

The smokehouse cellar was made of very dark stones that seemed to be fitted without mortar. They looked wet. The ceiling was low and there was only one small window—a horizontal, iron-grated slot just above ground level. One industrial, mesh-covered lamp hung down. A dungeon indeed. The cameraman recorded the thin mattress on the stone floor, a plastic bucket, then Clay, standing in the poor light, dressed in fatigues and a civilian windbreaker. With him was a dark, shaggy young man wearing a T-shirt and jeans. "Moe," said Clay. "One of our 'terps. You'll see other guys come and go."

"Who's shooting the video?"

"Don Tice. Who now works for Dr. Spencer at Arcadia."

"Interesting."

"He's a dispensing nurse. Nice guy."

An odd-looking plastic structure stood near the middle of the room. Beside it stood Aaban, stripped down to what looked like a dirty nightshirt. Hands cuffed behind him, of course. A crude wooden collar had been clamped around his neck. The collar had rope handles at opposite sides, and the interrogator—Clay Hickman— pulled Aaban forward across the room by the collar with both hands, then stopped and pushed hard, backward, sending him into the plastic wall. Aaban hit with a loud crack. The wall shuddered and Aaban crumpled to the floor. A moment later he was up, crouched and turning in a slow circle to find and face his tormentors.

"The walling wasn't to hurt them, it was to make them think they were hurt," said Clay. "The sound it made. The sound made them believe they were being seriously injured. Over and over again. And when they realized they were not, they began to doubt their own senses. To realize we could manipulate their senses. With enough repeated loss of self-control, they would reach the point of distortion and become totally helpless. This was based on Dr. Martin Seligman's experiments with caged dogs and electric shocks. You can break the will to resist. They learn to be helpless. That was when they were most willing to talk. But not Aaban. He never learned to be helpless."

I watched as Clay's co-interrogator—John Vazquez—snuck up on Aaban from behind, took the collar handles, and wrenched him around in a semicircle. Moe, the interpreter, hopped out of the way. Vazz hurled Aaban into the clattering wall again. And again the man struggled up and readied himself for the next attack.

"Next is Aaban chained to the ceiling in a stress position. This was one of our best EITs and it left no marks or scars. Visually, there's not much to it. I mean, you couldn't sit here and watch Aaban stand like that for the real-time period that we made him stand. Twenty-six hours was the longest. Of course, he couldn't sleep, either, and we didn't feed or water him much. Sometimes we'd release him to use his bucket. Other times not. Muslims hate being naked. They hate shitting and pissing into diapers, or worse, just on themselves. So those were enhanced techniques, too."

I sat there for a long while, watching Aaban. He was standing near the middle of the room, his arms raised over his head, wrists bound by a shackle that was roped to a fixture in the ceiling. His calves strained and his bare feet flexed, and sweat poured down his face and torso and into his diaper. He was big and well-muscled and he looked like a tortured Argonaut in an old movie. Standing in the background and watching were four men dressed as cowboys—chaps, yoked shirts, bandanas, cowboy boots, and 9mm semi-automatic pistols strapped to their thighs. Two wore black cowboy hats. Bodart's Wranglers, I remembered. And I recognized Bald Mountain from our early-morning encounter in downtown San Diego. In the video he wore what looked like the same leather duster. Same cowcatcher mustache. "Who's the bald cowboy?" I asked.

"Joe Bodart. The only CIA guy to lead an interrogation team."

"Why did you and Spencer allow that?"

"Crazy monster would do anything. Think Nell will like this?"

"I don't know."

"It's nothing compared to what comes later."

"Nell will wonder if the public should see this."

"The CIA destroyed all the White Fire torture video—twice. First was back in 2005, before my time. Dr. Spencer told me about it. The agency thought it would be devastating if the public saw the torture. Then later, just before White Fire was closed, our CIA handlers pulled the same thing on us. Confiscated all our phones and hard drives, all our flash drives and memory cards and notebooks—anything that could hold evidence. Searched our belongings, right down to wallets and dopp kits. But they missed the dolls. A lot of the guys had souvenirs. Vazz and I cut the stitching real carefully, underneath the dolls' garments. We worked in the flash drives good and deep, and restitched with the same thread. It took a while. But we were lucky. So this video is probably the last proof there is."

An uneasy feeling closed over me, like a stage curtain coming down. I'd been assuming that the men who tailed me to the Waterfront Bar and Grill, and later to Fallbrook Airpark, and who were waiting for me in downtown San Diego the night I was with Paige Hulet, were deployed by Spencer. But Spencer had only been one of several players at the black sites, and some of those players answered to higher powers than he did. And therefore had more to lose. So as I sat there with Clay, I understood the much colder fact that Joe Bodart was on my tail, protecting company interests, trying to find and destroy another "last" piece of evidence of what their agency had done at a black site in Romania.

"Clay? What motivates you? Why do you want Nell to tell your story and show these things?"

He was silent for a long moment while he looked at me. It was unnerving being stared at from that close, and all I could think to do was stare back. I watched his eyes—hazel on the left and blue on the right—as they roamed my face. It reminded me of the way Spencer had studied me that first day, speeding through the sky in his little copper helo. "It is not my story. It is mine and Dr. Spencer's. And Vazz's and Don's. All of us. You will understand when you see. So far, this is only context. Please be patient."

"What was Dr. Spencer's reaction when you told him you had 'white fire' for him?"

"He pretended not to understand what I was talking about," said Clay. "After I escaped from Arcadia, he hired a private investigator to find me. He admitted this to me on a pay phone conversation. I'm sure he told the detective that I may harm myself or others. And that I need the medications, and the security of Arcadia. But what Dr. Spencer really wants is for no one to know our story."

On-screen, Aaban was no longer dangling painfully from the ceiling. Instead he was strapped into a squat wooden chair, his feet locked into clumsy-looking steel boots fastened to the floor, his arms crossed in straitjacket sleeves lashed behind his back. He was wearing an orange jumpsuit again. His hair had been shorn short and his beard clumsily cut back.

"One night Aaban woke up screaming. I ran in and found him clutching the bars, breathing hard. No explanation from him, so the next day I cued up the surveillance video. They slept in the light, right? So I could see what had rattled him while he slept. It was just a cockroach inspecting his face. But it woke him and he went **off.** We realized how badly Aaban was afraid of bugs. Funny—strong guy like that, killed men face-to-face, probably cut their throats with a knife, but a bug totally freaked him. We used to have an approved menu technique we called Plague of Insects. We weren't supposed to use it anymore, but that didn't mean we'd forgotten how. That day we put Aaban back in the chair."

Across from Aaban sat Briggs Spencer, in a simple folding chair. Spencer held up a black cloth bag to the man standing next to him,

Timothy Tritt. I hardly recognized Tritt, looking so unlike the emaciated, long-haired man
living in the barn in Owens Valley. This Tritt
was trimly built and well-groomed. Still, I saw
the hardness in his eyes, the almost reptilian
smallness of pupil. The lack of emotion. He
held out a clear-glass gallon jar for Aaban to
see. The camera jostled, then came in closer to
capture the jarful of busy insects and Aaban's
face behind the glass. Some crawled, some beat
their wings, some raised their pincers, others slid
along the glass, legs working as Tritt tilted the
bottle. Aaban's eyes were wide and I could tell
he was trying to hold himself together. I recognized spiders and grasshoppers and cockroaches
but not much else. Some looked like scorpions
without stingers. Some were beetles. Some were
big, especially the roaches. Tritt unscrewed the
lid and dumped the creatures into Spencer's up-
lifted black bag, then smacked the bottom of the
jar to make sure they all made it in.

"Where is bin Laden?" asked Spencer. The
camera pulled back. Spencer held the bag closed
at the top with one hand, lightly patting the
body of it with the other, as if trying to disperse
the bugs.

"Allahu Akbar."

"Allah cannot save you from this," said
Spencer. His voice was firm but gentle, almost

condescending. **"I can. I can save you, Aaban. Where is bin Laden?"**

Aaban spit at Spencer. I couldn't tell if he hit him or not. Spencer leaned back, then stood up straight and looked down at Aaban. Spencer, back then, still looked like the slugging all-American first baseman captured in his college baseball pictures—wholesome and forthright. His expression showed pity. His eyes teared up. He held his chin high and I could see the moral quiver in it. I heard Tritt's words: **We were selling our souls; but we didn't know it yet.**

Spencer stepped forward, opened the bag, and quickly pulled it over Aaban's head.

Tritt circled a roll of duct tape around Aaban's neck, the tape rasping off to make a tight seal.

Aaban violently threw his head from side to side, wrenched his arms in their sleeves, strained to free his feet, which were locked by the ankles in the steel boots. Blood trickled down the steel. His screams were powerful and pitiable. The only word I recognized was "Allah."

I sat in the little motel room and heard the cars hissing by on Coast Highway while Spencer and Tritt and Clay and John Vazquez applied their "enhanced techniques." Back then, I'd known that things like this were going on in secret places, far from America. I'd rolled it into the price of freedom. We all did. We had our best people on the case, didn't we? They were calling the shots. But until now I'd never **seen** what we were doing. Up close. I'd never faced it. I felt a portion of Aaban's agony, a fraction of it—what I could handle. The rest ran off me. I also felt, very clearly, the pain of doing what Spencer and Tritt and Clay and Vazz were doing. I just now began to understand what it had cost them. "Christ," I said.

"Nell doesn't have to show this," said Clay. He sounded almost forlorn. "It's just background."

"He tells you nothing?"

"He told us about his mujahideen days in the summer of 1985—listed his friends and villages and the ways they died. He named the stars and planets he could see during each season of the year from the poppy fields in the Sangin valley. He described his wives."

Spencer stood with a finger pressed thoughtfully to his lips, contemplating Aaban as he thrashed. Tritt's primordial eyes seemed more drawn than repelled. Beside me, Clay regarded the monitor with what appeared to be blank resignation.

"I'll fast-forward."

Clay tapped the keyboard and the scene cut to Tritt, unwinding the duct tape and yanking the black sack from Aaban's head. Aaban looked up at Spencer with wild eyes and blew a cockroach into his face.

"We worked on Aaban like this for six months," Clay said. "He gave no actionable intelligence. The opposite. He taunted and lied and offered minor truths we already knew. Just before Christmas, Dr. Spencer announced that he'd dreamed of a new EIT. It wasn't new, really, just an escalation of things we'd tried before. We'd threaten their families. Threaten to kill their mothers and children and wives. Bullshit, of course, and most of them knew it. But Spencer wanted to take it further. He was naming it 'white fire,' after the idea that he'd found the one irresistible, infallible, undefeatable torture."

Of course, I knew. "Which was?"

"Aaban's son. It took six months, but Dr. Spencer brought him to Romania. Here he is, arriving at White Fire."

33

A rail-thin boy stepped down from the high backseat of the vehicle. He wore baggy Western trousers and a button-down collar shirt and athletic shoes much too big for him. He clutched a sun-faded backpack against his chest with both hands. His hair was short and lank, and even in the video taken from yards away you could see the fear in his eyes. Clay, dressed in jeans and a heavy jacket, stood waiting for him to climb out, and when he did, offered his hand. The boy shook it. Moe, the same interpreter who had been in on the walling, fell into step on the other side of the boy and the three continued across the courtyard.

"Roshaan," said Clay. "It means 'brightly lit' or 'bright-lighted.' He was eleven years old, Aaban's youngest child and only son. Which made him the most beloved person in Aaban's life. You'll see."

Next came video of Clay leading Roshaan to his father's dungeon in the smokehouse cellar. The video shooter trailed along behind, camera jumping. In a sere, snow-dusted barnyard, Clay and Roshaan descended stone steps and stopped at a heavy-looking wooden door with a window of steel mesh at eye level to an adult. Roshaan looked up at the window, then back at the camera, with an expression of hope that I'll never forget. Clay ordered Aaban away from the door, then swung it open and let the boy inside. The cameraman followed. Clay stood to the side and Roshaan ran to his father, who swept him off his feet and held him to his body. They whispered and spoke over each other, and I could see Roshaan working his head into the crook of his father's neck, the boy's black hair mixing with Aaban's growing beard. They were both crying.

"Day one of Dr. Spencer's white fire," said Clay. "Watch."

I didn't want to watch. I couldn't imagine what it would be like to be tortured in front of your young son. Or imagine what damage it would do to the boy.

The next video was again shot in the smoke-house cellar, and again the lighting was poor and the walls were slick and black. A water-board had been set up on the floor in the middle of the room. At one time it had apparently served as a door. Now there were ropes running through the knob hole midway down one side, and through a similar hole that had been cut out opposite. Through the holes sprouted leather straps, their buckles gawking open, ready for the arms of whichever miserable person was to be strapped in next. The original door hinges had been removed and I could see the screw holes and outlines of the hinge plates. At the opposite end of the plank were two more holes, and sets of ankle restraints, close together. The entire board rested on stone blocks at a mild slant—so the victim's feet would be higher than the head. Five white buckets stood in a row near the head of the board.

Aaban sat facing the camera, with his back to the contraption, wearing nothing but what looked like the same filthy nightshirt I'd seen earlier. His wrists were cuffed behind the chairback. Small clouds of condensation formed outside his nose. His head was up and his expression was proud. He looked as if he were about to offer his son a lesson in right behavior. Roshaan sat across from him with a worried expression on his face. No restraints. He wore a heavy black sweater, a watch cap, and mittens.

Spencer came into the frame, wrapped in a peacoat and a scarf. Moe followed behind him with a doomed expression on his face. John Vazquez and Clay were last.

"Don Tice again, shooting the video," said Clay.

Spencer stood over Aaban and his son and when he spoke his breath made faint cartoon bubbles that showed up clearly against the black rock walls. Spencer spoke English and Aaban spoke Dari and Moe the 'terp turned the words back and forth as nimbly as a fry cook flipping eggs.

"Where is bin Laden?"

"Paris."

"Where is Khairiah?"

"I think London."

"Khairiah," said Clay. "Bin Laden's first wife."

"Where is Amal?"

"New York. I'm certain of it."

"Amal," said Clay. "Bin Laden's last wife. His favorite. Aaban is trying to have fun with us."

Even with the watch cap pulled down for warmth, Roshaan's strange look of wonder and fear was easy to see. His mouth hung slightly open as he watched his father try to outlast his tormentors. His breath condensed into a small vague cloud, then evaporated.

"Aaban, I will have to drown you if you will not help me."

"Allahu Akbar."

"Allah's about to drown you in cold water, my friend."

With this, Roshaan looked disbelievingly at Spencer, then to his father, then to the camera.

The video jumped ahead: Aaban strapped to the waterboard, Spencer and Clay standing near the buckets, Roshaan out-of-focus in the background, still seated. Clay held Aaban's head in a two-armed lock. Spencer drew a dripping bath towel from one of the buckets and placed it over the man's face. Aaban exhaled, then inhaled sharply. He coughed.

"Aaban, I have not started with the drowning yet. Your son does not need to see you suffer. Tell me something easy, Aaban. Tell me what country is bin Laden in?"

"Afghanistan."

"What province?"

"Helmand."

"I'm so disappointed. Let us change directions. When and where is the next attack planned on the United States?"

"In the six months we'd had Aaban," said Clay. "This was the one hundred and eighty-seventh time we'd boarded him. Every time, he said bin Laden was in Helmand. But this was the first time with his son watching, and Dr. Spencer was hoping for something better."

On-screen Spencer sighed. Then he took up the bucket and splashed some water around Aaban's face, a little here and a little there, like a gardener trying to wet all his new plantings. Aaban snorted, coughed, then took a deep breath and held it. Spencer lifted the bucket and aimed a narrow stream straight into Aaban's nose.

It took twenty seconds or so for the man's breath to run out. An unbelievably long twenty seconds. Then his head wrenched against Clay's grip like something electrified. Suddenly he inhaled, his body telling him his life was down to its last thimble of air. Spencer tilted the bucket and doubled the volume. Aaban's head spasmed and his body convulsed. His legs rose off the board as if yanked by wires and his toes spread apart and the straps dug into his ankles.

"When and where will al-Qaeda attack the United States?"

Gurgled nonsense. Spencer righted the bucket and the water stopped.

"Where is bin Laden?"

Unintelligible.

Then a boy's voice, quickly followed by the interpreter's:

"Stop! Stop! Sto—"

Aaban's sudden inhale was loud enough to blot out the voice of his son. Then rapid breathing, almost tuneful with relief, if not gratitude— fast and high-pitched and fluttering. Again and again and again. I'd never heard a thanks so genuine.

"Where is Amal? The favorite!"

Aaban's breathing was so deep and fast he could only get the words out one or two at a time.

"To hell. You! To hell!"

And again, Roshaan through Moe: **"Stop, he doesn't know! He says he doesn't know!"**

Spencer looked down at Aaban for a long moment, then across the room to Roshaan. He looked at Clay and Vazz, who gave him vague shrugs. Then he set down the bucket and took up a new one. **"Bin Laden will be with his favorite wife! Where is Amal?"**

"Las Vegas."

"Where is your great Allah now?"

"He. Damns. You!"

"When and where is the next attack?"

"On your naked whore mother."

Spencer lifted the fresh bucket, directing the full heavy river into Aaban's nose again.

Five minutes. Ten. Spencer poured the water, and Clay steadied Aaban's head, and the man writhed and vomited, and the boy screamed in high-voiced helplessness, and Moe the 'terp made sure everybody was understanding everybody else.

34

We went on like that for about a month, mostly with the water," said Clay. His voice was softer now, and he seemed deep within himself. Working deliberately, he removed the flash drive from the computer, set it back in the drawer, and brought out another drive. He talked while he plugged it into the USB port. "Three sessions a day sometimes. In between the water, we used stress positions and nudity. You can't humiliate a proud man worse than stripping him naked and making him squirm with pain in front of his young son. At least, we couldn't find anything. He gave us nothing actionable. He toyed with us. He told us how to break down and clean an AK. He gave us directions to his home in Sangin. False, no doubt. He described the beauty of his wives. There's no use watching every minute of that. There's probably no reason for Nell to see it."

I didn't tell Clay that Nell would never show this video, because the federal government could charge her and KPBS with sedition or even treason. Nell could be the next Snowden. There was still a war on terror. And national security was as big an issue now as it had been then. Maybe bigger. Nothing had changed—or at least, nothing had gotten better.

"Do you still think she's going to like this?" asked Clay.

"She'll be fascinated, just like I am."

"But will she put me and Dr. Spencer on her show?"

"I don't know."

"Are you going to recommend it?"

"I'm still making up my mind."

"This is not the story," said Clay. "Not yet. You are about to see things that no one has seen or confessed to. Maybe then you and Nell will want the world to know."

"I've got an open mind."

Clay gazed at me. I sensed his attention leaving me, the room, maybe the whole country. Back to Romania? How could he not be drawn back there, over and over, like a moth to light? To white fire?

He turned and studied the bathroom mirror again, then stared out the crack in the front-window curtain. He looked at me with what looked like full focus and attention. In that moment he needed me. I saw in Clay what I'd seen in Tritt—an irresistible need to tell his story and confess his truth. It was stronger than their desires to forget, or to be understood or forgiven or even loved. Only Briggs Spencer seemed immune to the truth, in spite of the name of his book.

But, as the video rolled across the computer screen, Briggs Spencer began to change. I saw it first in his face, in the darkness around his eyes and the deepened lines around his mouth. His expression grew harder and more set by the day. His nose erupted in red acne. His movements became faster, abrupt at times, and this grim energy seemed to take him over. He cut off almost all of his thick gray hair. You could tell he'd done it himself because it was patchy and uneven. About that time he began shaving carelessly, or maybe using an older blade, because he had razor burns on his neck and nicks on his chin and under his nose. He also stopped wearing clean clothes. As the videos played on, Spencer's clothing was the same tan T-shirt and camo pants, dirtier by the day. He lost weight. There were times when he would talk to himself, then remember that there might be cameras running, and stop. Or, sometimes, he would turn to the camera and make faces or comments. At one point, while he held a snarling Malinois just inches away from Aaban's own snarling face, Spencer looked straight in the camera, widened his eyes, and said, **"All the better to see you with!"**

Sitting near him in the weakly lit room, I

covertly observed Clay, rapt and unblinking. His expression was of anticipation, as if he weren't quite sure what might happen next. "Clay? What are you thinking right now, as you watch yourself do this?"

"My first emotion is wonder. That Aaban could withstand all of that and never break. My second emotion is more wonder at how I withstood it. See, at Arcadia, I could hardly remember any of what we did at White Fire. From the first week I arrived at Arcadia, my mind got cloudier and cloudier, and my memories became very dim and uncertain. I'd ask Dr. Whipple and later Dr. Hulet why the pills were making my past fade away. And they told me the meds would not affect memory. But they were wrong. And Morpheus—that's a nickname for Don— he'd give me all sorts of special pills, plus the regular meds. He told me Dr. Spencer said I might appreciate them. The special meds made me see and hear things that, later, I knew weren't there. So, now, when I see what I did on video, it's like seeing these things for the first time. With my meds gone and this video to watch, I'm back there, Mr. Wills. I'm experiencing it again. It's hard to believe. It's painful. Even for me, the torturer."

Clay looked at me gravely. "I want you to watch this last part. It's the heart of our story. It's what I want the world to know. So please watch what happened. A lot of this Vazz and Tice and I shot without Dr. Spencer knowing. He was pretty much out of it by then. Vodka straight from the bottle as he worked. Plus the bliss bullets that Tice gave out. Dr. Spencer didn't care about anything but Aaban. Me and Vazz set up our Flips and phones and let 'em roll, so it's not real clear. I'll fill you in on what's going on. This is five weeks after Roshaan arrived."

At first, the video was just more of the same. A mood of near tedium hovered in the room as Spencer questioned Aaban, who was naked and chained to the ceiling. The same questions as before. Over and over. Bin Laden. Next attack. With every insufficient answer, Spencer slapped his face and Aaban either snapped and tried to bite him or laughed. Clay and Vazz sat across the room, on either side of Roshaan, who was sometimes silent and at other times crying piteously.

Then suddenly, Roshaan rose and charged toward his chain-hung father. He came from the background, a blur. Chaos. Clay tackled him at Aaban's straining feet, wrenching the thin boy into a choke hold and locking his legs around Roshaan for total control. The camera panned wildly to Spencer, then back to Roshaan and Clay, clinched tight together on the floor, Roshaan red-faced and bucking. Aaban kicked Clay in the back of his head, hard. Vazz rushed in and cranked Aaban up so high that he could stand only on the balls of his bare feet. The Malinois in the corner snarled and thrashed on its chain. Spencer cussed the dog while it tore at the air. Then he trudged over to Clay and Roshaan, and I thought he was going to kick the boy. Straining for balance, Aaban yelled his son's name.

Tice, the cameraman, shot Spencer face-on as he stared down at Roshaan with what looked like wild contempt. Clay held fast and the boy stopped thrashing as his father bellowed at him from above. Spencer stepped past Clay and Roshaan to stand directly in front of Aaban, and the two men roared at each other from inches away, Spencer cursing and Aaban yelling I knew not what, and the Malinois broke loose and leaped toward Aaban, and Vazz caught the dog mid-air and crashed to the stone floor with the dog's jaws clamped and ripping his shoulder. Tice abandoned the camera, but it settled with the lens aimed up, recording the mute black smoke-house ceiling and the screams and snarls below.

Two minutes went by. Just the ceiling and the unholy noise. Judging by the sounds, Tice and Vazz must have thrown the dog out the front door of the smokehouse.

Then came a gradually ominous silence.

In front of me, Clay stared at the monitor, transfixed.

By the time Tice could man the camera again

Clay was kneeling over the sprawled and inert Roshaan, holding two fingers to his carotid while Spencer threw handfuls of water into the boy's face.

"Clay, what the fuck?" demanded Spencer.

"No pulse."

"Roshaan!" Aaban boomed out from off-screen. "Gap zadam!"

"It's there," said Spencer. **"Find it."**

"No pulse, sir. Vazz, check his eyes."

The camera came in close on Roshaan's face. White and lifeless. Clay held out a dog tag to the boy's nostrils, looking for warm breath in the cold room. Vazquez, bleeding from his right shoulder, checked the eyes—clear and unfocused, and with the lids left open—unblinking.

"He's not breathing," said Clay.

"What is this bullshit?" snapped Spencer.

"Roshaan? Bedaar kardan!"

"I'm trying chest compressions, sir," said Clay.

"Do 'em. Do 'em, I said!"

Aaban yelled off-screen as the camera wheeled from Clay to Spencer to Clay again. Clay straddled Roshaan with his knees and went to work with the heels of his hands. The boy's slender body quaked with each compression, but to me it looked like it was Clay's energy going through him, not his own. Vazz hooked a thumb into

Roshaan's mouth, arched back the boy's head, and breathed into him between the compressions.

"How about Doctor What's-his-name?" asked Spencer.

"He went back to Washington last week, sir, remember?" said Donald Tice, loud and off-screen, behind the camera.

"Indeed I do." Spencer knelt beside Clay, took one of Roshaan's wrists, and pressed two fingers to the artery. **"This kid's flatlining on me. Harder, Clay! Faster!"**

Clay worked harder and faster, but the seconds seemed to drag more and more slowly as Roshaan's body shook and his head jerked with every push, and then Vazz descended for another exhale.

One eternal minute.

Clay hit the pause command and the screen froze on Roshaan's white-blue face. No more screaming man. No snarling dog. Just the car traffic on Pacific Coast Highway, Oceanside, California, six thousand six hundred miles away from where an eleven-year-old Afghani boy had died and a nineteen-year-old American boy had helped kill him.

"I worked on him for almost seven minutes, total," said Clay. "No response."

The monitor came back to frantic life around Roshaan's peaceful lifelessness. Clay continued the chest compressions. Spencer got up from beside the boy and strode off-screen. Vazz stood, too, and they argued, but I couldn't make out the words.

Then Clay and Vazquez lifted Roshaan's upper body from the floor and tugged off his jacket and underclothes.

I hoped the shock of cold might bring him back," said Clay. "Or maybe, I'd see that I'd been off on the compression site and I'd find a better place to press. I was desperate. I was willing to try anything. I started compressing again. I did the best, deepest compressions I knew how. Vazz went back to mouth-to-mouth breathing. Nothing. He was gone. Later we laid him on the waterboard and covered him with a blanket. By then everything was a blur."

The video froze on Roshaan on his father's waterboard, and Clay and Vazz spreading the blanket.

"Later I lifted the blanket and looked at Roshaan. Then at his father. I saw my soul fly away. It looked like a bat. I haven't felt or seen it since, Mr. Wills."

Cars on the highway. A distant siren. If I'd had any doubt about Clay Hickman's need to tell his story, it was gone. "It looked like an accident to me, Clay. Choke holds like that have killed before. That's why most cops don't use them anymore."

"What I think happened? Roshaan had a weak heart. Like mine when I was born. He couldn't have an operation. Or maybe he didn't even know."

He looked at me, then to the mirror taped to the wall, then out through the front-window curtain.

"Do you have more video, Clay?"

He glanced at me, then looked down, nodding. "Dr. Spencer ordered us to get rid of the body. He swore us all to silence. Penalty of death or worse, he said. Moe the 'terp disappeared the very next day. I don't know what Dr. Spencer did to him. Me and Vazz and Don decided to wrap Roshaan up and pack him in this wood-and-leather trunk we found in the basement. It was a heavy old thing. Like from another century. I can't play that video now. It's the hardest part to watch. But I'll play it for Nell and Dr. Spencer. I'm hoping Nell will want to show it up close. In slow motion. Maybe more than once. It was the end of the end, and the beginning of the beginning."

35

A nd so," Clay said quietly. "That's who I am and why I'm doing what I'm doing."

I thought about that. I'd just witnessed Clay Hickman's moral injury. His soul wound. I heard Paige Hulet's voice: **It is caused by something you** do. **Not by something done** to **you.**

In this stark new light, Clay wasn't quite the menace I'd thought he was. Victim? Not quite that, either. How about collateral damage? I felt old anger and fresh shame, like two snakes swallowing each other by their tails. I hadn't wanted to see what Clay had shown me, even though I had known the larger, more distant truth of it—like most Americans—for the better part of a decade. But Clay had restored my unwilling eyesight. He had called my bluff and drafted me in. Made me a partner. As Spencer had done to him. And others had done to Spencer and Tritt and many like them.

"You're me," I said finally.

"Not by a long shot."

"What I mean is, the story is about you and a

lot of other people, too. A whole country full of us who sent you in to do that."

Which is why the idea of Spencer pocketing twenty million dollars for his days at White Fire— for doing the hideous shit I'd just watched— brought Rage, Wrath & Fury running. That Spencer would now promote himself to hero in **Hard Truth** was the worst corruption of all. Truths hidden, lies magnified. For profit. Again.

"So what do you think? Is Nell going to want it?"

I knew if I was honest with Clay I might not see him again. But if I stayed in character, I could arrange one more meeting with him. By promising a meeting with Nell, I could deliver him instead to his parents. And they could get him out of Arcadia and away from Spencer. In my hands I felt the weight of Clay Hickman's precarious fate, and in my heart the sick fear of betraying his attempt at redemption.

"I think she'll want to interview you."

He turned to me slowly, hazel and blue eyes boring in. "If she doesn't, I can edit and narrate and post this on the Internet and the world can judge it. I can force Dr. Spencer to observe and comment, on camera. I understand there may be consequences for me. I will face the consequences, but not alone. Dr. Spencer must participate. I am not a terrorist or a traitor."

"I see that."

"I want my soul back."

"You've earned it."

He stood abruptly and went into the bathroom, looked out the window to the alley behind the room. He took out his phone, punched some numbers, then turned to me. "We don't have a lot of time now. They have found us. Company men. After White Fire, I can always spot them. They've probably bugged the GPS on your phone—feds can do it without a warrant. Patriot Act. They're twice as fast as cops, and sneakier."

Which meant the company had Clay's phone number, too. It had no GPS to track him by, but they would be able to communicate with him, and maybe find a way to fool and manipulate him, as I had.

Clay hustled back to the desk. He swept the first flash drive from the desk drawer and pocketed it. Then yanked the power cord from the wall and slapped the computer closed. Headlights came down the alley toward us.

"Take the dolls if you want them," he said. "I'll be in touch."

Through the cracked front-room curtain I saw movement in the dark, not the cars steady on the Coast Highway but human shapes coming our direction.

"I want that show with Nell, Mr. Wills. I gave you my truth and now it's up to you."

I heard a vehicle stop outside the bathroom window and a moment later a familiar voice hissed, "Clay! I'm here! They're coming!"

He hoisted himself up into the window opening, wriggled his shoulders through, and fell out, one arm leading the way, the other sheltering the computer against his flank. I heard him hit, grunt, and roll. I pulled myself up in time to see Sequoia Blain heading away in her little silver pickup truck, driving not fast but assertively, just another motorist with things to do.

The knock at the front door was loud. I pulled my burner, dialed 911, hit speaker, and set it on the desk where the computer had been.

"Clay? Open up! It's me, Don Tice!"

"One moment please." I knew he wasn't Tice. I'd talked to him long enough at Arcadia to remember his voice.

"I don't have all night, Clay!"

"Hang on, Morpheus."

"Hurry."

"Oceanside Police Department. Your name?"

"David Wills."

"Is this an emergency?"

"My motel room is being broken into. The Harbor Palms on PCH, room fourteen. I believe the men are armed."

"Are you inside the room?"

"Hey, Clay! Let me in. We have to talk."

"Yes, I'm in the room."

"Can you exit the building?"

A car screeched to a stop in the alley. I strode into the bathroom, slammed the window closed, and locked it.

"Not now I can't."

"I have units on the way. Can you hide?"

"Be right there, Don!" I said. "Did you bring some bad company with you?"

"Just me with some special treats from Deimos."

"Okay, give me a second."

"Is someone in the room with you now?"

Through the curtain opening I saw three more figures bunching up close to the door. Then I heard a thump on the bathroom wall and saw a man looking through the glass at me. I waved at him and called out, "Just a second, Don!"

"Hurry, Clay!"

"Can you exit the building?"

"I'm going to have to let them in. You guys better be fast."

"Clay, open up!"

I did. Joe Bodart barreled into me, grabbed at my coat collar, and tried to take me down. I used his momentum and flung him hard against the wall. Past me plowed three other men, the last of whom shut and latched the door behind him. The four looked late thirties to mid-forties, fit, focused, and itching to act. Their eyes roamed alertly and came quickly back to me. Two had drawn down on me. Bodart was wide-eyed and flushed. He righted himself against the wall and spread his hands, inviting everyone to cool it.

I knew that CIA officers couldn't arrest me, but plenty of other feds certainly could and would.

"Fucking PI," said Bodart. "Where's Clay?"

"Back in the wind," I said.

"Sir, can you hear me? Has another party come into the room? What's going on there?"

All four of them looked at my phone, sitting on the desk beside the dolls in the weak downcast of lamplight. "You guys look funny," I said. "She's my friendly 911 Oceanside PD dispatcher. Hi, I'm back. Yes, there are four of them in here and at least one more outside. Two are armed and brandishing weapons as we speak."

Bodart shook his head, went to the desk, clicked off the call, and tossed me my phone.

"They're on their way," I said.

"We've got one minute, men," he said. "Find it."

They spread out and searched the room in a storm of efficiency. Bodart stayed with me, eyeing the swordfighting folk dolls, then the suitcases on their stands. My phone rang and I had to figure Oceanside PD. I let it go to record.

"What does Clay Hickman think he's doing?" he asked.

"You know damn well what Clay's doing. Same as Spencer knows. You just don't know for sure what he's got. Or how much of it."

"Video, right?"

"Maybe."

"Christ, I hate amateurs." Bodart watched me while his three compatriots banged around the room, rifling the desk and night-table drawers, emptying the suitcases on the floor and tearing through the clothes.

"Spirited little primates," I said.

"Aren't they." A siren sounded south of us, coming up the Coast Highway. "Are you armed, Mr. Ford?"

"I'm not."

"Open your coat for me to see. Slowly and all the way. Then empty your pockets on this desk."

"No. And if you come at me I'll knock you cold."

"That's right, you're the jarhead heavyweight."

"And if you pull that gun, be ready to use it."

"Take a pill, hero man. Nobody wants to die for some puke like Briggs Spencer."

The siren came louder. "We're outta here!" He turned back to me. "Next time we meet, this will be different."

"Maybe I'll get to knock you out."

"**Much** different."

They ebbed from the room as quickly as they had surged in. At the doorway, Bodart the

Wrangler and one other man went north and the other two went south. The Coast Highway headlights came slow and bright while the taillights went likewise red the other way. Standing in the doorway I watched the northbound spooks cut left down the first street, heading toward the beach. I figured Clay and Sequoia were probably on I-5 by then, headed god knew where.

The sirens were closer, a few blocks away. Oceanside PD had my burner number but no GPS to ping me and no reason to think I was anyone but David Wills. I took one last look at the dolls locked in mortal combat on the motel room desk, closed the door on them. Then lit a smoke and strolled up PCH toward my car.

36

'm very disappointed about what happened with Clay yesterday," said Briggs Spencer. "You had him and you let him go. But I didn't ask you to my home today to tell you that. Rameesh!"

A young Afghani man came from the house. He was slight and clean-shaven and wore casual Western clothes. He had two cocktails on the drink tray. Spencer's home was three stories of white stucco that stood high on a bluff overlooking the Pacific and the city of La Jolla. The window planters overflowed with violet bougainvillea.

I saw a clay tennis court and a helipad on which the bright copper Sikorsky shined. From where we sat in a shaded backyard pavilion, a thick lawn spread all the way to the bluff's edge, drawing my eyes down to the black rocks, then across the vast ocean to the horizon. A half-dome of sky rose high and curved back overhead toward us.

Rameesh set two martinis on the thick glass

table, bowed slightly. "Lunch is almost ready, Doctor."

"Good," said Spencer with a smile. "I'm sure Mr. Ford is hungry. I hope you like octopus."

"More than it likes me."

Rameesh went back inside. Spencer watched him. "What does Clay **have**?" asked Spencer.

It was the second time he'd asked the question. So I answered it the same. "He says he has proof of crimes committed at White Fire."

"Video, correct?"

I said nothing.

"Did you see it?"

"I know what's on it."

His face hardened and darkened. "Crimes committed at White Fire—by whom?"

"All of you."

Spencer took a while to think about this. "Okay. All right. Then let me ask you this—can you locate Clay for me in the next forty-eight hours?"

"I believe so."

"How **much** do you believe so?"

"He's capable and unpredictable."

"I can't believe he gave five agency men the slip. Or maybe I can. Everyone is impressed by those spook types until they actually work alongside them. Then you realize they've been **classroom** trained. So, forty-eight hours is possible? To tell me exactly where Clay is? So I can take him back to Arcadia, which is my legal and moral obligation to the Hickmans?"

I sipped the martini. "He won't go with you quietly, Dr. Spencer."

"I know that. Under my contract with the family, I have legal authority to restrain Clay. As necessary for his and the public's safety. I'll have professional help and plenty of it."

"Nets and tranquilizer guns?"

He looked at me and raised an eyebrow. "At least."

"Then what are you going to do with him?"

"Reevaluate, adjust, and resume his treatment. Which, contrary to your amateur assessment, is probably the best available on the planet. Pharmaceuticals—no more shackles, cold baths, lobotomies, or straitjackets."

"You did squeeze in some electroshock."

Spencer shook his head slightly, as if shrugging off a bad idea. "Electroconvulsive therapy. Unilateral electrode placement, never bilateral. My first point is that I want Clay back within forty-eight hours."

"Noted."

"Mr. Ford, is Aaban on the video?"

"Clearly."

"Is his son, Roshaan?"

"Roshaan, too."

Spencer watched me closely as I answered his questions. His gaze seemed opinionless and penetrating at the same time. Like he was an impartial third party—a polygraph examiner or a high-court judge.

Rameesh brought out two bowls of octopus ceviche. On the side were avocado slices, lemon and lime wedges, tortilla chips, and a tray of salsas and hot sauces. "Ford, I saw a video not long ago of an octopus carrying a coconut shell across the bottom of the ocean. Really something. He held it up over his head, kind of like a construction worker carrying a sheet of plywood. You could see his other six legs conveying him across the sand. Slow motion, under the water. Very graceful. When he got where he wanted he stopped and crawled into one half of the shell, drew his tentacles in, then closed the other half over him. And there he was, safe within his coconut shell at the bottom of the sea. Where he'd wait for some unsuspecting fish to come nose the shell open, then he'd grab and eat it."

"I saw that one, too."

"Aaban was like that octopus. He'd go inside his coconut shell and you couldn't get to him."

"Which got to you."

"Everything got to everyone at White Fire. It was **war.** I don't have to tell you that. You know from first Fallujah—when they hung those

Blackwater men from the bridge. You must have felt the chaos in the air. Cruelty unleashed. A perfect storm of evil and opportunity. Evil and opportunity often go together."

I agreed with Briggs Spencer on that and told him so.

"How did you do in the war, Roland? Personally?"

I shrugged. "I followed the rules and accomplished my mission."

"Did you take out any innocents?"

"Not that I know."

"The kids would have been the toughest. Because a boy is a boy, but he can handle a gun or a bomb or carry a bomb pack."

I thought again of those door-to-doors—terrified Iraqis in their homes, hands up, eyes wild. I used to imagine what they saw in us. Murderous infidels? Liberators? Another plague to be endured?

After lunch Rameesh took away our dishes and Dawn Spencer brought out a plate of small bundt cakes that someone had spent some time on. She was pretty, plump, and blond, and carried herself apologetically. I remembered that she had been his high school sweetheart and they'd married young, which made her, like Briggs, just under sixty years old.

She sat beside her husband and offered the

cakes around. I took raspberry. "I hear you almost got Clay back."

"Almost, Mrs. Spencer."

"Just Dawn. Look. I've talked to Clay over the years, here and there. Nicest kid you could imagine. The feeling I got was the war took his mind but left his soul. With other people the war did just the opposite. Tim Tritt used to talk about those two types. Sound about right, Briggs?"

"Perfectly."

"So, I hope you can help him come back safely." She eyed me, then the cakes appraisingly, chose a lemon one. "I can tell you that my husband has had to climb back from those wars. Many times. And now that **Hard Truth** is coming out, he'll be able to answer the critics and set the record straight. Personally, I never thought Briggs owed the world an explanation for anything. He was saving American lives. Period. But now that I've heard his full story I'm even more proud of him than I ever was." Dawn ate the bundt cake daintily but steadily. "Honey, how did that sound?"

"Dawn and I have been training with a media coach," said Briggs. "For the tour. She's showing us the best way to say what we want to say. We need to be honest, first and foremost. But we need to be careful, too. If the liberal media can find a way to crucify us, they will."

"Did I sound believable just now?" she asked me.

"I believed you," I said. "But it sounded rehearsed."

"Well, that's no surprise," she said. She squinted out at the bright blue day. Without looking at the plate she took another cake and brought it to her mouth. "Every day I read my lines over and over but they never sound right."

"You're overpressuring yourself, hon," said Spencer.

"I know, but I just hate it when other people reach inside my head. Even our coach. Hate it."

"Well, the coach is just trying to make us feel relaxed with our story. Feel comfortable."

"All our story makes me feel is sick to my stomach." Staring out at the water, she finished the second cake. She stood, and we men did, too. "There. Nice to just say what I feel. And nice to meet you finally, Mr. Ford."

"My pleasure."

She offered me her hand, which was warm and soft, and a look, which suggested both anger and nausea. Her fair face was deeply flushed. "I can do it, Briggs. I can bring it."

"I know you can. Thank you, Dawn."

She headed back inside, walking past Rameesh, who held open the sliding screen door for her.

"She's a private person," said Briggs. "I've offered to do the tour without her, but she knows she's a selling point. Team player all the way."

"You might want to keep her away from that liberal media."

"I have a plan for that. It's why I asked you here today."

"I hope it's not about all those treasures you told me could be mine."

"Take a walk down to the cove with me. Hear me out."

37

Spencer swung open a tall metal gate that clanged shut behind us before we'd started down the stairs. The stairs were steep but wide enough for two, with a stout iron railing running down the middle. I saw the ocean boiling on the black rocks below.

"Once you've reunited Clay and me, I want to hire you as security on my book tour. Starting next week. Mr. Ford, as you might have noticed, there are a lot of volatile people in this world. There are people who hate me and hate America. I could transfer DeMaris from Arcadia for a month, let him protect me and Dawn. He's a good man. But I can't tolerate him close by for more than about ten minutes. You, Dawn, and I would travel by charter jet, then fly in as close as we can get to the actual events in one of my helos. Make an entrance in my Sikorsky, for instance. People are going to love me arriving at the helm of my own helicopter. Twelve cities, fifteen days, so far. That means talks, media, signings, media, parties, media, dinners. First-class hotels. All chop-chop. We'll be in and out the same day whenever we can. No downtime, no waste. I can get you temporary concealed-carry permits in every state. You'd need to stick close to me and Dawn when we're in public, keep an eye out for the crazies. My agency and NSA people have their ears to the ground. So far, okay, they're hearing light chatter. Maybe Portland. Maybe L.A. But you know how it is—you listen hard enough to SIGINT, you always pick up something."

"Why not just hire one of them to go with you?"

"I'd prefer a human being."

"You don't like or trust me."

Spencer stopped so I did, too. The ocean breeze blew his gray hair askew and he gave me his big-chinned smile. I'd seen it before, but it surprised me now, after his ice-blue interrogator's gaze over lunch. "I like you very much! And I know you're good. You found Clay's trail quickly. You kept Clay and the girl away from Rex Hickman's jackboots up in Ojai. You came damned close to tripping up whoever shot Vazz to pieces in his own home in Mendocino. **My** home. And you managed to get Clay past five agency men in Oceanside yesterday like they had their butts glued to the floor. So, my first draft pick is you."

"I like the work I have."

His smile gradually ebbed. The surf smacked into the rocks below. "How is Clay?"

"I saw a disturbed young man in a motel room."

"And video of Aaban and Roshaan."

I said nothing.

"What did you think?"

"I thought they should have had bigger parts in **Hard Truth.** I got an early copy. You mentioned Aaban, but nothing about his . . . son."

"Good strong stuff, though, isn't it—my book?"

"Not as strong as Clay's."

"That's why you have to bring him to me. Or me to him. Whatever works, Ford."

"You really don't feel guilt, do you?"

"I can't afford to. Truth **is** hard."

Again came the strong but weirdly detached pry of Spencer's blue eyes. He tried to work them into me, then turned and continued down the stairs toward the beach.

When we came to the sand Spencer led the way south, picking his way across slick black rocks and around shimmering tide pools. "I'll pay you a hundred thousand dollars bonus if you can bring me to Clay in the next forty-eight hours. Cash if you like. Then, with that bit of business successfully concluded, I'll salary you as security for the next three weeks—for fifteen days of tour, and for whatever might open up the week after. I think ten thousand a week is fair. Food, lodging, and ammunition on me. That was a joke about the ammo." Spencer stopped and looked at me. "What do you think?"

It was a tempting pitch and I hadn't seen it coming. But I wasn't going to work for a torturer again after this, our first and only engagement. Thanks to the video, I'd seen Spencer in action. I'd seen him descend into his heart of darkness and scamper away with his fortune. And there was nothing he'd done since White Fire to convince me that he couldn't go up that river again. Had he atoned? Had he even confessed? Soon, he'd be even richer, cashing in big on his fifteen minutes, years after Roshaan's young bones had been finally picked to nothing by the Dambovita. Was a hundred grand enough to help Briggs Spencer cover up his failed conscience and turn yet another profit on it?

"No, thank you."

"Think about what I've offered."

"I don't have to."

"You are not morally above me."

So many ways to answer that, but I kept them all to myself.

"You think you are but you're not. You know nothing of what we did and why we did it."

"Your conscience is hoarse."

Spencer took a deep breath and sighed loudly.

He looked west across the ocean, squinting into the sunlight and sea breeze. "Do you realize how important it is that I get Clay back under control?"

"Before he ruins you."

"Roland—think big picture here. Not just me. New president, new government. New cabinet. New director of Central Intelligence. So, no old ghosts in the machine. Every stone will be turned. Every whisper and rumor run to ground. Such as Clay Hickman's claims—whatever they are."

"He told me that you two have a story to tell together. The story of what happened to Aaban and Roshaan at White Fire. I don't know how it ends."

Again his gaze roamed my face for a way in. For a moment in that bright sunlight, I could see, standing on the rocks in the stiff wind, with his coat flapping and his hair blowing wild, the young Briggs Spencer who had played ball and married his high school sweetheart and wanted a family and loved America. But I could also see the older man, whose terrorized patriotism and greed had led him past the boundaries of what we think of as acceptable.

"You won't help me, will you?" he asked.

"I'll honor my contract, Dr. Spencer," I lied again. I'd been doing a lot of that lately.

"I will not let my future be sacrificed by Clay Hickman's imagined past. Nor the futures of men I believe in."

"Maybe discuss that with Clay."

"Call me when you have him ready for me," he said. "The bonus offer is good for forty-eight hours. And, if you change your mind about working for me after all this, let me know."

"I won't."

"Let's walk."

We continued on, skirting the tide pools, children and moms and dads, seagulls prowling.

"You know, Mr. Ford, some years ago, as I read about the shooting of Titus Miller in the papers, I thought that we were kindred souls. Because my behavior in a highly pressured situation had been questioned, and so had yours. We both stood up for what we thought was right. We were outnumbered but unashamed."

I stepped past a wad of seaweed, watched the sand flies lifting off, saw a sandpiper scurrying down-beach behind a receding wave. "Well, Dr. Spencer, when I read about Spencer-Tritt, I thought you were an opportunist with a good nose for dollars. I still do."

He glanced at me, smiling without humor. "Then, later, when I read that your wife had died accidentally in her plane out in this Pacific Ocean, I wondered what would happen to you. Untethered and free again."

Rage, Wrath & Fury stirred. "Now you know."

"They said it was a bad fuel pump, didn't they?"

"An intake obstruction. It was an expensive pump. Only a few hours on it."

"But of course, many fuel pumps are damaged when a light plane crashes. Especially from the estimated twenty-five hundred feet." We stopped, and again Spencer pried into me with his detached, unbiased gaze. "I wondered how you would deal with it. If you might feel responsible. If you ever regretted not doing something to keep her on the ground that day. With you."

"I never thought that," I lied.

He raised his eyebrows. "Of course you did. I became intrigued by the whole thing. Curious about you two. It didn't take me long to learn that she was an adrenaline addict and a drinker and a fan of cannabis. Considered a bit of a loose cannon around the public defender's office."

"She only flew sober. And she was always sober when she drove or climbed rocks or skydived or hunted lobster at night. Or argued in court. She was a great pilot. She respected the air and her plane."

"Of course you're angry at her for leaving you behind."

"I think I always will be."

"Do you curse and blame God?"

"Vigorously."

"What yearning drove her to risk her life in dangerous activities?"

"Flying made her feel more alive. Just like it does you and me."

He smiled his **You're going to like me** smile, seemingly satisfied with my answer. We headed back toward the house. Two young boys ran past us, splashing and screaming at the cold water for trying to get them. Spencer laid a heavy hand on my shoulder.

"Roland, say good-bye to your anger at her. And say good-bye to your fury at your god. These impede you. Come with me and I'll make you wealthy and you can remember Justine on your own terms instead of those the world assigns. You must learn to be free again. Freedom is the difference between victim and victor. Only when you do these things will she be **yours.** Now, that's an interesting expression on your face. You look intrigued by what I've said. The last time I spoke her name, up in my Sikorsky, you became childishly furious. I think you might be evolving, Roland."

He took his hand off my shoulder. "I expect a call," he said. "Soon."

38

Driving home I remembered Justine, on my own terms, and very clearly.

We met at a muted holiday party at the Manchester Grand Hyatt in downtown San Diego, in a banquet room overlooking the ocean. I was solo.

All nice: an ice sculpture of flying doves, a tower of poinsettias in the shape of a Christmas tree, holiday music from a chamber ensemble. A much-talked-about Alaskan storm finally hit, rain lashing the high windows and the lightning moving closer.

Not by accident I got in the buffet line behind a shapely woman in a red party dress. She stood all of about five-foot-six in her high heels. She looked at me, then went back to the food.

"Pretty dress," I said.

"Thank you." Sleek red hair, wide-set green eyes, and a half smile. "It's the same one I wore last night."

"I'd wear it two nights straight, too, if it looked as good on me."

"What a ghastly visual."

"It got your attention. I'm Roland Ford."

"I know. Justine Timmerman. I landed in the public defender's office about the time you ditched the sheriffs. If you ask me, your partner should have been fired **and** tried for that shooting."

We sat side by side at dinner, surrounded by people I didn't know. The party was thrown by my "personal-wealth advisor," who had put on much more of a spread than my modest investments deserved. I'd worn my best suit.

Justine was there with her friend Elke Meyer, who sat on the other side of me and told stories of Justine and her fishing in Baja the previous September. Justine had flown them to La Paz and back. Third year running. The women also snowboarded, skydived, and collected lobster together, at night, with headlamps to find their prey in the shifting black Pacific. Justine was a pilot, Elke a boat captain with a Master near-coastal license who "punched the clock" as an ophthalmologist.

They laughed and talked easily, a bit of competition in the stories. I sat between them like a stump. They'd known each other almost all their lives and were the same age—twenty-nine—and proud to still be under thirty.

They joked about pumping out some babies before too long, in plenty of time to get back to the careers and the fun.

They seemed interested that I'd lived up and down the coast, surfed and boxed and shot it out in the first Fallujah because I really did believe in service to country. They thought I'd done the right thing in regard to a trigger-happy sheriff's partner, and seemed intrigued that I could actually make a living as a private investigator. I had never wanted more to impress.

The three of us danced together after dinner. Happy chaos. But dancing is the one social skill at which I score above average, and I like it, so afterward I took them separately on sambas and fox-trots and swings. Elke was very good and Justine more intuition than skill, and I was proud to be the center around which they moved. When I finally took a break I downed my whole glass of ice water.

"Anyone up for a dip in the bay?" Justine asked. I looked out at the windblown rain and the bony fingers of lightning now closer to land.

"I'm in," I said. Testosterone pumping, compelled.

"Let's go," said Elke.

We checked our coats and valuables, then burst outside. The storm roared down extra hard, as if it had been waiting for people like us. Two blocks. The bay boiled before us. We ran across the small beach, shucked our shoes, and waded in. I remember the sharp cold, and the hard-to-forgive idea that I was willingly ruining good clothes to impress the redhead. Lightning cracked and thunder rumbled. We swam and splashed and yelled, then trudged across the sand to the boardwalk and back into the dignified lobby of the Hyatt. Got our personal things from the coat-check clerk. Justine's and Elke's party dresses were little more than drenched rags plastered to their bodies. People looked at us with amused disapproval.

At floor seven they stepped out of the elevator and blew me kisses while the door shut.

After that first unusual night, Justine and I became a two-person swarm. We were together almost constantly. I'd been a bachelor all of my thirty-four years, hot and cold, all in or all out, eager or bored, faithless or betrayed or both. I was never one for meeting the family. Neither was she.

Six months later we were married on a large motor yacht, **Cassandra,** offshore of San Diego. It was as fine a wedding as I can picture—good people filled with goodwill, all thankful for the present and bullish on the future. A genuine celebration. Justine was ridiculously beautiful.

The families got along. My mother and father were proud and blended in happily with the conspicuous wealth around them. As a former sailor, Dad loved the 248-foot **Cassandra**, with her helipad and "Balinese spa" and swimming pool. Grandpa Dick and Grandma Liz behaved themselves until well past midnight. We carried on late.

During the many congratulations I received that day, I secretly congratulated myself for having the good sense to love her.

Looking back I see our year and a half of life together as a half-crazy blur. Work hard, play hard. Sleep when you're dead. I regret not having considered that sleep might come to one of us much sooner than we'd thought. But we were young and in love and death cast no shadow that we couldn't outfly.

One Saturday in March, the first week of spring, two weeks shy of our anniversary, Justine woke up before me and came back to bed with two cups of coffee. She set one on my nightstand and took the other to her side and we propped up pillows and watched two orioles courting in the oak tree outside our window. "I've decided, Roland. I want to lay an egg, too."

We'd been talking about that—Justine laying eggs—for weeks. She'd never come right out with it until then. I told her the same thing I'd said before. "I think you should."

"You really do?"

"You'll hatch it, I'll bring the worms, and we can give him the whole bitchen world."

"Give **her** the whole bitchen world."

"Give all of them the whole bitchen world."

"Well, **that** was easy, Daddy Rolando!"

We made love with full abandon and no protection twice that morning before breakfast. It is an entirely different experience when a life is in the making. Nothing like it. After which, Justine, still in my arms and breathing hard, said we had to go celebrate with the cloud gods.

But I'd made an appointment for early that afternoon with an old friend, down on his luck and needing my help with an employee who might also be an embezzler.

"Oh, let's just fly instead," she said.

"He's a friend."

"Then he'll understand if you reschedule."

"I did that already. Last week, when we went to the concert."

"Just call him."

I did, but my friend really did need my help, and professional pride wouldn't allow me to postpone meeting him twice in a week's time.

With a smile and a wave Justine drove her convertible down the Rancho de los Robles drive. Sunshine glinting on her hair, music blasting.

In the time we were together she mentioned her mortality just once. "I'm not scared of dying," she said. "I'm scared of being forgotten."

Now, as I approached my home on that same long winding drive on which I had last seen her alive, Justine was not forgotten. She was everywhere.

39

Coming up the drive, I saw that things were wrong at the rancho. A black SUV stood outside the main house. Wesley Gunn, running toward me, arms waving. Dick and Liz, near the SUV, gesticulating at each other. Lindsey and Burt outside casita three, in animated discussion.

I punched the truck around the last curve and skidded to a stop as Wesley reached the window. "Weird guy with a gun came looking for you. We got him cuffed and locked in the empty casita!"

"Get in."

By the time we got there, all of the other tenants were now clustered outside casita three. Dick and Liz stood at one of the windows with their hands cupped, looking in. Lindsey leaned back against the front door, doing something on her phone. Dressed brightly for his thrice-weekly eighteen holes of golf, Burt waited on the front porch of the casita, feet spread and thick arms crossed. "I was putting my clubs in the trunk when he came racing up and demanded to see you," said Burt. "Opened the gate and drove past the no-trespassing signs. Gave me half a look at some federal ID and the gun in his holster. So . . ."

I butted through Dick and Liz and looked through the window at Joe Bodart, sitting on the living room couch. Dark suit, walrus mustache, shiny head. His wrists were bound with two plastic ties. Glaring at me, he raised them for me to see.

"Company man is my guess," said Burt. "I confiscated his gun and phone."

"Langley could have your ass for this, Burt," snapped Lindsey.

"I take full responsibility. But, Roland, that man approached me in a threatening manner. Disarming and restraining him was the most secure and humane course of action. I could easily have taken my driver to his knee."

I looked through the window again. Bodart now stood in the middle of the small living room, raised his wrists to me again. I stepped inside and closed the door.

"PI, you've put yourself in a bad position."

"At least I don't look ridiculous."

"If Clay Hickman has classified material from White Fire, he's guilty of a crime. If he makes it public, that's treason, and the DoD will send him to prison. He'll beg for his cushy digs in the nuthouse again, believe me. What did he show you?"

"Nothing," I lied.

Bodart looked down at the plastic ties. "Can you cut these fucking things off?"

"When I'm ready."

Bodart stepped in closer. He was a big man, and heavy. I didn't think he was foolish enough to kick me or take me down, but I was very ready. He stared at me as if in judgment, then moved away and sat back down on the couch. He looked past me at the Irregulars, who were no doubt watching the action through the window.

"I hope you're a reasonable man, Ford. If not, you'll get a lot of people hurt for no reason. Okay. Do you know where he is?"

"I haven't seen him since he crawled out the bathroom window on you guys."

"With your help. Which makes you a co-conspirator. I won't hesitate to have you prosecuted, Ford. And we won't stop until we have Clay and whatever his so-called evidence is. Top priority. We've been given wide latitude."

"Latitude."

"You know exactly what I mean. Cut these damned ties off me, will you?"

I shook my head no, returned his flat look. I was tempted to call him Wrangler, but Joe Bodart registered even higher on my scale of menace than Briggs Spencer. Especially where Clay

Hickman was concerned. I pictured him in his cowboy togs at White Fire. I feigned ignorance of him because I had to. "What's your name and who do you work for?"

"Bodart. And I work for the president of the United States. I have a number you can call. CIA, Special Activities Division. I'm the real deal, Ford, and I hate amateurs."

"What do you want from me, except for what I don't know?"

Bodart studied me. "I want Clay Hickman alive and well. In possession of no state secrets, no evidence of crimes committed at White Fire, and no plans to get vengeance on Spencer. Or whatever 'white fire to Deimos' is. I want to see Clay back in the hospital, which is probably the best place for him. And I want world peace, too."

"So **Hard Truth** can come out next week and Spencer can tell the world what a hero he was in Romania. How he saved American lives and foiled terrorist plots."

Bodart glanced at the window, then stood again. He went to the glass, pressed his face up close to Grandpa Dick's. "Who's that golfer?"

"Just a tenant."

Bodart turned back to me. "Ford? Our nation needs to know the truth from people **who were there**. The Senate report on torture only got a tenth of it. But not the tenth that matters."

"So **you** decide what matters."

He looked at me with a hint of exasperation. "I defend my country by protecting the people above me."

I thought back to Briggs Spencer's "new" government, realizing that some of the new people wouldn't be new at all. They would be the same people who had approved of White Fire, and places like it, in the first place. Rewritten the rules. Changed the game. They badly needed soldiers who could cover their butts or take the blame. "Does that make Clay more valuable to you dead, or alive?"

Bodart stepped in closer again and gave me an odd look—doubt and sympathy, maybe. His big mustache made him look somehow sad, but wise. "This is national security. Everyone's expendable."

"Like John Vazquez?"

A pause while Bodart's wheels turned. I was fishing, but I could see that I'd gotten to him. I immediately regretted it. "What I'm trying to reveal to you is that if you have any good will or affection for Clay Hickman, deliver him to me. Quickly. Not to Spencer. Not to Arcadia security. Not to his shrink. To me. If you don't do that, I can't even come close to guaranteeing his safety."

"But you'd kill him to get what he has."

"We are not killers," said Bodart. "But we have a mission to complete. We're not torturers, but we get the intelligence we need. If you are in our way, you are a threat to national security. Do comprehend this."

Again I pictured Bodart and his Wranglers loitering in Aaban's smokehouse torture chamber. Remembered Clay's description of him: **Crazy monster would do anything.**

I said nothing. Was going to ask him how a badass such as himself ended up in plastic ties carried by a small golfer.

He walked to the bed, stopped, and looked into the little casita bathroom, then turned to me again. "Who's the girl he's abducted?"

I told him her age and first name, and that she had paired up with Clay willingly. Bodart shook his head and exhaled with disgust, though I wasn't sure if it was for Clay or Sequoia or me. "One more time. What does Clay have? Video, right? Made by him and John Vazquez."

"He claims he has evidence of a crime at White Fire."

"And you claim not to know what it is?"

"He wasn't ready to trust me," I lied again. "He was still vetting me when you blitzed the motel."

A long and skeptical stare. He looked at the window again. I saw Wesley peering in up close, and Burt lingering behind him on the walkway to the pond. "If that little guy is a tenant, you must have done a background check."

I had actually done no background on him at all. Ditto the others. "Nothing came up."

"I've never seen a man move that fast. He had my gun before I realized what he was doing."

I led Bodart outside and toward the barn. The Irregulars fell in around us and we made our way across the sparse barnyard grass. On a workbench I found a pair of tin snips and cut through the heavy plastic ties. I asked Burt where he'd found the ties.

"Golf bag. I use them when I travel by air. You know, keep my sticks safe from those apes in baggage." Burt handed Bodart his handgun and phone. "Sorry I had to get physical. Being called an asshole dwarf set me off because I know three dwarves personally. Good people."

Bodart looked baffled, then tempted to attack Burt, then baffled again. He pocketed the phone, holstered the weapon, and rubbed his wrists while walking toward the barn door. At the threshold he stopped and turned and looked at us. He started to say something, then must have thought better of it.

"Next time, pay attention to those no-trespassing signs," said Grandpa Dick. "We don't want to have to go through all this again."

"Oh, come on Dick," said Liz. "You loved every minute of it."

40

Later that afternoon I hiked the Rancho de los Robles with Wesley. The day was cooling and the clouds tumbled in, heavy and gray from the Pacific. Wesley led the way, stopping often to scan with his binoculars, but I was the one who saw most of the birds first. His vision was fading and his pace was slower. My thoughts were troubled, filled with Clay Hickman and what would happen. I knew it was only a matter of time before Bodart or Spencer and their men caught up with him. And that if I could do anything on earth to help Clay, I would have to do it soon.

"You're quiet today, Mr. Ford. That CIA man got into your head?"

"He's some of it."

"Some of what?"

Where to start? I knew I could talk to Wesley as the bright young man he was without having to avoid the truth or change it or even lie. He wasn't a part of this. I was growing irate with deceptions, my own and everybody else's. They are intriguing, then tiring.

So I told him about Clay, and some of who Clay was and what he had done and how he'd escaped. How some people he worked with in the war did some bad things.

We ambled on. A kestrel circling high. A pair of band-tailed pigeons barreling along together.

"Clay has those bad things on video," I said. "Highly classified. They—the people he worked for—will go to great lengths to keep him from showing it."

"They? Like that CIA guy?"

"He's one. Others are military. Others are private contractors. None of them know where Clay is. But I do."

"What if they find out, too?"

"They'll lock him up somewhere, keep him drugged and quiet. To the government, Clay is expendable. We might never hear of him again. But the most important thing for them is to destroy the video."

Wesley stopped and turned around. "They would really do that to him?"

"They see it as their duty. They'd say if they didn't, national security would be threatened."

"Would it be?" asked Wesley.

I thought that question through again, for probably the thousandth time since I'd seen Clay's video. Same answer every time.

"No," I said. "But if the public saw the video, the national conscience would get roughed up. Badly."

"National conscience? Like, how America looks at itself?"

"Exactly that."

"Then these people must have done some pretty bad things," said Wesley.

"Very bad, Wes. Ugly and unnecessary. The country should know, because America is better than that."

"But if Clay shows the video before they get to him, what happens then?"

"They'll probably charge him with treason," I said. "That's prison time."

"Even though he's crazy?"

"That would be part of any trial."

We continued up the path in silence. Wesley, a couple of steps ahead of me, stopped and lifted his field glass to a very large sycamore tree growing in a low swale. Through my binoculars I saw the goldfinches flitting black and yellow amid the big green leaves. Behind the green the clouds piled in, blue-gray and fast.

"So Clay can't win, Mr. Ford. If he shows the video, they put him in prison, and if he doesn't they take it and put him back in the mental hospital. Or worse, even. Can you prevent any of that?"

"Maybe."

"You've got a plan?"

"Yes."

"Wow. Incredible." We walked on, Wesley a step ahead of me, scanning the trees. "Anything I can do to help?"

"There is. Friday, day after tomorrow, I'll need you to shoot some very important video with that nice camera of yours. We'll edit it in with some existing footage, taken by Clay."

"I'm slow with the video editing, Mr. Ford. Just learning."

"You'll have help."

Wesley stopped and looked back, smiling. "Okay, then. You got it. Will Clay actually be there?"

"With luck."

We forged ahead, moving slowly and quietly. Saw a female oriole in an old oak and a mockingbird jeering at us from a toyon. I looked up at a yellow Piper Cub descending toward Fallbrook Airpark. "How are your black eyes healing up, Wes?"

"Good. Kinda green now instead of black." He stopped and turned and took off his dark glasses. The sockets were the soft green of bread mold but the eyeballs were clearing of blood. Hard to believe that one of those strong young eyes would have to be taken. And maybe another. So that Wesley Gunn's life could continue. Just like it was hard to believe that Clay Hickman could either tell the truth and be considered a traitor, or conceal the truth and be considered insane.

"What a dumb thing to do down in Mexico," said Wesley, slipping his sunglasses back on. "I think those margaritas messed up my head."

Back home I started moving my other players toward the stage where they would perform on Friday. Good Friday.

The stage would be here, Rancho de los Robles—Ranch of the Oaks. Hide in plain sight. For one hour. One hour was what I thought I needed.

Burt Short agreed to help keep a possibly armed and very unpredictable Clay Hickman under control. If my ruse worked properly, we would have an hour without either Joe Bodart's Special Activities Division or Briggs Spencer's thugs, led by Alec DeMaris, bent on silencing Clay Hickman by whatever means necessary.

Lindsey Rakes would do some driving for me, then edit Wesley's video. She knew her way around video and audio from her Creech sensor ball days. Easy, she said. Her laptop was up to the task. And she was willing to help Burt handle Clay, if he needed help.

Dick and Liz would get out of Dodge in my truck, only so that I could sneak back into Dodge undetected. They would have to get along with each other for enough time to complete their tasks. They groused, then agreed.

Sitting in the eternal twilight of my heavily draped office, I called the Hickmans on a new burner phone. As they had said earlier, Rex and Patricia wanted a shot at convincing their son to come back home. Wanted it badly. They had said nothing yet to Briggs Spencer, but had talked at length with Paige Hulet, whom they trusted more than her boss. The Hickmans would fly down in their private propjet tomorrow. At my suggestion, they would bring two licensed security men with them the following day, Friday, when they would meet with their son.

Still on the burner, I talked again with Paige Hulet. She strongly wanted her star patient to try living at home with his mother and father, under the care of a psychiatrist—possibly herself. I could hear the excitement in her voice. She had already talked to the Hickmans about this, and she had agreed to handle the medical aspects of the transfer.

"I'd like you to be here when Clay arrives," I said. "He trusts you. If he doesn't like what he sees, you might be able to calm him down."

"Thank you" was all she said.

The only missing part was Clay Hickman.

I made the call on David Wills's phone at eight thirty-five that night and left a message:

"Clay? This is David, from Nell Flanagan's office. I have some very good news for you. Nell wants to do the segment. She is very excited about it. She wants to tape the day after tomorrow at noon, Friday, on location in north San Diego County. It will be you, Nell, Briggs Spencer, and Dr. Paige Hulet. Nell thought having your psychiatrist present would be important and fascinating. And, of course, I'll be there. When you call back I can tell you where to meet us, and what clothing you should wear, and give you some basic dos and don'ts about TV, okay? If you need a haircut, be a good time to get one. Absolutely no guns—that's a deal breaker and she'll have a bodyguard, who will search you. So be cool. Okay to bring the girl. Call me soon."

I was guilty of duplicity. Which felt close to betrayal. But betrayal for a good cause, right? Was it worth noting that betrayal for a good cause is the first small step on so many catastrophic journeys?

But this was my choice, assigned by fate or God or chance. I wasn't sure that it mattered which. The real question was: Could we do the right thing for Clay? Would he let us?

Wills's phone buzzed.

Clay's voice wavered with excitement. "This is excellent. And Dr. Spencer has agreed to be there?"

"He's very eager to promote **Hard Truth**."

"What proof can you give me that he'll show?"

"His greed and eagerness to wash his hands."

A long pause. "Imagine when he sees himself on video torturing Aaban while his son watches."

"It's dramatic stuff, Clay. It's true. **Your** hard truth."

"I never hated Dr. Spencer. Or even disrespected him."

"The best part of telling your story will be sharing your secret with other people. The world can help you carry it."

"You sound like Dr. Hulet."

Neither of us spoke. I searched for something to say that might prepare him to accept the offer I would make to him two days from now, an offer very different from what he was expecting. I tried to imagine his surprise and shock. "I have a favorable impression of Dr. Hulet from our correspondence. I know she's very concerned for you. She and Nell are somewhat alike, I think."

That was as good as I could do without giving anything away. Maybe his mother and father could convince him to come home. Maybe his doctor could. Maybe Sequoia. Maybe he was just flat worn-out and ready.

"When will the story be shown on TV?"

"We don't know yet."

"I want it to be before Dr. Spencer's book."

"Nell's show will make his book sell even more," I said.

"That's okay. This is about truth, not sales. What if you're one of Bodart's guys? Or Spencer's? Or the PI that Dr. Spencer hired and you're leading me into a trap?"

"Well, sure, lots of what-ifs. But I'm not."

"What proof can you give me?" he asked.

"None. Do you want Nell to tell your story or not?"

"Don't be ridiculous. Noon Friday. Where?"

I gave him the address and directions off both north and south interstates.

"Why there?"

"Nell likes the peaceful setting. Clay? No gun."

"No, sir."

"You'll be searched."

"You already said that."

"Do you plan to bring the young lady?" I asked.

"I don't know yet."

"Is she all right?"

"Why wouldn't she be? We love and take care of each other."

"What's her name?"

"I can't tell you until then," he said.

"Where are you going to go when this is over, Clay?"

"I can't tell you that, either. Why do you care?"

"I've gained a lot of respect for you since we met. I want the best for you. And the girl. After you two got away from the motel in Ocean-side, I had to stay behind and talk to Bodart and watch his guys search the room. I saw what a threat you are to them. I weighed them against what you had been through at White Fire. And I found myself on your side. I want you safe and I want your story told."

"Make it happen."

He hung up.

41

Good Friday morning, gray and still. Showers in the forecast. The kind of April day that can change quickly. Clay had been on the run for eleven days now and I was ready to bring him in.

Dick and I got into my truck. Liz was waiting for us in the backseat. I held up my Bodart-monitored smartphone to both of them, set it in the center console. Then I lifted out the DeMaris-planted transmitter and turned it on. The little black unit disappeared into the console's depths and the blue light vanished when I shut the lid. I explained to Dick and Liz how the bugs worked. "Looks like the pricks have you covered," Dick said.

"Roland knows what he's doing," said Liz. "Although the back of your truck is very small. Lucky I brought the pillow for staying low."

Dick turned to look at his wife. "Then why don't you use it and get low?"

Liz wriggled down onto the seat, stretched out as best she could, worked her head into the pillow. "Like camping when I was little. I always hated tents."

I guided the truck down the gravel drive and past the pond, toward the paved road. "This little trick won't fool them for long," I told them once again. "Remember, after you drop me off at Mercy Road, go south to the Eight, then east toward Yuma. Once they suspect you're not me, they might pull you over. If they do, call me immediately. Tell them you borrowed my truck to go see friends. Be as dumb as you can be. If you make it as far as Yuma before hearing from me, get a motel room and wait for my call."

"Don't worry," said Liz. "And, I'll need a room of my own if we make Yuma."

"You can have the whole motel," said Dick. "Good luck, Rollie."

"That's what this is for." I tipped Justine's lucky shantung fedora.

Half an hour later I pulled off Interstate 15 at Mercy Road. Sped down the ramp and gunned it into the gas station. Parked nose-out by the air and water area. Dick came around to take the driver's seat and Liz upgraded to the front passenger seat. I set my lucky hat on Grandpa Dick's head. He angled the brim to his satisfaction, using the rearview mirror.

I said, "If they make you, call me. If you **think** they've made you, call me."

"Got it."

"You look cute in that hat," said Liz.

"Keep your wits and stay calm," I said. "Chances are, when they see it's you and not me, they'll fall back."

I stepped away from the truck and Grandpa Dick gunned it away from the station toward the on-ramp. Liz waved. One thing I didn't have to worry about was Dick driving too slow. He'd always been a lead foot, like his son, like me.

I climbed into Lindsey Rakes's spotless black Mustang with the child seat strapped in back. She was dressed cowgirl chic again. "Hello, hotcakes," I said.

"Hello, handsome. Where y'all headed?"

When Lindsey pulled to a stop outside her casita, Burt Short pulled open her door and bowed. He was dressed from head to toe in black nylon-heavy "tactical" clothing of some kind. It was sized to show off his muscles, which looked comically dangerous on such a short man. His duty boots were old but well polished.

The three of us walked toward the palapa. "Don't worry about anything," Burt said. "After the pat-down, I'll be around, just in case Clay gets froggy. I am unarmed, as you ordered. Though I'd prefer a reliable sidearm."

"Keep an eye on Sequoia, too," I said. "She's under Clay's spell."

"I'll go with the flow, Roland," said Burt. "This is their show. And yours."

"Don't worry," said Lindsey.

"Why does everybody think I'm worried?" I rubbed the Y-shaped scar on my forehead, scratching the itch. Which led me to remind myself that neither I nor the beloved people around me were invincible.

"It's just pre-operation jitters," she said.

"We called it pucker time," said Burt.

"'We'?" demanded Lindsey. "Who was **we**? And when? When did you do all this stuff you refer to?"

"Before your time."

Wesley sat at a picnic table under the palapa, threading his video camera onto its tripod. Sunglasses on, a bottle of water on the table beside him. He glanced up at us, then went back to his task. He wore cargo pants and athletic shoes, a UCSB hoodie over a T-shirt, and an MTV ball cap. "If we set up in the shade here, I can get enough natural light for Clay's face," said Wesley. "But no glare off his monitor."

I asked Lindsey how much time she would need to edit Clay's old video into Wesley's new video, and upload the best ten minutes of it to YouTube.

"Hour and a half, minimum."

My mind was jumping thought to thought. "I've got you an hour," I said. "Maybe."

She looked at me but said nothing.

I watched through the binoculars as Paige Hulet came up the drive in a sensible white Toyota. Hair up, black suit, white blouse buttoned to the top. Dressing the doctor part for Clay. I thought of her that night in her penthouse, dancing in the swaying black dress, but couldn't hold the thought long. I waved her into the barnyard shade and took her hand as she climbed out of the car. She kissed me on the cheek, slung her satchel over one shoulder. A smile. Black running shoes instead of the usual black dress shoes. "I can't wait to lay eyes on him," she said. "I haven't not seen him twelve days in a row since he came to Arcadia."

"Well, your drought should end at noon."

The black Mercedes SUV came up the gravel drive slowly and heavily, a bear sniffing its way through the woods. Through my binoculars I could see the alert young man driving and the older man beside him, and barely make out the shapes of Rex and Patricia Hickman jostling gently in the back. Behind the vehicle, within a faint cloud of dust, the steel gate rolled back into place. I set the remote on the picnic table and checked my watch: 11:33 a.m. Clay was due at noon. I felt the .45 autoloader strapped inside my left calf. Sweaty and rough. Loose-cut cotton trousers and a black T-shirt, light jacket, and low-rise work boots to accommodate the gun. I hoped to be the only armed citizen at this convention but doubted that I would be. Especially if DeMaris and Bodart figured out my trick and decided to loop back and look for the smoke at Rancho de los Robles.

Rex got out first and marched straight toward me as Patricia climbed out of the vehicle behind him. He wore a dark suit and a white shirt. Patricia hustled to catch up, wobbling in dress shoes, the hem of her white dress lilting. The two security men flanked her, slowing their pace to hers, and escorted her into the shade of the palapa.

Rex pumped my hand, then Paige Hulet's. His two security men drifted from the shade to the sun but stayed within earshot. Compact men, sunglasses, the unsubtle signature of weapons under their windbreakers. Rex glanced dismissively at Burt, Lindsey, and Wesley. "Any word from my son?"

"None anticipated," I said.

"He's due here in exactly twenty-six minutes."

Patricia shook my hand and introduced herself to my tenants. She looked flushed and eager. She brushed a fingertip under one eye. "I haven't seen my son in a year. That's too long! I hope this all goes well. It has to go well."

"Explain your plan," said Rex.

I told them what had led us here and what they were about to see. I explained their son's assignment to White Fire, and his relationship to Briggs Spencer, Donald Tice, and Joe Bodart. And of Clay's gradual awakening, of the flash drives and the video they contained. I explained Clay's enthusiasm for **Nell Flanagan's San Diego**, and that I had impersonated a Nell Flanagan story editor to get Clay to come here to tape a show.

Last, I told them about the drugs that Spencer and his co-conspirators at Arcadia had secretly used to keep Clay numb and incoherent for three years, and unable to face his past, or his family's visits. Paige explained the altered formulary, the medication procedure, how she'd been duped by Spencer and Tice.

Rex and Patricia both stared at her silently, then turned to me. I could see the anger roiling on his face, and the astonishment on hers. "They gave him drugs to **make** him crazy?" she asked. "To make him afraid of us?"

Rex exchanged looks with his security men. "We'll deal with that son of a bitch Spencer later," he said to his wife. I thought: **Let him.**

"The video you're about to see is sickening," I said. "But we need to accomplish two things.

One is convince Clay to tell his story to us, in the absence of Nell Flanagan and Briggs Spencer. The second thing is to upload it to YouTube before Arcadia security or Joe Bodart's Special Activities spooks can intervene. I've thrown Spencer and Bodart off the trail, but probably not for long. We might not get more than a minute's warning if they figure their way here."

I told the Hickmans and Paige that if anyone threatened us here, in any way, Lindsey and Wesley would take them and Clay into the house and down into the wine cellar. "It's the safest place on the property. Burt and I and your two hired gentlemen will deal with whatever disagreements arise. Lindsey and Wesley will be there with you."

"Absolutely not," said Rex. "If there's trouble, I'm on the front line. Nonnegotiable."

"You want your son back?" I asked.

"Of course I do."

"Then do what I say and your chances go up."

"Front line, Mr. Ford."

"Rex! You can't—"

"I can, Pat," he said quietly. "I'm bringing him home."

In the silence that followed Rex Hickman's words I raised my binoculars to the paved road. Sequoia Blain's silver pickup truck came along it toward the dirt access road. Clay was at the wheel with Sequoia beside him, both looking intently up the rise to where the house stood. She pointed and said something and Clay drove past the dirt road, around the hill, and out of sight.

Five minutes later they were back. This time Clay slowed, swung onto the dirt road, and accelerated toward the gate. I took the remote off the barbecue and hit the button. The gate shuddered, and even at this distance I heard the faint clank of the chain as it rolled open. After a long pause the truck started up the drive. I felt a fragile, uncertain happiness that Clay Hickman was now on my property and the gate was about to close behind him. I'd finally bagged him.

I walked down the road and around the bend to wave them into the barnyard.

42

Getting out of the truck, Clay looked somehow larger than he had in the cramped Harbor Palms Motel room. Jeans and a black T-shirt, same camo boots, a fresh haircut. No bulge of a weapon. He looked at me, then took a nylon laptop case from the cab and went around to the other side. Sequoia got out. One look and I saw that she'd made me. I waited for her reaction. She took Clay's free arm in one hand and together they came toward me.

"Hello, Mr. Wills," he said, stopping six feet away.

"Hello, Clay. My name is Roland Ford and I'm the investigator hired to locate you."

His body tensed and he looked sharply at the girl. "Sequoia?"

"I didn't know, Clay," she said. "But this is the guy I told you about and I think we can trust him."

"Is Nell here?" he asked.

"Under the palapa over there," I said. "With Dr. Hulet and the videographers."

"And Dr. Spencer, too?"

"He's on his way. Come on. I'll introduce you."

Burt came down from the patio, introduced himself as Nell's security. "I'll have to check that case and pat you down, Clay."

"I said I wouldn't bring the gun."

"Then this'll be a snap."

Clay handed him the laptop case. Burt opened, inspected, and zipped it back shut and handed it to me. Clay spread his legs and raised his arms and Burt searched him. When he was finished, Burt stood back and looked at Sequoia, then to me. Her jeans and T-shirt were too tight to hide a gun.

"She's okay," I said to Burt.

"Sorry for all this," he said. He took the laptop and handed it back to Clay. "Welcome to the Ranch of the Oaks."

Burt led us across the barnyard, up the drive, and around the bend. I brought up the rear. Sequoia turned and gave me a hard look, then Clay did likewise. Gravel under our shoes, warm breeze. Climbing the railroad-tie steps to the patio, I felt the excitement rippling toward me from the people gathered under the palapa. Like high voltage in the air. I also sensed the jagged suspicion coming from Clay and Sequoia as they followed Burt up the last steps and onto the level ground of the patio. I was the last one up, ready to stop Clay if he panicked at the sight of his parents and tried to run back to the truck.

"Mom? Dad?"

"We're here to take you home," said Patricia.

I waved them over. Patricia threw herself into Clay's arms. Rex set a hand on his son's shoulder and waited his turn. Clay looked past them to me, his face a mask of stunned confusion. Then the three of them clenched like teammates, Sequoia still hanging on to Clay's arm, and Paige Hulet pressing into the pack.

A murmur of voices, soft and comforting. The pack swayed. Slowly and with collective resolve, it shuffled, many-footed and cumbersome, toward the big table, where finally Clay was deposited onto a wooden bench. Rex, Patricia, and Paige untangled themselves and stood close, hands still on him. Sequoia squeezed in by his side.

With the noontime sunlight hitting his face I saw that Clay's confusion was being beaten back by other forces. Curiosity? Surprise? His eyes—hazel and blue—looked up at the people around him, and I realized he was seeing them for the first time in years from outside the drug-induced cage in which Briggs Spencer had locked him. Wonder and doubt. Hope and fear. He flattened his palms on the table as if to rise, but the hands remained heavy on his shoulders, and Sequoia held fast to his arm.

I followed Clay's gaze to Wesley's video camera, waiting on its tripod nearby. Then to Lindsey's pink laptop, loaded with her editing software, and to Lindsey herself, who gave him a calm and welcoming look. "I hear you've got some video for us to see," she said. "And a story to tell."

"But where's Nell Flanagan? And all the TV cameras?"

"I'm Lindsey. I was a Reaper sensor ball operator for three years of my life. I've been in war, and I know video and what to do with it."

He looked at me, implosion on his face.

"She's not coming, Clay," I said.

"Where's Dr. Spencer?"

I sat down across from him, and looked him hard in the eyes. "He's not coming, either. His book is out next week. He wrote almost nothing about Aaban and Roshaan. It's up to you to do that."

"You betrayed me."

"I'm giving you a chance to tell your story to the world."

He looked at me with cold resentment but said nothing.

"Listen," I said. "You run your video and explain what happened at White Fire. Wesley will tape you. When you're done, Lindsey will cut your story down and edit it over ten minutes of your video. Then upload it to YouTube. Ten minutes is what they give you, Clay. To tell your story to the world."

I watched the emotions come to his face. Rolling beneath its surface like swells. Anger. Disbelief. Disappointment. Determination. Anger again. Then a long, indecipherable gaze at the pond. Clay Hickman's thousand-yard stare. His former selves seemed to parade across his face: the newborn not expected to live, the pained infant, the struggling boy, the determined adolescent, the healing teenager discovering the power of his own will, the young man gaining strength and trying to please, the scholar and the champion athlete who watched the planes hit the towers on TV again and again and joined the Air Force to fight back.

"Clay," I said. "You've got an hour of video and we've got an hour to make this happen. I know you wanted Nell and Spencer here, but your bottle is half full, young man."

"Come home," said Paige Hulet. "We want you back, Clay."

"Please," said Patricia.

"Bring the white fire to Deimos," said Sequoia. "Right now."

"Son?" asked Rex. "You can do this. You always did whatever you put your mind to."

Clay closed his eyes and lifted his chin. Like

a bird dog into the wind. His face was peaceful now and he looked asleep. The breeze shivered his white hair. "I got to the prison in March. It was cold. My first thought when I saw the old building was **You're not going to be the same when you leave here. If you ever do.**"

43

Clay's introduction to White Fire brought silence from his audience. The forbidding stone exterior. The naked trees and fretful sky and the blackening piles of snow against the courtyard walls. Clay climbing out of a Romanian government truck, puffs of condensation from his nostrils. Shuffling across the stones, raising a hand to the camera, an uncertain smile. Nineteen by then. Just a boy.

Soft exclamations.

Then a montage of interior shots: the "lobby" entrance and the mess and the small dark rooms where the Americans lived, then the cells and interrogation rooms with the ceiling chains and shackles, the plastic screens for walling, the isolation boxes and restraint chairs, the waterboards.

Murmurs and grunts. "Oh, Clay," his mother said softly. "You were never that."

Wesley wedged himself in closer to record Clay in response. "I was part of the team, Mom."

"He did what he had to do, Pat," said Rex.

Then Aaban arriving in the White Fire courtyard, glaring at the camera with hatred in his eyes. Next a blast of death metal music and Aaban writhing on his toes, dangling by ceiling chains as Briggs Spencer interrogated him. Then Aaban with the Plague of Insects being lowered over his head. Aaban in a wooden collar, walled, and walled again. Spencer's questions, patient and monotonous. Compliance blows, legs pulped. Aaban convulsing on the waterboard, Clay's arms locked around his towel-smothered head, torquing his body for breath as Dr. Briggs Spencer aimed the next rush of water. Gargled agony and Spencer's relentless interrogation.

Silence under the palapa.

A smash cut to the courtyard of White Fire and the arrival of a young boy. "Roshaan," said Clay. "Aaban's son. Eleven years old. Dr. Spencer thought we could exploit the boy to get to the father."

"Good god," said Paige.

"No," said Rex.

"You didn't," said Patricia.

My burner phone vibrated. I stepped away from the show and checked my watch.

Dick: "I got pulled over for speeding outside El Centro. Eighty-five in the seventy. Exactly thirty-eight minutes ago. Couldn't talk my way out of it so I stood there in the sun while the son of a bitch wrote me up. Kept an eye on the cars that passed me. So guess what? A black Charger and a white Range Rover went by. Blacked out windows, just like you said. Kind of close together, too, like a team. It took the cop forever to cite me, like he was just learning how to print or something. When he finally handed me the ticket to sign I saw the same black Charger and white Range Rover coming back in the other direction. Moving right along, this time. Back toward San Diego."

"Turn the transmitter off and keep going."

"Sorry, Roland. They had to have made me. I had your lucky hat on and everything."

"You did well. Keep going."

I rang off. My ruse had worked so far: by the time DeMaris and Tice had discovered that I was not the truck driver in the white hat, they were well on their way to Yuma. Now that they knew something was up, they would have to figure Rancho de los Robles, but they were over an hour away. Time enough. And more good news: Bodart, tracking the phone GPS in my truck, had the high-tech luxury of following from a much greater distance. Miles, in fact. So it was possible that he had missed the speeding stop altogether and was still headed west for Arizona. Possible.

I had my hour.

Back to the patio. Groans of disgust as Briggs Spencer aimed another flood into Aaban's anguished face. Young Roshaan stood in the background, plainly terrified.

The next minutes played out with all of the nightmare choreography I remembered. Roshaan's rush for his chained father, Clay's takedown and choke hold on the boy, the Malinois growling midair, the frantic scramble to revive Roshaan, and the staggering, unbelieving realization that he was dead.

For a long while I heard nothing but the hiss of the April breeze in the palm fronds of the palapa.

Then came the scenes that Clay wouldn't show me in the Oceanside motel. As they played out, I understood why. First, Roshaan's body, lying curled up and wrapped in blankets in what appeared to be a very old steamer trunk. Someone had combed his hair and placed bricks around him. The room was dark but Roshaan rested pale in a beam of icy light. Then a cut to Clay and John Vazquez. They were bulkily dressed against the cold—gloves, watch caps pulled down snug—and push-pulling the heavy trunk across a river walk caked in dirty snow. The trunk was wrapped in chains and padlocks and it scraped loudly. The Dambovita flowed just beyond them, high, black, and sullen. The two men grunted and their breath hung in the cold air, and Donald Tice's hands shook as he held the camera. Clay and Vazz grunted and muscled the trunk up onto the stone wall and rested for a moment, looking at each other. Clay glanced at Tice. Then the rasp of trunk and chain on icy stone, and the sudden dive. Roshaan made a neat, small splash and vanished.

Silence again from the living. I looked from face to face, their expressions so varied and strong.

Clay emptied.

Paige stunned.

Rex in grim shame.

Patricia in disbelief.

Sequoia in dull acceptance.

Lindsey nodding sadly, as if she'd somehow foreseen all of this.

Wesley still shooting video, and the two security men staring stoically at the screen.

Gradually, in that wrenching and frozen silence, I heard the distinct but distant chop of a helicopter. From the edge of the canopy I watched it descend from the western sky. Easy to identify because I'd seen it before—Briggs Spencer's bright copper Sikorsky 434 coming at some speed toward us. I got my binoculars, stepped outside the palapa, and watched it approach. It wasn't long before I could make out the rough outline of Briggs Spencer in the pilot's seat, aviator sunglasses on, headphones clamped over his bushy gray hair. Next to him, the unmistakable dome of Joe Bodart's shaven head. And behind them, in one of the backseats, a third man, obscured by sunglasses and a ball cap.

An arc of bitter regret jumped through me: the hour of time I had tried to steal was now cut in half. I'd bet everything on that hour. Bet that I could control dangerous men. DeMaris and Tice had taken the bait but Spencer and Bodart had smelled out the truth. Who would pay the price?

Spencer continued flying toward us, then banked away and lowered the chopper a quarter mile beyond the pond. Through the binoculars I watched the helo settle to the ground. Bodart and the Backseat Man climbed out. Another quarter mile to the south, dust rose in a faint cloud. A black SUV came into view, picking its way deliberately along the narrow road, heading toward the idling helo.

With my guts in an angry knot, I pieced it together: Dick was made by DeMaris, who called Spencer, who scooped up Bodart in the Sikorsky and headed here. Bodart hadn't fallen for my trick at all. He and his men had never set sail across the desert. He had let DeMaris take that risky bet, but DeMaris had made it pay. I raised the glasses again to confirm: two of Bodart's Harbor Palms Motel men in the SUV.

Spencer took the copper Sikorsky up fast, climbing back north. The machine was bright and somehow privileged in the sky, like something flown by gods or conquerors. It came straight toward us.

"Spencer," said Paige. "What is he doing?"

"Get under the tables, all of you. Take the computers and camera. Now!"

The Hickman security men scrambled off the patio and dropped into shooting stances on the embankment, pistols out but pointed down. I stood just under the palapa canopy, between the incoming helicopter and the tables. Through the growing noise of the rotor blades I could hear the ruckus behind me, table legs rasping on concrete.

Suddenly Clay ran past me and down the embankment toward the water, cursing. Paige ran after him. Spencer was half across the pond by then, lowering then hovering for a good look at them. I remembered the gun port and the pistol. Paige screamed, her words scattered in the rotor storm. The pond water whipped and Clay waded in to his knees, shaking one fist and yelling into the sharp clatter of the blades. Through the slop of whitecaps and rising mist Paige tried to pull him to shore. Through the glasses I saw Spencer with one hand on the stick, looking down at them with what looked like amusement. Then at me.

Like a cat losing interest in its mouse, he sidled the chopper my way, closer to the palapa, rotors whapping sharply, palapa fronds shivering as Clay's distant words blew across the water. Paige pulling, Clay not budging. Blade wind in my face and eyes, Spencer studying me, rising and lowering, forward then back. Suddenly the Sikorsky roared and rose, belly to my face, a suck of rotor wind as it reared up and backed away. Then leveled, and swooped down on Clay and Paige.

Chaos next, and the free fall of my heart.

44

Wesley and Lindsey slid down the embankment, leaning back for balance, sidestepping until they hit shore, then crashed into the water. The Hickman bodyguards followed them to the shoreline and raised their weapons. Slap of rotors on water, sunlight bouncing off the copper finish.

The helo lowered over Clay and Paige like a huge steel hen settling on her eggs. I saw the barrel of Spencer's coyote-killing pistol appear through the gun port and swivel down. Astonished at what he was about to do, I knelt and raised my pistol. Spencer's gun boomed. Clay and Paige both fell into the choppy water. I cut loose four rounds and heard the rapid cracks of the guns to my left. Bullets hit the Sikorsky in dull metallic thunks, hardly audible. Sparks jumped and the little craft shuddered. Then another blast from Spencer's gun.

Paige grabbed Clay by his shirt and they trudged—waist-deep and in agonizing slow motion—toward shore. Suddenly Clay wheeled and raised his fist, brandishing it at Spencer as if he could reach him with it. Across that distance, across the years. Spencer fired again and a plume of water jumped between them. Paige cried out and latched on to Clay again, pulling. Rotors whapping and the security men shooting methodically. I pictured Spencer behind the smoked-black fuselage and fired twice more. Burt Short appeared near my side, unleashing two thunderous rounds from an assault shotgun he must have kept in his casita.

The helo skittered weirdly, still sparking. A round from Spencer smacked into the palapa pole behind me and I felt the chips hit my neck. The Sikorsky belched a puff of black smoke as it banked high and fast over the pond and accelerated away to the west. Clay and Paige, clutching each other, clambered closer to shore with Wesley, Lindsey, and the two security men closing in around them. Paige's white blouse was a flag of watery blood and she moved with clumsy determination. Rex and Patricia waded out past the shoreline and helped pull Clay and Paige through the mud onto dry land. The muck had taken Patricia's shoes. Beside me, Burt was reloading without looking at his weapon, his eyes trained on the chopper.

"Call 911, Burt. **Now.**"

The Sikorsky wove through the sky like a big smoking snake, carving wider and wider until the tail swung around in frantic counterbalance. A slow nosedive. Through the glasses I saw Spencer fighting to land the helo, both hands wrenching the stick, jamming himself back against the seat for leverage as the craft whirled around and around. He got it back under control. Black smoke billowed, but the Sikorsky was stable again as it descended. Half a mile beyond the pond Spencer coaxed the wounded machine to the ground. Where it exploded.

Through the binoculars I watched him flail from the cockpit, covered in flames. Dragging one leg, he thrashed his arms wildly against the fire, then threw himself to the ground and rolled downhill through the dry brush. But the fuel that had drenched him burned viciously, and with each roll the dampened flames jumped to life on him again. Spencer finally came to a stop at the bottom of the small hillock, fought to his feet, spread his arms and raised his face to the sky. Hair broiling and mouth agape, he crumpled into a heap of joyous fire.

The black SUV approached from the far south. I could make out Bodart at the wheel and Backseat Man now in the front passenger seat, and the two Harbor Palms company men in back. They seemed to be arguing. The SUV hunched to a stop on a small hillock, and through my binoculars I could see Bodart jump out with his own field glass. He looked toward the smoking helo in the distance, and Briggs Spencer, who lay unmoving in his bed of flames. Bodart snapped something to the other men and climbed back into the vehicle. Which lurched off toward Spencer. I gauged that, after getting there and seeing they could do nothing for Spencer, it would take them less than ten minutes to descend on us.

Twenty minutes, max, I thought. Maybe less.

I helped get Paige to the house. She was shot above her hip—a small entry wound in her back and a larger exit hole between her ribs and pelvis. Her skin was already shock-purple and the surrounding flesh swollen. Bleeding freely but not hemorrhaging.

I ordered Clay, Lindsey, and the Hickmans into the barn to edit and splice. Told the security men to go with them and be ready for Bodart and his company thugs. Gave Lindsey her twenty-minute deadline.

Wesley, Sequoia, and I got Paige onto the long leather sofa near the living room fireplace, used two rolls of gauze to stanch her bleeding. Lots of isopropyl. Propped up on her elbows, she watched dispassionately as a doctor would. Sweat rolled down her face and her hair was a tangle of pond water and mud. She kept asking to see Clay. We wrapped her in blankets while Burt got a fire going, his pistol-grip shotgun propped against the fireplace rocks.

Heart thumping, ears ringing, but clear-headed—as on our door-to-door searches in Fallujah—I looked through a kitchen window to the pond and the hills and the narrow dirt road that would bring Team Bodart to us. No sign of them from this angle. So I scrambled to the front of the house, where I could see the long driveway that the sheriffs and fire department would use. I reloaded my .45, wondered who would arrive first—the deputies, fire and rescue, paramedics, or the Special Activities Division of the CIA.

When sirens wailed, I had my answer. I looked down to the road, saw the county convoy, then pressed the gate opener. A moment later five ve-hicles, lights flashing and sirens shrieking, raced through the gate and up the drive.

Back under the palapa I glassed the two-track and watched as Bodart brought the black SUV to a stop on the far side of the pond. He threw open his door and stood on the running board for a better look at Spencer and his demolished helo. I waited for what action they would take for their old friend and ally Briggs Spencer. Deimos, god of terror. And what they would do with Clay and his video, so close to them now, but so well protected. I had an opinion on both questions and I was right.

Bodart cursed, swung back into the driver's seat, and did a neat highway-patrol turn to reverse his direction. Put some gas into his getaway. The SUV bounced and skidded, the men inside rising and falling like crash test dummies. Brake lights, dust rising, tires swerving on the sandy, decomposed granite that would eventually lead them to the paved county road and the interstate.

In the barn Lindsey clicked the upload bar on the screen. She looked up at me with cool pride. Clay sat on a workbench between his mother and father, hunched in a barn blanket, pale and spent. His straight white hair plastered down over his forehead. Patricia held his hand. The security men stood watch at the windows.

"It'll take half an hour to upload, a few more minutes for them to get it ready to post," said Lindsey. "Is Dr. Hulet doing okay?"

"I think so. We got the bleeding slowed down. Paramedics coming up the drive right now."

"What do we tell the cops?" asked Rex.

"Just the truth," I said. "Spencer fired first. I'll keep them out of here as long as I can. If the upload is finished before they get here, come to the house. Make noise and keep your hands up. If you hear them coming here before the upload is done, hide the laptop up in the hayloft and let it finish. The deputies will be touchy, so be cool."

Clay caught me just outside. He worked a hand out through the blanket. Still shivering. I thought he was offering to shake hands, then saw his offer was something else.

"Thank you, Mr. Ford."

"We'll do it again sometime."

Clay cracked a small smile.

From under the palapa I looked southwest through my binoculars to where Spencer had died. No smoke now. Just a distant black stain with a gutted helo in the middle, bits of shiny copper catching the sunlight. And a blackened form lying downhill of the crash. Crumpled and small. Reminded me of the tormented figures in Clay Hickman's paintings. I thought of Dawn Spencer. Looked down at Paige's blood on the patio concrete.

Time to face the music.

Back in the house I pushed Clay's gifts under a couch cushion on my way to a window. Then watched the sheriff's vehicles block the driveway and park so no one could get in or out. Three deputies, guns drawn, crouched low. Two more covered them from behind the open doors of a cruiser. Lights blipping, sirens off. I recognized the team leader, a deputy who had been a rookie patrolman when I first worked with him eight years ago. Antwan Sheffield.

I opened the door and waited. Then slowly stepped out, hands up. Felt the barrels turn my way. Neck hair rising, race of heart. Sheffield crabbed toward me with a two-handed grip on his gun, aiming at my chest.

"Sheff."

"Don't move, Ford."

"There's a shot woman on my living room couch."

"You still don't move."

The next-nearest deputy took my coat collar and pushed me into the wall face-first. Cheeks and hands on old adobe brick. Through the open front door I could see through to Paige. The deputy frisked me high to low. Felt him pull the .45 free. Muttered something. He checked me all over again for a second gun, then yanked my arms off the wall one at a time. He pulled the restraints tight enough to hurt and keep me obedient.

Three other deputies clanked heavily past, guns out. Then the paramedics, who went straight to Paige and Burt. Burt started in telling them what to do.

Antwan holstered his weapon, took me by one arm, and pushed me inside. "What is this situation here, Ford?"

"A long story."

"How many more guns we walking into?"

I nodded to the shotgun against the fireplace,

told him about the two armed security men and the four innocents out in the barn.

"Anybody else hurt?" he asked.

I told him we had a dead man in the scrub brush half a mile away. And that he'd shot the woman.

"You saw him do it?"

"We all did."

He gave me a hard look. "You sure brought some bad heat to this department, man."

I shrugged, no bandwidth for any of that just now.

He turned me around and cut the cuffs off just as the paramedics wheeled Paige past me on a gurney. She lay covered to her chin in a blue SD County blanket, an IV-drip kit taped fast to one arm. I looked at Sheffield, then followed the gurney toward the ambulance.

"Clay?" she asked.

"He's okay."

"Get him home, Roland." She smiled weakly.

"I'll see you soon, Paige."

"Bullets hurt."

"Best doctors in the world in San Diego." I touched her hand as they glided her to the back of the truck. The gurney tucked into itself, and in she went.

Antwan had come up behind me. "It's show-and-tell time."

45

I sat up with Paige at Palomar Hospital that night. Her wound was painful but not life-threatening and she seemed serious about wearing the scar proudly. The drugs made her loopy and talkative. Then somewhere midsentence she'd close her eyes and sleep half an hour, then come to again.

"What about the video?"

"Posted and eleven thousand views, as of two hours ago."

"It's gonna really mess some people up."

"I talked to Rex. The FBI wants to see Clay first thing tomorrow."

"How is he? Clay?"

"Just fine. I told you."

"He's home from the war," she said dreamily.

"He took the long way back," I said.

"I was going to resign my position at Arcadia if Clay went home. Now I don't have to. Since my boss tried to kill me."

We watched the San Diego news. Details were sketchy, but early this afternoon a gunman in a

helicopter shot and wounded a woman near a remote Fallbrook-area residence before the helicopter crashed and burst into flames. The gunman
died at the scene but the unidentified woman
has been hospitalized and is expected to recover.
Next up, will the Chargers stay in San Diego or
won't they? It all comes down to money. Stay
tuned. I thought: **Just wait until they find out
who the dead gunman is. A whole new round
of stories.**

"I'm so happy they expect me to recover."

"I recommend it."

"Was it foolish? What I did—trying to protect him?"

"Well, you got away with it, Paige. And you
helped Clay get away with his life."

"I'm glad they didn't arrest you," she said.

"They still might. They have a lot to sort out."

She closed her eyes, a slight smile on her face.
Then sleep. I watched her for a while, thinking:
**Paige, I've been wondering about something.
I bet you know what. We'll talk, later. To-
night, sleep tight. I'm heading home soon.
Stiff bourbon and a smoke. I hope you feel
better in the morning.**

Squeezed her hand gently, touched her cheek.

I sat for a long while, listening to the chorus of
hospital sounds, the hums and beeps and bumps
and the quiet talk from the ICU nurses' station
outside. The pad of Crocs across the floor.

I was truly weary. Burnt out but on edge. Too tired to think clearly. But one thought was clear: I knew exactly where all of this had left me in relation to certain dangerous and guilty men.

Bodart knew that I suspected him of the murder of John Vazquez. Knew that I could drop his name to the Mendocino detectives any time. They could get him or his "short, stocky" partner on something as small as a fingerprint left in the Vazquez home. And Bodart also knew that I was a witness to his armed raid on an Oceanside motel room. If that wasn't enough, I could identify him as one of four men who left the corpse of Briggs Spencer smoldering in the hillside scrub near Fallbrook. Such facts if known would land him in court, possibly in prison, and certainly cast his agency in the public light they so loathed. I thought of Laura and Michael. I wanted someone to pay for John Vazquez.

Then there were DeMaris and Tice, who had conspired with Spencer to sedate Clay Hickman with powerful drugs to keep him silent. Three years of that at Arcadia, **an exclusive wellness community for treatment of mental and emotional disorders,** at twenty-five grand a month. With testimony from Paige Hulet and myself, any prosecutor I've ever met could prove that charge.

So what exactly was I, Roland Ford, in their eyes?

A threat. A serious one. The one person who knew what they had done, from White Fire to Arcadia to Mendocino to Rancho de los Robles.

Sitting there in the ICU with Paige, I tried to see me differently in their eyes. Maybe I had it wrong. Exaggerating my own importance. A small man with big ideas. But I couldn't figure it another way. Not with men like Bodart and DeMaris. Tunnel vision, on a mission. I was their biggest problem. And I believed they would try to make me go away. Quickly.

So I had the stay-alive plan.

Outside, the night was foggy and cool and the parking lot lights were wrapped in mist. Yellow, sickly lights. The lot was almost full. Windshields and windows sweating.

As I headed toward my truck a car door opened, then another. But neither shut. And no interior lights went on. Misty reflections off dark windows. Movement in the yellow light. A tingle on my forehead.

More motion, two figures coalescing near my truck—the approximate sizes and shapes of Joe Bodart and Alec DeMaris. I stopped and looked through the fog at them. I congratulated myself. **They've come for me.** Grim satisfaction in this, nerves sparking.

I stopped between two cars, partial cover, and dialed Burt. Slid the phone back into my trouser pocket. Then I wrapped my hand around the handle of the .45 in the right pocket of my baggy barn coat, took up the ultralight .22 in the left pocket, and walked toward my truck.

Fog drifting, asphalt wet. Bodart wore his leather duster as in his Wrangler days at White Fire. Thumbs hooked on his belt like a cowpoke. DeMaris in a hoodie, workout sweats, and duty boots, black gloves.

"The fun couple," I said.

"Clay's video is up to thirty-seven thousand views as of five minutes ago," said DeMaris. "Viral as Ebola. Nice job, Ford. You helped an insane traitor betray his own country."

"I thought his countrymen should see where their tax dollars go," I said.

"To torturers like us?" asked Bodart. "Who don't play nice?"

"What you did to Roshaan was a lot more than not nice. Live with it. Clay is."

"The FBI will arrest him tomorrow," said Bodart. "The charges will include treason, still punishable by death. If the girl won't cooperate they'll charge her, too. Co-conspirator. They might even go after you, Roland. Given how the video was created and uploaded on your property."

I thought about that. Concluded what I always conclude regarding people like the Hickmans. "Rex will get his son the best lawyers money can buy. I'd give them better than even odds against the United States government."

"And what about you?" asked DeMaris.

"I'll buy as much justice as I can afford."

"Better hope it's enough," said Bodart. "But we don't care about Clay Hickman anymore. Damage done. Now we care about us."

"I thought it would come to that."

"How much did you tell the sheriffs about Bodart and me?" asked DeMaris.

I reminded myself that they were here to kill me. Probably not right here in the light of a hospital parking lot. Somewhere a little more private. I was the only thing standing between them and blue skies.

"Just your basics."

They looked at each other. It was a lot like reading the dialogue in cartoon bubbles. Alec wanted to draw his gun and shoot me dead right there and then. Bodart wanted to stick with whatever they'd planned. An accident. A disappearance. A sudden heart attack from a practically untraceable drug.

"Well, Roland," said Bodart. "The San Diego County Sheriff's can't take on the CIA's Special Activities Division. That's a losing bet."

"He's dumb enough to take it," said DeMaris. "He's a witness to all of it. The formulary at Arcadia, you guys storming onto his property. He might even point the posse at Mendocino."

Bodart gave DeMaris an assessing stare. "We need you to forget us, Ford. Briggs was a lone gunman. Off his rocker and got what he deserved. You're the one person with the bigger picture. How can we make sure you keep it to yourself?"

"Couple million?"

"Thought of that," said DeMaris. "But you've got your dead wife's money. So I figured, keep it simple." He drew a thick black semiautomatic from the hoodie handwarmer. "Clean. Never registered."

So after shooting me in the head with it, he could put it in my hand. Arrange my body in the cab of my truck, just so. One of the several scenarios that had been playing through my mind the last few hours.

"We're going to take a drive in your truck," said DeMaris. "The three of us."

"Yeah," I said. "I figured you'd shoot me somewhere less public."

"If shooting was in the plan you'd be filled with holes right now," said DeMaris. "We're going somewhere we can talk some damned sense into you."

"Just let me go home," I said. "I'll take a shower and wash the stink of you people off me and never give you another thought."

Bodart smiled and shook his head. Right hand in the pocket of the duster. DeMaris had a stony expression and a small yellow glimmer in each eye. "Hands out and up, **real** slow."

My chance of shooting through the barn coat and hitting them both? Poor. Even worse if I tried to draw. My forehead scar was burning and my guts were knotting and my feet felt like I was standing in a cold river. Maybe the Dambovita. Roshaan.

I let go of the guns and raised both hands. DeMaris put the barrel of his autoloader to my forehead and Bodart took my weapons. "You should have stuck with divorces," Bodart said.

"I will from now on."

"You don't have a now on," he said. "Your fault. Here you are—amateur cop, amateur good guy. Amateur human. I explained to you out in your barn, very clearly, what you were up against. I told you point-blank that we're thorough and we don't stop until the job is done. But no. You wouldn't leave Clay to the pros."

He shoved me into the driver's seat of my truck, ran his free hand through the map compartment on the door, then slammed it. De-Maris was already waiting in the passenger seat, his pistol pointed at my ribs. He fished around in the center console. Then the glove box. Then under the driver's seat, switching his pistol to his left hand and holding it tight against my side. Bodart got into the backseat behind me, touched something cold and hard to the back of my head.

"Drive, baby."

46

South on Interstate 15, light traffic to Pala Road. Then winding through the farms to Pala village and past the casino toward the hills. Night close and foggy, moon a smudge. Windshield wipers framing the chaparral-covered hills. I thought of Justine on her last flight, just after she realized something was wrong. How she must have felt.

"Hey, Ford," said DeMaris, "did you ever get into Paige's pants?"

I said nothing.

"Wanted to myself, but I have a wife to consider."

I couldn't help it. "That was good of you, Alec."

A beat. Tires on wet asphalt. I could see half of Bodart's face in the rearview. Shining bald head and the cowcatcher mustache. Small eyes. He kept looking behind us.

"Ford, I can never tell if you're serious," De-Maris said. "It's another reason I can't stand you. That, and the superiority thing."

"I can't help it."

"Semper fi doesn't mean anything to you, does it?"

"It does. But I'm surprised the Marines would take an imbecile like you."

DeMaris nodded intently, seemed to consider this. "She's an odd one, that Dr. Hulet. Do anything for her patients. Not surprised she almost got killed for Clay Hickman today. Can't figure what goes on in that brain of hers. What a sweet piece she must be when she lets her hair down, though. And I mean exactly that—down from that damned bun. If she ever does. Maybe I'll give her another try."

"Did you help Spencer and Tice dope up Clay for three years?"

"Help? I supervised."

"Was it you or Bodart who let the Vazquez interview get out of hand?"

DeMaris stared at me, then glanced behind him. "Joe?"

"He can ask all the questions he wants," Bodart said from behind me. Touched his gun to my head again. "You wouldn't have that dwarf Burt try to follow us, would you?"

"No, sir. No dwarf."

"Amazing he got my gun. One of my few professional embarrassments."

"So what happened up in Mendocino?" I asked again.

"It was Joe and his buddy," said DeMaris. "You know how those company guys can get."

"They gave me a youngster to work with," said Bodart. "Turned into a mess. I liked John very much."

Silence then as the truck hummed along. Wipers clunking off and on. Solemn DeMaris lit by dashboard lights, animal twinkles in his eyes. Elevation rising. Pines now outside the windows, faintly darker than the night, tapered and tall.

"Coming up on South Grade Road, Ford," he said. "Make the stop, then turn left. Go nice and slow."

The road climbed, switchbacks and down-shifts. Through the fog I saw a wall of trees and three staggered yellow signs with warning arrows marking a curve ahead.

Bodart leaned forward. "There's a turnout on your right, just past the arrows. Pull in, shut down the engine and the lights. We'll see if your little friend is on his way."

We waited in the dark for five minutes. Cold at this elevation, the air humid and sweet. Only one car passed, going down-mountain and away. Another five minutes and no one.

"Onward," said Bodart.

Another winding mile to State Park Road. A sign for Palomar Observatory, seven miles.

Huge boulders pale in the darkness, scattered like some god or giant had tossed them there. Arcadia not far to the east. I wondered if they were planning to put me in Arcadian dirt. Good idea, really. Clay dug out. Roland dug in. Not many prying eyes, with Arcadia security on the job. **Requiescat in pace,** Roland.

Another turn onto an unmarked ribbon of asphalt, and I recognized it as the same way I'd come to Arcadia that first day. I remembered the morning, so April and hopeful. Up we climbed, the transmission gearing down on the steep curves, upshifting on the short straights. Then the unmarked Arcadia entry road, unpaved and obscured by trees. Half a mile of gravel until the asphalt started up again, thick and black and freshly resurfaced. We finally came to the guardhouse, closed this late. DeMaris aimed a remote at it and the barrier went up.

Arcadia, hunkered in forest and fog, rose from the base of the mountain ahead. Bevels of glass and concrete, dully reflective and shifting. "There's a turnaround," said DeMaris. "Swing in and park. Off with the engine and lights."

We sat in the dark for another five minutes. Nobody. Then we took the wide north loop around the buildings, which gradually angled west. The road pinched down to a bumpy two-track. Sixty acres of forest is a lot of ground. The truck straddled the trail, climbing through pines and manzanita until it leveled off in a small clearing. Oaks and toyon rising high.

"Circle around and park facing out," said De-Maris. "Good boy. There."

Engine and headlights off. Ticking under the truck hood. Under my hood, heart artillery. Ear sirens. Mouth of sand and eyes wired wide. Door-to-door, Fallujah. No M16. Nothing but the plan. Fight it off. Stay alert. Stay alive. Stay. Oorah.

Bodart stood back from the driver's-side window, gun holstered.

"Get out slow, Roland," said DeMaris. He waved the autoloader impatiently.

When I stepped out, Bodart got me by the coat collar and pushed me face-first and hard against the truck bed. I heard him step away. DeMaris took his place, gun barrel to my head. In the distance and through the trees twinkled Arcadia.

"Might want to get your thoughts in order," said DeMaris.

"Give me a minute."

"You bet."

Past the truck I could see Bodart standing inside the trees on the far side of the clearing, his phone utility light throwing a circle of bright white on the ground. Not exactly ground. Absence of ground. A hole. Longer than a man, and no bottom visible. A mound of red mountain dirt behind it. Two shovels jammed in.

"Donny used a Bobcat with a backhoe," said DeMaris.

"Thing's at least six feet deep," said Bodart.

"Don't do this, DeMaris," I said.

"Why not?" he asked. He sounded sincerely interested in my answer.

"It will cost you your life."

"You mean spiritually?"

"No."

"Then you're mixing you and me up," he said. "Probably the stress."

"No one has to die," I said.

"I one hundred percent disagree."

Bodart turned his utility light on us. Came in our direction. "Is Ford bellowing, bargaining, blubbering, or begging? We could always tell a lot about a detainee by what stage they were at, Roland. We called it the B list."

"You enjoyed it, didn't you, Joe?" I said. "White Fire."

"It got my monster up, that's for sure."

I thought for a moment before I spoke next. I saw no other way out. Bodart was upon me, gun in hand again, and I wanted to stay alive. The scar on my forehead was molten. "I'm going to ask you a favor."

"Ask away," said Bodart, aiming the gun at my head. "I feel gener—"

The toolbox in the back of my truck screeched open. Burt Short stood, pointed his combat shotgun at Bodart, and blew him off his feet. I wheeled on wide-eyed DeMaris, hit him with a left uppercut that started way down in my toes. His jaw shattered and his head snapped up and he went down, senseless as a bale of hay. I stood on his wrist and wrenched away his gun. Bodart lay on his back, arms out, hands slowly opening and closing. Face missing above his mustache, blood flooding out, the back of his head lying in the dirt ten feet away.

I looked from Bodart to DeMaris. Smells of blood and pine and fresh earth. Burt jumped out of the pickup, leaned in for a closer look at Bodart, and crossed himself.

"Got him."

"I'm glad you did." I heard my voice as if from a distance.

"We didn't ask for this," he said.

"No."

My body had a funny lifting feeling. Like it was a balloon and not tied down. But my soul weighed a thousand black tons and there was no way I was going to float off. My plan had worked.

"I'm going to offer you some free advice, Roland. Any time you feel bad about what we just did, you remember that hole in the ground and what they were going to put in it."

DeMaris moaned softly, scraped his fingers through the dirt. I went over to Bodart and retrieved my weapons from the pockets of his duster. Thought I owed him a look. Respect. Maybe that was a bad idea. Blood and dirt and shiny pieces of scalp. Bleeding less but the smell of it strong. Smell of a new grave ten feet away. Mine. I moved to the truck and leaned back against it. I'd felt like this a few times in my heavyweight "career." Late, between rounds, looking through swelling eyes at an opponent, measuring his misery against my own. You just want it to be over. But you will not give up because you are a fighter.

"We have a decision to make," said Burt. "Best-case scenario is DeMaris wakes up and buries Bodart, straightens up around here, and keeps quiet. But it's hard to keep quiet about something like this for long. DeMaris has a small conscience but a big mouth. Bodart's people will be all over him. So, worst-case scenario is he panics and runs off to the law. He and Tice would play this off as a bluff staged to scare you silent. Not going to harm a hair on your head. I think we'd beat them in court, but what a long, expensive, public headache. You could make bail, but your business would suffer badly. Details gruesome enough for the news at eleven. The Ford and Timmerman clans would not love it. And think how many hikes with Wesley you wouldn't have time for while you're sitting in the defendant's chair. More likely, DeMaris waddles off in a hurry to Bodart's handlers and tells them what happened. In which case, we might expect them to assign someone more capable to deal with us. In the long future."

I watched him, listening.

"The alternative is to white out DeMaris forthwith, dump him in the hole with Bodart, and use those shovels, you and me. Pack it down good. Spread some pine needles over it. Tice might dig them up later out of pure curiosity, missing boss and all. But I bet he'd take one look and cover them up again. What's he got to win? We could be out of here in less than an hour. Then back under the palapa at Rancho de los Robles, bourbons in hand, plenty of time to see the sun rising on a beautiful new day. I'll do the actual deed, since I'm one-for-one tonight anyway."

"It's wrong to kill him."

Burt looked down at DeMaris. "Don't forget my advice, Roland. This pathetic oaf was seconds away from shooting you in the head and dragging you to that hole."

"No."

Burt gave me a long look and I gave him one back. "Okay," he said. "You're the boss. It's endearing that you still care about right and wrong. I'm glad you let me help you out of this mess,

but I wish we could have come up with something neater."

I looked out at the grave and the mound of
dirt behind it. Just enough foggy moonlight to
see. Wanted to be gone from here. Up in **Hall
Pass** with Justine, free in the sky, alive in a beautiful world.

"Do you believe in good luck or bad luck, Roland?"

"Yeah."

"I only believe in good luck."

"Where did you learn to do this kind of
thing?"

He shrugged. "Born in L.A. but moved
around a lot."

47

One week later Paige and I sat across from each other at the picnic table under the palapa. I'd given her the pond view. I could see the rooflines of the casitas up on the embankment, and beyond them, the big house. She'd spent Good Friday, Saturday, and Easter Sunday in the hospital. Then another three days at home trying to rest, surrounded by FBI agents, Air Force Office of Special Investigations interrogators, and San Diego County Sheriff's detectives—the same humorless posse that tag-teamed me.

Freed from Arcadia, she wore a loose floral dress with a light white jacket, and her hair was down. The day was sunny and warm. I'd told the Irregulars I wanted privacy for this lunch and they'd decided to see a matinee and go bowling.

She flinched as she reached to pour more wine into my glass. A couple of fat red drops hit the tablecloth. "Ouch," she said.

"Here." I poured some wine for her. I served her some of the ahi salad that Lindsey and Burt had made for the occasion, pushed the baguette basket closer to her for an easier reach.

I broke off a piece of bread. "You invented Dan," I said.

She set down her fork and looked at me, her irises brown with some red in them—rust or cinnamon—and her expression flat.

"When did you suspect?" she asked.

"The first time you said his name."

"I thought you believed me."

"Not quite," I said. "But I didn't know what to believe instead."

"Yes. I invented Daniel."

"Remember, he went by Dan."

"Don't peck at me," she said. "I'm not proud of what I did."

I heard waterfowl skidding to a stop on the surface of the pond behind me. Figured it due to the brace of mallards that had shown up last week. Watched Paige Hulet's eyes tracking them right to left. "Why pretend you were married and he had died?"

She met my gaze, then looked away. "I wanted a way into you. So I made myself a widow in my mind. To understand yours."

"To heal me."

She touched her side very lightly. "You see what I did for Clay."

"I'm in awe of what you did for Clay. Were your five years without a dance invented, too?"

"No, Roland. I gave up dancing and what goes with it. It was all about my patients and my writing. I was thriving. But, when I got to know you, I thought you were beautiful and I wanted to dance again. I knew from the start that your heart would be in the right place."

"How did you know?"

She studied me over her wineglass. "Everything I found about you told me that you were a good and feeling man. The killing of Titus Miller. What you did and didn't do when your partner opened fire. What you said and didn't say. I admired you. And later, the **U-T** article about you doing well as a PI, and marrying a beautiful public defender—I was happy for you. What you said about her death a year after that. So, at the moment I met you, I already believed in you."

"Yesterday I looked at our contract again. I was trying to figure out how much money I'd return to Dawn Spencer. And I saw that you were the only Arcadia principal who actually signed the contract. Another light went on. It wasn't Briggs or DeMaris who thought to hire me. It was you."

She held my gaze.

"You amaze me, Paige. And I'm hard to amaze."

"Over time, I hope you forgive me."

She sipped the wine and looked at me. I could

feel the turmoil inside her. I expected her to say she didn't regret her deceptions because they had been done for good reasons. Ends and means. Protecting Clay. Getting what she needed. Dancing again. I felt a ripple of hurt pride as the facts of being researched and lied to sank in. But my pride was no match for Paige Hulet's passions.

"I forgive you."

"I know I've been reckless." She reached out and set a hand on mine.

I heard the blur of wing beats and turned to see a flock of red-shouldered blackbirds lifting off the cattails, a hundred black-and-red jewels rising into the blue. Wesley and I had had three good walks in the last three days. The hooded orioles. Quail paired up and the great horned owls moving into an unused hawk's nest, for the third year in a row. Wesley's vision fading.

We finished the lunch and I poured more wine. Light pours, given her performance during our previous social engagement. She smiled and lifted the glass, and in this moment, under this palapa on this day, Paige Hulet was beautiful. I thought of the pictures on her office wall. Girl. Camper. Tennis champ. Scholar. Biology summa cum laude with a minor in French. Medicine. Psychiatry. Moral injury. Dancer. Maybe I'd get my picture on her wall someday. I couldn't not forgive her.

"Does that rowboat work?" she asked.

"It's floating."

"Take me out?"

Justine in her floppy hat in that boat on spangled water. "Sure."

Paige sat on the bow bench, facing me as I rowed. Her dress rippled in the breeze. She hooked her hair behind her ears with both hands. "Rex and Patricia have hired me to be Clay's doctor again. I'll be moving up to their area soon. Quite a generous offer."

I congratulated her. I would rest easier knowing that this obsessive physician would be in charge of Clay's recovery.

"Thanks to you," she said, "I've got another chance to help him heal. I'll do just about anything on earth to let that happen. As you know."

"But would you take a bullet?"

She smiled and shook her head, turned her face up to the sun, and closed her eyes. I had that plunging feeling that is part biology and part mystery.

I manned the oars and let her talk. So much to do, she told me. The next few months were critical for Clay, though the most pressing question was where he would actually **be.** He was an obvious flight risk. The Justice Department, the DoD, and the Air Force all wanted control of him. The Bureau of Prisons provided a compromise—the U.S. penitentiary in Lompoc, California—an hour and a half drive from Ojai. As Clay's personal physician, Paige would have daily access to him. She had booked an extended-stay hotel in Lompoc for one month, easy to arrange in a prison town. Sequoia Blain had done likewise.

The sun was warm and there were hawks keening high up and golden poppies on the hills. She opened her eyes and looked at me. "Don't be a stranger. Lompoc is just over an hour flight from Fallbrook Airpark. I checked it."

"Okay."

"That look on your face now

"Just be alert, Paige. Alec is dangerous. And Bodart's people are worse. It's hard to know about men like that."

"Don't worry so much."

Itch on my forehead. "It's my job and I'm good at it."

I turned the rowboat back toward the dock. She squinted into the sunlight, much like that first day at Arcadia. "You brought something back to life in me. I'm going to miss you very much."

I held open her car door as she carefully lowered herself into the seat. I closed it and she wiped a tear. Shoulder strap, radio, window lowered for a gotta-go smile. Then the dust rising as she headed down the drive. Sun on chrome, music. Hand out the window, waving.

Flash of red, a voice but no words.

You.

A t twelve hundred feet the Pacific sparkled and heaved and the onshore flow pushed against me as I rose over Point Loma. Lighthouse and toy boats below, whitecaps and seabirds. Sails and wakes. I banked gently south to make the same loop we'd always made.

In the air my thoughts come and go more quickly than on land. I don't know why. Pressure drop? Temperature change? The ecstasy and risk of leaving earth?

I thought of Clay Hickman in Lompoc penitentiary. Of Paige on her way there. Of Sequoia already arrived. She'd sounded happy on the phone. Of Vazquez and Tice and Alec. Of Bodart. Of Briggs Spencer and his agony, of his sudden celebrity and **Hard Truth**, all of which had been the subject of endless news stories in print, on TV, and on the Internet. Everywhere you looked. Then not, sliding into the great yawning past of yesterday's news.

Funny enough, Nell Flanagan called me not long after Paige had driven away. Nell wanted to know if I'd do her show, talk about Clay Hickman and Briggs Spencer, the mysterious psychiatrist Paige Hulet, the shootout on my property, the torture video, White Fire. I declined politely, told her I loved **Nell Flanagan's San Diego**, and would donate as always to KPBS during pledge week. She said if I ever changed my mind she would love to hear my story.

Over the National City docks I began my southwest bank, which took me out over the Pacific. Engine drone rattling flesh and bone. Came around northwest as we always did, as she had on her sudden side trip to eternity.

Rage, Wrath & Fury lurched up inside me again, just as they had the moment I'd heard what had happened to her. And nearly every day since, many, many thousands of times. I looked straight down at the Pacific from 2,500 feet—approximately where Justine had begun her final descent.

I held that altitude and came toward the coast as she had, just south of Point Loma, headed for Coronado, whose elegant blue bridge now curved before and below me. I knew that by the time she had reached here she had been too preoccupied to notice that bridge. Preoccupied? How about disbelieving? Terrified? So I noticed the bridge extra, for her. She loved the beautiful.

My angry friends butted in again, haranguing God on my behalf:

You took her, You Son of a bitch. You. Took. Her.

But Roland doesn't want to hate You forever.

He wants to forgive You.

He believes.

Isn't that enough for now?

They were silent for a moment, and in that silence something finally either broke or healed. It felt so right. So necessary and overdue. Neutral buoyancy. State of grace.

Of course, Rage, Wrath & Fury couldn't just let it be. So they added a parting shot. Their voices softer:

You better leave Wesley one of his eyes.

We demand that You help Wesley.

Please help him.

Please.

Tough words from a history major Marine and mediocre boxer PI.

Tough words from a locator who knows he can't find the one person he most wants to find.

I ignored my counselors and listened for something better. For something beyond anger. For words that could throw a little light. Words that did not mean everything and nothing. I listened for seven things that I believed in, as asked of me by Justine in that lifetime long ago, and which I had been thinking about a lot lately. I heard them, mixed into the prop noise:

Gloves up, eyes open
Hold the living
Free the dead
Waste laughter
Save rain
Lower the volume
Give them the whole bitchen world

I push forward on the yoke and come off the throttle and send **Hall Pass 2** down. Like jumping off a mountain. Long fall, then speed building, Gs climbing, the rough constriction of gravity. Metal shudder and roar. A peregrine's stoop can reach two hundred miles per hour. Breathe now. Push. Down. Down. So easy. So fast. Justine taught me this. Could touch her now if I wanted. Stay the course and meet up with her. Together forever. No. Then full throttle and the blast of turbocharge, the haul of the yoke and the plane begins to level, slowly and steadily, grinding through air.

Gradually I feel the nose lifting and the invisible curve of bottom. All that has been charging up at me folds open and away. Parts around my propeller. Rushes past my windows, past me. Velocity so smooth and pure. Almost touching the green-jeweled chop that glitters for miles around. Bright hulls, billowing sails, rooster tails of motorboats on the mounding swells, and the black rocks of Zuniga Point hurtling past. Hold her steady. Push Clay's flash drives through the window, wind-snatched.

Then climb into the world again, headed home.

ACKNOWLEDGMENTS

The following books were illuminating and helpful in the writing of this novel. I congratulate these authors on their fine and sometimes disturbing work.

Madness in Civilization, by Andrew Scull

A Battle Won by Handshakes, by Lucas A. Dyer

Predator—The Remote-Control Air War Over Iraq and Afghanistan: A Pilot's Story, by Matt J. Martin with Charles W. Sasser

None of Us Were Like This Before, by Joshua E. S. Phillips

Torture Central, by Michael Keller

On Killing, by Lt. Col. Dave Grossman

What It Is Like to Go to War, by Karl Marlantes